DESERT SKIES

A Story of "Champions" in the Gulf War

30th Anniversary Edition

MICHAEL T. GREGORY

Desert Skies
Copyright © 2022 by Michael T. Gregory

ISBN
978-1-958122-85-3 (Paperback)
978-1-958122-86-0 (eBook)
978-1-958122-84-6 (Hardcover)

TABLE OF CONTENTS

AUTHOR'S INTRODUCTION

First and foremost let me say *'thank you'* for taking time to read "Desert Skies". I originally wrote this novel after digesting the Gulf War experience. I initially was going to write a non-fiction work about the War from my first hand experiences as an Attack Helicopter Company Commander in the 1st Armored Division. But, there were so many non-fiction books out there five years after the War that I decided to go with fiction.

That doesn't mean the book is all fiction. But I felt adding a bit more drama and conflict might keep a reader unfamiliar with war or the Army interested. That said, you just can't make sh . . . stuff like this up. There is a whole lot of truth running through these pages.

Nearly 30 years after the Gulf War, I re-visited "Desert Skies." This book is a raw look into the men and women that fought there. The relationships are based on people that I worked with and some that I had heard of. There is absolutely no ill will towards any of my supervisors, peers or subordinates from that time. There may be some regrets that I didn't do some things right, however my main goal as a Commander of men in War was to see my people home. In spite of the romantic philosophy of dying for one's country, I'm with Patton that American Forces make the other poor SOB die for his country. My goal was to bring my men home. I did that.

Now the Gulf War approaches the 25th year anniversary so I decided to re-publish the book. As for the ending, if you think about the Gulf War, you may understand why the book ends the way it does. It sets up "Desert Skies II" where art imitates life once more. You may say we didn't finish the job the first time. The job was to oust Saddam Hussein. We did that.

I was part of the greatest military force this planet had ever seen. We accomplished our mission in spades. As military might is merely politics applied with kinetic communications, our message was no force on earth could challenge us. If you are to go to War, the 'Powell Doctrine' is the way to go. That would be the doctrine that calls for overwhelming superiority.

If you are coming back for a re-visit to the book, may your memories be positive and your vision clear. If you are a new reader of "Desert Skies," I hope you enjoy the tale. Just remember. It's fiction!

And once again, thank you!

Michael T. Gregory

CHAPTER 1

June 19, 1990
Katterheim Caserne, Germany

"I WILL ALWAYS BE A CHAMPION!" With his final words choked out, CPT Charlton Sweat III crisply saluted, wiped his tears from each cheek, marched quickly to his position next to the squadron commander, and came to attention. LTC Charles "Chuck" Smithey extended his hand in the customary congratulatory handshake.

CPT Thomas Edward Lawton moved deliberately to the podium. Tom Lawton could be viewed as "average" in every sense of the word. Average height, average build, and average looks. Just another captain in the United States Army getting the opportunity to do what every captain wanted to do: take command of soldiers. To those that knew him, Tom Lawton was anything but average. To tell the truth, Tom Lawton was damn good at what he did. And the people that knew him knew how good he was.

Tom remembered his father's words from the previous day's phone call. "Soldiers appreciate it when the incoming commander's speech is brief and to the point!" Tom always found comfort from his father's perspective as a retired warrant officer. Will Lawton's twenty-four-year career as an army aviator was demanding and highly successful. Will Lawton was a decorated Vietnam veteran, and he had instilled in Tom the need to have a positive, honest relationship with his subordinates. He'd start this relationship by skipping the bullshit.

With a deep breath, CPT Tom Lawton began, "Colonel and Mrs. Denson, Colonel Steele, Lieutenant Colonel and Mrs. Smithey, distinguished visitors and guests of the C Troop, First Squadron, Sixth Cavalry Champions, I am honored to have the opportunity to command these outstanding soldiers at a time when the army faces many challenges. Cindy, Megan, and I look forward to the next two years with anticipation and excitement. I am proud to be a Champion and will do my best for my soldiers and follow the traditions of the US Cavalry."

Captain Lawton snapped to attention, marched to the head of the formation, and assumed his new role as the commander of C Troop, 1-6 CAV.

LTC Chuck Smithey shouted, "Take charge of your unit!"

Captain Lawton's salute was delivered sharply and held until Lieutenant Colonel Smithey's salute was dropped, and then his hand snapped to his side. *Much crisper than Sweat's salute*, thought Tom. *Just one more of his selfish insecurities*, he quietly reminded himself. CPT Tom Lawton was a very insecure man. This was one character flaw a commander of troops should never have.

Tom Lawton's about-face was executed flawlessly. He quickly scanned the eyes of his troop. Twenty-eight steely eyed, hard-nosed CAV troopers ready for war, or so he had been told. "I want the platoon leaders and the first sergeant to meet me in my office in an hour. Champions . . . dismissed!" CPT Tom Lawton received a thunderous "Hooaah" upon the completion of his first command. The soldiers moved out quickly to get in the food line before the visitors. 1SG Roberto "Bobby" Garcia, 1LT Hartley Osborn, and 2LT Hal Timmons demonstrated the appropriate patience before approaching their new commander. The first sergeant was the first to hold out his hand. "Damn good to have you aboard, sir!"

"Top, do you know how lucky I am to have you here?" The handshake was steady and firm, indicative of the mutual respect these two soldiers had for each other. SFC Roberto Garcia had known a wet-behind-the-ears second lieutenant named Thomas E. Lawton six years ago. As a new butter bar lieutenant fresh from the AH-1 Cobra qualification course, Lieutenant Lawton was wild and eager to learn. Garcia respected the new second lieutenant back in '84 because he kept his mouth shut and absorbed everything the unit was teaching him. Lawton was different because he took time to get to know things the other lieutenants didn't. He listened, he learned, and he grew into a leader. First Sergeant Garcia was glad to have this new boss. Hopefully, he would still listen.

1LT Hartley Osborn was next to congratulate his new commander. Hart Osborn could have served as an army recruiting poster. The lieutenant was tall, lean, and sculpted like a statue. Osborn was a dedicated officer and was serious about his profession and focused on every mission he was assigned. The fact that he rarely drank alcohol had not gone unnoticed by Tom. It was rare to find an army aviator that didn't drink.

To Lieutenant Osborn, CPT Tom Lawton was to be respected and admired. Lawton was a midgrade captain with over six hundred hours in the Apache. Lieutenant Osborn's 160 Apache hours were good, but with a whole year in the aircraft, he had expected nearly three hundred hours by then. He had worked with his new boss in the operations office or S3 shop as it was known. They often discussed training and operations plans at the office before Tom was selected to be the new troop commander for C Troop. Tom Lawton wouldn't be bad to work for. Hell, if Lieutenant Osborn played his cards right, he might just finally get to fly for this boss. "Welcome to the Champions, sir! Is it too early to ask you and Mrs. Lawton over to dinner?"

"Way too early, Hart. Let's take about a month to see how this bunch works and we'll have a nice little get-together with our wives. Perhaps your aero scout brother of diminutive stature could join us!" Tom joked, looking at the second lieutenant in the background.

Lieutenant Osborn moved to the side as 2LT Hal Timmons, all five feet, seven inches, angled up to the pack. "Sir, it's not going to be like it was in the Three shop, is it? I actually carry the respect and adulation of my troops here." Lawton broke out laughing and hugged his scout platoon leader. "Damn, sir, I thought you'd never get down to us line pilots."

"Screw you, Hal! I got more time as a platoon leader than you got drinkin' beer, and we all know you got a ton of time drinkin' beer!" Lawton laughed.

Lieutenant Osborn was surprised at the genuine affection his new boss was showing the scout platoon leader. Just two months ago, Second Lieutenant Timmons was the flight operations officer in the S3 shop. Hartley did not expect to see such informality between his new boss and the newbie scooter pilot.

"Gentlemen, I have festivities to indulge in, and I would greatly appreciate it if you would join me." *Enough of the clown*, thought Tom. "One hour, my office. The first and only topic for today will be aircraft maintenance. Bring your status reports and we'll talk."

Tom hurried over to the area of the hangar that had been set aside for the post-ceremony festivities. Cindy and Megan were there, and it was obvious that the little three-year-old wanted her daddy. "Doddy, Doddy!" Megan ran to Tom's arms. Tom effortlessly picked his daughter up, carried her over to Cindy, and gave them both little pecks on the cheek.

"Everything is in its place, Commander!" teased Cindy, bringing her hand up in a mock salute. Cindy Lawton was a tall, shapely brunette with almond eyes and a smile that was contagious. She loved Tom Lawton without reservation. And she never once doubted him or his abilities.

"That's enough out of you, woman. How are you hangin'?" Tom smiled.

"Oh! Finally concerned about little ol' me? I'm just fine. I see Colonel Steele made it here. It was awfully nice of him to come. Everyone else is telling me how happy he or she is for me that you're the new Champion commander. I haven't puked on anyone yet, but it's getting old fast," said Cindy Lawton.

"Patience was never one of your strong points, dear," teased the captain.

"Listen to you. 'I want it like this. I need that done like that. You need to be here on time.' This next two years is gonna drive me nuts," said Cindy. Tom cast her an understanding look and offered another peck on the cheek, which was promptly rejected. "Don't even try it!"

COL Barney Steele came over, excused himself, and said, "I just wanted to catch you both and congratulate you together because I know what a fine team you are." Colonel Steele was Tom Lawton's first commanding officer. He knew too well a single young lieutenant, a Cobra pilot that had demonstrated exceptional leadership traits while simultaneously displaying alcoholic tendencies. Barney Steele was glad Cindy had married Tom. Steele knew that she was the reason Tom had his command today. Lawton would have never made it without her steady guidance at home. Barney Steele was under the impression Tom Lawton would have either been kicked out of the army or dead if he had not have met Cindy.

"Thank you, Barney. No better half today?" Cindy was one of only a handful of people who could get away calling him Barney. She gave the six-foot-five colonel a big hug and a kiss on the cheek. Cindy respected her husband's former boss because he was the genuine article: a career army officer with a soft side and zero tolerance for bullshit.

"She's working at the hospital, and she sends her best wishes," said Colonel Steele. "And you, Young Captain, do you feel any different?"

"Sir, just between you and I, I'm a little nervous! It hasn't sunk in yet," said Tom.

As if on cue, CPT Charlie Sweat III appeared. Charlie Sweat was known around the squadron by many nicknames. Among them were the Turd, LSS for Lyin' Sack of Shit, and Tom's favorite, Courtney. Courtney came from "Courtney Massengale," the antagonist in *Once an Eagle* by Anton Myrer. Courtney Massengale was the type of officer that could best be described as a self-serving, manipulative bastard that spent more time worrying about his own career than he did taking care of soldiers.

Tom extended his hand, and the cordial handshake turned into a serious paw-pumping session. The show was obviously intended for the O-6 that Sweat "the Turd" did not know. "I can't think of anyone I'd rather turn my troop over to than you, Tom. You're the best trainer I ever worked with." With the ass kissing completed, Sweat turned to the real reason he came over. "Sir, my name is Charlie Sweat, Champ . . . formerly Champion Six."

Colonel Steele was an experienced warrior, and he could smell shit on a brownnoser from a mile away. He accepted the outgoing commander's handshake with firmness and respect. "What outstanding position does the army have lined up for you next, Captain?" inquired the colonel.

"Sir, I'm headed up to division to be the G3 Air," responded Charlie Sweat.

"Son, that's a damn good place for a man of your talents and abilities. Best of luck, young man." Gracious, even when cutting someone down, was COL Barney Steele. Sweat "the Turd" didn't get it. He considered the comment just as he considered the new job a chance to be seen by senior officers at Division Headquarters in Würzburg, a promotion, an effective step higher on the ladder to the top. He didn't realize that command is what got you to the top. Leading troops and soldiers in any capacity is a responsibility very few are selected to do. Colonel Steele had commanded on five separate occasions at various levels. Tom Lawton got the gist of Steele's comment and subdued his chuckle with a barely audible cough.

Barney Steele caught the fake cough of his former lieutenant, current Champion Six, and put him in his place also. "You haven't done anything yet to prove you're worthy of the position, my little friend." He bent toward Tom and added more seriously, "You screw this up, and I'll have your ass before Pete Denson does!" Captain Lawton nodded his affirmation and accepted his mentor's hand.

"Roger, sir. I'd like to be able to call on you for guidance on the basis I might actually need the help, sir," said Tom.

"I'd be pissed if you didn't. Fly safe, Tom." Colonel Steele in his role as the top aviator in the United States Army European Command headed over to visit with the brigade commander, COL Peter Denson.

"Who's that guy, Tom?" asked Charlie. Always the inquisitive one was "Courtney."

"Old boss. First squadron commander I ever worked for. Great, great boss. Works at Heidelberg now. He's the head army aviator in EUSAREUR. He owes me five bucks," stated Tom flatly.

It took a couple of seconds for the joke to set into Charlie Sweat's distracted mind. "Fuck you, Tom!" Then after a little pause, "Does he need an aide?" queried Charlie.

Tom shook his head. "I gotta go. Thanks for all your help." Tom bit his tongue to keep from adding, "Now piss off!" Charles Sweat III was the grandson of a West Pointer. It's said that his great-grandfather helped Robert E. Lee get through West Point. Tom Lawton could only picture Charlie Sweat offering U. S. Grant whiskey at Vicksburg. Tom accepted the fact that he would be Colonel Sweat "the Turd" at a minimum. Tom Lawton's intuition told him Charlie's integrity was locked up in a closet right beside his courage. Tom knew Charlie would continue up the ladder achieving his goal to become a general officer, leaving confusion and incompetence in his wake.

It wasn't only a West Point thing either. Tom had plenty of friends from the academy. He couldn't help but notice that some of the best aviators from his flight school class that were academy graduates had already left the army. Any source of commission could produce officers that were solely rank conscious, not just the military academy. It wasn't often an officer was produced that was as self-serving as Sweat. The academy didn't do that to him. Tom knew how good the academy was at producing leaders. Maybe he was jealous that he did not attend when Will Lawton said he could get him in. The source of his commission was just one more thing for Tom to be insecure about.

Tom continued to greet other invited guess as he mingled around the serving table. It seemed he was congratulated by every one of the 533 people in attendance. There were still two people he had to go thank. The first was his rater, the squadron commander, Lieutenant Colonel Smithey. Thanking Lieutenant Colonel Smithey would be enjoyable. The second one would not be quite so easy. The brigade commander, COL Peter Denson, would be a challenge. Captain Lawton had worked for Lieutenant Colonel Smithey in the operations office as the assistant S3 for a year, and he liked his boss. Colonel Denson was a totally different story. Denson was called "Darth Vader" by some of the junior officers. The difference between Denson and Darth Vader was that Vader had a heart. Denson lurked around the brigade area, popping up unexpectedly on units, in search of weak leaders and incompetence. Tom dreaded any meeting with Denson because he was stoic, monotone, and just plain unlikable. Denson had the knack of making everyone squirm at briefings. His favorite technique to intimidate his subordinates in meetings was putting them on the spot. Neither pleasant toward nor well-liked by subordinates, there was one damn good point about the man. He was a warrior. And warriors were getting hard to find. A brigade commander with a star on the horizon, Colonel Denson had many junior officers kissing his ass as they tried to ride his coattails up the ladder.

Most often, these ass-kissers could be found on his staff. At least two had wanted Tom's command desperately. Thanks only to Lieutenant Colonel Smithey's demands, Tom was given the command of the Champions, a command which was richly deserved. The problem was twofold: the chain of command, namely, Denson and Smithey, did not get along; and secondly, Lieutenant Colonel Smithey only had four months left.

Opportunity favored Tom for the moment as both men were together talking. Tom took a deep breath and moved toward them. Quick prayers to God, "Please, don't let me say anything stupid and get fired in my first hour!"

"The man of the hour," said Lieutenant Colonel Smithey. That warranted a grunt from Darth Vader.

"Gentlemen, please let me reiterate my thanks for the opportunity to command. I'll do my best," said Tom Lawton, immediately feeling as if he had screwed up by being sycophantic to some holier-than-thou beings.

"Everyone says that, Captain, but few actually do," responded Colonel Vader.

Lieutenant Colonel Smithey came to the rescue. "Sir, Captain Lawton will do a fine job. I'm very confident in his training abilities."

"You know as well as I do that training is only a small piece of the command puzzle, Chuck. And if that's all he can do, he won't last long," said the colonel. "By the way, Captain, you've inherited supporting me, and I fly whenever I can. I will let your instructor pilot know on Thursdays my schedule so you can work around it. Any problem with that, Captain Lawton?" inquired Colonel Vader.

He is one rude old fart, thought Tom. "Sir, the name is Lawton, and you can fly anytime you want." Tom bit his lip as he heard the words come out. The next thought that went through his mind was, "Maybe I should just kiss your fat hairy ass right here in front of Lieutenant Colonel Smithey!"

"Fine, Captain Lawton. I'll be in touch with Mr. Nichols on Thursday." On that pleasant note, Colonel Denson spun away to the crowd. He may have been one of the best warriors in the business, but he was still an asshole.

Tom shook his head from side to side and said, "Sir, I really have a hard time talking to him."

Lieutenant Colonel Smithey laughed. "So does his wife! I suppose the Champions are off the rest of the day?"

"Roger that, sir. I've got a meeting in my office in a couple minutes with the lieutenants and Top. Then we're all getting together at the O'Club to celebrate. Of course, you and Mrs. Smithey are more than welcome to attend."

Lieutenant Colonel Smithey shook his head and looked down at the ground with a smile. Slowly, he gazed up at his newest troop commander and said, "You've inherited a wild bunch, Tom. They aren't as good as they think they are. But . . ." He hesitated before adding, "You can make them the best."

"Damn, sir. I thought you said no pressure early on." Tom looked hard at his boss with his own little smile.

"I'm serious, Tom. The way they are now, they're dangerous. We'll talk more Monday." As he turned, Lieutenant Colonel Smithey couldn't help but get that last jab in. "I hope you don't get a call from the Polizei this weekend, Commander!"

"Nightstalkers, sir!" Captain Lawton saluted. Tom gave his boss a crisp salute and smiled as he responded with the squadron call sign. The smile faded quickly as he thought about a phone call from some German cop. He'd gotten what he wanted. Now he had to deal with it.

Tom arrived in his office about five minutes earlier than his troops. He unpacked a box of personal history. His left wall had I Love Me plaques, pictures, and mementos of six years of various aviation duties. The right wall had calendars and training schedules. Behind him was a window to look down on the hangar floor. A quick glance down on the floor and Tom saw Cindy and a couple of other wives cleaning up the leftover food from the party. Tom made a mental note to be sure to thank her for all she was doing for him. He knew he wasn't able to handle this job without her behind him.

As directed, Top Garcia, First Lieutenant Osborn, and Second Lieutenant Timmons approached Captain Lawton's office one hour after the ceremony. His contemplation was interrupted by light tapping on the door. "Sir, can we come in?" said First Lieutenant Osborn. In most army units, First Lieutenant Osborn would be considered an executive officer. But in an Apache attack troop, there is no position in the Military Table of Organization and Equipment (MTOE) at troop level. Squadron has an executive officer position for a major, but the MTOE was thin at troop level. The troop strength on paper is thirty-two soldiers of which there are three officers, fourteen warrant officer pilots, and fifteen enlisted soldiers. As the second-highest-ranking officer in the troop, Lieutenant Osborn therefore was charged to pick up the required duties as the executive officer of the troop.

"Come on in, take a seat," said Champion Six. The lieutenants took the couch, and Top Garcia took the easy chair. "First of all, let me say I am awfully damn happy to be here. The S3 shop was okay, but I'm ready to be with troops again."

"Sir, we can't begin to tell you how happy we are to have you here," said Lieutenant Osborn.

"Speak for yourself," said Second Lieutenant Timmons.

"I've missed you too, shithead." Tom couldn't help but smile. He was in the only job he ever really wanted. He had the best first sergeant in the army, the most experienced second lieutenant in the army, and a potentially outstanding senior first lieutenant as his attack platoon leader.

"Sir, you wanted to discuss maintenance," reminded Top, ever the professional.

The smile disappeared. "I've waited until today so as not to step on anyone's toes until it's my butt that's on the line." Enough dancing, thought Tom. "I don't believe we can launch what we carry up on paper." Tom caught the body language from both lieutenants and noticed a small smile appear on Top Garcia's face.

"Sir, we've got five Apaches up, and we can launch them within two hours!" said Lieutenant Osborn. "Three are fully mission capable (FMC), two can be fixed ASAP, and one is down hard for parts."

Tom didn't foresee the defensive outburst but was prepared. "The two that are down are not flyable within two hours. It'll take six hours to fix the nose gearbox on 956, plus a day to cure. As for 440, that is a leak on the number 2 hydraulic reservoir, not a drip. On Monday, have maintenance relook the system, fix it, or get the parts in order. Check the status of the part on 220 to see where it is. It's been down for nearly twenty days, and that's too long. Top, I want to implement the old reward system we had for crew chiefs based on monthly FMC rate plus hours flown per month. Starting today."

"Sir, I have the memorandum for your signature here," said the first sergeant.

"Roger, Top, thank you. As for scouts, Hal, what's up? No pun intended," quipped Tom.

"Sir, the three aircraft I have up are actually flyable, but only two are FMC. The radios suck on all of them to the point of being dangerous. The fourth one is in phase maintenance and won't be finished for two weeks. The phase is going well, considering they are about 80 percent complete with the rebuild. The D Troop phase team, headed up by Sergeant Kelter, is shit hot. I expect it to come out in better shape than it went in.

"There are only three of us to fly them anyway. Chief Warrant Officer 3 O'Toole, the aero scout IP, newly promoted Chief Warrant Officer 2 Cross, and myself. Do you have any suggestions, sir?" asked Hal.

God, he's smooth, thought Tom. "Just one. See if your beloved Sergeant Kelter will let you take the radios out of the phase bird so we can get two scouts talking. Focus on Havequick Ops." Havequick meant using UHF radios that frequency hopped and therefore provided more secure communications transmissions between aircraft. "I want the scouts talking secure Uniform radio by the end of the month. The next bird isn't scheduled for phase for fifty-five hours, so start working on write-ups." Tom changed the subject and did an impression of a priest. "By the powers vested in me by . . . the great aviator in the sky, you are hereby declared the C Troop 1-6 supply officer. You have thirty days to get the supply books from Chief Warrant Officer 3 Toretti." So Lawton's attempt at humor didn't fly. He chuckled to himself and got back to business. "We'll talk personnel and other issues next week."

Tom sensed damaged pride in the room. A quick glance at Lieutenant Osborn justified the feeling. He'd have to get thicker skin to be a commander, or he won't last. Clear the air, thought Tom, or it would eat at him all weekend.

"Lieutenant Osborn, the three birds that are up, can they fly a mission next Wednesday?" asked Champion Six.

"Roger, sir! We've got four crews ready to go. I could ask for another bird from A Troop?" the previously wounded lieutenant responded.

"Negative. You will have four Champion aircraft up by Wednesday, or you don't fly." Throw them a little incentive for success. The wound was healing right before Tom's eyes. "We need to get ready for the party at the O'Club. Does anyone have any questions?"

Tom looked for any expressions of confusion or hands and got none. All occupants stood and salutes given. Tom still needed to check the wound. "Lieutenant Osborn, could you stay here for a minute, please?"

"Sure, sir," came the reply.

"Look, I'm sorry if you felt I put you on the spot by disagreeing with you about the status. I expect nothing but honesty in all facets of this business. If I can't get honesty from my executive officer, who can I get it from?" Tom smiled a little waiting to interpret the wounded patient's response.

"Sir, by no means was I lying!" declared the lieutenant.

Whoa, wrong response. "I didn't mean to imply you were lying. It's just we have to speak from the same tongue, or this unit won't function. I only care about the success of this unit and the people in it," said Lawton.

"It's just that we have, I mean had, a way of working that I was used to. Captain Sweat wanted to make sure we made the Department of the Army standard of 75 percent FMC monthly, and I . . . started to say I assumed you wanted it the same way," explained the lieutenant.

"Were your reports honest?" quizzed Champion Six. Silence. "You told me you weren't lying. What's up?" the quiz continued.

"We would sometimes . . . make sure we were at 75 percent by midmonth. We would do the numbers or cannibalize parts to get there," explained the executive officer.

"Does that work?" the quiz continued.

"Heck no. The crew chiefs ended up doing twice the work. Taking parts off one aircraft, then moving them back again. We work eighteen hours a day doing twice the work and don't get anywhere." A pause. Then the light bulb came on. "You already know this, don't you?"

Again, the small smile, "Forty-two months as a platoon leader. Thirty-two of those months in Apaches. Yes, I know all this and more. You only got ten months in this unit. A unit that has less experience than the unit that taught me. I'll make you a promise. You keep tellin' me the truth, and I'll teach you more in the next three months than you learned in your whole career."

Finally, a broad smile from the wounded subordinate. "Sir, you're a lot different than Captain Sweat." A step back and one more question. "Will I get to fly more?"

"Only if you get your helicopters fixed!" shouted the newest troop commander in the army. More silence. "Lieutenant, you're gonna fly your ass off. If you don't have one hundred hours by Thanksgiving, we're doin' something wrong." Just one little thing was still bugging Tom. "Hart, I expect the warrant officers to refer to the previous commander for the next month. I understand they worked for Captain Sweat for two years. But I would greatly appreciate it if you didn't bring up Captain Sweat again. The Champions are my troop now. Okay?"

A pause, then a smile. "Roger, sir. I understand completely. We'll see you tonight."

As they walked to the door, Tom said, "Hartley Osborn, we're gonna have a lot of fun." He extended his hand, which the lieutenant took anxiously. "See you tonight."

Tom wasn't real sure if they would have "a lot of fun" or not. He knew the business well enough to understand that having fun and being a competent commander were one and the same. If he wasn't having fun as a commander, people's lives were in jeopardy. He was just happy for the opportunity to command. Tom would find out soon enough just how much "fun" command could be.

1830, June 19, 1990
Katterheim Officer's Club

THE OFFICERS OF C TROOP, 1-6 CAV, had a reputation as a hard-drinking, fun-loving, and happy-go-lucky group. Attributes which made for great morale, but a deadly combination when carried over to work. Helicopter pilots live life a little fuller than most people. Fast cars or four-wheel-drive vehicles and risky sports like skydiving, scuba, mountain climbing, and martial arts are ways of life for America's finest helicopter pilots. They are the epitome of "Live fast, die young, and leave a good-lookin' corpse."

When Tom Lawton was single, he agreed with the thought. He'd seen a corpse just once. And it wasn't a good-looking one. Helicopter crashes of any kind generally don't leave anything "good looking." There is something about the nonmovement of a lifeless body that lets you know death goes beyond the physical. It creates feelings that linger. Tom was fortunate not to have known the fallen comrade. But the experience was enough to leave Tom with one goal: if he ever got to command, none of his men would have to experience death. The goal was not just preventing training accidents, but surviving combat as well. If you flew long enough, you would experience death up close and personal. The challenge lies in taming something that is inevitable. Tom Lawton would do what he had to protect his unit in peace or war.

The party at the club was not about taming death, but about living life to the fullest. Something Tom Lawton was inclined to do every chance he got. This was one of those chances. Each command in the military takes on a new life. It is usually the character of the commander that drives the lives of his subordinates. CPT Tom Lawton vowed to always present a positive climate for his troops. He would not let his own personal insecurities jeopardize his men. Tonight, they all started new lives.

A Friday night at the Officer's Club used to mean drunkenness and debauchery. In the 1980s, the army determined that alcohol consumption was bad, and a conscious effort was made to slow down the booze. While this was a generally a successful policy, tonight, in Germany, the policy would have to take a backseat to tradition. The question was, would anyone other than the designated drivers remember it tomorrow?

"Hooooooah!" came a thunderous yell as Tom and Cindy entered the basement pub. The battle cry came from a booth in the back. Surrounding the table for two were four people. Two obviously inebriated twenty-something-year-old men and one attractive couple not quite as drunk stood up and hollered for the Lawtons to come join them.

"Christ, honey, it's only 1830, and Dean and Sheppard are trashed. It's gonna be a long night," noted Tom.

"Probably not so long for those two." Cindy chuckled.

LT Dean Alvin was the fire support officer in the squadron S3 shop when Tom was the assistant S3. Dean Alvin was a mustang officer. Being a mustang meant that Dean was a product of the Officer Candidate School at Fort Benning, Georgia, having started his career as an enlisted soldier before making the transition to the officer corps. At twenty-six, Lieutenant Alvin was tall and attractive; and with his stylish glasses, he could have been a model for *GQ* magazine. He was the glue that held the operations shop together since Tom left. The new S3 was good, but nobody was comfortable with him yet. The assistant S3 position had not been filled since Tom left over three weeks ago. Therefore, Dean was handling two jobs for the new operations officer, CPT Jerry Maurer.

The other very vocal young man of twenty-two was 2LT Steven S. Sheppard, Chemical Corps. Commonly known as Schlep, because as the butter bar in the shop, he had to go get anything anyone else was too busy to get. Schlep was the headbutt boy of the squadron. Any shitty little job no one else wanted, he got. As a nonaviator, he bore the brunt of many ground-bound jokes from his peer group and all the warrant officers. He handled the abuse well and gave as good as he got. One other little thing about the Schlepper: he was a physics major from Columbia, finishing with a 3.8 GPA. Not only bright, he was honest and very quick-witted with a tremendous sense of humor, and he loved beer. Germany was Schlep's paradise.

The couple was Jerrod and Betty Sue Stuart of the Alabama Stuarts. Jed (not Jeb, he hated to be called Jeb) was the former S2 intelligence officer of the Fighting Sixth. As the S2, Captain Stuart worked closely with the S3 shop whenever they went to the field for training. Jed and Tom became very close friends, and Betty and Cindy were nearly inseparable.

"You guys are trashed already! Look at you, I leave for a couple weeks, and you get sloppy. I love you, guys! Come here. Group hug." Tom gave his best Bill Murray impression as he rolled his eyes and moved his jaw like he was Carl, the Caddie. "I miss you guys like . . . cramps."

Betty and Cindy hugged and gave a disgusted look at their chosen ones. "God, it's gonna be a long night. He just got here, and he's doing that stupid Bill Murray impression already," said Betty. "I am so glad to see you again. Is that little one behavin' herself? I'll give our sitter another hour, then call. If she can still answer the phone, I'll know the twins haven't tied her up."

Cindy understood completely. Jacob and Isaac (Jake and Ike) were definitely a handful. "I think we deserve something to drink!" said Cindy.

"Gentlemen, and I use that term only because there are ladies present. Belly up, I think I'm buyin'. Drinks, ladies?" asked Tom.

"A Lichtenauer for me, please, Tom," said Betty. The locally produced German beer was excellent.

"I'll just have a Coors, honey," replied Cindy.

"Come on, fellas, time to assault yonder bar in force," declared Tom.

The four men moved through the crowd to the bar. Tom Lawton accepted handshakes from numerous people in the crowd on his way to the bar. *Just people out for a beer on me*, thought Tom. And that was okay, because tonight, he was on top of the world.

"Kind sir, perhaps you could get me and my friends here a little bit of your good stuff," said Carl, the Caddie. Naturally, he got a hoot from the three drunken sots by his side. "I believe to start, four shots of last month's finest Jagermeister! Followed by two Pils drafts, a Hefe Weissen, a Guinness stout, a Lichtenauer, and a Coors, please," requested Tom. He reached into his wallet and pulled out three hundred dollars.

Schlep was the first to speak. "Sir, could I get two? I mean . . . we're already here and everything."

Tom nodded. "Schlep, this is what flight pay does for ya," spouted Tom Lawton in mock arrogance.

"Sir, it's not your flight pay I begrudge you." A pause. "It's your base pay that you rip off from the taxpayers!" finished the chemical officer, to which Dean Alvin burst out laughing and provided a high five for Sheppard as the chemical officer shot down an army aviator.

"Good one, Lieutenant!" said Jed. "I haven't missed him, have you, Tom?"

"Like jock itch, my cavalry buddy. How's the new job?" asked Tom.

Jed shook his head and said, "Man, I miss the good old days of just bein' in my little S2 shop, takin' care of business. This ground CAV shit ain't what it's cracked up to be. I enjoy being the S3 Air of the finest ground cavalry squadron in the US Army. But I don't have time to deal with all the air side, and they got me doin' the ground side too!" He was recently "promoted" to a new position down the road to the first of the First Cavalry, the most heralded unit in the army. A no-bullshit, take-no-prisoners kind of unit with a fire-breathing commanding officer. A commanding officer that knew good soldiers, thus explaining Jed Stuart's move. LTC Angelo Signorelli needed an S3 Air. He wanted Jed, so he got Jed.

"You can handle it, stud! You . . . the maayan!" said Tom.

"Sometimes I wish I wasn't the maayan!" said Jed.

Joining the crowd came two of Tom's peers with their wives. The A and B Troop commanders were present and accounted for. CPT Phil Pearson, alias Assassin Six, and CPT Chris Wise, a.k.a. Werewolf Six, brought their wives up to meet the new C Troop commander. Phil Pearson and Chris Wise had attended flight school together, along with CPT Damon Winslow, another captain currently working in the brigade operations shop. Captain Winslow made no bones about the fact he wanted to command the Champions and work along with his two stick buddies from flight school.

Tom had a comfortable working relationship with Phil and Chris, but not so comfortable that he would sit while Winslow got command of the Champions. Aware of the Three Amigos' plan and the implications that he should wait for the next command to come down so they could be buds again, Tom went straight to Lieutenant Colonel Smithey. Chuck did what was right for Tom. He was already on to the plan the three captains had come up with, and he had confronted Colonel Denson. Denson reluctantly agreed that Tom could have the Champions. But with the acceptance came a disclaimer, "I think that Winslow deserves a shot to show his mettle, but if you think that Lawton's your man, Chuck, you've got him!" Needless to say, Tom was apprehensive about his new relationship with these "peers."

Chris Wise was the first to introduce the foursome to the small crowd. Tom did the honors for his pack of drunks. Chris said, "Welcome to command. The Champions are finally on track with a team player. Phil and I've been ready for you to come down to the line since last gunnery. Your predecessor was a good commander, but he sure was tough to get along with." Tom gave a friendly Roger-type affirmative nod and thought to himself, *Is there a punch line here somewhere?* "Team player" and "get along with" seemed to be emphasized in those statements. Tom wasn't drunk enough to say "fuck you, pal!" even though the thought crossed his mind.

On cue, Phil Pearson added, "We're hoping a new spirit of cooperation is formed in the hangar, and we can work together to get the staff off their asses to support us."

Tom fumed inside. Cooperation in the hangar was code for "let me use your aircraft when mine are broke." And just days before, Tom was one of the staff supporting these commanders. There were lots of things Tom Lawton wasn't sure about, but he was sure he hadn't spent time on his ass trying to support these two. He had worked for the operations officer and supported what was directed. One good thing about CPT (P) Jerry Maurer was that he didn't play favorites, so all five troop commanders were tasked and treated equally. But tonight was not the night for antagonism. In Tom's mind, he decided to go "George Bush" and be a kinder and gentler troop commander. Tom let the comments go and said, "Gentlemen, we are going to be the best attack helicopter squadron in the US Army. A toast . . . to the commanders of the Fighting Sixth!" Phil, Chris, their wives, and the pack at the bar raised glasses and toasted the squadron.

"Ladies, why don't you head on over and meet my wife, Cindy?" Tom yelled across the bar, "Hey, Cindy, I got somebody you need to meet!" A loud, rude, and generally obnoxious behavior was not new to Tom Lawton. Even when it was intentional. "Just head right on over to that booth. I'll bring you both a beer in a minute. First, it's customary I do a shot with your husbands, and you, ladies, don't need to witness this kind of debauchery!" Karen Wise and Shauna Pearson giggled as they headed toward Cindy and Betty in the booth.

"Gentlemen, no more business tonight. You two"—Tom pointed to Phil and Chris—"I'd appreciate it if you would drink a shot with me. We are in Germany, we are commanders, and we are thirsty. Therefore, we must meet . . . Mr. Schnapps!"

The party pack came to life. "Schnapps!"

Tom was in his element now and directed, "Let's see, Phil, you look like an apple-schnapps kind of guy. And, Chris . . . meet Mr. Peach Schnapps!" Within seconds, the shots were on the bar. "To the line, troop commanders!" toasted Tom.

Phil and Chris looked at each other and then at Tom. "To us!"

Tom drank quick, slammed his shot glass on the bar, and looked right into his peers' eyes. "Don't ever forget that it's us!" Tom lost his smile as he looked into their eyes to make sure the meaning was understood. In Officer Candidate School, the unwritten motto was elegantly referred to as cooperate and graduate. There, in the "real" army of 1990, it was better put, "Don't fuck me and I won't fuck you!"

Chris Wise was the first to get the message. A smile crossed his lips, and Tom could see he was tracking. Phil Pearson was a little slower to understand that the Three Amigos were now together, just with a different player. Phil acknowledged the alliance with a "Hooaah" directed at Tom. "Hooah" is army slang that means many things, and in this particular case, "Roger, message received!"

Tom smiled a big smile and stuck his hand out. "I'm damn glad to be here, fellas! Hell with the handshake." Carl, the Caddie, showed up again. "Give me a big hug. I got some nookies for you two! Let me buy you guys a brew ski!" The truce was declared.

Just as the beer arrived, the threesome entering the club distracted the men. Louise and Hartley Osborn walked in, followed closely by Hal Timmons.

"Woof! I think I'm in Love," declared Dean.

"Again! Lighten up, Dean. That's my new lieutenant's wife. Real nice couple. You guys behave yourself because I'm not sure if they'll like you," said Tom.

"Wait a second," said Jed. "They like you, and they won't like us? Six hours in command and he's already lost his mind." Obediently, the lieutenants nodded up and down and then burst out laughing.

"All right. I'll introduce you. Try not to embarrass yourselves. And another thing. I don't think they drink. But Hal will have enough for both of them," said Tom as he waved the threesome up to the bar.

Tom made the introductions at the bar, and Hart Osborn introduced his beautiful wife, Louise Annette Osborn. Mrs. Osborn was five foot seven, with auburn hair down to the middle of her back. Her smile was radiant but pale compared to her eyes. She was, in a word, beautiful. She preferred to be called Lou Ann or just plain Lou to her friends. Naturally, all the guys proceeded to be real nice to their new pal Lou.

"Hart, please excuse me as I take your lovely wife away from all this guy talk. Mrs. Osborn, would you like to go sit with the ladies at the booth? That way, we can indulge in the customary male bonding we came here for," said Tom as the drunken crowd grunted approval of the suggestion.

Lou looked at Hart to receive an approving glance, which was received with a big smile. Tom stuck out an elbow for Lou to grab. Smiling with glee, the pair moved to the back of the club where Cindy, Betty, Karen, and Shauna were sitting with a couple other wives that decided to join them.

"Ladies, may I introduce Mrs. Louise Osborn. I'm sure she'll give you all permission to call her Lou," said Tom. "Lou, you're in good hands, so excuse me as I go make sure they don't get too drunk . . . without me to supervise!" Tom blew a little kiss to Cindy and spun away.

"Hi, everybody, I'm Lou." She waved hello and then directed a question to the table, "Is he always so friendly?"

"Only around women and children," answered Betty Stuart.

Cindy gave Betty an understanding glance. "I'm Cindy Lawton. Pay no attention to the jerks at the bar. I saw you at the change of command today. I'm sorry we didn't get a chance to talk."

"I didn't stay too long. I don't know many people. Hart and I don't get out much. What did your husband mean about all of the guys and . . . male bondage?" inquired Lou.

The ladies roared with laughter. "I don't get it. What'd I say?" asked Lou.

"Sit down next to me, honey, 'cause we need to talk!" declared an obviously drunk Betty Stuart.

"Your husband is so funny. And those impressions he does. Is he always like that?" asked Lou.

Betty answered this one. "Yeah, he's always like that. Cindy tells me his best impression is of a large, well-endowed pool boy!" Cindy nearly spit beer out her nose. Both looked for the lieutenant's wife to blush or retreat. Not this one.

Lou looked at Cindy and asked with a smile, "Is he any good at it?"

Cindy and Betty looked at each other and burst out laughing again. Cindy said while shaking her head, "No, no, he isn't. But he keeps telling me he's willing to learn!"

The whole table joined in the laugh. Betty grabbed Lou and hugged her arm. "You're gonna be all right."

Tom returned to his pack. "Captain Stuart, I left you in charge, and I see these two don't have beverages yet. You always were a slacker," said Tom in mock anger. "Hal, are you doing Jack and Mountain Dew tonight or just beer? Anything for you, Lieutenant Osborn?"

"Sir, just Pils to start," exclaimed Hal Timmons.

"Sir, could I have a Michelob?" asked Hart Osborn.

Tom eyed Hart curiously. "I didn't think you drank beer? You don't have to drink if you don't want to."

"Sometimes I drink a beer or two. Tonight, I feel like celebrating. Just one and I'm done. I'm driving," explained Hart.

"Outstanding, Lieutenant! You might just be designated to drive us all," said Jed.

Drinks arrived for lieutenants Osborn and Timmons. The topic of conversation as usual ranged from helicopters to training, to alcohol consumption, and back around the cycle. The conversation was only interrupted by the occasional congratulatory handshake from other commissioned officers there for the party.

At about 1930, the warrant officers from the squadron arrived en masse. Tom was beginning to think they were going to blow him off. But they showed, about fifty of them, with all their wives in tow. Captain Lawton thought to himself, *Time for the club card to start charging the drinks.*

All the warrants came by to shake hands. Tom immediately ordered five pitchers of beer and provided each handshake a beverage. He noticed every one of the Champions showed up. Friends from the Headhunters (HHT), Assassins (A Troop), Werewolves (B Troop), and Wrenchmasters (D Troop/Maintenance) were all at the club.

It was about 2000 when Jed told Tom it was time for a speech. Tom, a bit inebriated by now, shook his head negative and indicated he wasn't speaking to a crowd this large about anything. "Tom, it's your duty. You're gonna spend hundreds of dollars tonight, and Cindy's gonna kick your ass, so you might as well say thanks!" As if on cue, the four lieutenants agreed wholeheartedly. Tom's head dropped down, and he said, "You guys are gonna make me do this, aren't you?" Small smiles all around. "I hate crowds this big. They're all gonna laugh at me 'cause I'm drunk."

"Not tonight, boss," said Hal Timmons. "Like you said, tell the truth and they'll like it."

With a heavy sigh and resignation, he said, "Okay. But it's not gonna be anything special."

In unison, the other drunks clapped Tom on the back and agreed this was the way to go. Jed Stuart banged on the bar and announced, "The new Champion Six has somethin' he'd like to say." Tom Lawton took a deep breath to chase away the insecurity monster.

The tiny, overcrowded bar slowly became quiet. Tom stood next to his barstool. "First of all, I'd like to thank all of you for coming tonight. I've been a part of this squadron for over a year, and I know most of you already. My experience tells me we are good at what we do. I like to think we can be better. I've got a great bunch of troops in the Champions. Cindy and I look forward to the next two years with excitement and anticipation."

From the back booth came, "Speak for yourself!" The crowd laughed off Cindy's heckles.

"No, seriously, she told me she loves this shit!" There was more laughter from men and women alike, the men believing it and the women in sympathy.

"Gentlemen, a toast to the ladies!" urged Tom.

"To the ladies!" came the response.

"A toast to the finest attack helicopter squadron in the world. To the Fighting Sixth!" said Tom.

"To the Fighting Sixth!" responded the crowd.

Tom began to feel the part he was playing. Why fight it? "To the best damn country in the world. To the United States of America!"

"To the United States of America!" came the return.

What the hell, thought Tom, she's gonna be pissed at him anyway. "On behalf of my lovely wife, who's helping me pay for this, I'll keep the bar open for another hour," said Champion Six.

"Hooooaaaah!" roared the mob.

"See, sir! They love ya," observed Sheppard.

Tom looked at his running buddies. "She's gonna kill me."

"Nice of you to oblige all these friends, Cindy," said Betty.

Cindy gave Betty a mock smile and said, "If I kill him, do I go to jail in Germany, or do they take me to Fort Leavenworth?"

"Cindy, it's his command. It's his chance to shine. Some officers never get this opportunity. He's gonna be a great commander. We'll all be right here beside you," said Betty. To her surprise, she got an affirmative nod from Lou Osborn too.

"You're right, Betty. I won't kill him . . . tonight. But two years of this is going to be an eternity," said Cindy.

"It's all downhill after that first command," said Betty.

Cindy nodded, looked at Betty, and said, "Okay, I'm better. I can handle this."

Feeling her beer, Lou stepped in. "I'm better too. Let's go break up the bondage!" The wives all laughed.

Tom's insecurities from public speaking had subsided when a new one popped up. Spousal communication. He had not discussed the cost of the party with Cindy, and after the fact, he felt remorse. He prided himself for his ability to communicate with Cindy but realized he stepped on his crank big-time. To top it off, she was coming to the bar with the other wives.

"Cheese it, fellas. Household Six inbound with reinforcements. No more war stories. Time to be husbands and lieutenants. Jed, don't let her kill me in public," said Tom.

"I'm with ya, buddy," came the drunken response.

The women lined up opposite the men at the bar as if there was going to be a shoot-out. Cindy looked at her husband and each one of his drunken clan with piercing eyes. The club grew quiet again. Everyone wondered what Cindy Lawton would do. Cindy looked around the crowd and back at Tom. "Well, if your buyin', Champion Six, I guess it better be the good stuff!"

The bar erupted with a roar. Tom Lawton felt a great weight lifted from his shoulders. He had negative expectations of his wife's reaction, but she fooled him. Cindy stepped into her role as the commander's wife and filled the part to perfection. Maybe she really did love this shit, thought Tom. Cindy grabbed her husband, hugged him, and whispered into his ear, "You owe me big-time."

Tom could only smile and say, "I guess I should start with a dance?"

"That's a start. Come on," said Cindy.

"Fellas, we're dancin'! Jed, Hal, rally time, 2200," said Tom. It came out more like an order than he wanted, but it was too late to retract the order.

At least it was a slow song, thought Tom. He was much more comfortable dancing slow. Cindy was a good dancer. Tom always thought of himself as awkward. He held her close. "Thank you, honey. I should have come and talked to you first, but . . ."

"You're drunk," she interrupted. Tom agreed. "I don't mind that so much, but under these circumstances, you need to control yourself," reminded Cindy. She was a witness to Tom's alcoholic tendencies and offered a gentle reminder of his new responsibility, to which, she was glad Tom had not taken offense.

Tom looked into her eyes, and her words registered. In his new leadership position, he could not be just one of the boys. His troops were here at the club, and they would be watching his every move. He had already noticed many of them dancing now. "Have I told you how much I love you?" said Tom.

"You are very drunk." Cindy Lawton giggled. "You only say that when you're very drunk or very horny."

"Yes, I am!" declared Tom.

"Which, very drunk or very horny?" asked Mrs. Lawton.

"Both!" responded Captain Lawton with a smile.

"You've already satisfied one urge tonight, so don't expect anything in that other area until you start using your brain head instead of your . . . other head," chided Cindy with a mischievous smile.

Tom loosened his grip around her waist and smiled. "Roger, dear." He looked deep into her eyes. "I still love you, very much."

"Play your cards right and you might get lucky," said Cindy. She was a sucker for his baby blues. She couldn't help but notice how much bluer they were now that he didn't drink as much.

They danced about twenty minutes and went back up to the bar with the crowd. The warrant officers from C Troop were there talking with the two lieutenants, the Stuarts, and their platoon leaders. Tom accepted handshakes and thanks for the drinks from all. Every warrant officer in his troop was there. Tom's instructor pilot was the first to strike up conversation. CW4 Mark Nichols said, "Sir, on behalf of the rest of the troop, let me say welcome and can we all get another beer?" Getting laughs and grunts from the crowd, Tom knew he was cornered.

"I think one more round on Champion Six will just about do it. Remember, the Lawton household is a threesome." Tom nodded to the bartender one more round.

"Sir, you got a lot of time in Apaches, don't you?" asked the instructor pilot.

"I guess that depends on your perspective of a lot. I've got over five hundred hours in Apaches and another hundred in Cobras. As far as a lot, I have a lot compared to other commissioned pilots, but not Warrants with six years in the aircraft. Let me see if I remember, Nichols . . . eighteen years in, fourteen in guns, over 3,300 hours in Apaches of which about 1,100 are under night vision systems," recited Tom.

"Pretty good, sir. Only it's up to 1,200 night system in Apaches. Do you have us all down according to our flight statistics?" said Chief Warrant Officer 4 Nichols.

"That's my job," answered Captain Lawton dryly.

"Sir, that is a lot of time for a captain," said CW3 John Walker, the troop maintenance officer. "But how much of it is night system?"

Tom glanced at his maintenance officer with a wry smile. "I'm sure I've got more NVS time than some maintenance puke. Not your 2,300 Apache hours, but I've got about two hundred NS hours. And you, Mr. Walker?"

"Try 627 pilot night vision system and another 250 with goggles," replied Chief Warrant Officer 3 Walker.

Tom snapped his fingers. "The task force. That's it. You flew with the task force before Apaches were in the fleet." The burly six-foot-four-inch, 250-pound warrant bowed. "I am impressed. I looked at your Officer Record Brief, but the ORB was somewhat blank from '83 to '85. It makes sense now. I'm lucky to have you."

"Yes, sir, you are," came the reply from the none-to-shy mountain of a man. "There are five of us left in this unit. Dr. Mengelson and Terry LaTear both in B Troop and Rick Todd and Jerry Croner in Alpha."

"I worked with LaTear in my old unit. Now I understand why he's so good. You guys all have a pretty good reputation. You and Croner are maintenance officers, and LaTear is an instructor pilot, but what is Todd doing?" asked Tom.

"Todd is both an instructor pilot and a maintenance officer," said Nichols.

"Both?" said Tom.

"Roger that, sir. He's the stud of the Assassins," said CW3 John Walker.

"That really pisses off old 'Dick' Needles." Nichols laughed.

"Oh, I can see why," said Tom. "Needles is the boss's golden boy, and I know how well the boss likes Todd. Chief Warrant Officer 4 Needles is perhaps a little jealous of Chief Warrant Officer 3 Todd's dual qualification. I'm surprised someone hasn't made him go one way or the other."

"Shit, sir, A Troop is so fucked up. They need all the help they can get," said CW2 Alton Berstein.

Tom gave the junior warrant a glance, trying not to show any emotion. "Mr. Berstein, did it ever occur to you that we too may be all fucked up?"

The senior warrant officers laughed knowingly. "Sir, you're gonna be all right," said Walker.

Tom smiled at that. Allies. With a little help from friends, Tom might just get by. "Look, gentlemen, I have to go mingle with the peasants. We'll talk more business one-on-one next week and as a group on Monday. Please don't drink and drive because I would hate to get a call on my first night. Champions rule!" Tom gave a quick little salute, shook hands, and headed to work the room. He noticed he was starting to sober up a bit. A quick check over his shoulder led him to the conclusion his senior pilots weren't.

"Captain Lawton!" It was CW2 Joe Petty. Joe Petty was the most junior attack pilot in C Troop. Hal and Top had told Tom Petty was a brownnoser. Tom hadn't had the time to tell, but so far, he thought his two friends had read Petty wrong.

"Hello, Mr. Petty. How's it going?" asked Champion Six.

"Sir, I'd like you to meet my wife, Crystal," said Joe Petty.

"Nice to meet you. If you get a chance, stop over and say hi to Cindy. Are you having a good time?" asked Captain Lawton.

"Oh yes, sir. This is a great party. I finally got Joe to come out on the dance floor. He's very happy to have you as his new commander," said Crystal Petty.

Tom couldn't help the thought. How many of these people were kissin' his ass, and how many were really glad he was the new C Troop commander? He took it for granted that these two really were glad he was there. After all, Joe Petty didn't get to fly much under Sweat. The kid was busting his ass to get noticed, and all he wanted to do was fly. Wrong approach, thought Tom. He was so good at computers and administration, Sweat had him locked in the office as a personal butt boy. The perception probably came from his many hours doing someone else's work. Time for a little test. Was Joe Petty a permanent butt boy or an army aviator in waiting?

"I'm glad you're both having a good time. Mr. Petty, when was the last time you flew night system?" asked Tom.

"Hell, sir, I haven't flown at all since the beginning of May. I've got five days until I go uncurrent," came the answer.

That's what Tom expected. Now the challenge. "On Wednesday night, I want to do a little mission. Just a little four-ship mission. Day out and a night return. Are you up for a multiship op?"

"Hell yeah, sir!" came the response.

Bingo, thought Tom. An army aviator in a butt boy disguise. Tom was sober enough to remember common sense. "I know you fly front seat with Chief Warrant Officer 3 Dolce. Since it's been so long, I want you two to do a day flight on Tuesday afternoon and at least an hour of night system Tuesday night. I'll talk to Lieutenant Osborn for the change. Take your time on your first day out and be ready to go Wednesday. Okay?"

Petty's jaw was visibly lower. Nothing for forty days and now twice in a week.

"Crystal, you might be angry with me, but I intend for your husband to fly a lot more. That means a lot of nights he'll come home late. But I promise you we'll be flying and not here." Tom wanted make sure this young couple knew what was going on and why. Definitely a positive pair. They were beaming. At least one couple would go home happy tonight. Tom erased the thought. "I've got to go find my better half before I get into more trouble. Very nice meeting you, Mrs. Petty. See you Monday, Joe."

Tom continued toward the back booth. He noticed one more table of Champions to visit. It was the biggest table in the bar, and at least five of his warrants were there, and they were playing drinking games. He watched for a minute and noticed four of his attack pilots and his newly promoted scout pilot engaging in a chugging contest. *Oh, to be young again!* thought the thirty-year-old captain. He thought back to the Fort Hood Officer's Club. It was 1984, and Tom saw himself as a fresh lieutenant doing the same thing. He was snapped back to reality by the call from across the bar.

"Hey, sir! Wanna chug with us?" yelled an obviously drunk CW2 Wesley Cross.

"Not tonight, Mr. Cross, I've got to wash the cat. He hates it when I puke on his fur." Champion Six smirked.

After the obligatory laugh, Wes Cross said, "Shoot, sir, we all heard about you. You've got a reputation as one great partier. We heard you're a wild man."

"That's reformed wild man, Mr. Cross. My liver appreciates me more every day. I still drink, but not with the same purpose I used to have," Tom said. For the life of him, Tom couldn't quite remember what that purpose was. He knew if he had kept doing what he was doing, he would probably have been dead by now. This was the most alcohol Tom had consumed in years.

"All I can say, sir, is I'm damn glad you and Lieutenant Timmons are my chain of command now," said Wes Cross. "Too bad you don't party hard anymore because Mr. Tucker is kickin' ass."

"As a true Champion should be. I see he has pretty good company with Mr. Hart, Mr. Toretti, and your mentor, Mr. O'Toole." Tom moved closer to the table and looked at the finest attack pilots in the world.

"Sir, come on, sir! Just you and me. Let's see who's fastest," challenged CW2 Carl Tucker.

Tom sized up the situation. Old urges to run with this pack of young guns started to swell inside him from places that were best left in the dark. He glanced across the bar toward Cindy. She was watching him. The look provided Tom the answer to Mr. Tucker's challenge. "Mr. Tucker"—Tom paused—"I concede. And based on what I just witnessed, I declare you the victor and forever beer-chugging representative for the Charlie Troop, 1-6, Champions." Tom started a mock golf clap that was picked up by the gathering at the table. Of course, Carl Tucker, with his newfound stardom, raised his hands in triumph and blew kisses to his fans.

Tom said in drunken Shakespeare, "Ladies and gentlemen, I bid you all a fond ado! 'Tis time for this Champion to depart. I must go yonder to meet my wife before there is no wife yonder to meet!" He changed the subject and got serious. "Please, drive safely tonight. I don't need any calls at three in the morning on my first night in command. Thank you all for coming. Good night." Tom shook hands and waved as he walked away to meet Cindy. She was still watching. Cindy was smiling again as she noticed Tom was coming back to her table.

"How are you doing?" asked Cindy.

"I'm still a little drunk," Tom said matter-of-factly.

"Are you ready to go? I've got to take Lisa down the street when we get home," said Cindy.

"Not quite yet, honey. I need about fifteen more minutes," said Tom. Cindy cast him a suspicious eye. "It's okay, honey. I'm not gonna drink any more tonight." He kissed her on the cheek. "I'll be back real soon."

"Operation Safety Net?" asked Jed as Tom approached the bar.

"Roger that," said Tom. He got the bartender's attention. "Two big ice waters please. It's time. Lieutenant Osborn, can you identify the vehicles of Mr. Walker, Mr. Dolce, and Mr. Cross?"

"Yeah, sure, sir. What's up?" said Hart Osborn.

"Come with us. Let's go, fellas," said Tom.

Tom, Jed, and the four lieutenants headed out to the parking lot. The natural-born leader in Tom Lawton took over. He was obviously on a mission. "Dean and Schlepper, you guys stand watch here. Sing us a little Stones, Schlepper, if somebody comes out. Sing loud. I bet they're parked out back, Jed."

The four men headed to the back of the bar. "Lieutenant, whose are those?"

"The '87 BMW is Mr. Walker's. I'm pretty sure the '83 Audi is Dolce's. I don't understand. What are you . . . we doing?" asked the confused lieutenant.

"Operation Safety Net, Lieutenant Jed. Hal and I cooked this up because we have a problem. Let me have it, Hal." Hal Timmons reached into his pocket and pulled out a tiny object too small for Hart Osborn to see in the darkness. Tom took it and squatted next to the visible tire on

John Walker's nearly new BMW 318I. "I guess divorced guys have lots of extra money." A loud hissing sound came from the tire.

"Sir, he's only separated, and I can't believe you just trashed his tire. Isn't this illegal or something, sir?" asked the lieutenant.

"Hart, listen to me. We have a collective problem in the troop. We are going to take actions to prevent bad things from happening to people we care about. Is that clear enough?" said Tom.

Jed Stuart explained, "The whole troop drinks and drives away from these functions, and we know they do. Captain Lawton did a recon to see who had designated drivers and who didn't. Hal knows they've been parking out back to slip the military police and the *Polizei*. Walker, Dolce, and Tucker are too drunk to drive, so their vehicles shouldn't be moved tonight. A drunk isn't gonna change a tire after drinking as much as they have."

"But, sir, are you gonna pay for the tires?" asked Hart.

"It's okay, Lieutenant. I'm just pulling the core from the valve stem. After the air is out, I put the core back in, put the cover on, and no one can tell the difference. The tire is all right. Tomorrow, when they get motivated, they'll change their tires, fix what they expect to be a flat, and realize it's not damaged," continued Tom.

"Not trashed, but you just screwed with the warrants in your troop, sir. They're gonna think it was you," said Hart Osborn.

"Doesn't matter. I picked a senior warrant of great respect, an obviously drunk Mr. Tucker, whose wife is a little drunk too. And finally, Hal's best buddy in the scout ranks, Mr. Cross. Three Champions that are part of our team. Three pilots we can't do without," said Tom.

Hart still wasn't with them. Hart said something Tom didn't expect. "I think this is a bunch of crap," said the lieutenant, either deliberately leaving out the sir or forgetting to use it. "This is gonna destroy morale and drive the unit apart. I think you should stop what you're doing."

Jed made a move toward Hart Osborn with a look in his eye that Tom could tell even in the dim light wasn't good.

"Whoa, Jed. Go get the Audi while Lieutenant Osborn and I have a little talk." Jed cooled down a little and headed toward the Audi. Over his shoulder, Jed was muttering, "If he fucks this up, I'll be the first one to . . ."

Tom let him go, not listening anymore as he focused on the problem at hand. His temper had spun up but was under control now. "I'll tell you what I think. I think you didn't have the guts to do anything about this before. Your previous, and I hesitate to say it, commander, couldn't, wouldn't, and didn't stop it! These guys are too important to me and you to be taken out by a DWI or killin' some unsuspecting deutschers by driving drunk!" Tom's temper picked up a notch. "You want to know what ruins morale. I'll tell you what ruins morale. Death ruins morale!" Tom took a deep breath to gain his composure. "So if this isn't the way you want to conduct business, your point is noted. Then I'll be clear to let you know this is *my* troop, not *our* troop. I'm not scrapin' any of *my* guys off the pavement or outta trees. From this particular moment, you can be in *my* troop, or you can pack your shit!" Hartley Osborn was hurt by his new boss's outburst. Once again, Tom had the urge to close the wound.

But the urge faded fast as he remembered one other thing. "And the next time you talk to me, use sir or don't say anything," said Tom as he looked for body language in the dim light.

Tom was still too soft to let it go like that. "If you want the Champions to be *our* troop, you, Hal, Top, and I have to speak with one voice. I'm sorry for being . . . such a dick on the first day. But this is the way it has to be. I'm the guy in charge."

"Yes, sir," was the only response.

Tom waited for any sign of reaction and got nothing. "Fuck it. You do whatever you have to do. Tell them or don't tell. They'll know. Hell, Walker will know as soon as he comes out!" Silence. "They'll figure out why it was done and . . . modify their behavior. Or else they're gone." More silence.

Just then, the awkward silence was broken by a chorus of Schlepper's piss-poor impersonation of Mick Jagger singing, "I can't get no . . . satisfaction!"

Tom glanced back at Hart. "Time to go." Reluctantly, Lieutenant Osborn joined his commander as they headed toward the screeching chorus.

"Is he okay with this, sir?" asked Hal Timmons.

"I don't know yet, Hal." Tom paused as he watched Hart Osborn head straight for his wife. His face was a little flush as he whispered in Lou's ear. It appeared she wasn't quite ready to go. Another whisper and up she came. Tom took a deep breath. "Bartender, another water please."

Back to Jed and Hal, "I guess we'll find out Monday." Tom finished the water quickly. "I'm outta here. Hal, do you need a ride?"

"Sir, I think I'll stay here for a while. Since my ride is leaving." Hal smiled. "I think I'll stick around and see what happens. Bein' how you don't want a call at three in the morning and all, sir."

Tom nodded and smiled. "Hooaah, Lieutenant Timmons." Tom skipped the handshake and offered up a high five to the lieutenant, which was gratefully appreciated.

"Keith and Mick, outstanding chorus, my good men. Please see that the bar is closed down properly and perhaps Hal will be kind enough to drive you home." Tom patted the two inebriated lieutenants on the back. "See you Monday."

"Come on, Tom. Let's go get our wives," said Jed Stuart.

The two captains made one last run through the crowd, saying good-bye to all along the way.

"Sir, see you at PT on Monday morning?" hollered Mr. Tucker from across the crowded bar.

"Nice and early, Mr. Tucker. See you at six thirty." *Is he pissed?* thought Tom. He remembered back to when he could recover from drinking like that in no time.

The two men arrived at the table and were ready to go. Betty and Cindy were ready, and the foursome headed to the parking lot.

"Is the Stuart Bar-b-que open tomorrow?" asked Tom.

It was Betty that answered, "How about 1600?" The Stuarts lived on the economy and somehow managed a whole German house with four bedrooms and a basement. The closed-in yard was perfect for cooking out and letting the kids run. The Lawtons were not so fortunate. Their accommodations were government stairwells on the Caserne. Convenient, but no room and no privacy.

"We'll see you then. Drive carefully," said Cindy as she entered the '88 Caravan.

"Hey, Jed?" said Tom, getting his friend's attention. "Thanks."

Jed smiled and shook his head. "Anytime." As he climbed in the Land Cruiser, Jed yelled, "'Cause you the maayan!"

"Take me home, beautiful, and then love me like there's no tomorrow," said Tom, laying his head on Cindy's shoulder.

Cindy looked down and, in a soft and caring voice, said, "You can just love yourself tonight."

Tom sat up and opened his mouth in mock amazement. "The pope says that every sperm is sacred. I can't do anything like that."

"If it's love you want tonight, you can. Don't try to butter me up. You probably spent $500 tonight. We don't have that kind of money, Tom," said Cindy.

Tom knew she was right. He started to think of some cute remark to break the mood but decided against it, lest he make things worse. Course of action 2. Time to change the subject.

"You want me to take Lisa home?" asked Tom.

"No, I'll do it," she answered. The rest of the ride was in silence.

"How was she, Lisa? I hope she didn't give you any problems," asked Cindy.

"No problems, Mrs. Lawton. She's already asleep," said the babysitter.

"Well, come on and I'll walk you home," said Cindy.

"Oh, that's okay, Mrs. Lawton. I can make it on my own. It's only two blocks up the street," said Lisa.

Tom listened and noticed that Cindy was quick to respond, "No, I insist. If you're ready, let's go. Bye, Tom. I'll be back in a few minutes." And in a flash, the two were out the door.

Tom thought hard about what just happened. Usually, Cindy wanted him to take the sitter home. Secondly, when she did take the sitter home, she would kiss him good-bye. And finally, she didn't go check on Megan. This added up to bad. Tom considered his options: go to bed and act as if nothing happened; stay up and wait for her to come home, talk it out, and make everything all right; or finally, wait and confront her on her attitude and how she needed to support her husband. Tom's decision-making process was in a streamlined mode due to alcohol, excitement, and just a little fatigue. He hadn't slept well the last week. Tom Lawton, being the man he was, chose the path of least resistance.

He went upstairs, checked on Megan, and went to bed.

CHAPTER 2

0630, June 22, 1990
Katterheim Caserne
Jordan Fitness Center

"LIEUTENANT, YOU GOT EVERYBODY?" ASKED CPT Tom Lawton.

"No, sir, I'm missing two," said LT Hartley Osborn.

Tom looked at Hal Timmons. "I'm only missing the three on reverse cycle, Mr. Cross, Mr. O'Toole, and Specialist Cryder."

"Roger. Let's get going," said Tom. The first sergeant called the troop to attention and immediately went into stretching. From his position in the back of the formation, Tom could see everything. He took mental notes of who was working hard at the exercises and who was not.

Tom turned around to see Mr. Tucker and Mr. Berstein trotting up from the parking lot. He intercepted Lieutenant Osborn. "I got it, Lieutenant."

Tom jogged out to meet the pair before they got to the formation. "Gentlemen, when's the 0630 PT formation?" Tom didn't wait for a response as he sensed the warrants' embarrassment. "As officers, I expect you to set the example. I'll be an asshole about timing. Don't be late and never miss a pitch pull. If we're supposed to leave at 2100, we leave at 2100 with whoever is ready to leave. Got it?"

Both warrants were at the position of attention, not knowing their commander's temperament. They looked at each other and then back at Captain Lawton. "Roger, sir!"

"Chalk it up as your first lesson. Let's go sweat," said Tom. The threesome jogged up to the formation.

After Top had finished the calisthenics, the troop closed ranks, and Tom Lawton took over. "Good morning, Champions!" Captain Lawton received a resounding "Good morning, sir!"

"I'm glad to see everyone here is in good spirits and ready to run. I love to run. I run for time, not distance. We'll do something a little different this morning. We'll run out for twenty minutes in formation, and it's every man for himself coming back. Any questions?" None came. Tom overheard some snide comments like, "Let's show the old man what we got." Tom looked at his troops and said, "All right then. Let's do it."

The pace was nice and easy going out because Tom wanted to make sure every one made it all the way out for at least two miles. He noticed Top, both lieutenants, and two other sergeants took turns singing cadence. He kept the unit guidon close on his flank, often making comments to the guidon bearer Staff Sergeant Turner about the pace. Top had obviously put Turner there for a reason. He was the senior aerial observer, which meant he was an enlisted aviator. Tom could tell by the sound of the cadence that the pace was too fast for the troop. He slowed down just before the two-mile mark and glanced over his shoulder to see the troop had spaced apart significantly. He took Staff Sergeant Turner and the guidon back and gathered everyone up. They continued to head out further from the Caserne. At the two-mile mark, Captain Lawton made a turn north down a dirt road through the woods, and picked up the pace just a little. This brought on a comment from Staff Sergeant Turner. "Sir, you trying to kill 'em?" Tom just laughed.

Twenty minutes into the woods, Tom turned the unit around. Of the original 27, only 18 remained. "Top, you and Lieutenant Timmons have straggler control. Staff Sergeant Turner, stay with me. The shortest way back is through these woods on this path to my left. Champions, you are on your own. See you at the finish."

Two soldiers took off immediately, stride for stride at what appeared to be a six-minute-per-mile pace. One was Staff Sergeant Ramirez, the aero scout platoon sergeant; and the other, to Tom's surprise, was Chief Warrant Officer 2 Tucker. How long could they keep that up for wondered Tom?

A mile from the Caserne, only Lieutenant Osborn and Staff Sergeant Turner were still with their commander. Tom looked over his shoulder. He could tell Turner was fine, but Hart Osborn looked a little green. Tom didn't say a word. He caught Turner's attention and nodded to see if he could pick up the pace. Turner smiled a broad smile and said, "Hoaah, sir!" They accelerated to their own six-minute-mile pace. Lieutenant Osborn faded. Valiant effort, thought Tom.

He could see Chief Warrant Officer 2 Tucker finishing up, but no Staff Sergeant Ramirez. He slowed the pace for the last quarter mile to cool down. As he finished up, he saw Hector Ramirez, all five foot, six inches of him, doing gut crunches next to the gym stairs. Chief Warrant Officer 2 Tucker was stretching out his legs and keeping the clock for Ramirez.

"Good job, guys. I'm impressed," said an out-of-breath Tom Lawton. "Sergeant Ramirez, what do you normally do your two-mile run in?" asked Tom.

"I did an eleven-forty last April. I feel really slow this morning," answered the sergeant.

"Feel a little slow, huh?" Tom shook his head. "And you, Mr. Tucker?"

"I did a twelve-twelve, but I didn't max the sit-ups," answered the warrant officer with a trace of a frown.

Tom chuckled. "Outstanding, fellas. Staff Sergeant Turner?"

"Sir, I busted thirteen, but I can't do push-ups. I only got a 278," came the reply.

"Same same for me, Sergeant. I can't max push-ups either." Then Tom noticed Lieutenant Osborn coming down the road, breathing real heavy. "Hey, Lieutenant Osborn, you gonna make it? I think he's gonna hurl, fellas," said Tom. Hart Osborn came in, breathing hard, and only waved as he walked around the side of the building. The small group got a good laugh at the lieutenant's expense. "Hey, he gave it 100 percent!" Tom chuckled.

Mr. Tucker said, "I think he's still giving!" That got another small round of laughter.

Slowly, the rest of the troop came struggling in. Top and Hal Timmons had a small group of six guys running in formation to finish up. Tom automatically checked his watch. Forty-two minutes for this group to finish up. He wanted to be upset but knew better. These guys didn't have a lot of time for physical training, and it was evident today. He couldn't be mad at them. PT was just something else that needed to be fixed.

Captain Lawton got the thumbs-up from Top Garcia. Top would form them up, and Tom would take over the formation to release the troop.

When Tom took the formation, he noticed many troops could barely stand. "At ease. Everybody, stretch in place. Some people are in better shape than others, and that's just fact. But a lot of you have been letting yourselves go to crap. In the helicopter maintenance business, you have to work out on your own, or you'll never stay in shape. Sometimes, like when we go to the field, you can only hope you don't get too far out of shape, so you lower your standard. Gentlemen, this is the lowest PT standard I want you to accept. What you feel right now, don't worry, it'll get easier because we were all in shape once." That got a small "Hoaah" from Staff Sergeant Ramirez. "When you are on reverse cycle, your place of duty at 1200 hours is this building. I will meet you here. I try to PT twice a day unless meetings take me away. I can't order you to do PT as much as you should, but four days a week is mandatory. Always stretch before and after because I can't afford to lose anybody for injuries. Get cleaned up and I'll see the officers at 0900 in the classroom. Top, get 'em started on fixin' aircraft and I'll talk to the enlisted soldiers at 1100. Sergeant First Class Pennington, we need four aircraft NVS capable for Wednesday night, okay?"

"Roger, sir!" came the response as Sergeant First Class Pennington sounded off.

"Champions, attention!" yelled Tom. "Top, you have the controls! I'll see you at eight forty."

The physical fitness status of a particular unit could be used as a gauge to see what their level of cohesion was or how good their morale is. As a gauge, this level is generally equal to the unit's status in other areas such as personnel actions, training proficiency, supply accountability, and especially their spirit. Besides the health benefits, physical training is meant to be fun and used as an outlet for the soldiers to enjoy unit camaraderie. It's hard for units to have fun at PT when it's kicking their asses. Tom was afraid this was an indication of the unit's overall status. His initial impression was the Champions were in pretty bad shape. His assessment was on the mark.

June 22, 1990
0840 Hangar 3010
Katterheim Caserne

FIRST SERGEANT GARCIA WAS ALREADY IN the office, doors all unlocked, coffee in hand, and ready to go. "Well, Top, I'd hoped they were in a little better shape. It looks like we have some work ahead of us.

But Tucker, Turner and Ramirez impressed me. Does Ramirez work as hard as he works out?"

"Yes, sir. He's the best junior NCO you got. Lieutenant Osborn has a packet in for him to be the small unit NCO of the year. As for the others," said Top with a pause, "we got work to do. We haven't had the time to do good PT. In case you can't tell, it wasn't emphasized before today."

"I could tell," said Tom. "Enough about that. How about maintenance? If PT is an indicator, my thoughts are we're sucking in a whole bunch of areas."

"Sir, in all honesty, I feel our maintenance practices are worse than our PT status. We're too scattered and just don't seem to be focused. We go twenty different directions at a hundred miles an hour. Typical Cav, half assed, full blast!" Top said without smiling. He continued, "This MTOE sucks." Garcia was doing a little venting this morning. The Military Table of Organization and Equipment was established by the army to provide a standardized amount of personnel and equipment to units of similar size and mission. The series MTOE the aviation troops lived with was Spartan, to say the least.

"Top, it's the same MTOE across the army, and everybody else has a problem with it too. We just have to work smarter. Number 1 on my hit parade is the maintenance. For three reasons, it's safer if they're maintained better, we get consistent flying in the long run, and finally, everyone's morale will improve."

Top nodded approvingly. "I'll talk to the platoon sergeants this afternoon and get them focused in that area immediately."

"Good deal, Top. Now I get to go meet the warrant officers. I'm looking forward to this," said Tom.

"Troop, attention!" shouted Second Lieutenant Timmons as Captain Lawton entered the room.

"Take your seats, everybody. Good morning." Tom gave them all a few seconds to get settled. "First of all, let me say thanks for coming Friday night. Cindy and I had a wonderful time. I'm also glad everyone made it home all right." He looked directly at Chief Warrant Officer 3 Walker with a big smile. Mr. Walker had no expression whatsoever. *He knew how his tire got flat*, thought Tom. *Good. He can spread the word.*

"I've got a few areas I want to discuss with you this morning. Safety, maintenance, and training. Safety six? Where are you?" asked Tom.

"Right here, sir," said CW3 Tom Dolce.

"Your assessment of our safety posture?" quizzed the commander.

"Sir, we're doin' pretty good. We had a class C last month, but it was due to a component failure. I'd say were doing well," came the response.

That wasn't quite what Tom was looking for. "How many flight hours in the last six months for the troop?"

Lieutenant Timmons was awake. "One hundred twenty by the scouts in the last three months."

Lieutenant Osborn took the hint. "We've got one hundred . . . twenty . . . nine in the last six months."

Tom nodded in affirmation. "Is that enough to be at the standard"—Tom looked for the proper words—"that you as army aviators would like to be at?"

The emphatic response across the room was negative, led most boisterously by Chief Warrant Officer 3 Walker's "Hell no!"

"You should . . . correction. *We* should fly over eight hundred hours next year. Of that, 300 to 350 will be NVS. I want 40 percent of our time to be night system. It is safer to fly at night, both in peace time and if we have to go to war."

A question. It was CW2 Joe Petty. "Sir, how do you figure it's safer to fly at night? I mean, you can't see better than in the day?"

"Good question. But I'll defer my answer to the experience in the room. Mr. Weimer, can you help me out with this?" said Tom.

CW4 Ron Weimer was a UH-1 Huey veteran of fifteen years. In the army's eyes, if he was to stick around for twenty, he needed to be tracked in an advanced-type aircraft or get out. In his fifteen years of Hueys, Ron was a maintenance officer and an instructor pilot for over ten years. He was sharp as a tack and had a very aggressive air about him. "Sir, there's a couple of reasons. One, stricter control measures and reporting procedures. Two, higher weather minimums," said the veteran. Then he added, "And around here, nobody flies at night." That brought a little chuckle from the pilots.

"I'll buy that. Plus one more thing. You are more likely to have your heads out of your cockpits looking outside at what's happening. The communication between crews will be much better because of anxiety."

Tom let that sink in. "The more you fly at night, the better you are at it and the safer a pilot and crew you become because you work together. Forty percent night system time is the goal."

Tom started on his second topic. "In order to do that, we have to have aircraft up. I am an advocate for aggressive preventive maintenance practices. I believe every officer is a maintenance officer." This got an "amen" out of Walker. "In the old cavalry days, everybody took care of their own horse. First Lieutenant Osborn, I want everyone's names painted on the aircraft by the end of the week, with the crew chief that's responsible for the bird on there too. Each pilot in command reports the aircraft status daily to the maintenance officer. Each crew knows its own aircraft better than the maintenance officer. The next issue is for the armament officer. Talk to me?"

"Sir, Mr. Berstein," said CW2 Alan Berstein.

"Gunnery is a year-round process. Not a biannual event where you get to fix what just broke. If a bird is in the hangar, I want you checking something. Upload and download some thirty-millimeter rounds, clean the rocket pods, or do some power on checks for the Hellfire systems. Run the gamete on armament. Check everything and then recheck it. Do you have an assistant?" asked Tom.

"No, sir, but I'll take two with that workload," said Mr. Berstein, drawing a laugh.

"I don't see that happening!" Tom smiled. "You are Mr. Walker's assistant, and Mr. Tucker is your assistant. Mr. Walker, you are hereby directed to train first Mr. Berstein and then Mr. Tucker as your assistants and successors. Stuff is going to break. But the stuff we say is up needs to be FMC. We have to develop confidence in our equipment.

"My final topic is training. Mr. Nichols, you're the senior instructor pilot here. What is your opinion of our training proficiency?" asked Captain Lawton.

"Sir, we're better than anybody else around here," answered CW4 Mark Nichols.

Everyone chuckled except Tom. Good spirit, but not very honest. Nichols deliberately avoided answering the question. Tom put Nichols on the spot again. "My question was, what is your opinion of *our* training proficiency?"

Tom literally saw Mark Nichols squirm in his seat.

A pause. Nichols started slowly as if it were painful. "Sir, we're not dangerous."

Silence filled the room. A surprisingly honest answer, thought Tom. "I think you need to expand on that answer a little bit."

The instructor pilot drew a heavy breath and began, "We can fly. Straight and level, a little instruments. Individually some nap of the earth (NOE) and NVS (night vision system)." Then he concluded with what Tom had already figured. "Nothing collectively."

That got some attention and an outburst from one of Nichols's peers. "Oh that's bullshit, sir!" said Walker. "We can do any mission we're ordered to do." This brought the room into a small buzz. Some thought the Champions were collectively trained and others untrained. Of particular note, Weimer and Nichols definitely sided against any semblance of multiship operations. Walker, Toretti, and Dolce all agreed the unit was capable of executing multiship operations. Tom also noted the lieutenants and junior warrants, to their credit, kept their mouths shut.

"Gentlemen," said Tom, getting control again, "I have the solution. Wednesday, 1600. Day out, night return. First Lieutenant Osborn, you have the mission. Plan on four aircraft and show me the crews later today. We'll see where we're at."

"In summary, the maintenance train will drive this unit. If maintenance is solid, we'll fly our butts off. The aircraft will perform better, we will perform better, and we will fly safer if we fly more. I'll entertain any questions, and then I need to see the lieutenants and Mr. Walker in my office," said Tom. No questions came. "Good. Let's go fix some aircraft."

"Troop, attention!" said First Lieutenant Osborn.

"Carry on," returned the commander.

Later that day, Tom had a get-together with some of the leaders. "Everybody, take a seat, please. Mr. Walker, I wanted to talk to you to make sure you are on the same sheet of music as we are. Apparently, shortcuts and inaccuracies in reporting were status quo before. I want you to know I don't need to have inflated numbers to meet DA standards. I need to have aircraft that are 75 to 80 percent FMC. We're worse off reporting aircraft up that are down than reporting a true status if that status is actually lower than the standard." Tom paused, looking at the maintenance officer for a response. "Does that make sense?"

"Sir, I understand what you're saying. Previously, I was told that we would meet DA standards at all costs," said Mr. Walker, glancing at Lieutenant Osborn.

"This isn't the previous regime. Working aircraft is the bottom line. If they are up and working, the numbers will naturally increase," said Tom.

Mr. Walker countered, "We need help then, sir."

"Name it," said Tom.

"As it works now, we get the new crew chiefs and train them. After a year, they go to D Troop to make up the phase teams. It should probably be the other way around. D Troop trains them, and we get them on an aircraft after six to eight months of training. Plus we're short two crew chiefs right now," said the maintenance officer. Tom looked at Hart Osborn, who nodded his concurrence.

"Good idea, John. I'll talk to Captain Rooks and see if he can help us out. After all, if we fix stuff at our level, that's less he has to fix in D Troop. Let me ask you something else, John. Have you ever heard of P4T2?" asked Captain Lawton.

"Yes, sir. That's a maintenance practice the guys in the Hundred and First use to keep their fleet up. Problem, plan, people, parts, time, and tools. Or something like that. We've never tried it here. Does it work?" asked Mr. Walker.

"I don't know. I do know the guys at Campbell have one of the best records for readiness in the army, so they must be doing something right. They have a maintenance company commander that developed this P4T2 plan, and it's obviously helping them. I think he mostly had it in mind for battalion—or squadron-level operations." Tom looked at the lieutenants. "We're going to try this at our level, both scouts and guns. Mr. Walker, you are responsible for identifying the problems and getting the parts and the tools to fix 'em. The lieutenants are responsible for the plan, the people, and the time. Just remember this. I don't think it succeeds unless you all communicate and all six items work as one." Tom got up and down nods and the "Roger" he was looking for. "Plus one more shot at you, Hal. Until we get some help in gun crew chiefs, your guys get trained in gun maintenance. I don't expect them to pull the transmission, but they can launch, do preventive maintenance checks with NCO supervision, and recover any aircraft returning at night. Will that be a problem?"

Tom could tell Hal Timmons didn't think much of the idea of his scout crew chiefs working extra hours to keep the guns flying, particularly since his four aircraft weren't in any better shape.

"Hal, I know what you're thinking. Scout crew chiefs shouldn't go home until the gun guys go home. We need to instill a team concept here. Not scouts against guns, but one whole unit." Tom studied the lieutenant. He knew he could order him to give up his people, but if the lieutenant supported the decision here, Tom knew that Hal would sell it to his crew chiefs. That way, Tom wouldn't hear about it later. "And if the guns are, for some miraculous reason doing extremely well, Hart, your guys gotta help the scouts."

"I don't have any problem with that, sir," responded Lieutenant Osborn.

Hal still hadn't completely swallowed the deal. Tom tried a stab at humor to break the tension and became an old man from Brooklyn. "You gotta trust me on dis. I'm not sellin' ya my grandmother's car." That got a partial smile from the skeptical lieutenant. "Work with me on this." Both the lieutenants chuckled. Mr. Walker smiled, but Tom could tell the impression meant nothing to his maintenance officer.

Reluctantly, 2LT Hal Timmons agreed. "Okay, sir. I want to make sure I understand that the scouts are equal in support needs to the guns." Tom nodded in agreement. "The scouts can help out," answered the lieutenant.

"Outstanding, Lieutenant. Then we all agree. We'll try this P4T2 for sixty days. With the crew chiefs working collectively and reporting in a long run, I think we'll be in great shape. Any questions?" Tom looked at the three men. "All right. Thanks. Let's see if we can practice what I preach. All of you meet me here at 1700 and we'll discuss your plans. One other thing, Mr. Walker. You are in the scout business too."

"Roger that, sir," replied the big warrant officer.

"Get outta here and go fix something," said Tom.

The lieutenants both got up to leave, but Mr. Walker moved a little slower. Lieutenant Osborn looked at Walker and then at Tom.

"Can I talk to you for a minute, sir?" asked John Walker. "In private."

Tom looked at the lieutenants at the door. He gave them a glance that they both understood. Hal Timmons continued out the door, but Hart

Osborn lingered. "It's okay, Lieutenant. Close the door on your way out please."

"Please sit down, John. What's up?" asked Captain Lawton.

"Friday, after the party, I came out to my car, and my tire was flat. You wouldn't know anything about that, would you?" asked the warrant. Tom noticed two things. One, Mr. Walker was not sure that Tom had done it, so Lieutenant Osborn had not told him. And secondly, the big warrant officer had not taken a seat. It was time for Tom to show his cards.

Tom looked into John Walker's eyes. "I did it."

The big man became angry. "What the fuck is that all about? What kind of chickenshit is that?"

Tom swallowed hard. The fact that the warrant had not called him "sir" was not important at that particular moment. He got up, walked around the desk, and got close to John. He looked up at him and smiled. "I can't afford to lose you, John."

"That's your answer." John Walker backed up a step. Tom stood straight, half expecting a swing. "That's your answer!" There was a pause for a couple of seconds, and a trace of a smile appeared on John Walker's face. Instead of the punch Tom expected, John Walker bent over laughing. Just as quickly as he lost it, John Walker regained his military bearing. As hotheaded as he was, he was always one helluva good officer. The warrant shook his head and said, "Hell, sir, I thought you were gonna lie about it!"

"You mean you knew I did it?" asked Tom.

"No, not really, sir," John added. "I guessed it was you. There was just too much coincidence going on. Three tires on three different C Troop cars. A new commander and your emphasis on not drinking and driving." John was still chuckling, and it was confusing to Tom. "Hell, sir, four of us wasted Saturday afternoon trying to fix tires that weren't even flat." He was still shaking his head.

Tom thought he understood the humor but needed to emphasize his point. "At least you didn't drive home drunk. Do you understand the reason?" Tom looked at him for a response.

"To get your point across about drinking and driving," said the burly warrant officer. It was the answer Tom hoped would come.

"Something like that. It's a little more than that. I can't lose you. Or Tucker or Cross or anybody else for any reason. Not for a DWI." Tom paused to let that sink in. "You're all too important to me and the unit. I admit it's a chickenshit thing to do, but I'd do it again in a heartbeat if it keeps you from fucking up your career. Or worse," said Tom.

John Walker stopped smiling, looked at Tom, and said, "I get your message, sir."

Tom stuck out his hand. "I'm in this for the long haul, and I want you at my back the whole way."

"Sir, if we'd found out Friday night . . . ," said John.

Tom interrupted. "You didn't because you were drinkin' until three in the morning." Tom let that sink in. "I'm not your dad or your brother. And I'm not gonna henpeck you like a wife. But you need to take better care of yourself and the junior warrants. They obviously respect you. And I enjoy a good party as well as the next guy. But there is a time for that. Just help me get these guys focused on flying. We could be damn good, but I need your help."

The big man took Lawton's outstretched hand and smiled again. "Maybe if we put as much energy into flying as we do drinkin', we will be good."

It was Tom's turn to smile. "You can bet your ass on that." Tom's smile turned flat for an instant. "You know, for a second, I thought you were gonna hit me."

"I thought I was too. No sense in ruining an already-mediocre career," said Chief Warrant Officer 3 Walker. Then he added, "You know I'm going to tell everybody else about what a chickenshit thing my commander did?"

"As long as you tell them the whole story." Tom gave the big warrant a stern look. "We need everybody. Besides, I have about six or seven more tricks up my sleeve to keep you guys from driving drunk. So go ahead tell 'em. I expect you to take care of the young guys."

"I got them, sir," said John. "And I got your back too." John Walker continued, "I heard you were a pretty big drinker. Somebody teach you that trick?"

"Yeah! Lieutenant Lawton slept in his car one night because he was too drunk to change his tire," recalled Tom. "One other thing along those lines, John. When we go out as a troop, I probably won't get drunk with you guys. Not because I don't want to. It's just that I can't. Do you understand?"

John thought about the comment. "Yes, sir, I do. It might be good having a commander that's not one of the boys."

Tom understood the comment and nodded. "Go fix something so these guys can train," said Tom.

Chief Warrant Officer 3 Walker nodded. He understood why it happened and understood where his commander was coming from. He appreciated the honesty and respected his new boss. This guy could be good because he gave a damn about his people.

1100, June 22, 1990
Hangar 3010
Classroom 3

"DID YOU GUYS ENJOY PT THIS morning?" Captain Lawton asked his enlisted soldiers. There was a mix of "Hooaahs," "Roger thats," and some looks of pain. "In case you couldn't tell, I like to do PT. We have some guys that are in pretty good shape." Tom walked around the classroom as he talked. He stopped behind one of the troopers who were hurting from the run. "Some others aren't in good shape. We won't mention any names." He noticed Specialist Jackie Thompson slide down in his seat. "No problem. We can fix that. As the commander, I owe you the proper amount of time to train, do your mission, and conduct PT. As Captain Lawton, I owe you time to relax and see Europe. I want you to live by the motto 'Work hard, play hard.' I know you all work hard. But I'm willing to bet only a handful of you get out and enjoy this continent or even Germany, for that matter. Because a lot of you are young and single, your tour will only be two years. Some of you have been here six months and haven't left the barracks. Get out. Get around and see this place, because in ten or twenty years, you may not have this opportunity. If you stay in the billets, you will regret it a few years from now."

Tom changed the subject. "As for work, I know you're working hard. Are you working smart?"

Staff Sergeant Ramirez sounded off, "We could always work smarter, sir."

"I'll buy that. Is there maybe just a little idle time in the middle of the day when things are kind of slow? I know the end of the day is hell because that's when all the parts show up." That got a laugh because it was true. It was amazing how on Fridays at about 1600, five or six parts would show up, usually meaning four to five crew chiefs had to stay late to fix the aircraft that could become FMC for the weekend. "We're gonna change that. I want a daily plan of ten to twelve things to get accomplished. Two to four people will be on night shift, and at 1700, the day shift goes home." This got positive nods and smiles from the crowd. "On Fridays, you can plan on working through lunch and being gone by 1500." Tom could see that got their attention. He had to give them the reality of it all. "This will not always happen. Parts will continue to come in late on Fridays, and we will work late to fix birds. But if you have plans to go out of town or visit friends, you tell your supervisor. Platoon Sergeants, we need to run a late Friday and Saturday work call roster because you know we're going to have to work then, so plan for it. Let's not work long hours just to be here. If we don't gain anything by being here, be somewhere else."

Tom walked a little more. "Does anyone have any questions for me?" asked Captain Lawton.

"Sir, are the warrant officers going to help out with maintenance?" came the question from Specialist Thompson.

SFC Doug "Penny" Pennington handled the question as any seasoned NCO would. "That's not their job. It's your job," snapped the sergeant.

Captain Lawton gave him a look which said, "I can handle this." But he wanted to show support for the NCO's authority. "Sergeant First Class Pennington is correct." But Tom didn't want to stifle the exchange either. Tom continued, "But, Thompson, you have a good point." This got the troops attention again. "I talked with the warrants this morning, and we are going to try some things to improve maintenance. That means more officer involvement and cross leveling of crew chiefs. We don't have enough personnel to do all missions 100 percent of the time. That's a fact. So some scout crew chiefs will crew guns and vice versa as necessary to accomplish the maintenance mission. We'll try some new things, get warrants on the flight line, and have a little bit more fun around here."

Tom enjoyed the excitement the soldiers felt at the possibilities of the changes. "One last thing. When I'm on reverse cycle, we still do PT. It'll be at noon at the gym, four days a week. Only Thursdays sergeant's time is exempt." Thursday from 0700 to 1200 was reserved for the NCOs to do training with the enlisted soldiers. It usually ruined Wednesday night flights, flights all day Thursday, as well as Thursday night flights because crew chiefs were required to attend the training. Tom had a plan for that too. "Flights will be down by 2300 on Wednesdays, and we will fly early on some Thursdays. Launches and recovery will be with minimal manning." This meant two to three soldiers. "We have to continue to fly five days a week. Any more questions?"

"Sir, we've had some problems getting paperwork processed up at Headquarters." It was Top. "Just little things like leaves and pay problems. We're losing a lot of man hours in the Personnel Actions Center." Top said it as a fact and didn't ask Tom to do anything about it. He merely was informing his commander of a problem the soldiers were having and used this format to ensure Tom knew a change was needed.

Tom nodded and said, "Got it. I'll talk to the adjutant this afternoon. Any more questions?" asked Captain Lawton while looking around the room. "All right then. Let's get something fixed this afternoon so I can fly tomorrow."

Top yelled, "Troop, attention!"

"See ya on the high ground, Champions." Tom left for his office.

Top gave the commander time to get down the hall. "If you had any questions, that was your time to ask."

Staff Sergeant Ramirez said, "Top, this seems too good to be true. Even if half these changes occur, we'll be in much better shape than we are now."

"I still think he's like all the others. All talk and no walk." It was Thompson.

Penny got out of his chair and started to move toward the troop. Top stopped him by putting his hand up. "Let me tell you something, you little maggot! This guy has been doing this for six years. He's earned this shot to command. You do what he says when he says, and you'll surprise yourself. You keep on the way you were with the last commander, and you're gone. This guy won't keep you around takin' up space. He'd rather go without a body in a slot if that body doesn't produce. Everyone just needs to pull together and give this commander some time. He listens."

Top's comments received affirmative nods and a couple of "hoaahs." "Now get outta here. We gotta have four aircraft FMC by 1500 Wednesday."

Tom Lawton was rather pleased with the morning's events. He got to run PT, be with his troops, and share his thoughts and plans with them. And he was happy with the reception he'd gotten. Now came something he didn't particularly enjoy. Monday afternoon was the scheduled time for the squadron command and staff meeting. Meetings where the staff and commanders sit down, discuss plans and events, and exchange information. Designed to last an hour, they sometimes ran for two hours or more and generally turned into bullshit sessions. Tom thought of them as a waste of time. Time that could be better spent with his troops.

Just as he expected, this one was more of the same. Lieutenant Colonel Smithey welcomed him as the new Champion Six. But everything else remained the same. The adjutant talked about personnel actions, incoming personnel (of course there weren't any), and outgoing personnel. The S2 talked about security of the aircraft and vehicles.

Then it was the S3's turn. Captain Jerry Maurer was new and enjoyed his job immensely. He was great at operations and pretty good at training. As the coordinator in the shop, his control was authoritarian. He didn't keep his subordinates informed of changes, so the conversations with the commander and the decisions made as a result of that communication were rarely relayed to the subordinates. This was evident at this meeting because at least three changes were made to the unit training calendars that were not posted. The five troop commanders were quiet as the squadron commander "heated up" at the lack of communication. Lieutenant Colonel Smithey had a lot of tact and didn't dwell on the discrepancies. It was always awkward at meetings when someone screwed up. It's up to the person in charge to set the tone for how mistakes are handled, and Smithey handled most minor faults with little fanfare, but an air of failure lingered.

The S4 went through the supply actions hastily. Unfortunately, the supply officer had a lot of information to distribute. And because he came after the S3, people were generally worn out and ready to go rather than listen. This usually resulted in somebody missing some piece of important information. He wanted to issue new computers to the line companies, and only Tom and the maintenance troop commander arranged to meet with him after the command and staff meeting to draw the equipment.

Then came the executive officer, MAJ Jim Bass, who was brief and quickly turned the meeting over to Lieutenant Colonel Smithey. "The only thing I'm concerned about is the gunnery in September at Grafenwoehr and getting this damn calendar under control. I don't want all these damn changes. We work hard to come up with long-term plans and were not sticking to them in the short term. Let's fix that, S3. Lawton, come see me in my office in ten minutes. Everyone else, dismissed."

"I'm sure glad I'm in the C Troop commander's chair and not the Assistant Three's chair, sir," said Tom.

"Unless the Three gets his shit together, you might just be back there. How's your first day going, Champion Six? It's got a nice ring to it, doesn't it?" said Lieutenant Colonel Smithey as he smothered a grin.

"Couldn't be better, sir. I've got a great bunch of troopers, and it's good to be in charge for a change," said Tom.

"Are you making any changes I should know about?" asked the commander.

Tom thought about the question and decided it would be better to tell his boss about the P4T2 he was borrowing from the 101st. "Well, to begin with, we're going to focus more on fixin' aircraft in an organized and systematic effort," said Tom.

"That P4T2 thing you mentioned to me?" asked the boss.

"Yes, sir. We'll try it for two or three months and see if it helps. We've got a good OR rate right now, but these guys haven't been flying any hours, especially at night. I could use your support to allow us more NVS time. I'd like to fly on Thursday mornings before sergeant's time," said Tom.

"Before sergeant's time? I'll have to check with higher on that. You know how the Germans love to support us with quiet hours and all," said Lieutenant Colonel Smithey. Tom knew all too well. The Germans were always calling Brigade Headquarters with noise complaints. They had 1300 to 1500 posted as quiet hours every afternoon as it was. "I'll support you on it, but fly friendly." This meant stay away from populated areas and stay at altitude whenever possible. "Your maintenance seems fine right now. So I don't know how your new "plan" will affect it. Please keep me informed, Tom."

"Roger that, sir."

"One more thing, Tom. You know the new commander is coming in soon. I'm afraid we're going to have to do an officer efficiency report on you," said the lieutenant colonel.

Tom knew exactly what he meant. Tom would end up with a four-month OER as a commander. This usually meant the dreaded "two block." As a commander, it was taboo to have anything less than the highest rating while you were in command. But with only four months to perform in a unit that had a "couple of problems" and worst of all Colonel Denson as the senior rater, Tom understood he had been dealt a bad hand. A hand he thought he could live with. Tom said, "We can cross that bridge in ninety days, sir."

Smithey shook his head. Anybody else would have pitched a major bitch and asked for a way out. "Tom, I'll see what I can do for you, but don't expect much."

"Roger, sir," Tom said as he stood up. "On Wednesday, we're gonna try a day out night return with four aircraft. I'll bring the mission brief sheet by tomorrow for your signature."

"Four ships! Already?" Lieutenant Colonel Smithey gave Tom a quizzical look.

"Sir, I've got to make an assessment of where we are as a troop. There seems to be some discrepancy, and I want to see for myself," explained Tom.

Smithey looked at Tom with a puzzled expression. "Discrepancy?" But he trusted Tom's judgment. "Okay, Captain Lawton. They're your guys. Just be careful."

"Always, sir," replied Tom.

The attack helicopter, type 64, was designed in the 1970s. Vietnam proved the usefulness of a helicopter gunship. Specifically, that war proved the value of the AH-1 Cobra gunship. Not that the AH-1 Cobra had a flawed design. The Bell aircraft served its purpose well in Vietnam. The main mission of the Apache was to kill armored vehicles primarily in the European scenario. Civilian contractors continually upgraded the technology, contractors such as McDonnell Douglas, General Dynamics, and Raytheon, to meet the mission specifications the army required. The weapons systems and the night visionics currently used in 1990 were products from designs two decades earlier. Because the army purchases products from the lowest bidder (everything from toilet paper to attack helicopters), when the product finally gets into the army system, it is no longer state of the art. In Tom Lawton's opinion, with the purchase of the AH-64, the army had done just fine. This helicopter was still state of the art.

Tom was fortunate enough to be in one of the first attack battalions to receive Apaches in the mideighties. Back then, he had been around just long enough to hear the old warrant officer's joke about the "lowest bidder" parts failures and initially agreed with their comments. Five years later, with a whole bunch of dedicated work by civilians and army personnel working together, the United States produced the best attack helicopter platform in the world. Tom Lawton was sure the bugs were out of the system, but what about the people flying them now? Were his pilots up to the abilities of the aircraft? Tom Lawton would soon find out.

1200, June 24, 1990
Hangar 3010
Katterheim, Germany

TOM LAWTON INTENTIONALLY LET LT HART Osborn run the first mission. First, to see exactly what the lieutenant knew, how he operated, and how he led the guns. Secondly, from the outside, Tom could observe objectively, evaluate, and see what level of training the Champions were at. Finally, Tom could work himself into the cockpit gradually. Tom knew he wasn't at the proficiency level he needed to be to effectively lead his pilots. This would give him the opportunity he needed to work his way up to his own high standard gradually.

Hart Osborn conducted the entire briefing flawlessly. It was the content that irritated Tom. The time schedule was too compressed. It didn't allow for little errors or "Murphyisms" that accompany military operations. His plan was wired down to a gnat's ass. He obviously had used the entire two days to plan the mission. In reality, he would have had only six hours to plan it, if that much. The army teaches everyone how to plan. The problem has always been executing the plan that has been developed. Today's army can plan mass artillery rounds on an eight-digit grid at the precise moment necessary but has problems getting a flat tire fixed.

For flight crews, Lieutenant Osborn selected himself and Chief Warrant Officer 3 Walker in lead, Captain Lawton and CW4 Mark Nichols as chalk two, CW3 Deano Toretti and CW2 Carl Tucker as chalk three, and finally CW3 Tom Dolce and CW2 Joe Petty in trail. CW4 Ron Reimer and CW2 Alan Berstein were on standby due to a lack of aircraft availability. Tom didn't like the order of the aircraft or the crew selection, but he committed himself to let the lieutenant run the mission and bit his tongue for the entire briefing. There was no contingency plan, refuel and rearm procedures were not mentioned, and an Instrument Meteorological Conditions (IMC) plan in case of bad weather was not addressed. This wasn't a safety problem because the forecasted weather through midnight was perfect.

The unit was to recover after only thirty minutes of night system operations. The plan was to be down by 2030. It didn't get dark enough for quality night system operations until 2100. The crews had been briefed to be in at 1300 for the OPORD brief, so no one had done a preflight on their aircraft (except Chief Warrant Officer 4 Nichols). Lieutenant Osborn completed the briefing and asked if there were any questions. Surprisingly, there were none. Tom knew the warrants had questions about the operation, but none were asked. The lieutenant failed to ask for a back brief from any of the pilots, which also made Captain Lawton nervous. Apparently, they were all satisfied that they knew what they were doing day and night.

Tom checked his watch and noticed there were an hour and fifteen minutes left until the briefed pitch pull time. The troop still had to preflight the aircraft, do a mission brief sheet and a risk assessment sheet, carry equipment to the aircraft, run up the aircraft, and roll to the launch positions. No way, thought Tom. The smart thing would be to postpone launch for an hour. Tom tried a little suggestion. "Lieutenant, I don't think I can be ready in time to pull pitch."

Tom got the opposite reaction he was looking for. "Come on, sir. You've got five hundred more hours in the aircraft than I have. Surely, you can be ready in an hour," said the lieutenant.

Mark Nichols coughed as he spilled his coffee. Tom started to get pissed. Somewhere, a kinder, gentler Tom Lawton took control. "Okay, Lieutenant. I'm sure Mr. Nichols can get me squared away." He didn't add "you cocky fuck."

"Damn, sir. I gotta hand it to you. You didn't get up and strangle him," said Mark Nichols.

Tom felt an impression coming on. George Bush appeared. "Mr. Nichols, I told you, a kinder, gentler kind of commander wouldn't be prudent at this juncture!" Then Tom shook his head as the president disappeared and added, "But it's gonna be tough." Nichols laughed and shook his head. "We have a mission, Mark. We're going to be ready to go in an hour. Of course, no one else will be ready!" Tom started out to the aircraft and said, "And if not, we'll fake it!"

Lawton and Nichols busted butt to get ready. Tom was glad Nichols had done their preflight earlier. It gave him time to get comfortable in the cockpit. Tom was always more comfortable when he had about five minutes to just sit in the aircraft and focus on the mission. He would spend the time studying the call signs, the frequencies, the time schedule, or the map. If time permitted, he would double-check the information he programmed in the aircraft, both navigation and targets. Mark had started the auxiliary power unit (APU) with twenty minutes left until the proposed departure time. This allowed the Forward Looking Infrared (FLIR) to cool down and the other necessary systems to get warmed up.

It was now five minutes prior to departure time. Lieutenant Osborn had briefed he would start the communications check. Tom looked around and saw two crews still outside their aircraft. Mr. Petty and Mr. Dolce's aircraft had just started the main rotor blades turning. Mr. Walker had their bird's APU running, but the lieutenant was just now getting into the front seat. Only the commander and the instructor pilot were ready.

At 1700, when the Champions were supposed to be pulling pitch off the runway, only two helicopters were running. Tom was silent as he waited for a radio call. Mark Nichols was rather chipper. "What the hell are you smiling about?" asked Tom.

"I just hate to say I told you so," said Nichols.

"You don't have to gloat," said Tom quietly.

Nichols chuckled. "How long you gonna let him go?"

"I think he needs more rope. You guys haven't done this very much, have you?" said Tom.

"Sir, the last full mission we did was stateside about thirteen months ago. I think we've done one three-ship day mission since we've been in Germany," said Nichols. "Needless to say, sir, I think we're rusty."

"It shows. Before we go any further"—Tom looked in the mirror to get eye contact with his instructor pilot—"you were right." Tom smiled. He didn't have to add, "I trust your judgment because you have proven your wisdom to me." Tom knew that wasn't what Mark Nichols was proving. The instructor pilot was proving he knew the status of his troop. That status was nowhere near ready for combat. "The lieutenant is still learning things right now, Mark. We let him go as long as I can without something unsafe happening." Tom made a conscious effort to emphasize "we." He liked Mark Nichols.

"Champion Six, this is Champion One-six on Fox." It was Lieutenant Osborn on the troop FM frequency.

"About time," said Lawton to Nichols. "Roger, One-six, talk to me," said Champion Six on the FM radio.

"Sir, I recommend we push back takeoff time for fifteen minutes. Commo check in ten," said the lieutenant with just the slightest hint of humility.

"I concur with that plan, One-six," said Tom. The captain looked back into the mirror to see the instructor pilot in the backseat. Nichols was shaking his head and smiling.

"Sir, I bet we still don't make it," said the instructor pilot.

"No bet here, Mark," returned the commander.

Somehow, the Champions managed to make the new "recommended" time work. The commo check was terrible, taking about two minutes with no one knowing exactly who could talk on what radio or who could hear. The pitch pull was made at the new time, but the formation was not what Osborn had briefed, and the pilots were constantly talking on the UHF and VHF radios. The proper route was flown, but the flight did not arrive at the assembly area on time. The unit formed a straight line in the assembly area and just sat there for five minutes. Most of the time was spent bullshitting on the UHF in the unsecured mode. The lieutenant finally called their arrival at the battle position. Occupation of the BP was ducks in a row as briefed, but for ten minutes, they sat there. Tom Lawton could take no more.

"One-six, this is Champion Six on 2. I've got two A-10s inbound in five mikes. I need you to conduct JAAT operations with them. Meet Thunder 47 on our Uniform push in two mikes," ordered Tom.

Tom got silence. He noticed Nichols was laughing his ass off in the backseat.

Ten seconds later, "Roger, One-six," said the lieutenant. Tom was testing to see if his lieutenant could conduct a Joint Air Attack Team engagement in a spontaneous setting.

That wasn't enough for the new commander. Tom continued the test. "Champion 23, this is Six on Fox, over."

"Roger, Six. This is Champion 23, over." Tom was surprised it was Petty that answered and not Dolce.

"Roger, Two-three. I need you to meet Redleg on this FM. I want immediate suppression on the bridge at one o'clock."

"Roger, Six," said Champion 23. Immediately, Joe Petty was on the Fox frequency, calling for artillery. Tom had Mark Nichols cover the fake artillery calls as he checked the map. Petty had the proper grid for the bridge, issued the proper call for fire, and called for an adjustment. Finally, the lieutenant called back with half of the Joint Air Attack Team nine-line format. He failed to identify the initial point for the A-10s or what the target was.

"Roger, One-six. Six is Winchester for Hellfire at this time," said Tom. Tom was telling the lieutenant he had fired all eight Hellfire missiles. *Winchester* was the code word used to tell the flight that more rounds were needed. A *Bingo* call would indicate he was out of fuel.

The lieutenant was obviously ready to depart. "Roger, Six. All Champions, this is One-six, execute egress, over."

Tom shook his head and looked at the instructor pilot. "I guess he wants to leave. I was hoping to use rockets or pretend to use the cannon, but I guess he's gotta piss!" Nichols just smiled.

The aircraft flew back in the proper order on the correct route and refueled without a problem. Fifteen minutes later, they lined up for departure for the night mission. It was the exact same mission to the same area. It was 1900 hours and not even close to getting dark.

The first thing Tom noticed was the radios were a lot quieter. Either they were tired or more focused or perhaps just a bit uncomfortable. Probably a combination of all three. The flight out was much better this time. They were at the two-hundred-foot aboveground level just as Lieutenant Osborn had briefed, tracking the route fine and making 120 knots ground speed. At the assembly area (AA), the darkness was complete. The Champions took ten minutes to get their FLIR systems functioning. To Tom's surprise, all of the pilots in command gave the lieutenant an "up." This indicated their pilot night vision systems (PNVS) were working properly. The aircraft had done surprisingly well, so far.

Lieutenant Osborn called for departure. The radios were virtually silent now. The formation for departure was awkward and slow. This was the beginning of a rough flight to the BP. The troop was unable to fly together in the dark. It wasn't a formation, as much as four individual flights. Tom noticed even Mark Nichols was quieter now. "Speak to me, Mark. What's up?"

"I'm just going to stay back here a little bit because I'm not sure what Walker's gonna do," said the instructor pilot. "I usually fly lead."

"No sweat. This is all training. I don't expect us to be the fucking Thunderbirds of army aviation," said Tom, trying to relax himself as much as his instructor pilot. Hell, who was he kidding? He was a comfortable ten-rotor disc back off the lead helicopter. It had been almost four months since he'd flown in a formation, at night, and under system conditions, and he was definitely tense.

As chalk two, Tom was backing up leads navigation along the route on his map as he was supposed to do. He would verify lead's call of air checkpoints and turns as necessary. With three points to go, he noticed lead changed his heading about five degrees to the right. Lawton was on it immediately.

"One-six, this is Six. Check heading," said the commander.

There was a slight pause, followed by, "Roger, coming right five degrees," answered the lieutenant.

"Negative, that's five degrees to the left for correct heading," said Lawton. Silence. Then came the correction. "Update over the next point. I've got you five mikes out on this heading."

"Roger, I'll update on your mark, but I'm showing seven minutes and twenty seconds to ACP," said the lieutenant. Tom became more nervous. Few things are worse than being lost in the dark with a flight of aircraft in unfamiliar terrain. Unless you add getting shot at, which would make it lethal. He didn't want to conduct a lead change in the dark. Lawton wanted to let the lieutenant maintain the lead on this mission, but too much could go wrong. He decided to get another opinion.

"Champion 23 or 27, say time, distance, and heading to ACP 7?" said Six.

"Six, this is 23. I've got 4:55, 16.7 kilometers, at 183 degrees," said Petty.

That was very close to what Tom had.

Two-seven came on the Fox radio, "One-six, we have the same, except 181 degrees."

"Roger, thanks. One-six, no lead change. I'll call the update point in 4:25 on this frequency, just follow this heading. I say again, *no* lead change," said Tom.

The flight slowed with the navigation error, which threw the time to the checkpoint off. It took nearly five minutes to get to the next point. Luckily, the lieutenant kept on course, and Walker tried to maintain 120 knots. Tom called the mark, and Lieutenant Osborn verified the correction, and his numbers to the next point were better. The flight continued to the battle position without further incidents but was inconsistent in its altitude and airspeed. The moon wasn't up yet, so the night was pitch black. Nichols said something about, "Darker than three feet up a bull's ass." But Tom was too focused to laugh at the joke. The formation was spread over a kilometer, nice and safe enough for this mission. They could work on closing it up later. The Champions hit the BP very slowly and descended to NOE flight three kilometers from the battle position. Again, they entered the area ducks-in-a-row in a slow and deliberate manner. All aircraft reported Set, and the make-believe attack commenced. Tom noticed lead and trail were at least 150 feet high, way too high to maintain visual contact with the ground. Also, chalk three was very close off Tom's right wing.

Everything seemed okay, so Tom decided to go heads down in the cockpit to look for simulated targets. He notified Nichols what he was doing so the instructor pilot knew he was no longer helping with visual clearance outside the cockpit. Through the FLIR, Tom could tell they were eighty feet aboveground level (AGL) in a nice, stationary hover. Tom pulled up his helmet visor to get his eyes closer to the optical relay tube (ORT) and looked for targets. Out of habit, he constantly told his back seater what he was doing.

About ten minutes into the engagement, Tom still had his head down looking for targets when he noticed the radios were eerily quiet. Instantly, the silence was broken when Mark Nichols yelled, "Fuck me!" Tom felt the aircraft jerk up and left hard. The movement was quick enough to bump Lawton's nose on the optical relay tube (ORT), which housed the screen Tom was looking in. The foam cushion that surrounded the ORT slipped under Tom's helmet into his forehead. He was momentarily stunned, and his heart skipped a beat as he listened for an impact that never came. He heard the whine of the engines as the torque soared. The noise was broken by the instructor pilot's voice on the radio. "Two-two, what the hell are you doing? Drop and slide right now!" said Nichols.

Lawton looked right and down just in time to get a terrific view of the glowing cockpit lights of chalk three. Jesus, he's close, thought Tom. He immediately looked to the main rotor blades, which created the illusion of meshing with the main rotor blades of Champion 22. Mark Nichols was still climbing gradually now. This gave Tom time to clear his head. He deliberately kept his cockpit dark to keep better night vision, but he was not seeing very well. As he rubbed his nose, he felt the pain and something else. He could smell his blood before he felt the cut. The ORT was covered over the top with a rubber cover to prevent the gunner from hitting any metal in situations like that. Between the sudden speed of the aircraft's movement and Tom's head position on the ORT and the unexpected movement, Tom was caught off guard. The contact was a freak occurrence but an eye-opener that Tom wasn't as "together" as he should have been. His helmet would have probably prevented the cut if he had worn it properly. The cobwebs in Tom's mind cleared. "Are we okay, Mark?" The first priority was to fly the aircraft.

"Yeah, we're fucking fine now. I probably overtorqued it. I didn't get a look at the gauge because I was too busy watching fucking Goober try to get outta fucking Mayberry," said a visibly agitated Mark Nichols. "Stupid fuck. The videotape for this is gonna be interesting," mumbled the instructor pilot.

"Chalk three, are you okay?" asked Tom.

"Uh, roger, Six. We may be having a little HARS problem here," said Dean Toretti.

"HARS problem my ass, you fuck!" Nichols said over the intercom. Tom was glad he hadn't said it over the FM. The Heading and Attitude Reference System was a black box that contains the gyros which tell the helicopter literally which way is up.

"I'm getting a flashing reticle, and I show us stationary, but we're obviously moving. To answer your question, yes, we're okay. How 'bout you?" asked Toretti.

Mark Nichols was in control of his emotions now. "We're okay too, but I think Six's fun meter is pegged."

Tom said to Mark on intercom, "You got that right." Then over the UHF, he announced, "All Champions, this is Six. We are mission complete for the night. We will egress direct to Katterheim at three hundred feet AGL and one hundred knots. One-six, if your Doppler is okay now, you have the lead."

"Roger, Six," said Osborn. "We are breaking left to the RP. Trail call clear."

Tom cleared the aircraft and told Nichols he was going inside the cockpit for a minute. He took off his glove and wiped the bridge of his nose. Definitely blood, but in the darkness, Tom couldn't see how much. He turned up the cockpit lights to full bright, which got a quick reaction from Nichols.

"Hey, sir, let me know when you're gonna do that!" said the instructor pilot.

"Sorry, Mark." Tom dimmed his lights because he had seen what he needed to see. "I got a little cut on my nose. My glove looks messed up, but the cut has stopped bleeding."

"Shit, sir. I'm sorry. I didn't think I pulled in that much torque," apologized the instructor pilot.

"I should know better. I have to watch that heads down stuff," said Tom. "I'm okay, no sweat. Let's just get this flight home and get a good debrief."

The flight back was uneventful. Tom still noticed the crews had problems maintaining altitude and airspeed, an indication they were not getting enough flight time in the dark. That needed to change.

Tom solicited Mark Nichols for opinions on the mission, and Mark didn't hesitate. He picked up on a couple of things Tom had not noticed. By the time refueling was completed, it was 2145. Tom, who knew the value of a good debrief, called for everyone to meet in the classroom in thirty minutes. He had no idea what to expect from the debrief. But if the after-action review was anything like the mission, it would be just as weak.

CHAPTER 3

AFTER POSTFLIGHT AND TYING DOWN THE aircraft, Tom stopped by the bathroom to wash his face. There was a small cut on the bridge of his nose. He was happy it didn't need any stitches. It hurt a little, but the headache didn't reflect how bad he really felt. The Champions didn't do very well during the mission, and that hurt more than his nose. He wasn't looking forward to the debrief.

After-action reviews are the army's ways of getting soldiers to learn from their mistakes by explaining their actions in their own words. This AAR was different to Tom in two ways. First, the troop was not real talkative about their mistakes. Secondly, trying to get them to tell the truth was nearly impossible. Usually, a soldier will tell you when he or she screwed up.

The day comments were on the mark and indicative of a mediocre performance. The crews knew when they were messing up and knew what needed to take place to improve their performance. Tom listened intently, letting Lieutenant Osborn handle the debriefing comments. He wanted to save his comments till the end. He heard various excuses about why so and so was late and such and such did not happen. More excuses why close air support and indirect artillery fire did not happen efficiently. The captain just sat there. He caught the glances from Mr. Nichols and Mr. Walker but never said a word. Tom Lawton was determined to let Lieutenant Osborn run with this mission, and that meant the AAR too.

After ten minutes of how good the day mission was and how well they worked together, Captain Lawton was squirming uncomfortably in his seat. This debrief was the epitome of what the army had become. The syndrome was commonly referred to as the Barney Army, named for the stupid purple dinosaur that Megan and other little kids were watching on

TV. The stupid title song "I love you, you love me. We're a happy family!" kept ringing in Tom's ears. It reflected the new army's inability to be honest and say when someone had screwed the pooch. Tom thought he was gonna puke.

The lieutenant started to debrief the night mission. Tom squirmed in his seat again as he listened to the comments from around the room. The pilots were obviously uncomfortable with the night mission when it started, but all continued the mission without addressing their fears. It was at this point that the comments became even less honest. Navigational errors were not discussed. The distance between aircraft and the inability to maintain the proper airspeed and altitude were never brought up. And chalk 3 never mentioned his loss of references or why his rotor came within a foot of chalk two. Tom Lawton started to get hot.

Lieutenant Osborn asked, "So, Chalk Four, your overall impression of the mission we ran?"

To their credit, Tom observed Joe Petty and Tom Dolce look curiously at one another. They both waited to see what the other would say. Joe Petty deferred to the more experienced warrant.

"I think it went all right. Considering we haven't done it since we've been in Germany," said Tom Dolce. Joe Petty did not agree, but he didn't say a word so as not to alienate his peers. He accepted the senior aviator's final remark, "Okay. All things considered," with his eyes looking away from his back seater. Tom Lawton could take no more.

"Bullshit!" he yelled. Tom's dad always told him never to cuss in front of the troops unless: (1) you were acting to get their attention, or (2) you really were pissed off. Option 2 was the ticket. "That's a fucking bullshit comment." Tom paused to glance around the room. The audience was sitting up and awake now.

"An 'okay mission' my ass! This mission was bull-fucking-shit!" yelled Tom. "You may accept 'all right' as a means of accomplishment, but not me! 'Okay' is even less than mediocre. *And* mediocre is *unacceptable*! We did Jack-fucking-shit tonight. We accomplished nothing." Tom paused to look around to see who understood what he was saying. About 50 percent of the room was stunned, and the other half knew he was right.

"First of all, the time schedule was *fucked*! Lieutenant, if you can't accomplish the pitch pull on time, you let somebody know about it! No way we make it off this airfield at the time you initially briefed. Next, what the hell are you guys doing at the BP? Logging flight time and looking at the cars go by. *Un-fucking-acceptable!*" Tom was worked up now and glaring at his pilots. "I know you guys are trained on how to call for fire, and I know you know how to call in a nine-line for close air support. So what happened?" Of course no one answered. The rhetorical question hit to the heart. Tom continued, "Let's get into the night mission. You're obviously not comfortable flying in the dark together. Somebody stand up and say so. We nearly had a midair tonight, and we skimmed right over it in this debrief. Well, fuck that!"

Tom got up from his chair and started pacing around the room. "I cannot accept mediocrity. Not from myself and not from you guys! We have too much experience and too much talent to wallow in fucking mediocrity." He started to say that mediocrity kills people, but he knew that wasn't true because he saw it every day. He got his emotions in check and continued, "I know we can do better than what I just saw tonight." Tom approached the blackboard and started writing. "Rule 1: Never miss a pitch pull! If we only have one or two aircraft ready, you launch when you're told because people are counting on you to do that. Rule 2: If you are messed up, tell someone immediately. Bad news does not get better with time. Rule 3: The nighttime is the right time! No one can see us in the dark. It is safer in the dark than in the day because nobody else is stupid enough to be out there." This brought a nervous chuckle to the audience and calmed Tom down a bit. "I could go on with some more, but I'm not going to inundate you with crap while I jump on a soapbox."

Tom looked at Lieutenant Osborn and saw a wound the size of Mt. Everest. "Lieutenant, you did good!"

"It sure doesn't sound like it, sir," said Hart Osborn.

"No! No! No!" said Tom emphatically. "You're not getting it!"

"Obviously, I'm not, sir!" came the reply.

"I don't expect you to be the expert at this, and neither does anyone else in this room. They expect me to be the expert, and I'll tell ya straight up . . . I'm not!" Tom saw this sink in. "For us to be effective, to kill the enemy, to survive on the modern battlefield, we have to move as one unit. We have to know each other's every move day and night. We aren't there yet. We have not trained together enough to be successful. And trust me, you did not fail the troop or me. You haven't been put in this position before, have you?" asked Tom.

Lieutenant Osborn looked around the room and saw the acceptance from the warrant officers because they knew the answer. "No, sir."

"It's 'okay' to make a mistake with me," Tom said this for the entire troop, not just Lieutenant Osborn. "It's not 'okay' to gloss over it like it never happened. We need to learn from this and not make the same mistakes again. That's the purpose of this AAR." Tom caught his breath. "Hell, man, we're all back alive, so this puppy was a success. Night air really does have lift. And I'm gonna be able to tell my grandkids about that night in Germany when I busted the hell outta my nose!" This took the edge off the group. "I did not expect us to be able to attack the dreaded Hun tonight. However, I will admit that I expected a little more." Tom erased his rules from the blackboard.

"So how do we fix it?" he asked.

"We have to fly more." It was Joe Petty.

"Bingo!" said Tom. "We have to fly more in the dark because if you can do it at night, you can do it in the day." Tom started scratching on the board. "Lieutenant, can you talk on the radios, call for fire, bring in CAS, know your exact position on the battlefield, and control the light team at the same time?"

Somewhat sheepishly, Lieutenant Osborn replied, "No, sir. Maybe three or four things at once, but realistically, no."

"If you could, you'd be the only guy in this room that could," said Tom. The senior warrants all smiled knowingly. "Hell, I have all I can do to keep the monkey fed at higher headquarters, much less know exactly where I am!" This drew the obligatory laughter. "By feeding the monkey, I mean keep him informed before he turns into an angry ape." Tom let that sink in. "This is the way I want it done." Tom proceeded to write on the board the crews and the chalk order. The troop was becoming noisy behind his back as the crews on the board and the new chalk order became evident. Tom put Petty and Dolce in lead, Lieutenant Osborn and Nichols in chalk two, Walker and Lawton as three, Weimer and Berstein as chalk four, and Toretti and Tucker in trail.

"I know you have questions, just give me a minute to explain. Mr. Dolce is not comfortable flying as a wingman, thus lead. Mr. Petty, you are going to be afforded the opportunity to lead this motley bunch around Germany. Lieutenant, you did nothing wrong, so don't take offense. I want you to be able to *command* the light team. You need to be on the map navigating and on the radios. Mr. Nichols will assist you because he is the most experienced pilot and needs to impart his knowledge into your beady little mind. Mr. Walker, you are with me because you have the next highest amount of experience and are the maintenance officer. The next time we have a maintenance problem, I don't want to tie up a radio talking to you about options. Plus, as chalk three, I'm in the middle and can talk to and see everybody when we're in the BP. Mr. Weimer and Mr. Berstein have demonstrated the best gunnery scores in the past, so out of selfishness and self-preservation, you are my wingmen. As for T-n-T, until we get another crew, they are the trail aircraft for all flights. Do you have any questions?" Tom heard the grumbling and thought he would get away without a question. Joe Petty raised his hand.

"Sir, I don't feel comfortable in lead. I think the unit would be better off if I was back in the pack or at trail," said the junior warrant.

Tom was tempted to cry bullshit again but maintained his composure. "Mr. Petty, what country are we in?"

Mr. Petty, obviously confused, responded, "Germany, Deutschland über alles and all that stuff, sir. Is that some kind of trick question?"

"Hell, Mr. Petty, you got that one right, so you're doing better than 50 percent of the gun pilots in Europe!" said the captain. The pilots around the room had to laugh at this. Helicopter gunship pilots are notoriously bad navigators. Since Vietnam, scout pilots have always been used to lead the guns to their assigned firing positions. And things really had not changed all that much in the last twenty years. The scouts were always on the map, and for the most part, the gun drivers had their heads up their asses. The Apache was equipped with a Doppler navigation system, which was no substitute for a good navigator with an accurate map.

Tom Lawton knew the answer was a lead aircraft with a crew member that could read a map, had the ability to picture the colored lines in his mind, and knew what to expect in day, at night, or in bad weather conditions. Joe Petty was the one who could formulate this picture and go it one further. He could develop the picture from the map and move through it at 150 miles per hour at fifty feet above the ground. An ability that is trained in pilots with years of experience but is rarely distinguished as the special gift that it is. Doppler made better navigators out of all pilots, but the best navigators used it as a backup. Doppler was merely an asset to the pilot and a means to get from point A to B. Captain Lawton knew that Joe Petty could navigate. And Joe Petty was going to be his troop's navigator.

"Until you prove me wrong, you're our man in front. And remember, it's a crew in the lead. Not just the front seater," said Tom, looking at Mr. Dolce. "We've got a long way to go and a short time to get there. Lieutenant, same thing in two weeks, my crews, in my order. Your aircraft and your mission."

As he headed for the door, the lieutenant responded, "Roger, sir," and called everyone to attention. Tom Lawton looked around the room and sensed something. He expected them to be defeated and down because of their perceived failure, but that's not what he felt. He felt his troops had accepted an unspoken challenge. As if he had dared them to improve. And they were going to rise to his challenge.

Walking down the hall, Tom reached up and lightly touched the cut on his nose. What would Cindy think about this? Not even one week into command and he was physically scarred. Tom felt the physical abuse was a piece of cake. It was the mental part of command that was already changing him. He wanted to go home, but when he saw his desk, his inbox began to call his name. Reluctantly, Tom sat down and began the nightly ritual of paper pushing. Daily status reports; maintenance, personnel, and equipment status reports; and previous paperwork he had procrastinated over earlier in the week sat there. Officer efficiency report support forms on the warrants were stacked up on a table behind him. All this and more quietly called for his attention. He really hated this part of the job, but that was what he got the "big bucks" for. So what if four of his warrant officers made more money than he did? Tom Lawton was the guy that swore to do the job. Command was all he wanted to do. Sometimes, alone at his desk late at night, it didn't seem worth it. His head was starting to hurt, and he wanted a beer. He hurried through his inbox, signed a couple pieces of not-so-important paper, and headed to the club.

June 25, 1990
D Company Commander's Office
Katterheim, Germany

CPT DARREN ROOKS WAS POSSIBLY THE best maintenance officer in army aviation. Perhaps it was his hockey goalie experience at the University of Vermont or his genuine concern for people. Darren Rooks was aggressive, dedicated, and without doubt, the best Blackhawk pilot in the world. All one had to do was ask him. As the assistant S-3, Tom Lawton rarely worked with Darren Rooks, but all his previous encounters had fostered an honest and carefree professional working relationship. Somehow, Darren had all the poop on army aviation happenings. The guy knew everything that was going on, not just in Germany, but also throughout the aviation community. Darren Rooks was in the know because he was personable and very good at his job. Not just in the maintenance arena. He was great with personnel because of his uncanny ability to communicate up and down the chain of command. "Rooksy" could brief a general about the dynamics of maintaining hydraulic systems in the world's most advanced helicopters one minute and in the next minute talk to a private about Prince's newest CD. His real joy was hockey, but lacking that outlet, Rooksy brought his aggressiveness to the basketball courts, where his six-foot-two and 220-pound build intimidated most everyone on the Caserne. Tom made of a habit of trying to get Rooks on his side and not just in hoop.

"What's up, Tom? I'm a businessman, and I got business goin' on!" said CPT Darren Rooks, snapping his fingers.

"I'll be brief, Rooksy, because I know your busy schedule." With that, Tom chuckled a little, as did the maintenance officer. "I need one, two if you got 'em, experienced crew chiefs. And secondly, I want to try that P4T2 plan we talked about at troop level."

"Done deal! When do you want the crew chiefs? Thirty days?" asked the D Troop commander.

Tom hesitated and looked Darren in the eye. "Tomorrow."

Darren burst out laughing. Tom only smiled.

"You're serious, aren't you?" asked Darren.

"Yeah, I am." Tom continued, "My troop is hurtin' for crew chiefs, and their aircraft shows it. I need two crew chiefs, and I can assign them an aircraft tomorrow." Tom continued his argument, "You know what kind of shape these birds are in. They suck due to a lack of attention. I know you're not fat in D Troop, but I'll take anyone you can give me." Tom looked at Darren hard and added, "That's not a dud!"

Captain Rooks rubbed his chin. "Your numbers are historically higher than A and B. How do I explain this to the boss?"

"Hey, we talked. My MTOE is short, and you see that you can help fix aircraft early at the line level! I get two crew chiefs. You get less maintenance and a better OR overall! You can't lose. Deal?" asked Tom.

Darren Rooks thought hard. "One crew chief on Friday and one more new guy to you in two weeks."

"I'll take it. And support for P4T2?" asked Tom.

"Roger. I think that's a great way to do business, but I'd like to see you use it first. We'll look at installing it at the squadron level around November if it's working for you," replied Rooks.

"All right!" Tom turned to walk away. "Hoops Friday?"

"Oh, definitely. Get there about 1130 or we won't get to play together," said Darren.

"Wrench 6" liked to play with Tom Lawton because he passed the ball and kept his mouth shut. "See you at 1125!" said Tom.

The first thirty days in command for Tom Lawton were excellent. He was in his element. He was training "his" pilots and teaching "his" guys attack helicopter tactics and operations. The maintenance program was slowly but surely improving. This was evident because the consistency of training and the reliability of the aircraft improved. Even though the OR rate was going down, the aircraft could be counted on for missions.

Lieutenants Osborn and Timmons were coming together on the work front, but they were on opposite ends of the personality and leadership spectrum. Osborn was distant and demanded mission accomplishment. Timmons, with his previous Grenada and Panama experience as an enlisted radioman, was more personable and tolerant of mistakes. Neither style of leadership was necessarily bad. Tom wished they would share some of their positive traits with each other. The soldiers were responding to both, and that's what counted. Plus, Tom didn't have to micromanage their platoons. They both were achieving the goals Tom had established for them. This gave him more time to stop by the club and have a brew.

The pilots' morale was noticeably improved. They had flown 45 percent night system in the first month, and their collective confidence was visible. Mr. Petty particularly had excelled in this new environment. He had flown thirty hours the first month of Tom's command, and Mr. Dolce's reports on his junior stick buddy were always positive.

At the end of July, two crew chiefs were given three-day passes at a formal payday activities ceremony. One Apache had been up 83 percent of the month and still flew 42.5 hours. Tom had been told a long time ago that the more you fly them, the better they work. In this case, the saying was proving to be more than some old warrant officer's tale.

The aero scout crew chief pulled 89 percent OR on his bird with forty-five hours flown. All three scout pilots were night vision goggle current and working on proficiency. Lieutenant Timmons was getting close to being ready for his NVG Pilot in Command (PIC) check ride, so he was a little tense, but always personable.

Morale was improving. The Champions were flying, and all seemed to be going fine. Tom Lawton diverted the attack pilot's attention to gunnery. In August, the squadron would go to Grafenwoehr for helicopter gunnery. Tom's goals were no crew less than the top 50 percent in the squadron and two of the three Top Gun crews. They were getting confidence in the aircraft, but his pilots needed to get confidence in themselves.

August 7, 1990
Combat Mission Simulator (CMS)
Katterheim, Germany

"MAN, WE'RE CRUISING RIGHT ALONG!" SAID Chief Warrant Officer 3 Toretti.

The aircraft was indicating 140 knots ground speed and between forty and fifty feet above the ground. CW2 Carl Tucker was in the front seat cockpit just a bit disoriented. "What's that vehicle we just passed? Go back and take a look."

CW3 Deano Toretti, not knowing where to go or what type of vehicle to look for, did what most attack pilots do in the CMS. He yanked back hard on the cyclic and proceeded to perform what is referred to as a Return to Target. During this maneuver, the aircraft is flown straight up until such time that the forward airspeed is decreased to zero. At that time, the aircraft is rotated about the axis of the mast 180 degrees, with pedal input and the forces gravity taking effect, bringing the aircraft back to earth at an extremely high rate of speed. From 2,500 feet, the Apache hurtled toward the computer-generated ground at five thousand feet per minute. This rate of descent was increased due to the fact Mr. Toretti did not have the aircraft in trim. With only a little over fifteen seconds to find the target and accurately identify and then engage with any weapon system, it was no wonder the target was never located. Mr. Toretti not only mushed through his pullout, his front seater was overcome with disorientation and asked the maneuver be terminated before he hurled. "What the fuck are you doin'?" said Chief Warrant Officer 2 Tucker. "I damn near blew chunks. Put this thing on freeze so I can get my shit together."

The civilian controller, Greg "Whitey" Whitehill, was kindhearted, and the machine was paused to allow the crew to get their act together.

CPT Tom Lawton sat in silence. Earlier, he had coordinated with Whitey and was in the simulator out of sight in the back of the pilot's station. The next thirty minutes of the flight produced more of the same. Typical cowboy flying. Pilots doing things in the simulator they would never do in the air. The unit's tactics called for hover fire from preplanned battle positions. This crew practiced running fire at targets they failed to identify and was rarely in synch. When they finally practiced stationary fire, they barely communicated with one another and misidentified the targets they could locate. The techniques used by the front seater were clumsy, awkward, and full of mistakes even Tom recognized. He realized that no one had taken the time or emphasized the importance of this training. No one had trained Tucker to do it the right way. After an hour, Tom could take no more.

"Take us off motion for a minute," he said privately to an obviously disgusted Greg Whitehill. The civilian contractor did the best he could to suggest techniques to the pilots. However, not being in the pilot's "food chain," Whitey was held with little regard. The cockpit grew silent as the machine came down off motion.

"Hey, Whitey, what the fuck you doin'? We done already?" asked Chief Warrant Officer 3 Toretti.

Tom remained calm as the cockpit grew quiet. Tom told Whitey, "Put me up on their radios please and reset from the BP."

Still disgusted, Whitey nodded his head, flipped the switch, and said, "They're all yours, Captain."

Tom smiled and decided not to explode but to try to teach a couple of little things to this crew to get them headed in the right direction. Getting pissed off would have only raised his blood pressure, and these guys would get nothing out of the two-hour training period. He made a mental note to ask Chief Warrant Officer 4 Nichols if this is the way he trained his crews. Deep down, Tom knew Nichols was too busy to come to all the CMS periods. As the only instructor pilot in the troop, he was constantly flying.

Calmly, Tom started, "We're going to pick this up from the BP and take it a little slower." Tom waited for a response and got none. He could have sworn he heard Mr. Toretti say "Oh shit!" The two warrant officers were taken completely by surprise. The fact that anyone was monitoring the period threw the crew for a loop. To find out it was the commander added another aspect to the drama. At least he didn't sound pissed off.

"Mr. Toretti, you have the controls. I want a stationary hover oriented on a westerly heading at 260," said Tom.

"Roger, sir," came the response.

"You've got three moving targets between two-five zero and two-seven zero degrees. Range is three thousand to thirty-five hundred meters. Identify and engage the targets," directed the captain.

Slowly, very meticulously, the crew found the targets, positively identified the targets, not killing the friendly M1 Abrams, and engaged and destroyed the enemy targets. Tom noted the whole process took over four minutes. He was glad they recognized the friendly, but the process took too long.

"Kudos, gentlemen, for not killing Tommy the Tanker. You took way too long to kill the Air Defense Artillery target. Mr. Tucker, the best way to track a moving target is with the linear motion compensator (LMC). You used the image auto tracking (IAT) gates, and when the vehicle went behind the trees, you lost it. Let's try the same thing again, but use the LMC to track and not that damn IAT. Be patient. You are at a far-enough standoff range, so they can't hurt you." The captain finished, "The speed of the engagement time will decrease with practice. Just stay focused on destroying the targets you currently engage." He continued, "Whitey, take the threat level up to seven."

"Shit, sir! Seven! We usually work at three, or we can't even get a shot off!" said Mr. Tucker.

"Well, I guess you need to kill the ADA first," said Tom matter-of-factly.

"Easier said than done, sir," responded Chief Warrant Officer 3 Toretti.

"I have faith in you. Stay in control, stay low, and work as a team," said Tom.

This time, the crew performed much better. Chief Warrant Officer 2 Tucker got the ADA vehicle with his first Hellfire. He used the linear motion compensator instead of the image auto tracker on the two moving tanks. Although he missed with his second missile, the next two were hits at three thousand meters. After this engagement, Tom made them repeat it twice more and then again under night system. The crew concluded the CMS period with an inadvertent instrument meteorological condition (IMC) flight recovery to the airfield.

On the way out of the simulator, Whitey said, "They sure responded to you. I just want to know how come you didn't rip 'em new assholes?"

"It wouldn't do any good," Tom answered. "They would have probably shut down mentally or not responded the way I wanted them to. This way, they knew I was pissed, and they kept their heads in the game and got something out of the period. And thanks for the compliment. I did want to chew them out, but it worked out okay. Thanks for your help. One more thing. If any Charlie, First of the Sixth crews come through here, give 'em 50 percent night system, the rest gunnery and an IMC recovery, okay?"

"You got it, boss!" said Whitey.

Tom stopped by the soda machine for his customary Pepsi after a CMS flight. In the debriefing room, the crew was silent. Usually after a period, a crew would be excited and talkative about their exploits. Not so with these two.

"Comments, gentlemen?" asked Tom.

"Shit, sir. We'd have done better if we knew you were there," said Toretti.

"So what your saying is, you only do 'the right thing' if I'm there to watch?" asked Tom.

"Um . . . no, sir!" said Chief Warrant Officer 3 Toretti.

"So what does it take to do what's right?" continued Tom.

"We just get bored doing the same thing in the CMS over and over," replied the senior warrant. Chief Warrant Officer 2 Tucker did the right thing now by keeping his mouth shut and deferring to the comments to his PIC.

Tom came back with anger in his voice, "Are you gonna be bored when he's lost as Hogan's goat? Are you gonna be bored when you shoot a friendly? Are you gonna be bored when your ass is in flames in the fucking trees?" Tom gained control and continued, "If this is boring, you're doing something wrong. Make this challenging. Don't do things in the CMS you wouldn't do in the cockpit. Know exactly where you are and what you're doing. Act as one crew, not as two pilots. You've got to communicate. Use all the things this multimillion-dollar toy has and become better pilots."

Tom let that sink in and got a "Roger" from the pilots. "You've got two weeks until gunnery. Use the time wisely and see if you can get focused on teamwork and killing the targets. I expect more from Champions!" Tom expected a "fuck you, sir!" but got a nod and a little smile from Deano Toretti.

"We can do better, sir," said Carl Tucker.

"Hell, Carl, if you worked half as hard in here as you do on your jump shot, you'd be a master gunner!" exclaimed Tom. That got a smile from the junior warrant. "Get your shit together," said Captain Lawton as he headed out the door.

Mission accomplished, thought Tom. The word of this little "training event" would spread throughout the troop. Naturally, Tom Lawton didn't have the time or patience to observe every crew or attend all the training flights. But the threat of the commander sitting in on your period and holding your hand was enough to produce the results Tom was looking for. The crews challenged themselves to keep it interesting and started to use the CMS with purpose.

Two weeks later, Mr. Nichols informed Captain Lawton that the Champion crews were in the best posture they had ever been in to perform a gunnery exercise. Tom Lawton simply smiled and said, "We'll see."

August 26, 1990
Katterheim Caserne

WHEN A UNIT DEPLOYS TO TRAIN for an extended period of time, it's customary for the families to see them off. This custom is probably best remembered watching John Wayne head off to fight the Apache Indians. The women and kinfolk of the old west would get together to watch the cavalry ride off to unforeseen adventure and danger. What the folks never understood was the soldiers really didn't mind riding off once in a while. They got an opportunity to get away from the garrison, their chain of command, and actually do what they got paid to do. They got away from the routine matters and got to do some soldiering. Be it patrolling or chasing Indians, that was the job, and that's what soldiers did.

The two-week gunnery exercise at Grafenwoehr was just what CPT Tom Lawton needed to get his crews fit to fight. Of course the goals he had set for his troop were lofty. They were goals that he told no one about. He was afraid that his crews weren't ready and they would not perform as he expected.

However tough on the family, getting away from the flagpole, executing quality training, and being a soldier was what Tom wanted to do. Shooting targets and challenging him to make his troop the best was his idea of fun. Sure, it was tough to leave his family, but Cindy knew the deal. She'd married a soldier and understood this was part of the job. In the back of his mind, he always pictured himself as John Wayne, the conquering hero making the world safe for democracy. In Cindy's mind, it was more like "Son of a bitch is leaving me here to go off and play soldier!" Somewhere between the two perspectives was the truth.

Cindy and Megan were at the hangar to see the troopers off. Cindy was helping the other wives get snacks and sodas for the soldiers before they left, lest they all starve to death in the two-week absence. Cindy was cordial and helped out as much as possible. She did all the things a commander's wife was supposed to do. This made Tom happy, but he could tell she didn't enjoy these separations one bit. Too soon for Cindy, it was time for Tom and the Champions to go.

As he bent to kiss Megan good-bye, it dawned on Tom that little Megan had no clue that Daddy was going away for two weeks. It struck a nerve, but it was quickly chambered away to a hiding spot that Tom never opened. Tom kissed her on the cheek and looked into his wife's eyes. "You two try not to forget me and we'll be back as soon as we can."

"Oh, we'll be here. Just us girls. Waiting patiently. Quietly. Alone," said Cindy somewhat tersely.

"Honey, look, can we talk about this when I get back? We have to get going," said Tom impatiently.

Cindy looked at Tom and grabbed his arm. "You mean that, right? We'll actually talk about this whole 'command' thing?"

Tom interpreted the question as worry for her man to come home. "Yeah, sure." He smiled back at her. Actually, what she meant was, "We will talk about this, and you will listen to my point of view, right?" She desperately wanted to talk to him about the way things were getting between them and the changes she had seen. Tom was clueless.

Cindy just shook her head and let go of his arm. "We'll see you when you get back." Dutifully, she kissed him on the cheek and turned away. Tom, for his part, realized she wasn't smiling. He missed the smile that she usually gave him when he left on a trip like this. Tom tucked the missing smile in the same hiding spot he put Megan's innocence. He swore to himself he would really talk to Cindy about what was bothering her. That would have to wait until he got back. It was time to take charge.

August 27, 1990
Grafenwoehr Training Center, Germany

THE UNITED STATES MILITARY MACHINE SPENT millions on laser-guided weapon technology. Everyone expects laser-guided munitions to be one-shot, one-kill type of rounds. The problem, which most people tend to forget, is these weapons rely on people to fire them. People make errors. While the missiles were manufactured to hit the target over 90 percent of the time when properly fired, the fact was the army was only achieving about seven hits out of every ten missiles fired. Tom Lawton used this thought on his pilots to help them to understand what to expect. They all expected to go eight for eight with their Hellfire shots. In reality, six for eight would be excellent, and seven of eight was outstanding. Eight for eight under the allotted time meant the crew was probably a combination of Davey Crockett and the Red Baron.

The Apache gunnery scoring system was based on a two-thousand-point total, of which one thousand points came from videotaped engagements in the aircraft. These points consisted of seven hundred points for accurate and timely Hellfire shots and three hundred points for accurate and timely firing of the 30mm chain gun and the 2.75-inch rockets. By combining these points with the written gunnery test, a vehicle identification test, and a hands-on weapons loading test, the instructor pilots could calculate the unit crew members score to determine which crew member had the highest score. Add the written test scores of the two crew members together with the scores of the live helicopter firing and you get the score used to rank the unit's best crews in aircraft gunnery. Keeping up with Hollywood, these were called Top Gun crews.

Training missiles were used to produce live and accurate data, which was recorded on the videotape. These "seeker" missiles sent information to the fire control system that worked exactly like a live Hellfire, displaying the same information on the ORT that the gunner would use to fire a real missile. The distance, time, and tracking information displayed were necessary to score the crew during a target engagement. Most crews could find, track, engage, and destroy the moving targets (range dependent) within forty-five seconds. Two targets during one engagement proved to challenge crews the most. The challenge during multiple-target engagements was maintaining situational awareness of the targets, including the number of missiles fired and the time of separation between the missiles. Factor in time to locate, positively identify, put crosshairs on the target, track it, destroy it, and get the helicopter back down to a covered position provided leaders a pretty competitive scoring program. Everything was recorded on the omnipotent videotape machine mounted in the aft section of the aircraft. A machine that could make even the most religious man curse in disgust.

Each crew used their own aircraft to fire. There were more crews than aircraft, so some crews had to use the same aircraft twice. Word got around quickly, letting everyone know which aircraft fired the best. You could tell the good aircraft because they flew twice as many hours as the weaker aircraft. Every crew did a practice table day, then again at night, then a scored table for day and night. Minimum standards were to be met to get live rounds and subsequently qualify as a crew. Without qualifying on the lower tables, crews could not proceed to higher tables of firing multiship or combined live fire exercises called CALFEXs.

The first day of gunnery, Charlie Troop was on standby. In the morning, they checked over their aircraft and reported problems or write-ups to the crew chiefs that needed to be fixed. That afternoon, Tom Lawton called all the pilots together for a quick meeting. "Gentlemen, we have some additional time to get ready, so let's not waste it. Take the next two hours to study the program. Get it down so that it is second nature when you're in the cockpit. Rehearse your crew conversations. I mean to the point of a written script. The instructor pilots have given us the engagements. It will never be this easy on a two-way range. After you've got the engagements down, go out and check your aircraft one more time before dinner. Tonight, talk to A Troop and B Troop guys and see what they did today. Find out what positions have hard-to-see targets and the positions where you can make up some points. Remember, this ain't rocket science, and you ain't Einstein. Have a little fun, but watch what you say. Every word you say is on that videotape. When the instructor pilots review it, they may miss something you've done until they here you say, 'Oops!' Remember to turn it on and off for the engagements and try not to cuss." Tom could tell they were ready. "And go kick some ass!"

That was as close as it ever came to a speech from Captain Lawton. After that meeting, the gunnery was in perpetual motion for ten days. Of course, it couldn't be gunnery in Germany without rain and fog wreaking havoc on the timetable. Many hours were spent with the auxiliary power unit (APU) running. This kept the aircraft's weapons systems powered up for up to thirty minutes. One or both engines were started as needed to keep the transmission cool.

The weather held, and only two training days were completely lost due to rain and low ceilings. The Champions were the last troop to start to fire, but the first to qualify all five crews. What were more impressive were their scores. The troop average for aircraft firing was 938, twenty points higher than A Troop. B Troop had problems with aircraft, and one crew failed to qualify. The squadron commander flew thirty hours on the sixth C Troop aircraft. Lieutenant Colonel Smithey and CW4 Richard "Dick" Needles didn't qualify for score, but their videotape showed the gun and rockets were firing great. On the last three days of the gunnery, the staff pilots were using the only aircraft left shooting. Of those, four were C Troop birds.

Tom Lawton was ecstatic. His troop had far exceeded his expectations. C Troop had the first, third, fourth, eighth, and tenth rated crews of the seventeen in the squadron. His boss was happy, his men were happy, and the aircraft were in great shape. The whole exercise could be categorized as a success simply because there was only one minor aircraft mishap. B Troop had a tail rotor strike at the holding area. Luckily, no one was injured, and the aircraft was fixed in three days.

Lieutenant Colonel Smithey was pleased with the whole exercise. He gave impact Army Commendation Medals to Chief Warrant Officer 3 Dolce, Chief Warrant Officer 2 Petty, and Staff Sergeant Ramirez as the Top Guns of the Fighting Sixth. CW3 Jerry Hunt, CW3 Robert Kilgore, and SGT Steve Waltrip from A Troop were second in scoring. The Champion crew of CW4 Ron Weimer, CW2 Alan Berstein, and Specialist Leon Hoard came in third.

The awards ceremony was great for the troops. Unit morale was excellent due to the success of the gunnery and the imminent return home. But Tom noticed Lieutenant Colonel Smithey appeared to be down for some reason. He had his smile, but his voice was lower than normal. Lieutenant Colonel Smithey only had two weeks left, and Tom expected him to be higher than a kite going out on a successful exercise like this. Captain Lawton went over to him after the ceremony.

"Well, if it isn't Hawkeye!" said the squadron commander.

Captain Lawton blushed a little. "Shit, sir. Nothing you and Mr. Needles couldn't have done if your score counted."

"Fourth place in this squadron is pretty damn good, Captain. You should be happy," said the squadron commander.

"Don't get me wrong, I'm happy, sir! But I'm happier for my pilots. They came through better than I expected," said Captain Lawton. Time to cut to the chase. "I was just wondering, sir, you seem a little down or something. Is everything okay?"

"Is it showing?" said the squadron commander.

"Something seems wrong, sir," said Tom.

"Well"—Lieutenant Colonel Smithey looked around to see that no one else was listening—"let's walk a little, Tom." As they walked, the colonel talked. "Even though it's time for me to go, I don't want to. I've done this for two years. I've seen the highs, and trust me on this, the lows too." He smiled a little. "I guess you might not understand until you get to this level."

"I don't see that happening, sir. I'm happy right here at troop level," said Tom Lawton honestly.

"At this level of command, you become so much a part of the unit and its people that you may become . . ." His voice trailed off. "I've become too close and too fond of my people." He paused for a moment, and his voice took on a different tone. "There are some things in motion that, given your position, you don't need to know about. But I do. Your new commander is a good one, and I know he'll take care of you guys. What you've done with the Champions in such a short time can only be described as outstanding. Don't stop training them because of this minor success. You keep pushing them, and you'll all do fine."

Tom was confused. There was a message there somewhere, but Tom didn't get the connection. "Do fine at what, sir? I'm not sure I understand." Tom felt like Luke Skywalker trying to get answers from Obi-Wan Kenobi.

Without another word, the squadron commander's mood changed. He slapped Tom on the back and said, "You'll understand a hell of a lot more in the next couple months. You did an outstanding job, Tom. Keep it up."

Tom didn't want the boss to leave, but before he could think of anything to say, the boss had turned and started toward his aircraft. Everything had been going so great, and now Tom was more confused than ever. What was Lieutenant Colonel Smithey talking about?

September 6, 1990
Katterheim Caserne

THE TROOPS RETURNED HOME UNEVENTFULLY. WHEN units came back from field training exercises, there was always excitement with spouses and families reuniting. Children running around the hangars, excited to have Mom or Dad back with stories of what great things were done to protect freedom's frontier.

This return would be different. Tom Lawton didn't see anything different, but he certainly felt something different. There was an uneasy civility in the atmosphere, almost as if something, an accident or injury, had happened and all the wives were aware, but not the troopers. Tom noticed the smiles were a little more strained and the talk was generally chattering, not full of happiness or relief that normally accompanied these returns. Tom also noticed LTC Stanley W. Hawk and his wife making their way through the crowd with Laura Smithey. Hawk was Smithey's replacement.

What the heck was he doing there? The change of command was still three weeks away. Usually, the new commander was not visible until a day or two before the official change of command. Laura Smithey looked very happy. She actually looked relieved to see everyone back. Chuck Smithey came up and received a very warm reception. The army frowns on public displays of affection, but Laura obviously didn't care. Introductions were made, and Chuck Smithey was warm and cordial to his replacement.

Tom saw Cindy and Megan headed toward him as he left the helicopter. Tom hesitated to run to them. He still had his postflight inspection to do. *I'll do it later*, thought Champion Six. *I deserve this welcome. Conquering hero and all.*

"Hi, baby. Man, did I miss you two!" said Tom.

Cindy Lawton hesitated. A tear was trickling down her left cheek. Tom couldn't help but notice something was definitely up. She was always happy and in control at these things. "I'm so glad your back. We both missed you very much."

Megan managed something like, "Miss you, Doddy!" with a big smile. Tom could only smile at her bliss.

"What's up, hon? There's something going on around here, isn't there?" asked Tom.

"Nothing that anyone is positive of. Just a whole lot of rumors and speculation," said Cindy.

"Rumors? What kind of rumors?" said Tom. It was amazing how the wives always found out things before the soldiers. For the most part, their "rumor mill" was accurate.

"That you guys are deploying. That this whole gunnery training exercise was to get you ready to go," said Cindy.

"Of course it's to get us ready to go." Tom was still a little lost. "We've got annual requirements. This thing's been on the calendar for a year. As for deploying? We couldn't get to Ramstein right now if we had to. Somebody is overreacting, sweetie. Let me hold Megan."

Cindy reluctantly gave the little girl to "Doddy" and wiped her cheek. "Hussein has invaded Kuwait."

Tom looked at her. Terser than he intended, Tom said, "We hadn't heard that." He looked around at the crowd and could see the news was spreading throughout the assembled crowd. Tom looked back to Cindy to comfort her. "Nobody has said a word to us, baby." Then he added, chuckling, "Shit, they'll send the Boys Scouts from stateside before we go anywhere!" Tom reached out for her and hugged her tightly. As he looked around, many more couples and families were hugging. What normally was a carnival-type atmosphere was somber. Quiet crying and sniffles could be heard. Tom saw the Smitheys and the Hawks working the crowd like politicians. The old man knows what's going on. Tom was going to find out as much as he could. But now was hardly the time or place.

"Come with me, honey. Let's go meet the new boss. Trust me. Everything is going to be just fine. We ain't goin' anywhere," said Tom. He almost believed it himself.

September 7, 1990
Hangar 3010
Katterheim Caserne

"CPT TOM LAWTON, I'D LIKE YOU to meet LTC Stan and Mrs. Susie Hawk. Stan, this is Tom Lawton and his wife, Cindy. That little one there is Megan, and she is definitely a daddy's girl," said LTC Chuck Smithey.

As the ladies exchanged pleasantries, Tom saluted crisply and reached out to take the incoming commander's hand. He had a firm grip and a broad smile. Tom could tell he was happy to be getting his command, and it appeared that he worked out quite often. Tom looked back at Chuck Smithey and then to Stan Hawk. Stan Hawk looked young, very young compared to Lieutenant Colonel Smithey. Not just young, but confident and full of energy. To Tom, Chuck Smithey looked tired. He wasn't the same man that took command two years ago. Not only had time taken its toll, but also command as well. Worrying about subordinate actions, the safety of the soldiers, and of course, answering to higher headquarters at a moment's notice had worn Smithey out. A commander needed faith. Some men handle leadership without a problem, and you never see an effect. Chuck Smithey couldn't hide the effects of command anymore. Tom understood what his old boss meant back at Graf. At least some of it. The command part and getting too close to his people. It was the last part that he didn't understand.

"Chuck's told me a lot of good things about you two. I heard you had a terrific gunnery, Captain Lawton," said the new boss.

Tom picked up on two things. Chuck and Lieutenant Colonel Hawk had met before and talked probably in depth about the squadron. And secondly, they had discussed wives. "Well, you've got me, sir, because I don't think any of us in the squadron know a thing about you," said Tom honestly.

"We'll have lots of time to talk about me later. What kind of shape are your aircraft in?" asked Lieutenant Colonel Hawk.

Tom read faces pretty well. Hawk wasn't just making conversation. He really wanted to know. Tom looked at Lieutenant Colonel Smithey, and Smithey just smiled. Damn the old man! Tom knew why nobody wanted to play poker with him. "Actually, sir, we're in pretty good shape. We came back with five of six still shooting and one headed to phase . . . probably on Wednesday. The sixth one has a seep in the nose gearbox, and we canned a PNVS to get one other FMC." Tom added without wanting to sound like he was bragging, "And the crews all qualified well above average, sir."

"The crews I'm not too worried about. It's the aircraft that are of concern after an exercise like this." Tom nodded affirmatively and smiled slightly in acknowledgment. But he was real curious why these particular questions were coming from his future boss and not his current boss.

"I'd like to believe it was my crews that rode 'em hard and put 'em away dry. We've been focusing real hard on maintenance the last couple of months, sir," said Tom. He was very pleased with the progress. On paper, the numbers reflected a drop in operational readiness rate. In actuality, the success rate measured by aircraft launched as scheduled was at 92 percent.

"That's probably because they were taken care of very well before you took command," said the new boss. Ouch! Where the hell did that come from? Then it hit Tom. This guy knows Sweat. Tom couldn't help but draw back at the remark. He was probably Sweat's boss in a previous life. "Don't take me wrong, Captain Lawton. I know the history of your troop, and before you took command, it led the brigade in OR rate." The history was probably slanted by the source of his information, thought Tom.

Tom's jaw slightly dropped. He looked to Lieutenant Colonel Smithey for support that never came. At least he wasn't smiling anymore. "Well, sir, we've been working on some new procedures that are getting us back to that standard again." In one brief comment, Stan Hawk had unknowingly opened a wound that had taken Tom three months to heal. The comment stung more severely than Tom had realized.

"I'm sure they will be. I need to go meet your peers. We'll have more time to talk in the next few days. Pleasure to meet you, Tom. And you, Cindy," said the new boss.

"Roger, sir. Ours too. Lieutenant Colonel Smithey, a moment of your time, please, sir?" asked Tom.

"You all go ahead. Champion Six needs my critical wisdom and guidance on some major issue of importance," said Lieutenant Colonel Smithey. The Hawks and Laura Smithey moved on to the rest of the crowd. Lieutenant Colonel Smithey said to Tom, "What is it, Captain Lawton?"

Such formality. Tom looked at Cindy and Megan, then at Lieutenant Colonel Smithey, a man he thought he knew well and admired. Then he looked down at his feet like a kid who had been scolded. "What's goin' on here, sir?"

"What are you asking, Captain?" responded the squadron commander.

Tom looked at Cindy, who immediately understood an unasked request and walked away. "I didn't expect that, sir."

"Expect what, Captain Lawton?" asked the commander.

"Damn it, sir!" Tom was pissed to be getting the third degree from somebody that isn't even his boss yet. "He's knows a helluva lot about us, and we haven't even met the guy. And thanks for your support on the

Champions' maintenance program too! Shit, sir. I haven't worked a single day for this guy, and he thinks I'm a dud. And another thing! What the fuck is goin' on around here? It's like a funeral or something." Tom looked hard at the boss he loved and respectfully added, "Sir." He was looking at a different Chuck Smithey.

Lieutenant Colonel Smithey reached in his pocket for a cigarette. "I told you to keep up what you're doing with the Champions, and you'll do fine. Same with him as it is with me. He's a good man, and he'll be a good commander. Give him a little time. He knows what you're capable of. As for what's going on here . . ." His voice trailed off. The response was not what Tom had expected. "It's a welcome home party, Captain."

Tom Lawton knew that was all he was going to get. If the boss did know anything and Tom was sure he did, he wasn't giving it up to this "captain." Lawton ran through a quick decision-making process. Press him. Let him go. Set up a time to talk later. Tom studied the man hard and looked deep into his eyes. Lieutenant Colonel Smithey knew exactly what was going on. He knew everything. Tom felt like a pawn. He was so tempted to snap, "Well, thanks for nothin', you old . . ." But he couldn't. He loved this man like his father. Decision made. "Roger, sir. Good-bye." The good-bye had such finality to it that it took Tom by surprise. He wouldn't press his mentor anymore. The mentor would provide no more answers. Things had changed.

"Did you find out anything, honey?" asked Cindy.

"Nothing that can answer your questions, Cindy. I've got more questions now than before." Tom touched her softly on the arm and looked into her eyes. "Let me get all the guys headed home and tie down the aircraft. I think cordon bleu and Jaeger schnitzels at the Greek place in Ansbach are in order. I'll let you 'hack' a little Deutsch, and I'll smile approvingly like a tourist."

"Can we ask the Osborns?" said Cindy.

"Sure. I don't know if Hart will want to go or not. He's pretty sick of me right now. Besides, you know the two of us will end up talking about work," said Tom.

"But if they come, I don't have to listen to you talk about work," replied Cindy.

Tom nodded. "You've got a point there."

"I'll ask them, and I'm sure they'll come," said Cindy.

Tom looked down at Cindy. She and Lou Ann had already planned to get together. It was just a matter of the time and place. Tom mockingly came to attention and saluted. "Yes, ma'am!"

Cindy smacked his arm and smiled. "Jerk!"

September 7, 1990
Ludwigstubbe Restaurante
Ansbach, Germany

THE MEAL WAS TERRIFIC AS USUAL. Tom's cordon bleu was the perfect combination of chicken, ham, cheese, and grease, washed down with two of Germany's finest pilsners and a mineralwasser. Cindy had a huge Jaeger schnitzel that she shared with Megan. Lou Ann indulged in a schnitzel that she couldn't come close to finishing. Hartley Osborn was more adventurous and ordered something from the Greek menu. Nobody could interpret the Greek waiter's gestures, but the group eventually agreed it was lamb. Cindy and Lou split a carafe of wine, and Hart stuck to coke. The conversation managed to stay off work and the army. It was focused on backgrounds of the foursome, hometowns, and plans for the future. Typical things army families talk about when they avoid discussing the army.

Hart ventured into the work arena when the dessert arrived. "What did you think of Lieutenant Colonel Hawk, sir?"

The table grew quiet. Tom didn't want to go into this tonight. He was actually having a good time. So he tried to lighten the mood by putting down his fork full of black forest cake. He managed to do a semblance of an impression. He put his index finger to his temple and became the scarecrow from the *Wizard of Oz* when the wizard told him he had a brain. "The politically correct thing to say to my subordinate is, I think the lieutenant colonel is an outstanding officer, and he'll do an outstanding job as our commander." The girls both chuckled, which Tom enjoyed because it eased the tension.

Hart didn't chuckle. "C'mon, sir. What's he doing coming around the squadron so early? And why all the questions? He wasn't even trying to be cordial. He was looking for pinpoint answers to serious questions. I talked to lieutenants Hightower, Blue, and Rison, and they said the same thing. He asked the other commanders in-depth questions. Especially Captain Rooks."

Tom thought hard and looked at the lieutenant. He didn't want to talk about work with the wives there, but he had been put on the spot. "In all honesty, I'm not real sure why he . . ." Then it hit him. Maintenance. The rumors. The Nightstalkers weren't ready to go anywhere. Being between a new commander inbound and their current training record, that schedule couldn't be changed. The personnel status couldn't be changed. But their aircraft were the best in theater because of Rooksy and the maintenance guys. Smithey probably asked to extend and was denied, which explained his testiness. Hawk was coming from the test facility at Fort Rucker and knew as much as there is to know about how to fight and maintain Apaches. It was just a guess on Tom's part. Suppose Hawk was told his first mission was to support the Middle East Theater with aircraft. He needed to know the unit's status immediately. That's why Smithey had him so pooped up on the unit status. Some unit in theater was on alert, which explained the wives' chain of rumors. This unit didn't have the aircraft to go and were looking for aircraft support. Tom smiled. Somebody needs our Apaches.

Then he shook it off. He was so full of shit sometimes. Time to play the jerk again and keep the air light. "He wants to make you the squadron maintenance officer because you're doing such a fine job keeping your birds up." Tom tried to keep a straight face.

Hart Osborn turned white. "No, sir! You can't let him . . . I don't want to go. I'm just now figuring out what the heck I'm doing, and you want to let me go?"

Tom couldn't hold it anymore. He burst out laughing. It was the first time he'd seen Hart Osborn really show emotion, and it was refreshing. "Just kiddin', Lieutenant. I wouldn't trade you for two lieutenants." More seriously, Tom added, "I honestly have no idea what's going on."

That ended the work talk for the evening. Cindy and Lou were in their element, enjoying each other's company and being with their men. Hart was more relaxed than Tom had ever seen him. But for the remainder of the night, Tom Lawton was somewhere else. His mind was in perpetual motion. If he was right, the deploying unit was probably not just short on working Apaches but probably needed people. Maybe they needed a whole troop. If Hawk asked him, what would he say? *Yes, the Champions are ready, and I want to lead them into the jaws of battle.* Or no. Honestly, there is no way in hell his guys could face up to a seasoned fighting machine like the Iraqi Republican Guard. Either way, there was a lot to do in a short time.

Usually, after a terrific night like this one, a husband and wife would top if off with a tremendous exchange of renewed vows and serious lovemaking. Cindy was willing and gave off the proper signals. Tom was missing all the signs. His mind was miles away. When Cindy put on her sexiest nightgown and came to bed, Tom didn't even notice. He had a Soviet threat manual in bed and was memorizing weapons capabilities. He had just finished reading which Soviet-based air defense systems had been sold to Iraq.

"Hey, tourist boy! Why don't you come on over here and experience some foreign terrain?" said Cindy playfully.

Tom looked up from the book. His mouth fell open a little as he saw Cindy standing next to the bed completely naked. "I . . . guess this can wait a while longer."

"'Bout time. I was beginning to wonder if I was losing my charm," said Cindy.

"Not you, baby. You'll never lose your charm. Or me." Tom came across the bed, grabbed her around the waist, and kissed her on the neck. Slowly, knowingly, he kissed her all over, remembering each and every hill and valley. Cindy was in heaven. But she felt something wasn't right.

Physically, Tom was there and doing all the right things. But she knew this man, and mentally, he was somewhere else. It felt so good to have him back and paying some attention to her that she shook off the feelings and let herself enjoy the moment.

After they finished making love, Tom couldn't sleep. His mind was still racing. So much to do, so little time. He didn't want to wake Cindy. As quietly as he could, he got out of bed and went to the living room.

Cindy wasn't sleeping. She couldn't sleep without Tom next to her. What was a terrific evening had turned right back to the way it was before he went to gunnery. He was so absorbed in this whole command thing. Didn't she and Megan matter? Was she losing him? Did she need to change?

For just an instant, Tom thought he heard a sob come from the bedroom. He was still and listened intently. No, just his imagination. Cindy was definitely asleep. Now what was the range on the ZSU 23-4?

September 22, 1990
Hangar 3010

THE WEATHER WAS PERFECT FOR THE ceremony. The change of command was a thing of beauty. The Fighting Sixth Cavalry band came up from Ansbach. The squadron had practiced for two days and pulled the event off like clockwork. Commanders from all over Germany came in to witness the exchange of colors that symbolized the passing of unit responsibility from one man to another. Tom got a chance to talk to old friends and visit with Barney Steele. He was a little down on himself for not engaging in meaningful conversation with Chuck Smithey. He couldn't bring himself to do it. There was still pain there from Smithey's distant attitude after returning from gunnery. It had been three weeks, and neither squadron commander, incoming or outgoing, had said anything to any troop commanders about what was happening. The rumor mill was rampant, and uneasiness could be sensed throughout the community. But no one said a word, lest the rumor becomes fact.

LTC Stanley Hawk was a West Point graduate, class of '73. He was hard charging, confident, and friendly. His Officer Record Brief (ORB) was filled with command jobs from the time he left flight school. Lieutenant Colonel Hawk had two tours with different armored cavalry regiments, Second and Eleventh, and was very familiar with Germany and cavalry tactics. His position at Fort Rucker enabled him to put his experience to paper and produce the doctrine army aviation would use in the next decade. It was his first Apache unit, but this was not a liability by any means. His cavalry experience combined with his natural aggressiveness augmented his attack helicopter pilot mentality. The man was mission focused.

Immediately after the ceremony, Lieutenant Colonel Hawk called all five troop commanders together. "Enjoy the festivities, give your troopers the day off, and be in my office at 1300. Gentlemen, we have work to do."

The five commanders looked at each other. They smiled, saluted, and offered up a gung ho "Roger that, sir!" That was the first time Tom had ever seen all five captains together on anything.

1300, September 22, 1990
Office of the Commander, Nightstalker Six
Katterheim Caserne

"GENTLEMEN, IT IS WITH GREAT PRIDE that I am here. I don't want to bore you all with any more speeches, so I'll get down to business. At this particular time, aircraft maintenance is the priority. Not training. Not ground maintenance. Not check rides. Fixing aircraft." Tom Lawton looked at Rooksy. They both smiled. "I've gone over the OR rates of the respective troops, and I see A Troop has the best readiness rate, followed by B Troop. C Troop, what seems to be the problem?" inquired the commander.

Lawton was ready for the inquiry. "Sir, we don't have a problem. We have some parts that take time to get, but when we get them, we fix what's broke. My numbers are just that. Numbers. If an aircraft is down, I talk to Captain Rooks, and we fix it ASAP. If it's FMC, I report it FMC. If it's only partially mission capable, I report it PMC. The rate reflects my readiness."

"I'm not looking for the book answer here, Captain Lawton. I'll ask my question again." The gloves came off. "Why are you broke?" asked Nightstalker Six.

Tom was taken aback by the directness of the question. It was his first day as squadron commander, and he was already screwing with one of his troop commanders. Hawk wanted to play hardball from the start. Tom brought his bat. "I'm not broke, sir. I'm fixed," he said flatly.

"I don't get it. The numbers have been down three straight months since you took command. What's fixed?" asked the commander.

Here goes nothing. "The numbers before I took command were a little off. Since then, I made my personnel read the regulations, apply what they read, and interpret the situation accordingly," said Tom. "Not to mention, we've tripled the amount of flight time from the previous quarter."

"Are you saying, before you took command, the reports were lies?" asked the commander.

Tom sensed everyone in the room squirm except himself and Rooksy.

Rooksy joined the conversation. "Sir, I took all those reports, and the priority at the time was meeting DA standards." Rooksy offered himself up for sacrifice.

"Captain Rooks, you already defended him before. I want to hear his answer," said the commander.

Tom stared back at Lieutenant Colonel Hawk. Remembering that Sweat and Hawk knew each other, he said flatly and tactfully, "Not lies, sir." He searched for a word. "Inaccuracies." Tom continued, "There was some . . . pressure to meet DA standards every month."

Not taking his eyes off Lawton, Hawk said, "And you, other gentlemen, had . . . inaccuracies to report as well." A couple of coughs and some foot movement under the table broke the silence. Hawk looked around. "The silence speaks volumes." Tom had survived his first test with Stan Hawk.

"Captain Rooks, I've got to have accurate reports. Pearson, Wise, and Lawton need to keep you informed at all times what are FMC, what are PMC, and the parts they need." The colonel looked at Tom with a smile that came out of nowhere. "Captain Lawton, I'd like you to know that Captain Rooks said the same thing you did, only with much less tact, last Friday," said Lieutenant Colonel Hawk. "I believe the quote was, 'The numbers are down because that's all we got up!'" Lieutenant Colonel Hawk looked at Tom and said with a huge grin, "I was just testing you."

Tom smiled, somewhat relieved by the results of the "test," but still not quite sure where he stood. He had to know. "Sir, I know you've done your homework on us, and you are familiar with previous troop commanders." Tom was trying not to be awkward or put his boss on the spot, but guts worked before. "You've obviously researched our history and have formed an opinion. I guess my question is . . . where does C Troop stand with you?"

LTC Stan Hawk tilted his head to the side and looked around the room at all five captains. "Let's be clear on one thing. Troop commanders are special. Any of you can come to me and talk to me about any subject at any time. And another thing, you are all equal." Then he looked directly at Tom. "What happened past is done. Collectively, we move forward and reach the standards our bosses set for us. Captain Lawton, C Troop is doing great. You stand right beside me." And he smiled.

Tom exhaled audibly. "Without sounding too much like an ass-kisser, sir, that's where you'll be able to find us," Tom said, hoping he spoke for the others. For just a while, all was right with Tom's world again.

The meeting concluded with Captain Rooks briefing the new commander on aircraft status. And contrary to "numbers," the implementation of P4T2 was working. Surprisingly, Lieutenant Colonel Hawk was very receptive and ordered the other two troops to implement the maintenance program as well. He vowed to see what he could do to get parts for aircraft down for over thirty days but couldn't promise anything.

The commander concluded, "I'm looking forward to the next two years. I hope we can make a lot of great things happen, no matter what our missions are."

To Tom, this seemed like a peculiar thing to say. "No matter what our missions are." It was as if he already knew there were missions the unit would not like. As everyone rose and rendered the salute, the commander said, "Captain Lawton, could you stay here for a couple minutes?"

"Roger, sir," said Tom. He caught Rooksy's attention before the maintenance officer could leave and grabbed his arm. Quietly, Tom bent over and whispered in his ear, "Thanks, man. I owe you one."

Rooksy slapped him on the arm. "Yeah, you do."

Tom could only drop his head in mock shame and smile.

"Sir, is there something else I can do for you?" asked Tom sincerely.

"Yes, Tom, there is." The colonel grabbed a piece of paper from the top of his desk and began to read. "The following personnel in your command are in debt to the Officer's Club in the amount posted next to their respective name and troop."

Tom scratched his head and looked at the commander.

He continued, "This list has twelve names on it. Within the brigade, eleven of them come from this squadron. Five are in your troop. As a matter of fact, three of the top 4 are in your troop." The boss paused for effect. "Does your troop have a drinking problem?"

Tom wasn't quite sure how to answer. For a brief second, he worried that his name was on the list. He was sure it wasn't because he paid cash most of the time. Which Champions were on the list and how could he smooth it over for them? It was obvious by the squadron commander's demeanor that the situation didn't call for humor. Tom went with sincerity. "Not that I'm aware of."

The lieutenant colonel handed over the paper, and Tom could see why he was serious. "The top guy there has a $1,200 bar bill!" said Hawk.

Tom Lawton's jaw dropped. There it was in black and white. Five of his warrant officers had overdue bar bills between $500 and $1,200. "Sir, I had no idea. I'll fix it. Can I get a copy of this, please?"

"Roger." The commander continued, "That's bad stuff. They have to be drinking a lot to get their bills up that high. This problem may be deeper than you realize."

"Sir, let me fix it. This is a problem I can handle at my level. The club should never have allowed them to run up a bill that high in the first place. If you think we have a bunch of drunks, I'll fix that too. My problem, my solution. Okay, sir?" said Tom.

Lieutenant Colonel Hawk hesitated. "Okay. You've got thirty days. Report back to me on the status of these individuals, the status of the bills, and if you have any drunks. All aspects of their lives are your responsibility."

Tom thought about that but didn't add, "Shouldn't they be *our* responsibility?" Tom knew when to keep his mouth shut. "Roger, sir." He came to attention and said, "Is there anything else, sir?"

"Just one other thing. You do have the best aircraft in the brigade. Keep 'em that way. Dismissed, Captain Lawton," said the commander.

"Yes, sir. Thank you, sir," Tom said with a smile. With the ass chewing came some slight praise. Tom saluted and moved out before he took any more fire.

"One more thing, Captain," said Hawk.

Tom winced and turned to face the commander. Lieutenant Colonel Hawk said, "Being how they're in such good shape, I'll be flying one of them, right?"

Tom wanted to protest. He already had to fly the brigade commander. He only had one instructor pilot. Was he getting tested again? "Sure, sir. I've got 956 without a crew. It's all yours. Just let us know when you want it and I'll have the crew chief there for launch and recovery, sir." Biting his tongue after he said it, Tom had no idea how much he would regret this casual offer.

CHAPTER 4

SEPTEMBER WAS USUALLY A GREAT TIME for American troops in Germany. Octoberfest was a mere alcoholic memory. The country was a happy place for German citizens at harvest time because US troops and foreign visitors chose to provide income to the Federal Republic of Germany's economy. This particular October was different for American forces.

It had been a week since the squadron change of command. The rumors had not gone away. They merely intensified as the soldier chain became involved. The rumors would say, "I got a buddy up in Hanua, and he says . . ." or "My brother back at Hood says something else." It wore on the whole military community. The commanders at squadron or battalion level, even if they knew something, couldn't and wouldn't say anything. The wives chain always conjured up information, valid or not, that spread like wildfire from one caserne to the next. In the small communities, there were no secrets.

Naturally, the word got out throughout the brigade that the Champions were all alcoholics and they collectively owed ten thousand dollars to the Officer's Club. Tom blew off all the comments he received about his troops and their so-called bottle problem. The solution for the troops wasn't as easy to blow off. He thought about how to solve it, casually mention it to the senior warrants, and let the warrant officer chain take care of it. Not enough time. Bring in the five culprits for one-on-one counseling or as a group and rip them a new ass. That wouldn't work because it might split the troop. If he briefed the whole troop, the warrants would be embarrassed in front of the enlisted soldiers, who may or may not handle the information in a professional manner. Tom decided to brief all the officers on the situation and provide answers to Top for the enlisted soldiers.

It was an awkward situation. Tom's men were running up bills that high at the Officers Club. The timing was never good for something like this. Just when things were coming together, an external event of this type could drive a unit apart. On the other hand, it could bring them together and provide a commander some ammunition.

1000, September 29, 1990
Hangar 3010, Classroom 3
Katterheim, Germany

TOM CALLED ALL THE OFFICERS INTO the classroom. "Gentlemen, we have a little problem to discuss." He walked around the room and looked at the faces of each man to keep their attention. He told the truth. "The new commander gave me a list. On this list are names of people throughout the brigade who owe money to the O'Club." A nervous movement rippled through the room. "Apparently, some of you go to the club and drink. And I do mean *drink*." Nervous laughter. "The problem is the audit trail. When you charge there, they know they'll get their money with interest. They don't tell the troop commanders. They don't tell the squadron commander. They go straight to the big guy. The brigade commander. Now I don't know how many of you have had the pleasure of his company, but it ain't pleasant. And I don't want it!" Some more laughs. "I don't want that guy giving me a visit or coming to visit you unless it's on terms we are prepared for. If it's on his terms . . . we're screwed! The bills are the responsibility of the individual, but collectively, for better or worse, we have established a reputation as hard drinkers. But that's okay! I can handle that. Even good old Lieutenant Osborn's been known to have a beer now and again." The lieutenants blushing could be seen across the room. More laughter and smiles from the Champions. "The outstanding bills are a different story. To make what needs to be a short story even shorter, pay 'em off! If you don't have the money, go talk to the manager and work out a payment plan. Hell, we haven't had time to go there that much lately. How long have they been this high?"

It was a rhetorical question, but Chief Warrant Officer 3 Walker answered. "Sir, my bills been over a thousand dollars for six months. They never charged much interest until lately and didn't send us any bills. I understand the problem, sir. I'll have it paid off ASAP."

"They never sent you bills yet kept serving you?" asked Captain Lawton.

About six heads nodded in affirmation. The reply "We're good customers!" came from Mr. Berstein.

What could he say? Tom laughed. "I'll say your good customers!" He paused as he got his composure and the room quieted down. "Man, we got people calling us the champagnes and welchers and other names I never heard of. Please pay these puds off." Tom walked to the front. More serious than he wanted to be, he said, "Without the pot calling the kettle black, I've been known to imbibe a little myself." Tom looked around again, tugging at an imaginary tie. More nervous laughter. "Some people might consider the amount of alcohol consumed to cause those bills a problem! And don't tell me its food 'cause I know it ain't food. That vast amount of booze could constitute a drinking problem." Tom looked hard at Walker, Tucker, Cross, Berstein, and finally Weimer. Silence. Too uptight, thought Tom. "I know what the problem is. You drink so much you think your flight pay will cover it!" The crack broke the tension again. "I've said it before, and I'll say it again loudly so all of you can hear me. You are too important for me to lose you!" He let it sink in. He continued walking. "Injuries. Judicial punishment. Medical problems. I can't lose anyone for any reason. I don't want to make that determination for you, but I will if I have to. If you think even for a moment that you have a problem, come see me."

That should do it, thought Tom. Get the back brief. "Mr. Weimer, would you care to sum up our little meeting for the crowd."

CW4 Ron Weimer rubbed his chin and said, "Pay your bills off, you bunch of drunks."

Tom could only stare at Weimer. The pilots looked at Weimer and then back to Lawton and began to laugh, slowly at first, not knowing how Champion Six might take the assessment. Tom chuckled. The pilots started to laugh out loud. Tom joined in and shook his head. Laughing with his hands up, he said, "I took all that time . . ." The room erupted in laughter. "You guys kill me."

The laughing continued, and Mr. Walker added, "So what you really want is for us to charge all our drinkin' to your account?"

"No, no, no! Don't even think like that. My wife would kill us all." Tom smiled, barely able to contain his laughter.

As he started to leave, he was still shaking his head. "You guys are too much. Dismissed!"

Tom got a thunderous "Hoooaah!" from the Champions as he headed for the door. He heard Mr. Cross say, apparently to Lieutenant Timmons, "So, sir, can I use your club card?" The place erupted again. Tom stopped in his tracks and lowered his head. He looked over his shoulder at Mr. Cross.

"Just kidding, sir," said the scout pilot.

"Guys, stay out of trouble. Get your maintenance status to the lieutenants before you go home." Tom shook his head and smiled. What more could he say. They were together again as a unit should be. His unit.

October 12, 1990
Hangar 3010
Katterheim Caserne

"MAN, ROOKSY, YOU GOT THIS PLACE spic-and-span. We havin' some kind of inspection I don't know about?" asked Tom.

"I wish. Fucking Darth Vader himself showed up unannounced for a visit to B Troop. Colonel Denson's got B Troop in the classroom, giving them the riot act. I wish that S1 at brigade would give us a courtesy call when he comes down here for these unexpected visits of his," said Captain Rooks.

"She probably doesn't know where he's going," said Tom.

"Oh, she knows. She just doesn't want to give us time to get ready for one of his tantrums," said Rooksy.

"What's the visit for?" asked Tom.

"He's pissed about the low gunnery scores and low OR rates," said Rooksy. This was as disturbed as Tom had ever seen Rooks.

"Hammerin' him for the truth?" said Tom.

Captain Rooks shook his head. "No. Hammerin' him for not having his shit together. There's a difference."

"Well, let's talk phase bird and he might be gone by the time we're done," said Tom.

"I hope so. I don't like Denson in my AO. Makes the troops do stupid shit," said the maintenance officer.

Thirty minutes later, Tom walked outside. Across the parking lot, Colonel Denson had Lieutenant Colonel Hawk and CPT Chris Wise involved in a one-way discussion. Tom could see it was one way because Denson was about two feet from the B Troop commander, poking his finger in Chris Wise's face and talking with a real pissed-off look. Both Hawk and Wise were "at ease" if you could call it that. Denson wasn't hollering, but he was obviously making sure Wise got the message Denson was transmitting. He turned to Hawk and reiterated something. Tom had no idea what was happening, but he was glad it wasn't happening to him.

As he walked to his car, he noticed a small cluster of troops watching the tongue-lashing. Finally, Denson left. Hawk was alone talking to Phil Wise. Phil was shaking his head and breathing heavy as if stifling a sob. Tom heard a group of soldiers about ten feet away talking. "Man, I think he's crying. Shit yeah. Look at that." Tom looked over at Chris Wise and saw a fellow commander in distress. Wise probably didn't deserve what he just took, and he didn't need some jerk-off dickhead running his lips off to other soldiers about what may have just happened. Lawton reacted quickly and without mercy.

"At ease that shit!" Tom yelled a little more forceful than intended. He walked over to the group. It just happened to be five lieutenants. He'd never seen any of them before. He said to the mouth that made the comment, "What's the matter, Lieutenant? Forgot how to come to attention and salute?"

"Uh, uh, no, sir!" came the timid response.

Tom took a step closer. "Do you know what that little conversation over there was about?"

"Uh, no, sir," he said a little quieter this time.

Tom stepped closer and looked around the group. "If you don't know what the conversation was about"—Tom looked right at "the Mouth"—"then maybe you should keep your thoughts and play-by-play comments to yourself." Tom continued, "Maybe the colonel informed him a relative died."

From Tom's left came, "I don't think that was it, sir."

Tom looked left and snapped, "I don't give a fuck, Skippy!" Tom got his composure. "You got that. What you saw or thought you might have seen doesn't need to get around. Someday, if you use that one cell you call a brain instead of your mouth, you might be in his shoes. And when you lay your beady little brain bucket on your pillow tonight, you better fucking thank God that the captain over there took that ass chewin'. Because somewhere, a lieutenant that worked for that captain probably fucked up and got him that ass chewin'! So unless you have some omnipotent power that allows you to know everything that's happening on this planet, why don't you keep your mouths shut and take care of the soldiers around you. That means up and down your chain!" Tom waited for a response. None came. "You all better thank God you don't work for me. Now get your asses back to work or wherever the fuck lieutenants go!"

"Yes, sir!" came a chorus from the captive audience.

Tom turned and started walking away. Over his shoulder, he said, "Carry the fuck on, Lieutenants."

Why had he gotten so upset? It seemed like a minor thing. Another captain getting his ass reamed from a brigade commander. At least Darth Vader had the tact to pull him off to the side and not do it in the hangar in front of troops.

Deep down, Tom knew exactly why he reacted so angrily. It could have been him. It might have been CPT Tom Lawton, or any commander, getting his ass chewed out for something. It's never pleasant, it's never anything you can plan for, and it's rarely anything the commander can control. It just comes with the territory. And it pissed Tom off to see some junior, no time in the army, officers getting a laugh at the expense of a peer. He was mad at himself for losing his composure, but he was downright pissed at the lieutenants for their behavior. He didn't know what Chris Wise had done to deserve the visit, but he knew Chris didn't deserve what he got.

October 12, 1990
Hangar 3010, 1930 hours
Katterheim, Caserne

TOM WAS WRAPPING UP HIS EVENING paperwork and looking forward to getting to his quarters. Cindy usually had supper on by 1900. He would be late again, and she'd have a right to be angry. Lieutenant Osborn had the mission for the night. He had two scouts and three Apaches doing a movement to contact. Tom had to admit, Hart was a damn good platoon leader. The warrants had problems with him because he was pretty straight and by the book. Hart was also talented and conscientious and had become extremely loyal to Tom. That was all he asked for.

There was a knock at the door. Tom wasn't expecting anyone, so it was a surprise just to have someone else in the hangar. He was even more surprised when he saw Chris Wise standing at his door. "You got a minute?"

Tom hesitated. He remembered that Cindy was waiting, but that would have to wait . . . again. "Yeah, sure." Tom stood up and showed Chris into the office. "Take the couch. You want me to close the door?"

"I don't think anyone else is here. It's fine. Everybody else is out at the aircraft," said Werewolf Six.

"You want a soda or something?" asked Tom, not sure what the topic of discussion would be.

"I'd really like a beer . . . or six!" Chris Wise smiled.

Tom smiled back. "How 'bout a Pepsi? I've got candy too. Snickers, M&M's, Chips Ahoy cookies, you name it. The troops love to come see me. Besides, it keeps me on the borderline for the 'fat boy' program."

Chris laughed and shook his head. Then his mood became serious. "Is that how you deal with it?"

Tom wanted to say "Deal with what?" But he had too much respect for his peer. He knew exactly what Chris meant. Tom smiled back, thought hard about his answer, and cleared his throat. "Not really. But it helps for me." He nodded and continued, "Of course there are the other things. Drinking heavily as time permits works too. Working late hours trying to anticipate what the highers will want next. Delegating like a big dog works." That got a smile from Chris. That was enough to loosen him up. Tom had to know. "Chris, what's up?"

Chris Wise didn't want to share what he interpreted to be a problem with anyone. He wanted to keep it to himself and "handle it." Tom knew Chris needed to talk to someone. Tom could see Chris deciding "How much can or should I let him know?" Time to get him to come clean. "Look, man." Tom smiled. "You had a bad day today. But it ain't the worst day you'll ever see. Trust me on that one."

Chris let go. "I don't think there can be a much worse one. It may very well have been the worst day of my life." He got up off the couch and paced a little. Tom was silent, letting Chris sort his emotions. "Of course you know about the Jesus meeting today, right?"

"Yeah, most everybody in the brigade knows by now," Tom said honestly.

"Denson came into the classroom and asked point-blank if any of my troops had a problem with me, now was the time to say so. To their credit, no one said anything. To me, that was a relief. You know the kinds of problems we're having. We can't seem to get anything fixed, so we aren't training enough, and we don't fly enough because we don't have aircraft up. Our gunnery scores weren't anything to write home about," said Chris.

Tom sympathized. "Hey, man, you've done this long enough to know it's a cyclic business. It's like the spokes on a bike. Sometimes you're up, and sometimes you're down. You're going through a down period. It isn't anything to get down about. Next month, it'll be me!"

Chris smiled and continued. It went deeper than that. "After the meeting, he called Hawk and me outside for an earful. Denson basically threatened me with my command." Chris let that sink in.

Tom thought back to what he saw in the parking lot. He remembered how glad he was that it wasn't him. He didn't tell Chris that he saw it or about the encounter with the lieutenants. "Did he actually say he would fire you?"

"In so many words, I believe it was, 'I'll get somebody else in here to square this outfit away because you are one fucked-up captain!' The Hawk tried to calm Denson down, but he doesn't have the same rapport with Denson that Smithey had." Chris gathered himself a little. "He was pissed. I haven't been treated like that by anyone. My father never talked to me like that."

Tom laughed a little to try to lighten the moment. "I heard he was one of the all-time greats." Chris sat down. "You got to remember, Denson's from the old school. He is a warrior. He won't tolerate anything less than a warrior mentality to surround him." Tom got up and reached into his jar for some Hershey's Kisses. "Denson's tough because he wants us to be the best." Tom offered Chris some of the chocolates. Chris would have none as he continued to pace. Tom asked, "So what are you gonna do?"

"I don't know, Tom. Should I quit? He listens to the rumor mill. Somebody up at brigade fills him with garbage, and he believes it." Chris swallowed hard. "There is nothing in the world I want to do more than command soldiers. This is what I want to do with my life. But . . . I don't see how I can. I feel like the deck is stacked against me. If I screw up just a little, he's going to relieve me. I don't know if I can take it."

It was Tom's turn to walk. He thought for a minute. "I can't tell you what to do, and it's not fair to say 'If it was me . . .' because I don't know what I'd do with a hand like you've got. But I do know I wouldn't quit. I don't think you should even consider that as a viable option." He paused. "Nah. Fuck him. You want to channel your emotions toward success in whatever direction works, but don't make it that easy for Denson. You've worked your whole career to get to this point, and you're considering throwing it away because you're in a numbers slump and you got your ass ripped. There isn't anything you can do except be honest. And that means be honest with yourself. You can't control every action of your soldiers, you can't keep aircraft from breaking, and you can't change who you are." Tom sat down. "Damn it, Chris! You worked too hard for this. Don't give up without giving it your best shot." Tom thought about how he'd fix the problem. "I'd like to make a couple of recommendations. First, go see the old man. Not tomorrow. Let it set a couple of days. Focus on flying. I can give you a couple of birds this week. Get your aircraft up. Give this whole situation time and it will be over in two weeks. It will get better. Hell, it can't be any worse, right?" Tom got up and put a reassuring hand on Chris's shoulder.

Chris smiled and sighed heavily. "You're such an optimist."

"Hey, man. Like I told Hal Timmons, don't sweat the petty stuff. Pet the sweaty stuff!" They both chuckled. It was quiet for a moment. "And next month, you can give me some aircraft 'cause I won't have shit up!"

Chris smiled and extended his hand. "You got a deal."

Tom took it and said, "You probably need to let Karen in on the situation too. You know how word gets around in this place. She probably already heard about it from somebody!"

"You got that right!" Chris headed out the door and stopped. "Thanks for listening. I do think your right about one thing. It can only get better."

"Next month, it'll be my turn to get an ass chewin' for something I can't control!" Tom smiled. He got serious. "Hey, Chris. We can do this."

Chris Wise smiled back and replied with a solid "Hooah!" Tom knew Chris would be okay. Better off than Tom, because Cindy was going to kill him for being late again.

October 31, 1990
16 Bundestrasse
Heilbronn, Germany

THE STUARTS DECIDED THEY WOULD HAVE a Halloween party at their humble abode on the edge of Heilbronn. The house was big enough for two families, so they had plenty of room for the whole crowd. All the *Kinder* stayed with friends and sitters in the posthousing, thereby freeing up the adults to party with reckless abandon. There were about twenty couples from the brigade that the Lawtons knew and about ten couples from Jed's cavalry unit, plus six or seven single officers with a couple of dates thrown in. A predetermined plan was implemented not to have field grade officers, warrant officers, noncommissioned officers, or enlisted soldiers at the party. This lack of invitation was not a slap or disrespect for the grade, merely a necessity. The captains had gotten together and decided it was a damn good time for all the junior officers to get rip-roaring drunk. And they did just that.

LT Steve "Schlep" Sheppard decided that a good theme for this Halloween party would be *The Rocky Horror Picture Show*. Those that were aware of the cult classic would come dressed as their favorite character. Those that weren't could come dressed as anything they wanted. It sounded like a good idea at the time.

Cindy was all for it. She highly encouraged Tom to go dressed as Frankenfurter, the part of the Transvestite character played by Tim Curry. Of course Cindy went as Janet. The crowd at the party was relatively straight at first, so there were many Janets and many Brads and some Magentas, but only one Dr. Frankenfurter.

Upon entering the stylish home, Tom Lawton was very nervous. As one of the senior officers, he was a leader, therefore responsible for the behavior of the group. He didn't know everyone there and was uncomfortable with the thought that his first impression with many peers and subordinates would be as the guy that was the transvestite at the Stuarts' Halloween party. To Tom's rescue came the host. Jed Stuart arrived with a bottle of Jagermeister, followed closely by lieutenants Alvin, Sheppard, and Timmons. The "Pack" was reunited.

"Great costume, sir!" said Dean Alvin, chuckling.

"Sir, I didn't know they made nylons that big," said Schlep. Naturally, they all had a good laugh at the comment. Tom just shook his head in disgust and looked down at the black nylons that covered his legs. The lieutenant continued to jab because he could see how effective it was. "And the lipstick, sir! Is that Rouge-de la-Merde?"

"Fuck you, Schlep! Fuck all you guys!" Tom continued to shake his head, but he knew deep down, it was all in fun. Let them have a good laugh. Hell with it. Tom decided early to go with the flow and have some fun. The Champions had been working hard, and he deserved a break. By design, this was the time for the captains and lieutenants to let their hair down and have some well-deserved fun.

Tom grabbed the bottle of Jagermeister and took a pull as they went inside. "Ya know, I never planned on being the president of the United States." He looked at himself in the hallway mirror. He took another long pull on the bottle. "You guys will respect me in the morning, won't you?" Tom batted his made-up eyes and burst out laughing. Somewhere in the background, Prince was singing "1999," and the party started hopping. "Gentlemen, shall we dance? Let's get this party goin'!"

The stage was set. Liquor flowed, and beers were chugged. In many ways, it resembled a fraternity party with organization for the first hour. Then it was all downhill.

Cindy was having a great time talking to Betty and Lou and an occasional lost single lieutenant. Generally, the lieutenant would leave after five minutes, red in the face and holding his mouth closed, trying to keep the shot of tequila in. The women would laugh hysterically at someone that tried to drink a shot and couldn't take it. They had another habit, which they found extremely humorous. If the men were talking about work or the army, they would interrupt the conversation and "sentence" the participants to "penalty shots." These penalty shots varied and often included tequila, rum, or vodka. If they liked the violators of the well-known rules, the penalty would be flavored schnapps. But if they didn't like the offender, 151 rum or scotch was served.

Luckily, about 2300, many of the partygoers had to leave. Kids needed to be picked up, sanity needed to be restored, and general order put into perspective for the revelers. Soon after the first group of twenty or so left, the Pack found themselves in the kitchen, discussing life in general, lest they be forced more shots from the party patrol.

Tom was leading a discussion on things they had done in their past. He was orienting his comments to Hart Osborn, but Jed, Schlep, and Dean Alvin were listening intently, catching their breath before another song came on. "I played rugby in college. We spent many nights doing this same thing." Tom laughed and punched Hart Osborn lightly on the shoulder. "I don't even remember my sophomore year. I went to school in September and started drinking. Next thing I knew, it was May." Hart Osborn's mouth was open. "Hell, I got a 2.8, and I don't even know what I took!" All laughed except Hart Osborn. He was confused. He respected Tom Lawton. But here was his boss and mentor dressed like a transvestite, drunk, and bragging about an eight-month blackout.

Tom could see Hart's confusion, so he tried to clear things up for him. "I used to drink a lot, Hart. These guys know me. They know my past. I trust them, and I think they trust me. I don't drink as much or as often as I used to because I've grown out of that." Looking at Jed, he added, "For the most part anyway." They laughed. "I know my responsibilities, family and work, and I'm very happy with them," said Tom as he became thoughtful and serious.

"Sir, I don't understand . . . how you got from being a drunken college kid to where you are today?" asked Hart Osborn.

The Pack quieted down because they had never heard the story either. Tom didn't want to talk about it but felt he owed his lieutenants an explanation. "I was going to be a physical education teacher after college. I wanted to coach basketball and track. But the starting salaries and opportunities just weren't there. After two years of literally hanging out, I decided to enlist in the army."

"So you enlisted?" asked Schlepper.

"Sure enough." Tom drank a little beer and continued, "I went to basic training and advanced individual training in Alabama. I wanted to be a crew chief, and the army afforded me the chance to do that." Tom sighed heavily and smiled. "A guy named CPT Wallace C. Pilthrow. No shit, that was his name. Ol' Wally told me with my degree and my leadership abilities, I could be an officer and fly helicopters rather than crew them. It sounded like a good plan. I put my packet in, went before the board, and was accepted for Officer Candidate School. After OCS at Benning and the officer basic course at Fort Knox, I went right back to Rucker for flight school."

"Sounds like you had help, sir," said Hal Timmons.

"Yeah, I did. I was Wally Pilthrow's company clerk. He didn't have a single person that could type, so I squared away his office. In return, he squared away my desire to fly. It helped that I scored the highest Flight Aptitude Test score for the year at Rucker, but I don't want to brag." Tom smiled. "And here I am today, a leader of men, a warrior . . . dressed like a transvestite and talking to you schmucks!" They all laughed, even Hart Osborn.

"And might we say, you're our favorite transvestite too, sir!" said Hal Timmons.

"You brownnoser!" It was Hart. Tom was caught off guard. Hart Osborn cut down his fellow platoon leader in front of his boss. At that moment, Tom saw that Hart had become one of the group. He laughed and hit Hart Osborn on the back.

"Hart, you're one damn good guy and an even better lieutenant. Just between us guys," Tom said, looking around the kitchen, "you are ready to take a troop right now! And if you tell anybody I said that, I'll deny it."

"Thanks, sir!" replied the shocked lieutenant.

Jed brought him back to earth. "Not that anybody in his or her right mind would offer you a command, but you could do it! Shit! Nobody would work for you either!"

Hal Timmons piped up, "Sir, he's more ready than some of the other captains that have commands now!" It was a surprise because the two lieutenants were usually at each other's throats.

Tom looked at Jed and merely nodded at the comment. He didn't want to go into this either.

Maybe it was time to change the subject, and Hart Osborn did it as if on cue. "Sir, what does it take to be a great pilot?"

Tom smiled. "What does it take to be a good pilot?" Tom started rubbing his chin and grabbed his crotch, naturally forgetting he was dressed as a transvestite. "Hell, sonny, it takes balls as big as coconuts and nerves of steel!"

The crowd laughed, and Jed just had to comment, "How'd you make it? I see you're lacking in those departments."

"I'm wearin' this stupid costume, ain't I?" fired back Tom.

But Hart Osborn pressed the issue, a bit more serious this time. "Come on, sir. What does it take to be a great helicopter pilot?"

Tom thought and looked at Jed. "You might have to back me up on this one and see if I'm talking out my ass or not."

"Go for it, brother! I got your six!" replied Jed.

"There are four categories of helicopter pilots. We'll start at the bottom and move up. There's the sorry-ass dog that no one wants to fly with because (a) he's dangerous, (b) he's stupid, (c) he thinks he's a great pilot, or (d) some combination of those three. Stay out of the cockpit with him at all cost. Then there's the average pilot. He's competent, efficient, works hard at the books. And on a good day, he doesn't scare anyone he's flying with. This pilot is usually described by his peer group as being a sandbag. Then come the good pilots. Generally speaking, the pilots in command. PICs with experience, confidence, and knowledge. The thing that keeps them from being great pilots . . ." Tom looked at Jed.

"They don't have *it*." Jed smiled.

"That's exactly right. They don't have *it*!" Tom said flatly.

"Come on, sir. Is this more of your bullshit? I'm asking a serious question, and you're playin' with my head," said Hart Osborn.

Tom smiled and tried to explain. "*It* . . . my dear Lieutenant, is the ability to become one with the helicopter." The crowd laughed a little until they could see Tom was serious. Hart Osborn looked at his boss quizzically, as if saying, "You're so full of shit." "*It* is the ability to feel the helicopter. To understand and know not just what's happening, but what is about to happen. The ability to always be ahead of the aircraft, in control, and not have to use the instruments. The helicopter becomes part of the pilot's body."

"Shit, sir. I know your drunk now!" said Hal Timmons.

"Yeah, I'm drunk. But hear me out. Because you guys may or may not have flown with someone that has *it*. This is how you can tell. In a helicopter, especially the Apache, the pilot constantly struggles to stay in trim." Tom pulled a chair in the middle of the room at this point and sat in it. "Trim is always kickin' our ass." His feet were moving as he talked, simulating pedal inputs. He stopped and looked at Hart. "A pilot that has *it* . . . doesn't fight with trim. He can simultaneously control the three axis of the helicopter in any environment. A perfect example is landing in a confined area. Great pilots become the helicopter as it enters the area. With only inches between the rotor blades and the trees, they are in perfect control. Smooth with all three inputs moving in a steady, controlled movement. They feel the aircraft." Tom acted as if he was in the simulated cockpit while sitting in a kitchen chair. "They become the aircraft."

Jed entered the conversation when he saw Tom was not reaching the lieutenant.

"It's the same on approaches. Some people stair step an approach down to the ground. Great pilots have the ability to enter the approach and maintain a steady angle all the way to the ground. It's an automatic function to input pedal requirements and cyclic input equal to the amount of reduction in collective. Hell, they don't even look at the torque gauge or trim ball because they feel the aircraft. They know automatically what has to be applied for the glide path. The movements are smooth and effortless. 'The force' is with them," Jed said, smiling.

"The force?" said Hal.

"Shit, sir. Now you're telling me I've gotta do some kind of . . . 'Vulcan mind meld' with the damn helicopter to fly it," said Hart Osborn.

"No, Lieutenant, that's not what I'm saying. I'm saying the great pilots do that. They can become one with the aircraft," said Tom. "On rare occasions, when I'm flying a lot, I mean twenty hours a week or more, I can tell the difference. I feel as if I'm a part of the aircraft. I know what it's going to do. All my limbs work without thought." Tom shook his head as he tried to explain. "The best way to get that feeling is to practice landing on slopes. Next time you try to land the helicopter on a slope, try to feel the helicopter, anticipate its movements, and be a part of the maneuver you're trying to do. Don't focus on the upslope or the downslope. Focus on the whole aircraft, look outside, and feel what's happening to the bird." Tom looked at him. "Guys, that fly a bunch, instructor pilots, maintenance officers, and the like, they have this quality. As far as I can tell, this ability to 'be the aircraft' can be learned, but some guys are just born with the natural ability to be great pilots." He shook his head and ended the topic. "Keep flying the way you are with the amount of time you're getting and you'll feel it. It takes time in the seat, in the air, and doing the maneuvers. And the feeling is a tremendous asset in the dark."

Hart Osborn shook his head in agreement with his boss but still looked skeptical. The two nonaviation lieutenants looked back and forth at each other in disbelief.

"I know you guys don't know what we're talking about, but it's something you have to experience," said Jed.

"Sir, I'm afraid that if I told anyone that I experienced anything remotely like what you guys are saying, I'd be taking piss tests myself rather than giving piss tests to pilots until my commitment is up," said Lieutenant Sheppard. The crowd laughed. Among the other not-so-flattering jobs Schlepper had to do was to administer routine or random urinalysis testing to soldiers as a deterrent to drug abuse.

Three obviously inebriated ladies showed up. "Talking about work, are you?" said Cindy. "Penalty shots all around!"

Betty looked at Tom and stepped between him and Jed, "You bitch! Get away from my man! I'll kick your ass!" The room erupted in laughter.

Lou Ann was the giver of penalty shots, and the whole room got strawberry schnapps, killing the bottle.

"It's that time," said Cindy.

"What time?" asked Tom as he finished his shot.

Cindy grabbed his hand and pulled him out of the kitchen. "Time for 'Sweet Transvestite'!"

"No, no, no, honey! Don't make me do this. Please. Don't make me do this!" Tom begged.

"You have to, honey! Besides, all the 'sticks in the mud' have left!" she cried.

The crowd that was left was chanting, and the Pack was clapping their hands and cheering.

Again, Tom relented. "All right. But no cameras!"

Jed already had the CD out and was starting the song "Sweet Transvestite" from the movie *The Rocky Horror Picture Show*. Tom smiled at Jed and shook his head in a negative manner toward the crowd. The cheers and taunts compelled him. He grabbed a bottle of schnapps that just happened to be handy and took a long pull. "Hell, I guess I can trust this crowd!" he yelled. Tom began to dance and sing in time with the music. The crowd loved it. Tom loved it too. He was the center of attention, and the party was going great. Everyone there was having a terrific time. For just a short time, he wasn't Champion Six, defender of democracy, techno-warrior of the twenty-first century. He was just Tom Lawton, having fun and enjoying himself with his wife and friends. It all seemed so innocent. With the music blasting and everyone clapping and dancing, Tom Lawton was too drunk to notice everything going on around him. The alcohol had taken control. Something caught his attention in the corner of his eye, and he thought he saw a flash go off, but it just didn't matter at the time. He was dancing and having fun. He took a bottle and turned it upside down, emptying what was left of the Jagermeister. That was the last thing he remembered about the night.

CHAPTER 5

November 3, 1990
Katterheim Caserne

IN THE LATE SUMMER OF 1990, Saddam Hussein's Iraqi Republican Guard forces had rolled south through Kuwait and threatened the Kingdom of Saudi Arabia. American forces from the Eighty-second Airborne Division and the 101st Air Assault Division were deployed to protect the kingdom from possible invasion. Hussein had taken Kuwait by surprise, and now the entire world wondered how far he would go. Tension was high throughout the Middle East, and fear was spreading to other parts of the globe. The United States initially deployed stateside units, so units in the European theater were not compelled to prepare for deployment. Assets were being shifted from stateside, and it was widely thought that the "Defenders of Democracy" in the states would be in Saudi before any units from Germany would go. With NATO commitments and "real missions" in Europe, it was generally accepted that no unit in Germany was going anywhere. Still, the rumors of units in Germany deploying to Saudi Arabia persisted. It came as quite a surprise when the rumors became fact.

As tensions mounted in the Middle East, they continued to mount in the United States and Europe as well. These tensions affected world leaders, military units, families, and individuals. At the individual level, these tensions manifested themselves in the form of withdrawn personalities, short-temperedness, or increased alcohol consumption. Some individuals may have suffered through all these symptoms simultaneously. Tom Lawton was one of these individuals. He seemed to be losing his sense of humor. He was often short with his subordinates, particularly Hart Osborn or Hal Timmons. Tom spent nearly eighteen hours a day at work and usually stopped by the club on the way home "just to check on the warrants." He rarely talked to Cindy. The pattern had developed where he'd go to work all day, go to the club immediately after work, get home late, and go to sleep. The rumors played on everyone's minds and Tom's in particular. He wanted to make sure if the Champions were called on, they would be ready. They flew as much as maintenance would allow. Tom expected the unit may get called upon soon and put pressure on himself to get the Champions prepared enough for war. The time had come for the rumors to stop and reality to start. As fate would have it, the reality of the situation is never what one would expect.

1400, November 3, 1990
Office of the Commander, Building 13155
Katterheim, Germany

"GENTLEMEN, I'M GLAD YOU COULD MAKE it," the commander said as a winded Captain Rooks came into the office and grabbed a seat. All the company commanders and platoon leaders were on hand. "Corps has finally determined what they want from their aviation assets in Germany."

Chris Wise nudged Tom. "Here it comes. We're goin' in." Tom wondered to himself, *If that's the case, are we ready to go?*

Lieutenant Colonel Hawk, with just a trace of disgust in his voice, continued, "In their infinite wisdom, corps has decided the squadron should be piecemealed out to support division operations." The room erupted in confusion and anger.

Hart Osborn grabbed Tom's sleeve and spoke into his commander's ear. "What does that mean, sir?"

Tom raised his hand and looked into Hart's eyes. The look was all the lieutenant needed to calm down. Tom spoke flatly to his lieutenant. "I'm sure he's about to tell us."

"Corps wants us to provide one troop to support the First Armored Division's Aviation Brigade. All assets will be afforded that troop, and we will support this action wholeheartedly." Tom looked hard at the commander and could tell his boss was upset with the decision. He wondered to himself which "one troop" the commander had decided on. "On top of that," the commander began to get red in the face, "we have been ordered to send six aircraft to support a unit in Hanua." The room erupted. Lieutenant Colonel Hawk rolled the paper he was holding into a ball and threw it across the room. "Listen. Listen up!" yelled the commander. "I knew the army was capable of giving us 'shit sandwiches,' but I didn't expect we'd have to eat it." The boss's tone let the troop commanders know he obviously was not in favor of the higher headquarters' plans. "This is the mission we've been given, and this we will do to the best of our abilities."

The commander got up from his desk and walked around the room. "Now I know what your next questions are. Who's doing what, when are we doing it, and what is my role in this plan?" He paused to let the comment sink in. "I talked with the XO, the S3, and Captain Rooks, and they all provided information with various pluses and minuses for each of the troops regarding the two requirements. The decisions rest with me. This is my squadron, and I decide who does what, so if any of you have a bitch, you pitch it to me behind closed doors." Lieutenant Colonel Hawk went to a butcher-block chart and pulled up the top two pages. "This is all classified information, so I'm sure by the time you get home tonight, it will be all over the Caserne. I've chosen A Troop to go and support the division and C Troop to give their aircraft to 3-225th in Hanua." The room was again filled with murmurs and muffled conversations. Tom looked at Hart Osborn, who was flushed with anger. Hal Timmons had a poker face. Chris Wise was visibly pissed at the omission of B Troop. Phil Pearson smiled contentedly. Tom wondered to himself if the Champions had been chosen to go to the desert with the division, would Tom have had a smile?

Hart Osborn tried desperately to get his boss's attention. Tom bent over to Hart and whispered somewhat angrily, "Not here and not now."

Hart eased up some, but his expression indicated what Tom was thinking. *Why are we giving up our aircraft?*

"I will talk to each of the commanders after this individually. Right now, time is not an asset. So I need all of you to go to the briefing room, and we'll timeline this out and figure who's doing what and when. Let's move with a purpose," said the Hawk.

Chris Wise sat still and stared at the boss as everyone else started moving out of the office. Tom grabbed Hart's arm and saw that Hal was hesitating. "Let's go, guys! This is not the time or the place to protest or put the old man on the spot."

"This is a bunch of bullshit, sir!" said Hart.

Tom stopped abruptly, got close to the lieutenant, and looked him in the eye. Through clenched teeth, Tom said, "Not here. Not now." The mood was set, and the lieutenant finally started moving. Tom noticed over his shoulder that Chris Wise, face red, remained in his seat. Lieutenant Colonel Hawk moved around to the front of his desk. He apparently was ready to take the B Troop commander's questions. He nodded to Tom, and Tom looked at his peer.

"Close the door on your way out, Captain Lawton," said the squadron commander.

Tom did so and continued down the hallway. He knew Chris Wise was upset because his troop was selected on all the support missions, and that probably meant splitting them up. This could have been interpreted as a slap in the face. Tom felt lousy too. The Champions were being asked to supply aircraft to some other unit so they could fly them into war. Why the hell was that unit going into combat if their maintenance was messed up? He understood exactly where his two platoon leaders were coming from. They had worked damn hard to get to the level of training and maintenance that they had achieved, and it appeared to have been taken away from them by some clueless desk weenie from corps headquarters. They would talk in depth about this at a later time, but being the soldier he was, Tom wanted to be in control of the mission at hand before they tried to second-guess the decision makers higher up.

For his part, the S3 had a good plan. Maurer obviously wasn't given much time to prepare for the tasks at hand, but the plan was solid. A Troop would begin training immediately with their new battalion. C Troop would take their six aircraft up to Hanua. B Troop would provide "fillers" in the form of personnel to A Troop and one aircraft to C Troop to go to Hanua. The more Tom thought about the whole thing, the more he empathized with his boss. There was no good answer, but the support accomplished the tasks the squadron had been issued. Somewhere, someone didn't think too much of the squadron or army aviation in general to decide to piecemeal a unit like this. The AH-64 is designed to provide a knockout blow to the enemy. That blow is to be delivered en masse. To break up an already-established attack helicopter squadron did not make any sense. But these were drastic times, and they called for "thinking out of the box." It didn't matter that the current box was pretty damn good.

Reluctantly, Tom Lawton sat through Captain Maurer's briefing, thinking of the best ways to support someone else's fight. On one hand, Tom was elated that he and his men would not be put in harm's way. And in another, he was disappointed he wouldn't get the opportunity to do what all commanders want to do, and that is lead his troops in combat. Deep down, Tom wasn't sure he or the Champions were ready to be tested. Reality told him the test could wait.

Lawton thought about McClellan marching troops all around Washington in 1861. Was he justifiably cautious or just chicken? Tom shrugged off the similarity. Different war, different requirements. Better to err on the side of caution. Something still nagged at him, and he couldn't quite place his finger on what it was. In college, he thought McClellan was a coward. Faced with a similar situation on a much smaller scale, Tom Lawton wanted to march his troops on the parade grounds and keep them away from the war too. Did that make him a coward as well? He filed the question away and tried to focus on the briefing. But like a question with no right answer, the thought would not go away.

November 5, 1990
Hangar 3010
Katterheim Caserne

"HE TOLD ME TO QUIT MY sniveling and drive on," said Chris Wise. "I wanted to protest a little more, but it wasn't getting me anywhere. I was just managing to piss him off more, so I let it go."

"Smart move, amigo," said Tom. "Thanks for the aircraft. I'll see that the homeboys in Hanua take good care of it."

"Gee, thanks. I wish we were taking good care of it," came back Captain Wise.

Tom looked down from his cockpit and extended his hand to Chris. "Look, man. We do what we're told. This is somebody else's plan, and we are the executors. Remember," Tom said in his best John Wayne accent, "a man's gotta do what a man's gotta do. And if that means squaring away somebody else, pilgrim, we're just the guys to do it!"

"You're too damn rational about this whole thing." Chris Wise smiled back as he took Tom's hand. "Have a safe flight."

Rational, thought Tom. That's a different way of looking at it.

November 5, 1990
Building 6308, Office of the
Commander, 3-277th
Fleigerhorst Caserne, Hanua, Germany

"SIR, CAPTAIN TOM LAWTON REPORTS." TOM held his salute until Lieutenant Colonel Gill Reilly saluted. Reilly was a CAV trooper from the old days, and his office was a testimonial to the old cavalry ways. Tom's first impression was positive, and he immediately liked this commander. "Sir, I've got six of the finest attack helicopters in Germany parked outside your hangar and was told to report to you upon arrival." Tom remained at the position of attention.

"Well, I think you better just hold on there, Soldier," said Lieutenant Colonel Reilly as he leaned back in his oversized leather chair. Tom's eyes averted down to focus on Gunfighter Six. "I think there has been a change in plans," said the lieutenant colonel.

Tom wanted to say, "What the fuck, over?" But military bearing was one of his strong points, and a somewhat audible "I don't understand, sir?" was all that came out.

"Seems the fellas up at corps have decided to let the Fightin' Sixth come and play with us," said the lieutenant colonel.

"Sir, I'm still not sure I . . . ," stumbled Tom.

"In English then, son, pack your shit," said Gunfighter Six. "You fellas are comin' along for the party."

Tom noticed his mouth was open and immediately closed it. It was amazing how fast shit moved when it hits the fan.

Tom gathered his composure. "When I left, sir, they didn't say anything about us going to the show."

"I received the call on that red phone over yonder about fifteen minutes ago. You're more than welcome to call your boss. But I can assure you, your whole squadron is going to Saudi Arabia," said Reilly.

Tom thought about it, and it finally sunk in. Someone somewhere had figured out what a mistake it is to separate an entire squadron of Apaches. A moment of exhilaration swept over him as the thought set in. The Fighting Sixth was going to war. His Champions were going to war. Then the reality sunk in. He was going to war.

Tom got back to the aircraft as fast as he could. As he ran, he thought about the call back to Katterheim. The boss was excited and wanted the troop back immediately. Naturally, the Champions were laughing and joking in the ready room. The UH-60 pilots that had accompanied the flight had already filed the flight plan and were reviewing the flight route back.

Tom entered the pilot's lounge and took a deep breath. "Everybody, listen up. We're taking the aircraft back to Katterheim." Confusion swept the room. Everyone was talking at once. "All right, just shut the hell up and I'll explain!" Tom let the room get quiet. "We have orders to bring all six aircraft back. All indications are the Fighting Sixth will be gettin' orders for deployment to Saudi Arabia." Tom let that sink in. The room grew even quieter. He looked at his the faces of his pilots for emotions. He found Chief Warrant Officer 3 Walker and got a reaction he had not expected.

"Well, it's about damn time!" said the big warrant. "They ought to let the best attack helicopter troop in the US Army do their job." John Walker was standing up and walking around the lounge now. "Let's go kick some Saddam-worshippin', Kuwait-invadin', toga-sheet-wearin', Muslim hippy ass!"

The comment took the group by surprise but was exactly what they needed. The outburst brought energy and togetherness to the pilots. Tom Lawton could only smile and nod at his maintenance officer.

The group looked at the commander for a response. Tom looked back at his pilots, nodding up and down. "Hell, if anybody needs an ass kickin', it sounds like he does." Tom went over to the big warrant and offered a high five. "And we're just the guys to do it!" The pilots erupted with a resounding "Hoooaah!" "Let's get focused on what we need to do. I want the front seaters to go preflight. Remember, it got you in here, so I'm sure it can get you back. PICs, let's review the route and file back as a flight. I want to be outta here in thirty minutes. Let's move with a purpose, fellas!"

Tom was proud of his pilots. They were focused and motivated, which was all any commander could ask of his soldiers. A quick thought rushed through Tom's mind. Was he good enough to lead men of this caliber? He wondered about that thought for just a moment. If he had any doubts about himself or his abilities, these guys would surely see the weakness. *Just like Dad said, if I take care of them, they'll take care of me.* Tom knew he had started taking care of them months ago. He'd find out real soon if the Champions would take care of him.

November 5, 1990
Hangar 3010
Katterheim Caserne

WHEN THE CHAMPIONS ARRIVED AT KATTERHEIM, Lieutenant Colonel Hawk was there to meet them. He pulled Tom Lawton to the side and told him everything he knew. The plan had changed, and the whole squadron was going to the desert. Only the timeline was up in the air. A Troop was no longer assigned to the division, and B Troop was whole again. The squadron commander was upbeat, and the conversation excited Tom. To be a part of everything that was happening, from deploying to the thought of actually leading his troops in combat. The boss informed him of long days and many challenges ahead. Tom knew what to expect in that area, and he was ready for that. It was the actual fighting that made him apprehensive. Tom Lawton wasn't sure the Champions were ready, but he couldn't tell his boss that. So he did exactly what everybody else did. He showed all the enthusiasm he could, nodded, and smiled. Now he had to get up the courage to tell Cindy. A quick trip to the club for a couple beers would help him get ready for that.

When he got home, he found out the alcohol was not needed. As he walked in the door, Cindy was there to greet him with open arms and a concerned look. He didn't have to say a word. The wives chain had seen to that. She already knew as much as Tom. There was a tear in her eye. Tom smiled and wrapped his arms around her. "It's gonna be all right, honey."

"I don't want you to go," she said.

"I don't want to leave either," he said.

"Do you know when?" asked Cindy.

"Nothing yet. But we know it'll be soon," said Tom meekly. "When did you find out?"

Cindy looked up at him. "This morning. The phone was ringing off the hook. The whole Caserne knows." She smiled and fought back a sob. "I'm gonna miss you so much!"

"Hey, I haven't even left yet. We've got no timeline, and I'm not going anywhere anytime soon! So you'll still have me to kick around for a while. Okay?" Tom pulled her chin up to him and looked at her soft, beautiful face. "It's gonna work out. I promise."

"It's just not fair," said Cindy.

"Not a lot of things in life are fair, honey. What's fair is me having you and Megan. That's all the fair I need!" Tom smiled.

"What do we tell her?" asked Cindy.

"Nothing for right now. When the time comes, it's 'Daddy's going away to work for a while.'" This led Tom to think of something else that came out before he could stop himself. "God, I hope she remembers me."

Cindy slugged him on the arm. "Of course she'll remember you, you jerk!" Cindy was half laughing and half crying. "I'll make sure she remembers you."

"Honey, I'll spend as much time as I possibly can with you two before we go. I swear," said Tom.

"You better." She pulled away from Tom and smiled. "You big jerk."

"I'll always remember you two," said Tom. "Jesus! Listen to me. Sounds like I'm already gone or something!"

Cindy shook off the comment without a second thought. "I guess you expect supper now. Come home for a couple hours, sleep, eat, back to work, and off to war. All so routine." Tom could tell Cindy was back to her normal iron-willed self.

"Sure, honey. Routine." He added, "As far as you know!" and smacked her on the butt as she headed to the kitchen. Cindy was doing all right with this. On the outside, she was handling it better than Tom. She merely packed away Tom's imminent departure in the same place Tom tucked away things that disturbed his routine. If it stayed in that spot long enough, it would go away and not be a problem. Unfortunately for both of them, his departure would not stay "packed away" for much longer.

The Champions continued to train as much as they could. The aircraft were doing well. With one attack bird in phase and one scout coming out of phase in mid-November, the unit had plenty of aircraft hours for training, but not enough hours in the day for everything they needed to work on. There was always a meeting for the pilots or the crew chiefs. As the war machine spun up, classes were scheduled to discuss everything from hygiene to threat radar systems or the Iraqi culture. Naturally, the brigade and the squadron weren't on the same sheet of music. Brigade would schedule classes for an hour or two in the morning, which eliminated the opportunity to train at night. Then the squadron would turn around and schedule afternoon classes that prevented day collective training. This wore on the units' morale, and time was running short. The questions on everyone's mind were when would they be leaving, and how much time left did they have? And one not talked about out loud: were they ready to fight?

November 26, 1990
Enlisted Dining Facility
Katterheim Caserne

ONE OF THE NICER MILITARY CUSTOMS is that commanders at all levels eat their Thanksgiving meals with the troops, and this was still the case before deployment. Tom didn't mind this event one bit. He enjoyed getting dressed in his Dress Blues and serving the Thanksgiving meal to the troopers. What bothered him was the fact that this was the first day in three weeks he got to spend any time with Cindy and Megan and he was spending it glancing at them across the dining facility. He had promised Cindy he would spend more time with them, but there never was any. He was always at work or too tired to play with Megan, or they would be asleep when he got home. Cindy was working hard trying to keep things normal. But as hard as she tried, the more time Tom found to be with the troops. Mentally, Tom was already in the fight in Southwest Asia. He was oblivious to the fact he had already mentally deployed. He had packed up his mind, his heart, and his soul and left Germany behind.

The time was coming when the physical deployment would happen, and it couldn't happen soon enough to suit the warriors. A part of every soldier was already there. They lived, breathed, slept, ate, and crapped the Southwest Asian theater. In essence, Tom, just like many other soldiers, had already left his family before he left the country.

The troopers were all cordial and enjoying the meal. Lieutenant Colonel Hawk arrived about 1415 hours. He motioned for the troop commanders to rally at his table. Susie Hawk and their kids had been at the dining facility for two hours. Tom could tell by the colonel's demeanor something was happening. He handed over his ladle to Lieutenant Timmons. "Hal, you have the controls, buddy. Looks like he has some news."

After all the commanders had arrived, the squadron commander got everyone's attention. "I see we have everyone here, including the wives, which is good. Everyone can hear what I have to say all at once." He cleared his throat and motioned everyone to come closer. The dining facility became somewhat quieter, but for the most part, the soldiers kept on packing in the chow. "We have a tentative deployment schedule. Due to the amount of time it takes to get the ships to Saudi, we will have to get the aircraft to port next week. We leave in three flights, staggered takeoff times on Tuesday. S3?" He looked for Captain Maurer.

"Here, sir!" said Jerry Maurer.

"Brief me tomorrow on the routes and times. I want A, B, and then C with the support 60s split among the three troops. After we get the aircraft to port, we come back here and wait for our unit to be sequenced into the flow. The way things are going right now, I expect that departure to be somewhere around mid-December." Lieutenant Colonel Hawk let that digest with the crowd. "It doesn't give us much time together, but on the positive side, we now see things happening. I don't know about you all, but the suspense is killing me!" He chuckled. Everyone smiled and nodded along with the commander. Then the reality of what he said sank in. The group that had gathered all looked at their loved ones and pulled them a little closer. He continued, "Gentlemen, as soon as you can, wrap things up here, go home, and spend some time with your families. Meet me in my office at 0900 tomorrow for the OPORD. Thank you all and we'll see you guys tomorrow."

Tom looked at Cindy, and she turned away to gather up Megan. "I'll go tell Hal we're leaving. I'll just be a minute."

"Yeah, sure. I'm heading outside." Cindy went over to where Lou Ann Osborn was playing with Megan. He thought he saw her wipe away a tear as he headed to the serving line. But she was smiling by the time she got to Lou. She was a rock.

November 28, 1990
Apartment 4, 112 Gruberstasse
Katterheim, Germany

THE PHONE RANG. IT WAS JUST after suppertime, and Tom was finally going to play with Megan. Cindy came out of the kitchen with a disgusted look on her face. "It's for you. I think its Dean Alvin." When she handed him the phone, she immediately went back to the kitchen.

"Captain Lawton. What's up?" said Tom.

"Hey, sir. It's Lieutenant Alvin. I was wondering if you could come over to Hal's, sir?"

"What for, Lieutenant?" said Tom rather impatiently.

"Well, sir . . . it's kind of hard to explain," stammered the lieutenant.

"Well, Dean, why don't you explain it in a way I can understand," said Tom terser than he wanted.

Tom heard loud music in the background on the other end of the line. "I just think you need to come over here. Tonight. Right now," said the lieutenant.

"Look, Dean, I don't have the time or the patience for any bullshit right now. What's going on?" asked Tom Lawton.

"It's Hal, sir. He's really drunk. He's pulled out his pistols, and he's talking a lot of shit about Grenada and Panama." The lieutenant paused. Tom looked at Cindy who had entered the hallway and was still frowning. "He's in a weird mood, sir!" said Dean Alvin.

Tom wanted to snap "What the fuck is a weird mood?" but something in Dean Alvin's voice told Tom exactly what that meant. "Let me talk to him," said Tom.

Lieutenant Alvin tried to cover the phone, but Tom heard him ask Hal to come to the phone. Tom heard a loud "Screw him!" come from the background.

"He says he doesn't want to talk to you right now, sir," said the lieutenant flatly.

Tom looked at Cindy who was scowling now. He quickly went back to the phone. "I'll be right over." Cindy threw the towel she was holding at Tom and walked away.

Tom hung up. "Hal sounds kind of drunk, honey. I need to check on him."

"Is this just another reason for you to go out and drink with those drunks you hang out with?" said Cindy as the tears welled up in her eyes.

"Not at all, honey. I think Hal's gone a little bit over the edge, and I need to go talk to him. That's all," said Tom, trying to convince himself as well.

"You son of a bitch," Cindy said flatly. Shaking her head, she added, "I thought tonight we might have some time together. You just go ahead. You go drink with your buddies. You're such an asshole, Tom!" Then she turned and ran to the living room.

"Honey!" Tom started after her but knew it would do no good. He thought about Dean's voice on the phone. This better not be a joke, or there'd be hell to pay.

2045 Hours, November 28, 1990
BOQ, Cranston Caserne
Ansbach, Germany

"GLAD YOU MADE IT, SIR," SAID Dean Alvin.

"If this is some kind of—" said Tom, who stopped short.

"Trust me, sir. It isn't." Tom noticed that Lieutenant Alvin was a little bit white in the face and seemed sober. He looked past Dean Alvin into the apartment, which was a mess. Then he noticed the stereo was blasting "Back in the Saddle" by Aerosmith. Sprawled on the couch, head back, screaming in time with Steve Tyler, was Hal Timmons. There was a fifth of Jack Daniels with about two inches left on the coffee table in front of him. Tom Lawton noticed his scout platoon leader was clad only in his briefs. The tattoo from the Eighty-second Airborne was visible on the lieutenant's ample biceps.

"He's been drinkin' hard since four o'clock, sir. He's trashed," said Dean. "I can't get him to talk to me anymore. He was babbling some garbage about Grenada and how screwed up that operation was. You were the only person I know that can talk to him. I didn't call anybody else. I'm worried about him, sir."

Tom could see why Dean was worried. "Thanks for calling me, Dean. Anybody else in here come up or complain?" asked Tom.

"Yeah, some fuckin' field artillery puke started some shit an hour ago. I told him to piss off. No military police yet, so maybe we're okay?" explained the lieutenant.

"Good, good. I want you to stay here for a little while longer in case that same guy comes back again." Tom looked around and said, "Shit. You might as well get me a beer. Maybe I can calm him down. Here goes nothin'."

"My man! How the hell are ya?" yelled Tom across the room. Hal looked at his boss and started to get up. "No, no, no, man, don't get up on my account. How you doin'?"

"I'm toasted, sir," replied Hal Timmons. "I couldn't get up if the room was on fire." The lieutenant finally sat up on the couch. "I . . . am drunk."

"Roger that, Lieutenant! You got cruise control on. You and Jack goin' to town by yourselves, or can anybody come along?" said Tom as Dean Alvin showed up with a beer.

"Shit, sir. We're all goin' to town. Hell, we're all on a rocket ship ta hell!" came back the lieutenant.

Tom laughed and thanked Dean for the beer. "Well, at least we're all going together, right? Mind if I turn this down a little, Hal? I can hardly hear you." Tom went to the stereo and turned down the music. That's when he noticed Dean Alvin pointing at the coffee table. A .45 caliber pistol was lying there with what appeared to be a full magazine lying next to it. Tom looked back at Dean and nodded.

"Talk to me, man. What's eatin' you?" asked Tom.

"Isn't that what the cannibal said to the tourist?" Hal Timmons burst out laughing at his own joke. Tom smiled and looked at Dean. "At least his mind is still working."

"In that ever so abstract way that his mind works." Lieutenant Alvin smiled.

Hal Timmons finished laughing and looked at his boss. He took a deep breath. "Hell, sir." He paused and looked back at his shot glass. "Want to join me?"

"I think I'll stick to beer, Hal," said Tom, still smiling.

Hal nodded. "Okay." Lieutenant Timmons raised his shot glass. "Here's to me and men like me. If you ain't CAV . . ." Tom joined Hal, "You ain't shit!" Hal downed the shot. Tom took a big gulp of beer.

"You know they won't let us drink in the desert, sir," said Hal matter-of-factly.

"Yeah, Hal, I know that." Tom saw an opening. "You know they won't let us take our own guns either, right?"

Hal was real drunk, but not totally gone. He looked at Tom and then looked at the coffee table. Then he looked back at Tom. "You're not gonna let me take Wilma?" Tom shook his head back and forth in an exaggerated negative. "Hell, sir! I gotta take Wilma! I'd be lost without her!"

"That's one of the rules, Hal," said Tom.

"I wish I'd have had her in Grenada," said Hal.

"Is that what this drunk is all about?" asked Tom. "Hal, this isn't gonna be anything like Grenada. This is huge compared to Grenada. Or Panama." Tom could see he wasn't reaching his friend. Hal was still far away. "Talk to me."

Hal Timmons got up off the couch and walked over to the gun. He picked it up. Tom looked at Dean, who had taken a step forward. Hal picked up the magazine and slammed it in the .45. "Those fuckers!"

Dean stepped back, and Tom put his hand up toward Lieutenant Alvin to indicate relax. "What fuckers, Hal? The Cubans?"

Hal thought about the question for a second. "No, sir." He was still for a moment. "The fucking brass, sir!"

"Come here, Hal. Sit down. Tell me what you're talkin' about," said Tom.

Slowly, Hal Timmons moved to the couch. He sat down where he'd been previously. "They were so fucked up." This time, he drank straight from the bottle of Jack Daniels. Tom sat back and waved to Dean to take a seat. Hal belched hard and started to talk.

Hal was a radioman in a field artillery unit as a forward observer in Grenada. They'd been assigned to air assault in with a flight of Blackhawks.

Apparently, the recon photos they had used to plan the mission didn't have a direction posted, so the planners had the insertion flight enter the intended landing zone in the wrong direction.

"When we came in . . . we came over the horizon expecting a long axis to land on. It was the short axis, and the UH-60s started stacking up to try and make the LZ." Hal paused for a drink and finished off the bottle. "No go-around. No missed approach." Hal got angry. "Just pieces of shit flying everywhere!" He wiped his nose with his free hand and continued, "Stacked two of those fuckers right on top of each other." He put the gun down on the coffee table and got up to walk. "Then the goddamn LZ got hot. We tried like hell to get the damn medevac bird in. I couldn't get on the damn radio. Everybody was yellin' and . . ." Hal sobbed a little. Tom got up and went over to him. Hal continued, "The radios were . . . nuts. I couldn't talk to anybody. Lieutenant Henson was freakin' out." Hal got mad again. "And those fuckers from brigade, they ate the fuck up . . ." His voice trailed off.

Tom softly grabbed his shoulder. "That was a long time ago, Hal."

"It seems like yesterday," he said softly.

Tom nodded to Dean to get the gun. "Dean, see if there's any coffee in that mess he calls a kitchen."

Hal chuckled a little. "It is a mess, isn't it, sir?"

"No sweat, man." Tom turned the lieutenant around and pointed him toward the couch. "Come over and sit with me." They walked toward the couch and sat down. "That must have been a hell of an experience, buddy. But it's in the past. What would you have done differently now if you could have?"

"Aviation all the way, sir! Above the best and all that crap," said Hal, mocking a salute and giggling.

Tom looked at him hard and made eye contact. "What would you do different now that you know better?"

Hal's smile faded, and he thought hard. "I'd have talked on Uniform or Victor!" Tom smiled now. "You'd talk on UHF or VHF! Outstanding!" Tom continued his praise, "You would have used alternate communication and gotten through to higher."

Hal looked at Tom and said, "I'd have told that old fat ass how we screwed the pooch in that LZ and to get us some help ASAP."

"And when I'm screwed up, you're gonna be able to tell me how to fix it, right?" said Tom.

"You bet your ass!" said a smiling Hal Timmons. Then his smile faded as Tom's words sunk in. "I won't have to tell you shit, sir. You know what's goin' on."

"Look, Hal. I'm not a magician. I can't be all, know all, and do all like the army expects a commander to do. I'm tellin' you straight up. I need help. And I need your help. Your experience is a tremendous asset. Help everybody else understand the past mistakes so we don't repeat them," explained Tom.

"Like that shit bird Hartley?" said Hal. "He don't know half what he thinks he knows."

Tom nodded. "Like that shit bird Hartley." Tom continued after a small drink, "He only knows what we can teach him. And admit it. He's getting better."

"Roger, sir. But he's still a shit bird," said Hal.

"Yes. He's our shit bird though." Tom slugged Hal in the arm lightly. "How about a Coke?" asked Tom.

Hal stared straight ahead and then turned slowly to Tom. "Don't trust higher, sir. They'll screw the dogface in a heartbeat."

"I guess that's why the dogfaces have us in aviation. To save their asses, right?" said Tom. The music was still loud, and Tom thought it might be better to change the mood. "Can I play something different? We probably need to turn it down some. For a while at least. How 'bout some Buffet?"

"Sure, sir," said Hal as his eyes closed a little.

Tom looked at his platoon leader and whispered in his ear, "I only trust Champions." Timmons smiled and laid his head back on the couch. "We're all gonna get through this, Hal."

Hal's head rolled over to Tom, and his eyes popped open. "As long as you're in command, sir," said the lieutenant.

Dean Alvin came back with three Cokes. The crisis was defused for the moment. The three officers talked for a couple more hours about music, drinkin', fightin', and women. This turned a light on in Tom's head. He needed to get home. He didn't want to leave until he was sure the situation was calmed down. The music had gotten progressively mellower, and Crosby, Stills, Nash, and Young were singing in the background when Tom decided to make his exit.

"Everything all right with you now, Hal?" asked Tom.

"You're still not gonna let me take Wilma, are you, sir?" asked Hal. He was horizontal on the couch now, and the hangover was setting in.

"Not my policy. It's the rules. You can't take your gun to war! Somebody might get shot!" Tom smiled.

Hal smiled. Dean Alvin looked at Tom Lawton and gave him a thumbs-up.

Tom walked over to Hal who was almost asleep now. "You're too damn good to be locked up for something stupid. I'm not gonna let you take Wilma, Hal. There will enough guns to go around. Get control of yourself because I need you. Your guys need you. Don't come in tomorrow." Tom started in with a mock German accent, "Ve vill see you in two days, meine freund! *Auf Weidersehn!*"

Hal smiled a broad smile from the pillow. His head popped up. "Thanks, sir. I'm gonna appreciate this someday."

"Just return the favor for me when I need it. Bye, Hal." Tom headed for the door.

"I think I'll just spend the night here, sir," said Dean Alvin.

"Good idea." Tom paused. "Look, I'm sorry for being so short with you on the phone. I didn't realize the situation. But thanks for calling me, Dean."

"No problem, sir. Thanks for coming," said the lieutenant.

"Please don't let anybody else in the unit know about this. They'll be a lot of questions and bullshit speculation. You know what I mean?"

"Oh! Sure thing, sir." The lieutenant nodded. "Lieutenant Timmons tried to kill himself or shoot you or some other stupid rumor! I know the deal."

Tom nodded. "You know the deal all too well. I gotta get home. Cindy is gonna kill me. Bye, Lieutenant," said Tom.

He hurried down the stairs and drove like hell to get home. It was after midnight, and all the lights were out. He hurried up the stairs and got into the house. All was quiet, and Tom checked on Megan. She wasn't there. For an instant, he panicked. He hurried to the bedroom, and there she lay next to Cindy, who was snoring softly. Tom exhaled and got control of his heart. Rather than wake them, he headed out to the living room and lay on the couch. Cindy was going to kill him, but it would have to wait until the morning. Tom knew she thought he merely ducked out of another night at home to go party with the boys. It would be awfully tough to convince her otherwise, but she had always stuck by him in the past. She wouldn't abandon him now, would she?

As he lay on the couch, something else was bothering him. His mind kept going back to the night's events, and he thought about something Hal Timmons had said. "Never trust higher." Hal Timmons was not your everyday, average second lieutenant. He had a tremendous amount of military experience and rarely talked trash about it. At what level do troops stop trusting higher? When or why? Is there something a leader does that makes a soldier lose confidence or trust in his commander? Tom was confident his troops still trusted him. But what about the higher ups? What happens when a military leader is no longer in touch with the soldier and no longer remembers the soldier's sacrifice or understands the effort given by their subordinates? There was no answer to the question, and Tom didn't dwell on it. He vowed to never forget his roots. Always remember and think about the soldiers that worked for him. If a leader that Tom Lawton ever worked for forgot his roots and no longer worked for the soldiers, Tom swore to himself he would never work for him.

Hal's statement made him ask more questions. Did he trust Hawk? Did he trust Denson? Without question, he trusted them. Somewhere sometime you have to trust somebody. He thought about the OER he had just received. Colonel Denson had placed Tom in the two block on his senior rater profile. Justifiably so. It was only a ninety-four-day efficiency report. A two block worked out to be center mass on Denson's profile. Not a "career killer," as Hawk put it. Denson never even spoke to Lawton, and even Lieutenant Colonel Smithey told him it wouldn't hurt him. He'd probably have two more command OERs and another command before he was looked at for promotion to major. The colonels all had experience. They knew the army system and were taking care of their subordinates. Tom thought hard about his own questions. He swore an oath to obey their orders. But just as he was questioning his own courage, Hal Timmons's doubts began to make Tom question the leadership he was working for. This was something Tom would never have thought of doing until he was put in a command position. He was responsible for the lives of his men. That meant being honest with them at all times. He felt he was a top block officer. Tom Lawton had never been told he was anything but a "one block."

His mind began to race. How much of this deployment information did they know, and when did they know it? What else weren't they telling the subordinates? Tom wondered to himself at what level do they forget that they were once troop level commanders. Screw it. It came down to lanes of responsibility. Tom knew what his lane was, and he was damn good at it. He'd take care of his men because he trusted them without a doubt. Tom made a second vow. If he ever lost the troopers' trust or the ability to lead them effectively that would also mean it would be time to go. He was comfortable with that. He rolled over on the couch and tried to sleep.

December 1, 1990
Katterheim Caserne

C TROOP WAS THE LAST TROOP to depart for Amsterdam. The aircraft needed to get to the port and get turned over to the port operations officials and packaged for delivery to Saudi Arabia. The mission itself seemed simple enough on paper. Fly from point A to point B, turn over equipment, hop on the bus, and return to point A. Nothing in the army is that easy.

Weather reports had indicated visual flight rules (VFR) weather all the way to the port. A trip that could be made from Katterheim in about five to six hours. With an hour separation between troops, the Champions were scheduled to depart at 1100 hours and arrive NLT 1800. This took into account slower than planned routes due to weather, two fuel stops, and any maintenance Murphyisms that usually occur on long flights.

Captain Lawton was pleased with Lieutenant Timmons briefing. He had the routes briefed by time, distance, and heading legs and covered an alternate route and two additional sites to land in case of inclement weather. The warrants asked a couple of good questions about fuel at the sites and if it would be paid for with multiple receipts of the government credit card. Hal surprised some of the veterans and had the answers to their questions.

"We'll get Jet A at Eindhoven, and Captain Lawton will pay for all the fuel with his flight pay!" cracked the second lieutenant. The pilots all chuckled and looked at Tom.

"Up yours, Single Lieutenant, with no kids and no car payment!" scoffed Tom. He headed to the front of the classroom. "We'll sign for the gas at Eindhoven, and the junior warrant, Mr. Cross, is the POC for that action."

Wes Cross's mouth fell open. "Why always me?" complained the junior warrant.

"Because you are so damn good at it!" yelled CW4 Mark Nichols.

Tom smiled and closed out the briefing. "Look, guys. The weather isn't the best. We are not obligated to get there tonight." He looked at Chief Warrant Officer 2 Petty and Chief Warrant Officer 3 Dolce. "You guys are up front. If it goes to shit, I want you to put us on the ground. We're not gonna mess around in Germany or the Netherlands with nasty weather. Put 'em down. We'll regroup and get there when we get there. If anyone, I say again, anyone is uncomfortable now, during, or after the flight, do not hesitate to talk to me." Tom looked around the room. "I'll probably be more uncomfortable than all of you put together." Some chuckles around the room. "Let's make our pitch pull and take care of your wingman. See ya on the high ground!"

1443, December 1, 1990
Thirty-seven kilometers east of Eindhoven

"I CAN'T SEE A GODDAMN THING!" said Tom Dolce. "This is messed up."

The flight had slowed to eighty knots. Joe Petty's head was on a swivel in constant motion of searching, scanning, and always keeping the flight clear of obstacles. The ceilings had dropped to a hundred feet about ten kilometers back and the flight was headed into a fog bank. The temperature had dropped, and ice was beginning to form on parts of the aircraft.

As tense as he was, Joe Petty didn't let the rest of the Champions know it. "Flight, this is lead. We are slowing to sixty knots, and I'm going over to the road junction at ten o'clock so we can all update our Doppler."

Damn good idea, thought Tom. There were no snide comments, no bitches or complaints. Simply execution by the Champions. The scouts were trailing the Apaches and monitored all the radio conversations. Without Doppler and limited visibility, it was difficult for them to navigate.

"Champions, this is 23," said Mr. Petty. "I can't see much past this point. We have a good update, so I'm going to move over to the field on the northwest side of the intersection and hold until we're all together."

The flights acknowledge the plan in chalk sequence.

"Two-three, this is Six," called Tom. "That's a good call, but I want to put everybody on the ground before we try to go on."

"Roger, Six," replied Champion 23. All the other Champions responded in chalk order, acknowledging the order.

Tom had Mr. Walker turn the aircraft so he could see all the Champion aircraft land in the newly designated assembly area. He looked in all four directions for visibility and ceiling height. The troop had crossed a river, the visibility was getting worse, and the ice was getting thicker. Tom shook his head. If they waited too long, the troop would end up shutting down right there. If they went in as a flight, it promised to be a cluster. They were still too far away to talk to Eindhoven tower.

He looked back toward the river. That's when he noticed an OH-58 slowly emerge from the low clouds. Then there was another. And finally a third. The flight of three turned slowly south, and Tom noticed markings on the side of the airframe. They were B Troop aircraft. He quickly dialed up the B Troop FM frequency and made a call to Werewolf 26.

"Werewolf 26, this is Champion Six on Fox, over," called Tom in the blind. He repeated the call once more, and LT Albert Rison called back.

"Champion Six, this is Wolf 26, over," said the B Troop scout platoon leader. "I've got you in sight on the ground!"

"Roger, 26," said Tom. "Want to fall in trail with us? We're outta here ASAP!"

"That would be great, Champion Six," said the lieutenant. "When we came down out of the mountains, the weather started going to crap, and we couldn't keep up. We slowed down, and the next thing I knew, we couldn't contact anybody on the radio." The lieutenant paused, searching for the right words. "Sir, we're real low on fuel and lost like big dogs!"

Tom looked at Chief Warrant Officer 3 Walker who smiled at the commander and said, "At least he's got the guts to say it."

Tom called back to Wolf 26, "No sweat. You did the right thing by not flying faster than you can see. Do you have everybody?"

"Roger that, Six," said the lieutenant.

"Good. Come up 245.8 on UHF and 134.5 on VHF," Tom directed. "Call me on those frequencies when you're up."

Tom waited about ten seconds. The three scout aircraft were landing behind his flight. The clouds were getting thicker and starting to roll in behind the flight.

"Champion Six, this is Werewolf 26 on UHF." The lieutenant paused as he switched radios to Victor. "And Werewolf 26 on VHF."

Tom came back on UHF because he knew he had every aircraft up on Uniform frequencies. "All Champions, this is Six on two. We have added three little brothers. We are now a flight of fourteen aircraft. If we wait here, we'll get socked in. We will split into two flights with two-minute separation between the trail bird of flight one and lead of flight two. Flight one will be Champion light team. Lieutenant Osborn is in charge with the Blackhawk, followed by the Werewolf team that is almost Bingo. Flight two is the heavy team, with the Champion elements picking up the rear. Airspeed is no greater than eighty knots, lest if you can't see. Max altitude of 150. Don't be afraid to put them on the ground again if it gets too bad. Lead and trail elements for both flights call identified, as well as when clear of towers or wires. Pitch pull is from present positions. I show destination to be 36.2 kilometers at a 278 heading. Champion 26 has radio contact with Eindhoven tower for his flight, and Champion 27 has the radios for flight two. Acknowledge mission change in new chalk order, over." Everyone responded in the proper order, which surprised Tom.

Lieutenant Rison answered for the entire Werewolf flight. "Champion Six, this is Wolf 26. All my elements are green for mission change. But I need to tell you, the clouds are really rolling in back here. I can barely make out lead, over," said Lieutenant Rison.

"Roger, Wolf 26. We're outta here in a couple of mikes. Everybody, check fuel, and, Flight One, move out," said Tom.

"Roger. Champion 26 has flight one, and we are set for pitch pull in ten seconds. Champion 23, call the flight off, and, Champion 16, let me know when we're all up, over," said Lieutenant Osborn.

Ten seconds later, Champion 23 was in the air and headed west. In the proper order, the entire first flight was off within a minute. Tom zeroed the cockpit clock and started it again to get the two-minute separation. He heard Hal Timmons report, "Flight one is up!" Out of habit, he watched the flight move to the west. About a mile away, they were no longer visible. He looked behind him and could barely make out the last scout in the new flight order.

The two minutes seemed to take forever. With fifteen seconds to go, Walker got light on the wheels. "Flight Two, pitch pull in ten!" A quick glance back showed all the scouts were already at a hover. They were definitely ready to move.

"Let's go, John," said Tom to his back seater.

"Roger, Six," came back Walker as he pulled in torque. Smoothly and effortlessly, the seven-ton aircraft picked up and turned to the west. After ten seconds, Lieutenant Rison informed Tom the flight was up. Tom exhaled audibly. "Now if we can just get this group to Eindhoven in one piece."

Only two sets of wires were between the flight and Eindhoven Airfield. Luckily, they were both only one-hundred-footers. Both flights called the wires, and trail responded when the flight was clear. Twelve miles out, Tom heard Champion 26 contact Eindhoven Tower for his flight. He heard the position report and quickly verified on the map flight one's location and plotted his own position. The separation was still good. He monitored the landing direction and determined the best way to approach the runway. Then he heard Werewolf 6 call the Eindhoven Tower to call the B Troop's position. Tom checked the map, and it appeared they were real close to flight one. Tom quickly got up on the B Troop frequency and called for Werewolf 6.

"Roger, Champion 6, this is Wolf 6. We have negative contact with your element, over," said Chris Wise.

"Say direction and airspeed, over." Tom was nervous because the air traffic controllers had done nothing to separate the flights.

"We are eighty knots, heading two-seven-zero. Ten miles from Eindhoven to land on the 250 runway," came back Chris Wise.

"Roger. Any contact with my first element, over?" asked Tom.

"Negative contact," came back Chris flatly.

Damn it, thought Tom. He switched his FM and called Champion 26. "Two-six, this is Champion Six. Do you see the Werewolf element?" asked Tom with a touch of panic in his voice.

"Negative contact, Six," said Hartley.

"You need to slow down and let them get in. Slow to sixty and let me know when you have them in sight," said Tom.

There was a pause. "The tower has cleared us in, Six."

"I don't give a damn. Let them go. I'm showing your courses converging, and they are flying faster. Have you got the visibility to see a mile out?" asked Tom.

"Negative, we have about a half a kilometer. We're slowing at this time," said the lieutenant.

Tom said to Walker, "He damn well better slow that flight down." Then there was silence on all the radios for thirty seconds. They should have seen each other by now. And the damn tower wasn't helping a bit.

Tom thought about the third dimension. Altitude. He quickly called B Troop and got back from Wise that B Troop was at one hundred feet. Then he heard Osborn say they were at one hundred and he would descend his flight to fifty. Only two of the three flights were on the Command Fox frequency. Chris Wise said the B Troop flight was going up to 120 feet. Ten more seconds passed in silence.

"I got 'em, sir!" said Chief Warrant Officer 2 Petty. "I've got an AH-64 at my one o'clock position. He's about a hundred meters out. Plenty of separation, 26."

Tom continued to hold his breath. That was plenty of separation as long as that's the trail bird of B Troop.

"I have negative contact with your element," said Chris Wise.

"Roger. I think they may be at your six o'clock. Have your trail turn off his strobes for five seconds," said Tom Lawton.

Ten seconds later, it was Osborn on the FM. "Roger, sir. That was the trail of B Troop Joe picked up in FLIR. He got close enough to see the markings on the engine cowling. We're two miles out and slowing for separation."

"Good job, fellas. We'll see you on the ground. Switching frequencies to monitor tower. Champion Six, out!" called Tom. To Walker in the back, he said, "Damn it! I know we can do what we're supposed to do. But those guys should have been in an hour ago. And his scouts are in our formation." Tom shook his head and sat up taller in his seat. He got his military bearing back and started looking outside the cockpit. The way things were going, this flight would never end. The ceiling was down to a hundred feet and visibility only a quarter of a mile. Three more minutes was all they needed to make the runway.

He heard tower call flight two clear of the runway and looked for the lights. Nothing. He slowed the flight to fifty knots. Doppler showed them to be two Ks out on a 250 heading. The radios were quiet. The entire flight was searching. And the clouds somehow seemed to be getting thicker.

They crossed a hardball road, and Tom saw a six-foot chain-link fence. Seconds later the runway lights. Finally, the runway appeared, and Walker rolled 220 on the runway.

The UHF radio squealed, "US Army flight 444 should have the runway in sight?"

Tom looked at Walker and shook his head. "You got the runway in sight yet?"

Walker laughed and said, "You want the controls, sir? My bladder's about to bust."

"I need a beer after that," said Tom.

"I think I need about six!" The warrant grinned.

"Roger that. Let me talk to my contemporaries. I don't think we're going anywhere. Batten down the hatches. Check out all our maintenance issues and we'll discuss this little adventure as soon as we can."

"Hey, sir, we didn't kill anybody," said the burly warrant.

Tom just shook his head.

1830 hours, December 1, 1990
Eindhoven BOQ Pub
Eindhoven, Netherlands

INSTEAD OF A FULL-FLEDGED AAR, TOM talked to his peers Rooks and Wise. They decided to do troop level AARs, and Tom chose to have his at the Eindhoven Officers Club. Needless to say, it was very informal.

"It's a darn good thing you told us to slow down, sir. We didn't know they were out there," said Tom Dolce.

"The altitude change was a great idea too. If they'd have been any closer, we would have both been at one hundred feet," said Hart Osborn.

"That's why you're not lead, Lieutenant. You were on the map and knew where you were. The next thing you should have been doing was monitoring the calls to the tower and picking up the Wolf flight when they called their position. If you hadn't slowed down, you would have been a lot closer. They were supposed to go in first. That was the plan. As soon as you heard him talk to tower, you should have found out his position and let him go in," said Tom.

"Roger, sir," said the lieutenant. He could smile at the comment now. He hadn't quite so understood an hour ago.

"As for you, Lead!" said Captain Lawton to Chief Warrant Officer 2 Petty. "Damn good thinking. Having the FLIR up and looking was a great idea."

"Sir, that Apache was so much hotter than the clouds. It stood out like a whore in church!" The warrant grinned.

Tom smiled and grabbed the junior warrant officer on the back of his neck. "Good job, Joe!"

The AAR concluded with smiles and handshakes all around. The D Troop crews arrived, and B Troop had just concluded their AAR across the room. Tom stood up from his table and nodded to Darren Rooks. "Gentlemen, if I could get your attention please. Having talked it over with my peers Captain Rooks and Captain Wise, they have informed me that I am not the senior man here." There was a big "Aaawwwww!" from the crowd of fifty. "Captain Promotable Rooks is the senior man. The commander and the Alpha Troop guys made it to Amsterdam. We are at the whim of Wrench Six!" Tom looked at the stout captain standing ten feet away. "You have the controls, Rooksy!" The group mocked a small golf clap.

"Hold the applause until I do something, will ya?" The D Troop commander beamed. "I just got off the phone with the boss at Amsterdam, and he told me to use my judgment and discretion." Rooksy paused and looked at all the troops. "So I talked to these British guys, and they're gonna get us rides to town!" The crowd roared with approval. "And besides that, Champion Six said he's got the first round!" And the crowd roared again and started for the doors.

Tom looked down at his feet and shook his head. "I never said that!"

"Hey! I was caught up in the moment," said Rooksy as he turned to leave.

It was going to be a long night. Lawton looked for Hart Osborn and Hal Timmons. "I want to make sure we can get outta here by 1000 tomorrow. Get all the paperwork, flight plan, risk assessment, and everything else done tonight. Then we can get a beer or two. After this afternoon, I think we all need a little break. Reiterate to everybody, twelve hours, bottle to throttle. That includes the aftereffects!"

It was a nice try. But these were attack pilots, and they had a reputation to keep.

2115, December 1, 1990
Eindhoven Officer's Club

AFTER EATING IN TOWN, THE CROWD returned to the base club. This was the first mistake.

"Whooh, Doggy Jed! Look at all the big bad Blackhawk pilots!" The yell came from an obviously inebriated CW4 Michael Leslie, more commonly known as Safety Six. He had flown in with Rooksy.

"Oh, Christ!" said Tom Osborn to no one in particular. The warrant was gesturing rudely to a group of relatively young warrant officers over at the far end of the bar. Captain Rooks and two other warrant officers from 1-6 were drinking large bottles of Weissen.

"Come on, boys, I think we can all get some new ass tonight!" hollered Safety Six. Mr. Leslie was referring to the group of about fifteen warrant officer ones and twos that were pretty much minding their own business at the far end of the bar.

Then an even louder voice yelled from the Blackhawk pilot's area, "If anybody gets any of this ass, it'll be me. Not any stinkin' gun bunny."

Rooksy's two cents popped in. "Oh yeah! Just who the fuck are you?"

Tom had a bad feeling that this was no longer a jocular bantering that pilots are known for. He was right. From out of the crowd of Blackhawk drivers, a captain appeared. He was about five foot six and 150 pounds. But he did have a 250-pound mouth. To Tom, he looked like Jiminy Cricket.

"I'm the guy who owns these outstanding army aviators!" bragged Captain Cricket. "And if anybody wants to fuck with these guys, they gotta go through me first!"

Tom saw Safety Six start toward the crowd, but Rooksy grabbed his arm and whispered in his ear. Safety Six roared with laughter in obvious approval as he let Rooksy go first toward the crowd at the bar.

"How you guys doin'?" questioned Darren Rooks to his Blackhawk brethren. "My name is Darren Rooks. I'm the D Troop commander of the Fightin' Sixth, the best damn attack unit in Germany. I'm also probably the best Hawk pilot in the country. My good friend here is Chief Warrant Officer 4 Michael Leslie. Mr. Leslie is the best damn safety officer in EUSAEUR! Can we buy you a drink?" said Rooksy in his New England accent. Tom turned back to the bar with a smile. That damn Rooksy knew everybody. He must have known one of those guys. Thinking all was well, Tom turned his attention to his drink and started to answer Hal's question when he heard Jiminy Cricket sound off again.

"We don't need any drinks from you goddamn Apache pilots! You fuckers can just go on down to the other end of the bar and tell your goddamn war stories about how goddamn great you are!" yelled Cricket.

On that note, Tom got off his stool, nodded to his lieutenants to join him, and headed to the other end of the bar. His actions were duplicated at about five other locations in the bar. The bartender was calling for peace. His pleas were falling on deaf and intoxicated ears.

"Sir, I think the captain envies our big gun!" said Chief Warrant Officer 4 Leslie, egging on the drunk Cricket.

"What kind of fucking name is Leslie? You some kind of Kansas City faggot?" asked Cricket, trying to be humorous. No one laughed as his stab at humor failed and Mike Leslie's broad smile faded. Mike Leslie survived two tours of duty in Vietnam in Special Forces units. Good-natured, often comical, Mike Leslie was a friend to all and an enemy to none. But Jiminy Cricket pushed a button in Mike Leslie that no one in the Fighting Sixth had ever seen.

Rooksy put a hand solidly on Leslie's chest as Leslie had raised his fist and had it cocked to the throwing position. The warrant looked at the captain holding him back, and his expression said it all. Anger and frustration combined with a longing to punch the shit out of the loudmouth asshole, Leslie produced a barely audible "Please."

Rooksy shook his head, and to Tom's surprise, Mike relented to the captain's negative headshake. "Not in here," said Rooks, looking at Leslie. "Go outside and cool off." To everyone's surprise, the totally pissed Vietnam vet put his fist down, stepped back, chugged his beer, and headed for the door. The crowd that had gathered breathed in a collective sigh of relaxing air.

Jiminy "Fucking" Cricket would have none of it. "I think I'll go outside with you, you old fart!"

Rooks's head snapped back at Captain Cricket. "You pompous little fucker! I ought to turn him loose on you! But because you're drunk and in front of your troops, I won't let you or him embarrass yourself. You want to go outside so damn bad, you come with me, you little bastard!"

Rooksy had turned and was heading for the door. "I'll take you too, you fat piece of crap!" snapped back Cricket. Rooksy stopped dead in his tracks. The tension increased again as Blackhawk pilots and Apache pilots looked at each other nervously. Sizing up opponents, the crowd faced off for a fight that no one wanted.

Darren Rooks took a deep breath and said over his shoulder, "Outside, you little peckerhead. Now!"

The crowd rolled toward the door. The bartender was glad to see it head that way but was on the phone in an instant. As soon as the crowd had gathered outside, a circle formed. Tom Lawton was trying to think of a way to stop it. It was happening way too fast. The beer and the atmosphere had played up the event to a point where no one could turn back. The crowd watched with baited breath as Darren Rooks told the CAV pilots to stay out of the circle. It was just between him and the Cricket.

For his part, the Cricket didn't say a word to his men. He just kept talking trash about Rooksy's weight. Wasn't he good enough to fly with real Hawk pilots? After a little more taunting, the Cricket addressed his foe. "All right, fat guy! Give me your best shot!"

Without hesitation and with merely tremendous speed and aim, the former University of Vermont hockey star crushed the Cricket's jaw with a hard right jab. The Cricket stood straight up, and his head wobbled from side to side. He started to fall to the right as his eyes rolled up into his head. The crowd was totally silent as the Cricket fell backward like a dropped board. His head landed on the mushy, wet ground with a splat. The crowd was stunned. No one could move.

"Damn!" yelled Mike Leslie. He looked at Rooksy and yelled, "Damn! I can't believe you hit him!"

Rooksy wasn't too shaken by the outcome, and he still had his fist clenched and was ready to battle more. Then it sunk in. He'd just knock the hell out of another officer. An event that was not only career threatening, but punishable under the Uniformed Code of Military Justice.

Realizing what had just happened, his jaw hung down, and he looked at Leslie. "I didn't hit him that hard! God, I hope he's all right. Please, God! I didn't mean to hurt the little guy!"

About ten seconds later, as some of his soldiers bent over him, the Cricket's head began to wobble again as he regained consciousness. He closed his eyes and opened them in disbelief. He shook his head hard and looked around. The crowd held its collective breath again in anticipation.

What was this guy going to do next? His pilots helped him up. The Cricket shook his head again and tried to focus on Rooksy. He regained his balance and looked directly at Darren Rooks and said, "Let that be a lesson to ya!" Then he looked at his men and slurred, "You guys can party with them if you want to. They're okay. But I think I'm going home now."

Darren went to the Cricket. "Hey, I'm sorry. But you said, 'Give me your best shot!'" He looked down at the other captain who was rubbing his jaw. "I hope you're okay."

"I guess so!" He shook his head one more time as the circle started to break up. There was a lot of laughter and some "Can you believe that?" Jiminy Cricket stuck out his hand toward Rooksy. "I'd like to keep this between you and I, okay? If anybody hears about this, I'll probably get relieved or grounded."

Rooks just shook his head. "No sweat." He squinted and looked down at the Cricket one more time. "Are you sure you're okay?"

"Yeah. I'm goin' home now," said the wounded captain.

Rooks looked around and said to no one in particular, "I'm gonna go have another beer." With that, he headed inside.

Tom Lawton just shook his head at the display. He just knew if it'd been him, there would have been a brawl, and his head would have been handed to Denson on a silver platter. Some guys just have more luck than others. The crowd headed inside for more beer.

December 2, 1990
Eindhoven

THE NEXT DAY, THERE WERE DIFFERENT views of what happened and the tales became taller in the following months. The one that got the most attention was about the knife fight between Blackhawk pilots and Apache pilots. Other tales told of Brits fighting Yanks. And another rumor indicated a gun came into play. There were all kinds of stories about the events of that night, but never the truth. The truth was too simple. One captain punched another, and that was that. No brawl, no knives, and no guns. After the Fighting Sixth left the airfield, the incident at Eindhoven was only mentioned at beer parties. The chain of command in Katterheim as well as Stuttgart, the home of the lift pilot's outfit, never found out.

The whole unit looked like death warmed over. Hangovers were part for the course. Only Hart Osborne had a smile on his face. He took the opportunity to needle his commander.

"So, sir, is there anything I can get you before we take off? Aspirin, Tylenol, Alka-Seltzer, or maybe some Pepto-Bismol?" chided the lieutenant.

Tom smiled and shook his head. "No, Lieutenant. Maybe a round for my .38 because my head is killin' me," said Champion Six. The great defender of freedom didn't feel too good at that particular moment. His head was pounding. He had a bad case of heartburn, and the greasy morning eggs weren't sitting to well.

Hart Osborne continued to pick on his boss. "I talked to everybody else, and they don't seem to have any aftereffects." He had to stick the knife in one more time. "I've got a cheese omelet MRE, and it's yours if you want it." He chuckled.

Tom grabbed his stomach and burped loudly. "No, thank you, Lieutenant. And quit smiling so damn much. Your face will freeze that way." Tom changed gears and got serious. "Is everybody ready to go?"

"Roger that, sir. They're quieter than usual and a little tired, but everybody wants to get to Amsterdam and head home," said Hart.

"Let's do it. I know I look pretty green, Lieutenant, but I feel a lot better than I look," came back the captain.

"I hope so, sir. 'Cause you look like hell!" Osborne smiled. He saluted his boss, still smiling.

Tom returned the salute and said, "See ya on the radio, wiseass!"

Hart Osborn turned and ran to his aircraft. Tom looked around. The crews were moving a bit slower than usual. They deserved the break. They had been kept on a short leash for over a month, and the drunk front that just came through Eindhoven was good for morale. God help them if anyone busted an aircraft or had a mishap. The blame line would start and stop with Tom Lawton. He took a last walk around the aircraft and nodded for Walker to crank the APU.

Thirty minutes later, they were airborne. The flight was much smoother that day. Great weather. Everything went according to the briefing, and they arrived at the port of Amsterdam at 1245 hours. Hawk was pleased that everyone made it. He called Rooks, Wise, and Lawton off to the side for a quick commander's debrief. Tom was expecting an ass chewing.

Hawk couldn't help but notice how rough and tired the crews looked, including the three commanders. The good thing was that Hawk was smiling at the observation. He then informed the three troop commanders that the mission was complete for the day and the host country had a beer tent set up.

Rooks couldn't contain himself. "Damn, sir. We had enough beer last night to float these fuckin' boats to the Mediterranean!" said Rooks sheepishly.

"I expected that with you in charge." Hawk slapped him on the back. "Don't feel bad. We did the same thing here." The group sighed relief and shook their heads. "The main thing is, you're all here, and the aircraft will be on the way ASAP. Our mission is relatively complete, except Rooks's stay back force. Good job, gentlemen. You and your men deserve a break."

Chris Wise said, "Sir, we had a break last night."

"Have another break then, Captain. The buses roll out of here at 1800. Your next mission is to have all your soldiers on them. Darren, run this plan by me again and then you all can go join your troopers," said Lieutenant Colonel Hawk.

Because he was the squadron maintenance officer, Darren Rooks was responsible for the breakdown, "shrink wrapping," and loading of the aircraft. He received three crew chiefs from each line troop and had a team of twenty soldiers of his own to accomplish the task.

"The port guys are the controllers here, sir. They run the timetable and scheduling and locations of which ships our aircraft go on. Our function is to merely assist them in the execution. I have four four-man teams, each working on an aircraft, with an NCO supervising. Each of these teams removes blades, marks them, gets the aircraft to the civilians that shrink wrap the airframe in protective plastic, and move it to the staging area before it is loaded. Another team walks the aircraft onto the ships, and my senior NCO and a paperwork nug monitor the loading and location of our birds. We have three teams of three soldiers that will depart on board the ships that have our aircraft when they depart from the port. Each team has an NCO. The latest information says we will be on three ships, not two. Thus, the need for the third team. We can anticipate the whole process taking two days and the ships to leave next Friday or Saturday at the latest."

"Good. Good deal," replied Nightstalker Six. "When will your rear detachment be coming back to Katterheim?"

"Not until the last bird is on board the ship. Then there is nothing we can do from that point. Probably late Wednesday, sir," said Captain Rooks.

"I don't want you or your people here any longer than you need to be, got it?" said Lieutenant Colonel Hawk.

"Shit, sir. That's what we get the big bucks for!" Darren Rooks laughed. "Honestly, sir. Nobody wants to be here one minute longer than he needs to. And I've already coordinated with the S4, Captain Krause, for transportation. Larry said it would be ready and gave me the number to call, and I'm set, sir." Rooksy was just too damn good.

"Call me immediately if there are any changes. You guys get your troops to that beer tent. I'll see you at 1800."

December 2, 1990
Amsterdam, Netherlands

TOM FOUND THE LIEUTENANTS AND SENT them and the rest of the Champions to the beer tent. Most were none too anxious. Six of them wanted to observe the port operations and the shrink-wrap process, as did Hart Osborn. They were told to rally at the tent NLT 1700. Everyone else headed to the hospitality tent for more cheer.

At 1800, the buses departed with all assigned personnel. The mood was definitely festive. Some singing, some jokes, and a whole lot of trash talking took place for the first hundred miles. Slowly, the atmosphere changed. As the miles rolled and the minutes turned to hours, the jocularity and enthusiasm gave way to reality and nervousness.

The Fighting Sixth had just left their entire squadron's worth of Apaches, three Blackhawks, and ten OH-58 scout helicopters in Amsterdam to be placed on ships for transport to Saudi Arabia. The equipment was packed in Sea-Land vans for storage on the boats. It took over twenty tractor-trailers to carry the squadron's support equipment and supplies. All those helicopters and all that equipment for one squadron. Eventually, there would be over thirty squadrons of attack helicopters in Saudi Arabia. The organization and effort involved in this operation was unlike anything undertaken in decades.

The fact that all the aircraft were on one ship and that ship could sink or be destroyed by terrorism or an act of God was the focus of discussion by the pilots during the bus ride to Ansbach. Two hundred fifty million dollars plus per squadron, plus the additional equipment and soldiers, multiplied times thirty, staggered Tom's mind. And that was just the attack helicopters. It would be a miracle if they ever saw any of the mill vans.

The bus became quiet as the crews slowly drifted off to sleep. Tom couldn't sleep because he knew there was something he had to do when he got home. He owed it to Cindy to sit down and talk to her. He had kept putting it off, and too soon, he would be gone.

As the bus pulled up to the hangar, there were no wives or family there to meet them. They staggered off in silence. Tired, hungry, and grouchy to a man. The departures were hasty, and Tom headed to his car. He wasn't looking forward to talking to Cindy, but it was time.

CHAPTER 6

0415, December 3, 1990
Katterheim Caserne

TOM LAWTON WALKED IN THE APARTMENT tired, weary, and somewhat confused. Tired from the ten-hour bus ride, weary from a lack of sleep, and confused because Cindy Lawton was up reading a book on the living room couch. He looked at his wife and could see she was neither tired nor weary. Simply put, she looked pissed.

Tom thought he'd try the glad-to-be-home line. "Hi, sweetie. What are you doin' up?"

Cindy would have none of it. "You look like hell," she said.

Tom was surprised by the comment and didn't find it amusing. The comment did provide him an opportunity to attack before she did. "Great to be fucking home, dearest! I missed you too."

The reaction put Cindy on the defensive. "I didn't mean it the way it sounded," Cindy tried to explain. "I meant it like . . ." She fumbled for the words. "You look tired."

"I get what you meant." Tom put his bags down and went to the refrigerator. Cindy followed him into the kitchen. He got a glass of iced tea from the fridge, hoping it would give him the caffeine he needed to stay awake a few more minutes.

"Can we have that talk now that you've been promising me?" asked Cindy. "I just need to know what's going on . . . inside your head."

Tom reluctantly nodded, then turned around to face her. "I guess so."

"Do you want me to start, or do you have anything you want to say?" she asked.

The fatigue smacked Tom in the back of his head like a hammer. "I don't have anything to say. So why don't you just go ahead and get whatever the hell is bugging you off your chest." It came out harsher than he intended, but it was the way he felt. He didn't intend the comment to be mean, but it was. Cindy closed her mouth tightly, turned, and headed for the living room. Tom shook his head and muttered, "Nice start, asshole."

He followed her into the living room and said, "I'm sorry, honey. Look. I'm just a little tired right now. Do you want to wait until this afternoon and talk?"

Cindy was ready for that one. "No, I want to talk now," she said calmly.

Tom thought to himself, *This is gonna suck.* "All right. Go ahead."

"I know we don't have much time together until you go. But I'd like you to do one thing for me until then," said Cindy as she walked around the couch.

"Sure, hon. Name it," he said.

"Sleep on the couch," said Cindy.

Tom wasn't ready for that. "What's that supposed to mean?"

"Just what I said." A tear formed in her eye, and she wiped it away. "Until the Tom Lawton I married shows up in this house, I want you to stay away from me!"

"Oh, come here, honey! What are you talking about? I'm still me." Tom was visibly shaken by her comment. "I've just been . . . preoccupied with work, that's all."

Cindy was visibly angry now. "Preoccupied with anything but Megan and me. I don't understand how you can be . . . so distant. So cold toward us. It's like we don't even exist to you."

Tom thought about what she said. He didn't get it. "Look, Cindy. I've got a job to do, and I'm doin' it the best I can."

Cindy walked over to the hallway, turned, and yelled, "To hell with your job!" She added icily, "And to hell with you too!"

Tom walked quickly over to her. Cindy rarely cursed. "You think I enjoy this. You think I want to go and get my ass shot at?"

"Not that part of it. But it's awfully convenient for you to put Megan and me far away while you run off to some stupid war," she snapped.

"Goddamn it! I'm in the army, and that's the job I signed on to do!" Tom yelled back.

Cindy could take no more. This wasn't the man she married. She resorted to the only thing she could to get him back. She pulled her hand back and slapped him as hard as she could. Tom didn't move and caught the slap full force across his face. Calmly, with gritted teeth, Cindy said,

"You signed on to be a husband and a father too." She turned and walked slowly to the bedroom. "It's obvious that you can't handle that part."

Tom was too stunned to move. The comment hit home. She was right. Hell, she was always right. What a jerk he had been. Why hadn't he seen this coming? Because he was so absorbed with the unit. "Command" had him obsessed with the mission. He was so focused on war, he forgot about peace. *Damn it!* It wasn't too late. Surely, he had time left to salvage his marriage. He needed to tell her the truth. Tell her what he felt. All the things he was keeping inside. She had a right to know. As he rubbed his cheek, he slowly walked down the hall to the bedroom.

With a deep breath, Tom started, "I apologize. I've been wrong. You're right. I've been so . . . focused on commanding the Champions that I've neglected you and Megan. Honestly, honey, it wasn't my intent to hurt you."

"You did," came the response. She didn't look at him.

Tom felt the words rather than heard them. They were like an ice pick in his heart. He gathered his courage to tell her the truth. "I'm afraid." A tear appeared in his eye.

Cindy looked up, confused. "You? Afraid? You've never been afraid of anything."

"I am now." Tom choked out and rubbed his eyes.

Cindy turned toward him. "What are you afraid of?"

"I'm afraid . . ." He struggled for the words. "I might never see you again."

Cindy knew Tom Lawton. And this was him. This was no impersonation to win her over. He really was scared.

"I'm scared for myself. I keep thinking . . . I'm not good enough. Or that I'm gonna screw something up." His words trailed off, and Tom seemed very far away.

Cindy got up off the bed and went to him. Tom nearly collapsed in her arms. She pulled him to the bed and held him tightly, and Tom let go of his emotions. "I'm not so worried that . . . I'm gonna die. Just that . . . I'll make some stupid decision and someone else will. Or that I'll end up a prisoner and . . . you won't remember . . ."

Cindy rubbed his head. "Well, we know that the last one is not gonna happen. You think your family would let me forget you. I don't." She rubbed his neck. "I would think you would be afraid . . ." It was Cindy's turn to search for words. "Of dying."

Tom gained his composure. "For some reason, I don't feel afraid for myself. Maybe it's because I grew up an army brat or death in war is . . . romantic or something. My own death is not what I'm afraid of." He got up to get a Kleenex. "I just feel like I can't take care of all the things I need to to keep everyone alive." He added, "And I obviously haven't been taking care of y'all."

This was the Tom Lawton that Cindy had married. One more jab. "We've been getting along just fine without you the last three months."

Tom laughed. "I know what's been happening to me. I just seem to be powerless to stop it."

"Maybe . . . ," Cindy started, "if you stopped drinking so much and got some more sleep while you can, you'd be in better shape, you know, mentally to deal with everything."

Damn her. Tom hated it when she was like this. Always right. "Yeah, I know."

"Look, Tommy. Everyone I talk to tells me you're the best. Why can't you accept that for what it's worth? You know the aircraft, you know people, and you know how to put them together and make a team work," said Cindy.

"The term is *unit*, honey," said Tom.

"You know what I mean, shithead!" And she playfully smacked his arm. "You're not gonna make mistakes. I have faith in you. You've worked too hard to get to this point to make mistakes." She got up to hug him. "Your guys will do whatever you tell them to do. You just need to bring yourself home to me."

"You gonna be here?" asked Tom.

"I ain't going anywhere," she replied.

Tom remembered his father's experience in Vietnam. "I'm a little worried that I may not be the same when I come back. I think that maybe none of us will be the same."

"With or without this war, we all change, Tommy," she said. Tom thought about it, and she was right again.

He nodded his agreement but could tell she was concerned. It was Tom's turn to be supportive now. He could see she was the one in need now. He pulled her close. He put his fingers under her chin. Gently, he wiped a tear off her cheek. Tom did his best John Wayne. "Well, I think ya need a man to take care of ya, little lady. I'm just the guy to do it."

It seemed ages since Tom had done a stupid impression. To Cindy, as bad as the impression was, it was the best one Tom had ever done. He was back. At least for a while. She fully intended to take advantage of him too.

Slowly, they kissed. A long, hard, passionate kiss. They undressed each other, not with abandon, but deliberately. It had been quite some time since they had made passionate love. And neither ventured to guess how many more times the opportunity would present itself. Effortlessly, Tom picked her up and carried her to the bed. For the first time in years, they made love from the heart. The kind of passion that can only be generated when two people are totally in tune to each other's desires and needs, committed to satisfying the person you lay with without reservation, without distraction. Committed to the moment. Each knowing that they may never make love like that again.

December 3, 1990
Katterheim Caserne

TOM WOKE UP WITH A SMILE on his face and looked at his digital clock. It read 5:23, but he wasn't sure if it was a.m. or p.m. The shades were drawn, so the bedroom was dark. Cindy was nowhere to be found. Tom put his head down on his pillow and closed his eyes. He listened and heard the clanging of pots in the kitchen. Tom realized that for however long it was, that was the best sleep he'd had in months. His nose told him that Cindy was cooking chili, and it smelled wonderful. Must be p.m.

Quietly, the bedroom door opened. Tom could tell it was Megan peeking in, so he pretended to be asleep. Megan came in, holding her stuffed penguin and sucking the middle two fingers of her free hand. Slowly, she shuffled toward her daddy, trying not to wake him up. The man played possum until she got next to the bed. Megan's hand came out of her mouth, and she reached over to her dad's face. She slowly grabbed the closed eyelid of Tom's left eye and pulled it up. Tom turned his head quickly and said, "What are you looking at?"

The little girl squealed with excitement. "Doddy!" She smacked him on the arm. "You top that!"

"Come 'ere. I was just playin' with you," said Tom as he picked her up and placed her next to him on the bed.

"You cared me," said Megan, still not able to make the *s* sound in *scared*. But then she smiled and laid her head on Tom's shoulder.

Then the door came open again, and Cindy came in. "Is everybody all right? About time, sleepyhead. It's been ten hours. You won't be able to sleep later tonight."

"We're fine. That's the best sleep I've had lately. I can go for another twenty-four hours now!" declared Tom.

"Megan, you need to go pick up that mess you made in your room," said Mommy.

"No," came the reply from the Lawton Angel.

"Megan, I said go pick up those toys, or I'm gonna spank your hiney!" came the stern response from Mommy Dearest.

Megan looked at Doddy for support that only partially came.

"How about Daddy comes and helps you in a few minutes, okay?" said Tom.

She studied Tom for a second and guessed that that would be a good solution to Mom's request. "Oh-kay!" She got up and slowly rolled off Tom and took off out of the bedroom down the hall.

Tom patted the bed next to him and slid over to give Cindy room to sit down. "Thanks for letting me sleep, honey."

"You needed it," she said. Then she started to rub on Tom's stomach. "This gut's gettin' a little big, Soldier!"

Tom looked down and had to agree with her. "I haven't been working out as much as I should be."

"And you've been drinking more," said his wife.

Tom thought about the comment. Naturally, with the increased alcohol consumption came the expanded waistline Tom hated. She was right again. Tom knew better than to try and deny it. "You never told me about your . . ." Cindy looked for the proper, nonalienating-type verbiage. "Meeting with Hal and Dean Alvin the other night before you left."

Tom nodded and rubbed her smooth arm. The vision of Hal with the gun popped into Tom's mind. He didn't want to tell her about that, or she'd be worried sick. "In spite of what you're thinking, it wasn't a drink-a-thon." Tom coughed and looked at her. "Hal had been drinking. A lot. And Dean thought he might try to hurt someone or . . . hurt himself."

"What?" asked Cindy in disbelief. "Hal? The veteran?"

"Yeah. He was really drunk. And pissed off too. A bad combination," explained Tom. "He was thinking about his past, and it made him . . . worry about what might happen in the future."

"Everybody's doing that. Why's he so worried?" asked Cindy.

"He had a bad experience in Grenada that I wasn't aware of. There was a midair collision between two Blackhawks, and he saw it all," said Tom. "He blames the planners for not having their shit together, and it's been eating at him for a while. The fact that we're headed to the Gulf merely brought those feelings to a head, and he needed to let it out."

Cindy Lawton studied her husband's face. She was sure he was telling the truth but wondered to herself about the sanity of his subordinate.

Tom could see her concern. "He's fine, honey. He was just venting, and I was glad I could help him do that." Tom could see this didn't settle her. He thought about it and decided to give her an explanation that he hoped would clear up a couple of other things too.

"A navy captain came to our unit in Texas about five years ago. His topic was pilots and their relationships. We weren't married then, so I only paid minimal attention to him. But now that I'm older and more mature"—he coughed again and smiled at her—"I understand better what he was talking about. He said pilots tend to compartmentalize their feelings and emotions." He could tell that didn't register. "We try to put things like emotions, problems, or troubles into little convenient boxes and tuck them away to deal with them later. We leave them in these makeshift compartments to allow us to focus on being pilots. It's a convenient way to deal with things that at the time may be unacceptable or that we would rather not address unless it's on our own terms. Hal, aided by Jack Daniels, chose this time to pull this . . . trouble out of its compartment."

Cindy nodded as if she understood. Tom wasn't sure that she did, so he continued.

He cleared his throat. "I've been putting you and Megan in a compartment." He could see the light come on in Cindy's eyes. It made her sad, but she smiled a knowing smile anyway. "I've kept you two in a place that I could reach but didn't want to. Last night, you made me pull you out of my . . . storage space and forced me to deal with emotions and reality that I had been putting off." Tom looked into her eyes for recognition. "Do you understand now?"

It was obvious that she did. Her cheeks were flush. "I don't want to be in some place that I'm not real to you. That's the pilot and Commander Tom Lawton talking. Not the man I married."

Tom nodded in agreement. "It's just a . . . technique for maintaining—"

"Tom," she interrupted him, "just don't do it anymore."

Tom nodded. "I'm sorry, hon." He understood her feelings completely. "I see now what that navy captain was trying to explain, and he was exactly right." Tom added, "I promise I won't put you in my . . . 'compartment system' anymore."

Cindy was a realist. "Now that I understand, I know that you will do exactly that. Besides, you are who you are, and I can't change you. If you were any different, I probably wouldn't love you so much." She smiled. "When you're flying around down there, I don't want you thinking about us. I would rather you take care of your business and get it over as soon as you can." She let that sink into his thick skull and then added something Tom needed to hear, "I'll be here when you get back."

"Damn, Cindy." Tom got up and gave her a big hug and kiss. "I have to admit, that's been in the back of my mind too. A whole bunch of the guys' wives are talking about going back to the states. I was worried you would leave."

"Look, Tommy. I love you. I'm not leaving." She smiled and shrugged. "Hell, I'm in for a penny and in for a pound on this whole army thing. You just keep remembering me as a person and not . . . something less." She added, "You big jerk, Lou and I discussed this, and she's gonna stay here for Hart too."

"Great. I think that's great, honey." Tom smiled.

She still had a question. "About Hal, are you sure he's gonna be okay?"

"You mean down there?" Tom asked. She nodded. "Yeah, he'll be fine. It was just something he needed to get off his chest." Tom said, not sure if he was trying to convince Cindy or himself. "He won't have any problems."

Then it was Tom's turn to clear the air. "About last night? I am truly sorry for being so outta touch. The last thing I want do before I go is make sure you understand nothing in this whole world matters more to me than you and Megan."

Cindy nodded but knew that soon enough her husband would mentally depart to that far off place and she would be boxed up and "compartmentalized." It was only a matter of when. But this was Tom talking, and he was back for now. Cindy was glad to have him there. "I know you do. Just remember us."

Tom nodded and looked her in the eyes. "Always."

"I've got some chili cooking, so let's get to it, sleepyhead!" she said.

Tom jumped out of bed and started to go help Megan. For some unknown reason, he was compelled to turn and grab Cindy one more time. Without a word, he pulled her close and gave her another passionate kiss. He moved away and smiled. She smacked his butt playfully and said, "Get goin'!"

Tom mocked a salute and double-timed down the hall.

Dinner was great. Tom's favorite, Texas chili, cornbread, and beans. Tom spent the evening playing with Megan, but his thoughts would shift to what was to come, and as they did, Cindy could see what he was doing. After they tucked Megan in, they immediately went to the bedroom and made love. It wasn't the same as it had been the night before. It was great, but it was just sex. Cindy could tell Tom was mentally gone again. He was distracted by thoughts of what needed to be done. She resigned herself to the fact he was the commander again. It was so good to have him back, even if it was only for one day. But her Tommy was gone. God, how she missed him.

December 9, 1990
Katterheim Caserne

THE DAY CAME THAT NO ONE was looking forward to. Deployment shots. Over a two-day period, the entire brigade lined up at the gym to take deployment shots. It didn't matter if you had shot records or had taken shots recently. You were going to get more. Inside the gym was a small army of doctors and nurses and medical techs that had one purpose: make a pincushion out of any soldier headed to the desert.

Of course the warrant officers in C Troop found a way to pass the time in the three-hour line. Odds were established, and bets were made on who would pass out after the infamous "silver bullet." Every trooper had to get injected in the buttocks with an ice-cold 15cc of some jellylike crap. Tom Lawton was happy to hear no odds were drawn on him. However, the odds on Hart Osborn's passing out were three to one. Tom heard if you could warm "the bullet" up for two minutes, the substance wasn't as solid and was almost turned to a liquid. As soon as he got close, he asked for his "bullet" and began to roll it between his hands to warm it up. It didn't matter. It still hurt like hell.

Whoa be it to the trooper that held up the line to inquire as to the substances that were about to enter his or her body via their ass. The medics had a job to do, and they had little humor when it came to doing it. They could be gruff, or they could be full-fledged assholes. They didn't enjoy sticking needles full of jelly in over five thousand asses, but it was their job, and they did it without fanfare. A mere five thousand asses in Katterheim, another five thousand in Hanua, and another five thousand in Wiesbaden. After a while, it had to drain on their sense of purpose.

John Walker made an observation that by the time they got to his ass, over 17,386 asses would have passed in front of his specialist's view. He would have to inquire with his medic about exactly where his ass stood on the "Beautiful Asses for Shots Scale" (BASS). This didn't endear him to his young female medical technician one bit. His "bullet" was not warmed up, which caused the medicine to enter his butt as Jell-O rather than jelly. A significant difference on the butt pain meter. The young lady rammed the needle home and, without hesitation, injected the large and rather obnoxious warrant officer with the whole thing in a record three-point-two seconds. The howl he generated was heard downstairs. Apparently, three newbies passed out right behind Walker upon hearing the large warrant officer howl in pain. For his part, John Walker limped off, shaking his head and cursing under his breath. A golf-ball-sized mass was protruding from his right butt cheek. Tom couldn't help but notice the sadistic young specialist was smiling. But no one in her line had any more comments about her duty.

As Tom limped back to his office, he pondered all the things that were happening. In his mental checklist, everything was caught up. They were as ready as they could be to deploy. There was just one thing he personally had to do. He needed to take the time to write a letter.

To Tom, it was something he had to do to be ready to go. In case something bad did happen to him, he wanted to let someone know what he wanted in case he did not return. The person he chose for this "reward" was his brother and sister-in-law. Sherry Bolden was Cindy's sister, and her husband, Gary, was like a brother to Tom. When they were in Texas, the two went everywhere together. Gary flew Blackhawks in the Texas Guard. He and Tom would always tease each other about how good attack helicopters were or why lift aircraft were better. The rivalry was always good-natured, and they formed a mutual admiration and trust. Cindy and Sherry would just sit and laugh at the antics their husbands would create.

Tom went to his office and locked the door. He got out paper and pencil and wrote a letter that served one purpose: to let them know how much he loved them and how much faith he had in them to see Cindy and Megan would be looked after if something bad were to happen to him. Gary and Sherry were the people Tom wanted to look after Cindy and Megan. It was an emotional event for Tom. As he sat and wrote, he was conscious that a tear had formed. But he stayed focused on the task at hand. After he was done, he hastily reread it, sealed it in the envelope, and placed it on the desk in front of him. The fact that he had written the letter and it was physically there made Tom feel better. It would be in the mail first thing the next day.

Tom took a deep breath and sat back in his chair. He looked around his office. Tom looked at his I Love Me wall. He looked at the plaques, the awards, and the commendations and thought about his past. He'd done a lot of things in the military and been to a lot of places. Tom remembered Reforger '86. He thought about how screwed up the Apache operations had been and how much they had improved since he was a lieutenant. He knew what he was doing, and he knew what he had to do. Any doubts he had about his ability or competence would soon be answered. He subconsciously rubbed the cut over his nose and smiled. Tom Lawton was as ready for war as he possibly could be.

December 17, 1990
Katterheim Caserne

THE SQUADRON HAD GOTTEN TO THE point that transportation, or lack thereof, drove their schedule. They were ready, but the helicopters weren't. The operation was huge. Aircraft from the United States and all her allies flew round the clock to bring warriors to battle. A scheduled time would be announced. Excitement, anticipation, anxiety, and subsequent predeployment depression would all culminate in an emotional meltdown as the inevitable announcement of a cancellation would come. This went on for two weeks, and the tension was becoming incredible. The emotional roller coaster of peaks and valleys played hell on the minds of the troopers. But that was nothing compared to the turmoil it placed on the families. The swings of emotional highs and lows only contributed to the mental anguish.

Rumors of a unit movement swept through the tiny post like fire. Before the command could stop one, another started the next day. Individual soldiers began to lose faith in the command's ability to know what was happening and the "assumed" ability of the US Army to even get to the fight.

The pressure mounted. In another unit, a pilot mysteriously shot himself in the thigh while cleaning his personal .45 at his quarters. The bullet did not hit any vital area, merely flesh. Whether an accident or intentionally done to avoid duty, the soldier was immediately considered a coward. He might as well have shot himself in the head because his reputation as a man and as a soldier would be forever questioned.

One of Rooksy's troopers went off the deep end. Drunk out of his mind, the single sergeant first class and Vietnam veteran ran up and down the halls, hollering he'd done his time and he wasn't going. The junior troopers immediately called the military police and Captain Rooks. The inebriated sergeant didn't have to listen to no captain. He was "stayin' in Germany and ain't no mother fuckin' body gonna tell him any different." Rooksy watched helplessly as the four military police subdued, then carried off his avionics platoon sergeant. Three weeks later, the private entered the stockade at Mannheim. The kicker was the sergeant would have been eligible for retirement in nine months.

The Champions had no incidents that prevented anyone from deploying. The fact that many of the men were just as scared as Lawton was never revealed to Tom. The Champions had formed a terrific team under Tom. That "team" concept was a tremendous multiplier in a combat unit, especially a unit that had never faced the fire of a hostile enemy.

Still, Tom Lawton felt anxious because of all the little problems, the anticipation, and the constant ups and downs. He didn't think he would ever get over the anxiety associated with all the waiting. Every day Tom would be ready to get the word they were leaving. When the word finally came, it was much earlier than he wanted.

CHAPTER 7

0100, December 23, 1990
Twenty-eight thousand feet over
the Mediterranean Sea

THE PLANE RIDE WAS SMOOTH, YET tense enough to keep everyone on edge. Low muffled talk on the jet had the older soldiers, veterans of Vietnam, Grenada and Panama, calming or reassuring the younger troops. In all honesty, no one knew what to think about the coming fight. Desert warfare, combined arms operations, or air-land battle was still untested. All the talk centered on what was about to happen. The past was a continent away.

To Tom, it was just one long damn ride. The flight did allow Lawton time to think. He thought about Cindy and Megan for the first couple of hours. But after that, it was time for business. Tom's demeanor changed. He no longer was Cindy's caring husband. No longer Megan's loving father. He became what he needed to be—a warrior.

After three hours into the flight, Tom Lawton could take it no more. He got up and circled the plane. He didn't really need to stretch. He just felt the urge to be moving. Helicopter pilots are like that. Tom didn't feel in control, so he got up and moved around. He visited with his troops, all the time assessing the faces he saw and the attitudes of the men. He concluded that they were as ready as they could be. The plane ride was the epitome of what camaraderie should be. Backslapping and high fives were everywhere. Each soldier's emotions fed off the other. After his first trip around the plane, Tom made a habit of the "recon" every hour or so. Finally, the drone of the engine got to him, and he fell asleep.

It wasn't a sound sleep. He couldn't dream. No matter what position he was in, he couldn't get comfortable. What Tom really wanted was a beer to take the edge off. A nice, cold beer or two would help him sleep. But there was no beer on this flight. No beer in Saudi Arabia. Lawton wouldn't have another beer for a long time. If ever.

0430, December 23, 1990
Riyadh, Saudi Arabia

TOM WAS STARTLED AWAKE AS THE huge jet touched down hard. "Welcome to Saudi Arabia," said the flight attendant over the loudspeaker. He couldn't help but notice she didn't add, "Enjoy your stay."

As they taxied, the troops were all trying to get to windows to see outside. It was dark, and no one could see past the lights of the airport. From the sanctuary of the jet, they could have been anywhere. But they were in a combat zone. All the curiosity and expectations would soon be answered.

The first thing they noticed as they got off the plane was the smell. Cutting through the burnt jet fuel of the airport was the scent of a foreign land. The night air was full of strange sounds and odors from a time long ago. Not bad smells, simply unfamiliar. Smells Tom Lawton could only describe as . . . unwelcome.

Then they noticed the sounds. Unfamiliar language and strange faces looked at the Americans as they departed the plane. The faces were rough and hard looking, and many were unfriendly. It was obvious the people live a tough life. Between the jet engine's roar and the uncertainty of where to go and what to do, the appearance of mass confusion was created. Soon enough, an American Air Force sergeant got the CAV troopers pointed in the right direction. The grueling transition from the plane to the first station began.

Two hours later, the troopers of the Fighting Sixth were on buses headed through a security gate. The sun was up now, and the strange country was illuminated with bright sunshine. Wherever the buses went, the soldiers were met with stares. The civilians, the Arabs away from the airport, weren't unfriendly. More simply put . . . they were ambivalent. They seemed confused by the presence of so many foreigners dressed in "chocolate chip" BDUs. Many of the soldiers were laughing or smiling. The confidence of the American soldiers, their collective cockiness, kept the Saudis away. The only people the troops talked to the first few days were the hired help. They were usually Indians, Pakistanis, or Filipinos. And the help definitely enjoyed the American presence. The airport was the only modern thing in the area. Outside it, the unit may have flown into any third world country in a completely different century. There were shacks, goats, an occasional palm tree, and people in haggard clothing riding bicycles. The bikes appeared to be the only modern conveniences the locals had.

The first thing familiar that Tom recognized was the Pepsi can the bus driver was drinking. The coloring definitely indicated a Pepsi. But the Arabic writing made it look strange. If they had Pepsi there, he knew it was still the twentieth century.

The bus ride was a steady drone on a two-lane highway through the Saudi desert. Once they were out of the city limits, it all looked the same. Beyond the highway was nothing but desert on either side of the road. The scenery didn't change for 230 miles. At that point, the change was amazing. A few miles before the coast, the highway became a wider two-lane system. There were farms, animals, and shacks that apparently sprung up from nowhere. In the distance, a city could be seen with high-rise buildings, antennas, power lines, and traffic, things that were familiar to the soldiers. At the coastal city of Ad Dammam, the buses got on a four-lane highway and headed northeast.

Two hours later, they arrived at their new home. The place was named Al Jubayl. It was in the area of an oil refinery built on the coast about sixty miles north of the port of Dammam and seventy-five from Dhahran. The area immediately took on an ominous and more fitting name. The initial comment came from CW2 Carl Tucker from Georgia. "Holy shit, man. This place looks like Andersonville!" The people that knew of the reference to the infamous Confederate Prisoner of War camp of the American Civil War got a good laugh at the joke until they looked out the window and understood what Mr. Tucker saw. The laughter became strained, and the bus became quiet. The camp was wall-to-wall tents. Simple, OD green tents, General Purpose Medium, and they were only three feet apart. There were twenty-three rows on the left side of the bus and twenty-three rows on the right. More rows were being added on each side. They couldn't tell how deep the rows went, but it was at least ten deep. Hart Osborn did some quick calculations. He concluded from what he could see, 460 tents, which housed ten, maybe twelve people, that Andersonville held between 4,600 and 5,520 people. He was wrong.

Captain Krause met every bus and informed the Champions of their location and the direction for the troops to their new "castles in the sand." The Champions and some of the troops from HHT rode in on a bus together. Krause informed the people on the bus that C Troop was assigned C17 and C18. The HHT soldiers would be split between B7, B8, and B9. Tom did some quick calculation and could tell from the uproar in the back that the warrants had their calculators out too.

"Uh, Larry, we only get two tents? I've got thirty-two guys now. How we gonna fit everybody in two tents?" asked Tom. Wrong question. Obviously, Captain Krause had been asked this question before because his answer was canned.

He looked at Tom as if to say, "Give me a break!" and then addressed the bus. "Listen, fellas. We're lucky. We got fifteen tents assigned to us. They thought we had more people in our squadron than we have. Some of these guys have twenty in a tent, so quit cryin'!" explained the S4.

"How long do we have to stay here?" asked Tom.

"Expect two weeks," said Larry Krause. Krause was obviously busy and didn't have time to explain anymore. "There's a meeting for us at 1700 in B6. I gotta go. This place is nuts." Then he was out the door and running to the next bus.

Tom nodded and yelled out the door, "I can see that. See ya at 1700." Tom turned to face the troops. He expected a bunch of complaints and bitching. No one said a word. Tom looked from face to face and smiled. "*Os* will be in C17 and *Es* in C18. Top, I want you and the platoon sergeants on the end facing outside, and the lieutenants will be with me on that end in 17. Everybody listen up. We've only got thirteen officers, so we'll take three EMs in our tent to keep the space even." There was a mild protest, and Top Garcia got his boss's attention.

"Sir, if it's all the same to you, I think we'd all like to be together. There's gonna be more people coming, so if I can get all my people together now, we can get settled," said the Top.

Tom thought. Ran the numbers again. Damn. He was right. There'd be more people coming into the tents when the trail party got there.

"Roger, Top." He looked up at the Champions. "Let's go stake our claims, gentlemen!"

Thirteen people in a GP medium was too crowded for anyone to be comfortable. The nineteen enlisted soldiers in C18 were downright crunched in. Each tent had one stove that was placed two-thirds of the way into the tent, away from the main entrance. Three feet out the back exit was another tent. The officer's tent had at least two feet of space between the cots. Tight quarters for all concerned, but not unacceptable. The temperature got down to the thirtys at night, so the closeness was good. The folks that chose to sleep by the stove soon found out that the heat it generated was more than they needed.

Tom Lawton went to the meeting and listened to the status of the other units and how crowded they were. Sometimes, it was good to be the smallest troop. A Troop was overstrength by three people. They had nineteen in each tent. HHT was hurting for space, particularly the S3 shop. Tom swallowed hard and volunteered to take the Assistant 3, the Chemo, the S2, and the FSO. Hawk was surprised to see such team spirit. Tom had ulterior motives. By having the staff with his troop, chances improved that he would know what was going on and could prepare for movement or the inevitable changes quicker. Besides, they would be out of the tent at the TOC most of the time. His guys might bitch, but his thought process told him to take someone you know and could use rather than four unknown guys.

No one knew anything about the departure timeframe or plans to leave "Andersonville." Larry Krause said there were 7,300 people at the camp, and it could peak at ten to twelve thousand within two weeks. A huge meal was planned for Christmas Eve, and everyone would be there to eat. There wasn't much else to talk about. Maintain accountability, track hygiene, and keep the weapons clean. There was a little PX toward the front of camp for necessities and sweats, but not much else. Finally, the commanders were all told to have the troops keep their protective masks on at all times because the chances of SCUD missiles being fired with chemical munitions were "highly possible."

When Tom showed up with lieutenants Alvin and Sheppard; the S2, LT Corey O'Connor; and the new Assistant S3, CPT Nathan Brustad, he caught quite a blast of disgruntled warrant officers' comments. He and the new "guests" heard various remarks including, "Why we suckin' up to the staff? They don't do any work anyway!" "They don't get equal space, do they?" and "Are you guys homeless?"

But the "Schlep" was equal to the good-natured barbs and would quip one for one with each slur. Schlep returned the barbs with comments like, "I'm writing a book on discipline and wanted to get pointers from Mr. Walker. He didn't need to be homeless. He was from New Jersey." And then he started with sexual comments like, "I'm gonna sleep with cheap women when I get back, so I need to learn as much as I can from the warrants!"

As long as it remained good-natured fun, Tom would let it go. It took their minds off the challenges they were about to face. Andersonville was not the place for them to get focused. The time would come for that. Andersonville was a chance to adapt to the country and a routine. A grotesque, yet necessary stop on the road to war.

1730, December 24, 1990
Jubayl, Saudi Arabia

CHRISTMAS EVE, SAUDI-STYLE. THE HOSTS FOR the Christmas Eve dinner were very hospitable. Someone had done a good job preparing the Saudi hosts, and the dinner was outstanding considering the situation. The wind was howling off the Gulf, and the temperature had to be about twenty degrees with the windchill factor. Three Toyota pickup trucks were lined up, and the food was distributed off the back ends. Plenty of turkey, potatoes, beets, stuffing, and gravy were available. Not like home, but the attempt was nice.

The meal started at 1800. The line started at 1730. There wasn't much else for the soldiers to do. The lieutenants waited for Tom after the nightly command and staff meeting before going to dinner. At 1845, when they got out, the line was one single file for a quarter of a mile.

"Goddamn, sir! Why didn't you guys bullshit for another thirty minutes?" said Hal Timmons. "We might get a piece of bread by the time we get to those trucks!"

They laughed and continued to head to the end of the line. It moved fast, and when they got there thirty minutes later, there was still plenty of food, and the Pakistani servants had somehow managed to keep it warm. Two Saudi sheiks were at the end of the line, and at least three colonels were conversing with the hosts. Their English was surprisingly good, and they took the time to thank as many of the soldiers as they could and wished them well.

After the terrific, yet somewhat-tasteless meal, the small group of men found they were freezing. They hurriedly went to the "water pile." This area was a stack of *Evian* water bottles. It was stacked in cases about six high. Each officer grabbed two one-liter bottles and headed back to C17. The chain of command was always hot on "hydration," and keeping plenty of water handy was a task unto itself. The Champions would soon find another use for the trusty, ever-handy water bottle.

The close quarters inside C17 had become even closer with the addition of the staff. The space between bunks had become a mere six inches. All the gear, kit, and duffel bags and everything else were now stored under the cots. Outside C17, it was a two-hundred-yard walk to the nearest latrine. The wind was still ripping through the camp when the troopers had lights out. The soldiers still weren't into the sleep pattern yet, and no one could sleep. Some small chatter took place, but for the most part, it was quiet.

Suddenly, from about the middle of the dark tent came a strange sound. It got real quiet, but the sound persisted. Tom propped up on his elbows and listened intently. It was a sound he was familiar with but couldn't quite recognize.

From out of the darkness, Lawton heard, "Allen? What the fuck are you . . . ? Holy shit! He's pissin'! I don't fuckin' believe it? He's pissin' in that bottle!" cried out Tom Dolce.

As if on cue, sixteen flashlights were turned on and focused on CW2 Allen Berstein. Dolce was absolutely correct. Berstein was standing at the end of his bed, holding an Evian water bottle with one hand, and peeing into it with the other. The flashlights were all targeted on Berstein's crotch as he relieved himself. Everyone exploded in laughter. The flashlights became shaky as everyone started to jerk from laughing. Allen Berstein, now unable to control himself, began to laugh too. As he did so, his aim became unstable. "It's Christmas Eve, I'm in fucking Saudi Arabia, it's ten degrees outside, and I'm pissing in a water bottle," said Al Berstein. "This fuckin' sucks, man!"

"You piss on my fuckin' fart sack, and I'll show you something that sucks! I'm gonna rub your nose in it like a little kitten, you douche bag!" said John Walker. Everyone lost it. The lights turned into strobe lights pointing at the shaking man's groin from every direction. The whole tent joined in the frolic and showed Berstein no mercy. For what must have seemed like an eternity, Allen Berstein urinated in the water bottle while being relentlessly tormented by eighteen juvenile men chanting, howling, and shining flashlights on his now-forever-infamous manhood.

When he was done and the tent calmed down, Allen explained how he'd forgotten to go and he wasn't about to walk all the way down to the latrines in the cold, blowing wind.

Walker offered him an option. "From now on, 'fore we go to bed, I'll shove one of them fuckin' bottles on your dick, and you won't even have to get up!" That got the tent howlin' again. "You better have good fuckin' aim too! And don't you get it switched with my drinkin' water or I'll kick your ass!" continued the burly warrant, showing Berstein no mercy.

For the next five nights, nobody went to the latrines to pee. For the first two or three nights, everyone got out the flashlights and shined them on whomever the poor soul was that had to go. Eventually, the chuckling stopped. Within a week, the flashlights stopped coming on. By then, it had become routine, and everyone did it. They were cavalry soldiers doing cavalry things. As hygienically unsatisfactory as the act was, it saved precious sleeping time, and it was great for morale.

December 25, 1990
"Andersonville," Saudi Arabia

CHRISTMAS DAY WAS SPENT GETTING ORIENTED on the camp, talking to other soldiers and units, and getting some physical training in. Top was smart enough to bring a football, so the Champions got together to play some NBC mask football. Everywhere they went, soldiers had their protective masks with them. The Mission Oriented

Protection Posture, or MOPP level, called for everyone to keep the mask at the ready in case a SCUD missile attack came.

At the edge of camp, in a sandpit, the unit set up a field. The uniforms were standard army gray PT garb, the sand kept everyone from running too fast, and the mask was always in the way. Other units would show up to watch, and some soldiers would play. It took everyone's mind off the threat. After a couple hours, the games became more physical. When the soldiers started playing tackle, Top Garcia collected the ball and all the Champions on the field and headed back to C17. One protective mask was crushed during a pile on, and it took the rest of the day to get it replaced.

At the center of camp, all in a row were wash points. They alternated between shower points and sinks. They were in constant use. Troopers and soldiers, officers, and enlisted formed continuous lines at the points for shaving, brushing teeth, or washing clothes or bodies. The shower stalls were separate, and it was rare to find one with water that had been warmed at all by the sun. If there was water in it, someone was willing to use it no matter how cold it was. Few of the CAV troopers opted for showers. Most warmed about a gallon of water in the tent, poured it in a plastic bucket specifically designed for the hole, and carried it to the wash area. The buckets soon became hot items, and after two days, they were rationed by the logistics weenies that ran Andersonville.

Because water for the stalls was hard to come by, the guidance was issued that women would take showers every two days and men every three. Naturally, there were minor bitches pitched about equality. But for the most part, everyone accepted the guidance and executed it without reservation.

December 29, 1990
"Andersonville," Saudi Arabia

THE STAFF MEETING WAS ACTUALLY FRUITFUL that night. Information on the whereabouts of the squadron aircraft had come down. The ships had made it through the Suez Canal and were expected into Dammam any day. Lieutenant Colonel Hawk ordered Larry Krause, Darren Rooks, and CW4 John Townsend, the senior maintenance warrant, to go to the port for a recon. Krause had been to the warehouses that would house the Fighting Sixth and knew the location. There was ample space, but two days prior to the meeting, it was still occupied by a unit from Hanua. Rooks and Townsend were to get to the port and gather information on the off-loading and set up and launch procedures for all the aircraft.

Andersonville was beginning to wear on everyone. The closeness, the constant treks for everything from latrines to water, and long lines were causing even the best soldiers to become foul tempered. Lieutenant Colonel Hawk knew this and issued the warning order to prepare to move. The units' spirits were lifted immediately, and a more relaxed temperament fell over the unit again.

Replacements also showed up. Tom Lawton was amazed to find out the Champions had received two new soldiers. One was PFC Keith McFarland, a scout crew chief from Seattle, Washington. He was in the Individual Ready Reserve, a working civilian, when he got his letter. Three weeks later, he was in Andersonville. Lawton was worried that the newbie would be clueless, but to his surprise, McFarland had only been out of the army for six months. He was at least six feet two inches tall and obviously overweight. He must have weighed 250. When Tom interviewed McFarland, he found out he was a vehicle mechanic in the civilian world and a part-time drummer in a rock band. Before Tom could ask him about drugs, the large redheaded young private informed his new commander that he was not into "that scene" and he was "damn glad to be here." Tom was momentarily ashamed of his stereotypical thought. To his credit, the newbie was aware of the image his part-time job presented and understood his new boss's reservations.

The second new guy was a warrant officer one, fresh out of the Apache aircraft qualification course at Fort Rucker, Alabama. He was five foot eight and appeared to be about sixteen years old. WO1 Timothy Harmon was instantly designated Boy Warrant by his brethren. Mr. Harmon was from some backwoods area in southern Missouri. He liked "both kinds of music, country and Western; watching things blow up; and Walt Disney movies." A strange combination for a young man with a contagious smile and a down-to-earth manner. Tom told him he didn't have a PIC for him yet, but he promised he'd get Harmon in the air as much as everyone else. The new warrant understood, and he too was simply happy to be there.

Although welcomed with open arms by the rest of the troop, both newbies were immediately tagged as butt boys from their peer group. If anything had to be done, water, fuel for the stove, more MREs, these two were the first choices as the gofer.

Their timing was great. They only had to spend one night in Andersonville. The next day, the Fighting Sixth moved to Ad Dammam.

December 31, 1990
Ad Dammam, Saudi Arabia

THE TWO-HOUR BUS RIDE SOUTHEAST WENT by fast. The time to leave the cluster of Jubayl could not have come soon enough. Morale increased immediately, and the talk changed to aircraft and fighting Iraq. A new breath of camaraderie swept through the unit.

Upon arrival at Dammam, the buses drove around the area for a quick recon. The warehouses were built on a man-made point that went out into the Gulf about a half mile. There were five huge buildings close to the edge of the water. Rumors ran through the warehouses that the waters had poisonous sea snakes in them. No one knew for sure, but no one tried to go swimming either. The observation was made that the locals didn't get in the water, so that added to the rumor. The talk then changed accusing the chain of command of starting the rumor to keep the troopers from swimming. Even though the water was cold, Tom thought for sure some idiot might try it and briefed his people accordingly.

Because the point the port was built on was man-made, the ships could pull right next to the warehouses where cranes were located to off-load the cargo. Two of the Fighting Sixth's three ships were lucky enough to be ROROs. These ships had the ability to roll cargo on and roll it off. The time to off-load or on load these types of ships was reduced by half over the standard freight carriers. Dammam at first appearance seemed to be unorganized confusion, but the transportation boys knew what they were doing, and they did their jobs well. Those folks wasted no time or effort.

Larry Krause waited until the whole unit was off the buses to address everyone at one time. "Welcome to the port of Dammam. The warehouse to my rear is the site of our new home until the aircraft are ready to fly out.

The whole squadron will be in there along with the 227th. They will only be here for another three days. I have maps for all troops, and they will be issued to you by the S2, Lieutenant O'Connor. The situation is almost the same as Jubayl. The latrines and showers are behind you, but the food will be served at the far end of the warehouse. The first shipment of aircraft and equipment is expected in tomorrow morning, so Happy New Year." That got a big cheer out of the assembled crowd.

Captain Krause turned the formation over to the troop commanders, and the process of occupying the warehouse began. Space was reconned, and an advanced party was established to set up cots. It was amazing to watch how orderly the routine of occupying living areas had become. An unwritten standard operating procedure (SOP) had been established, and no one was dumb enough to try to organize it or write down the process. At that point, it worked better letting the soldiers do what was natural to them.

That night, the squadron was fed another terrific meal catered by the hosts. Though most troops turned in, the commander, staff, troop commanders, and some of the senior warrants stayed up till midnight to toast some "nonalcoholic" wine and beer for New Year's. Tom had the urge for a "real beer" but didn't mention it to anyone else. Every so often, he would find his hands shaking a bit, and the feelings associated with the involuntary movement made him anxious. He wasn't sure if it was DTs or his nerves.

Lieutenant Colonel Hawk thanked everyone for their effort to date and reminded the assembled crowd that it was getting time to get "their game faces on." Everyone agreed with the boss and soon turned in.

Tom lay on his cot and thought about how his previous New Year's were spent. He would have been two sheets in the wind by now if he were home. He quickly dismissed the notion and made his New Year's resolution for 1991. There was only one. He was going to bring everybody back from this, no matter what it took.

January 3, 1991
Dammam, Saudi Arabia

NEARLY EVERY ITEM THE WAR MACHINE needed came through the port at Dammam. Every class of supply from water to tanks, medical supplies to artillery shells, and everything in between. All the materials needed some place to be stored. There were so many tons of materials that the time came when it could no longer be stored in a controlled area, so the material began to stack up on the side of the pier.

Time is a terrible thing in the hands of idle soldiers. Not that they become mischievous or anything. Man is that way by nature. The troopers of the Fighting Sixth just happen to have an abundance of time on their hands that sunny afternoon.

Freshly off-loaded from one ship were one hundred tons of 155mm cannon rounds. The port operations personnel had no place to move the rounds, so they sat on the dockside until the proper personnel were available to relocate the ammunition.

Not intent on mischief, a small group of Champion warrant officers managed to stumble upon the neatly stacked rounds. The felt pens came out, and the artistry commenced. Messages for Saddam, pictures, graffiti, and military poetry (colorful to say the least) were added to the ammo.

That night at the command and staff meeting, the word was put out. No one goes near the ammunition. Tom had already gotten word about the good time the troops had, so rather than speak up or ask stupid questions, he kept a low profile. Lieutenant Colonel Hawk said that someone was pretty damn pissed off about the whole deal and that if it continued, the units in port would pull guard duty on the rounds to "prevent vandalism." He was damn glad that none from his troopers had participated. Immediately, the assembled crowd turned their heads to Tom and smiled. Lieutenant Colonel Hawk was not amused.

Conversation then turned to actions in case of a SCUD attack. The crowd grew silent and looked around the area. No location was designated as a bomb shelter. The thought dawned on Tom, *What if the top of this hangar had a great big target painted on it? Hell, the whole port was one big target.* Chris Wise quipped, "I didn't come all this way to die twitching' in some hangar with shit in my pants!"

Lieutenant Colonel Hawk said that a Patriot missile battery protected the entire city and there was nothing to worry about. Nothing had happened yet that indicated a need to be alarmed. That satisfied everyone for the time being. But as the meeting broke up, Chris Wise's off-the-cuff comment hit home. Everyone wondered about the effects of nerve agents or blister agents. The off-the-cuff comment was no longer that humorous. How soon could they get out of the port?

January 4, 1991
Dammam, Saudi Arabia

THE AIRCRAFT FINALLY ARRIVED IN PORT. Each troop sent a team of six troopers to the download area to help assemble aircraft for test flights. Another three troopers were sent as part of the team to download other equipment. The operations were round the clock, so day and night teams were established. All the aviation maintenance personnel and IPs worked during the daylight hours. It took three straight days to download all the ships. Yet the real work had only begun.

Someone somewhere decided it would be a great idea if "environmental protection material" were placed on the rotor blades. Apparently, units already in the desert were experiencing a tremendous amount of wear on the leading edge of the rotor blades. To combat this environmental damage, a four-inch-wide strip of rubber was glued to the leading edge of every blade. The material covered the main rotor and the tail rotor from the tip to within a foot of the root. The rubber strips were put on the blades in a separate hangar location and then mounted onto the waiting airframe that was then rolled out for engine run-up.

The man-hours used to place the rubber stripping on the rotors could not really be assessed. Different teams worked on different blades, and every aircraft that came through was having the process done. The intent was to save wear and tear on the blades. It was a good idea, but the process kept the unit in port for another week. And that wasn't the only problem. Soon enough, the unit would find out how well the strips worked.

January 9, 1991
Dammam, Saudi Arabia

LIEUTENANT COLONEL HAWK WAS FINALLY SATISFIED the unit was ready to launch. Only two more Apaches and one Blackhawk needed to be test-flown. The advance party of Larry Krause, Steve Sheppard, and three troopers departed at 0700 in two Humvees. CPT Richard Blakely, the HHT commander, would be responsible for closing the port operations and the warehouse when the unit completed operations in Dammam. Paperwork needed to be taken care of because the squadron had signed for twenty-four new Humvees. The last Blackhawk would stay behind with one Hummer to bring the trail party out to Assembly Area Gomez.

Preparations were made for early-morning departures on the tenth. A Troop would leave at 0700, B Troop at 0800, and C Troop at 0900. Lieutenant Colonel Hawk would depart with A Troop in the first Blackhawk. C Troop would have the trail maintenance Blackhawk with them. Routes were planned, double-checked, and triple-checked. The aircraft were preflighted that afternoon, and the mission was briefed before dinner. The entire unit was put to bed early that night, but very few people slept.

0900, January 10, 1991
Dammam, Saudi Arabia

THE CHAMPIONS DEPARTED ON TIME WITH six Apaches, four OH-58s, and the Blackhawk. Chief Warrant Officer 4 Townsend and Warrant Officer 1 Harmon flew the sixth aircraft. Because Townsend was an instructor pilot as well as the senior maintenance pilot, he could fly with the new aviator. Lieutenant Colonel Hawk had to approve the crew, which he did without hesitation. The mission was simple: get the squadron to AA Gomez.

One thing that struck Tom as ironic was the fact that they departed without ammunition. There wasn't even a FARP established to get ammunition. No 30mm, no rockets, and definitely no Hellfire. They were headed to a war zone and didn't even have rounds in their pistols.

The route took the squadron up the highway past Jubayl. It looked bigger from the air. About eighty miles past Andersonville was the refuel point. It was set up directly to the northwest of the only road intersection in the area. The Champions spotted the Werewolves headed west out of FARP "Junction," so occupying the unfamiliar FARP area was not a problem.

At the FARP, the refuelers looked worn out and tired. Tom got out, used the latrine, and talked to the NCOIC. Some of the soldiers had been there on and off for three months. The sergeant said they weren't allowed to go into the town three miles away. Apparently, only ten years ago, the village had to be relocated because a bubonic plague had wiped out the original location. A scant twenty-five miles to the north lay Kuwait. Marine Corps Cobras patrolled the area along the coastline, but only a few army helicopters ever stopped there. The NCO did say that business was picking up, but he had little else to talk about.

Forty-five minutes later, the Champions were off the ground. Hal Timmons called the flight was clear, and they headed west into Indian country. The route called for the unit to follow the Trans-Arabian Pipeline Highway, or Tapline Road, to Air Check Point Hotel and maintain two hundred feet AGL. This point was five miles short of a village named Hafar Al-Batin. Thinking the enemy may have spies or sympathizers in this town, the ACP was planned short of the town to prevent anyone in the area from seeing the occupation. A good plan in theory. However, the desert terrain didn't allow success in this area. After the junction, the area to the west was thousands of square miles of nothing, just miles and miles of perfectly flat sand. There were no terrain features of any kind. The highway was the only known point for miles. Ten miles prior to ACP Hotel, the Champions saw Hafar Al-Batin. Anyone with binoculars could have seen the unit come into the area. At ACP Hotel, the unit turned directly south for twenty miles to enter AA Gomez.

Ten miles away, they could see the dust clouds on the horizon. There were no other vehicles in the AA. The aviation assets were the first to occupy, except for advance parties. The squadron was to occupy the area furthest to the south in the AA. It was smack dab in the middle of nowhere.

As briefed, the troop overflew the entire area and flew to the area that would be C Troop's location. Fuel HEMMITs were planned to be rolling into the area no later than 1500. Until then, they would have to sit and wait. The only thing in the Champion area was the three-man shower stall and a three-hole crapper. Captain Lawton decided they shouldn't burn any more fuel. The unit landed in an area that resembled the surface of Mars.

One at a time, the aircraft landed. Passing through seventy feet, the dust kicked up. At twenty feet, visibility was zero. Walker literally planted the bird into the desert, and the dust eventually cleared.

"Sorry, sir. But I needed to put it on the ground. I couldn't see shit!" said Chief Warrant Officer 3 Walker.

"No sweat, man. I think it's going to take us all some time to get used to this," said Tom.

He looked out to see the Champions landing. Sometimes, he could only see the dust clouds, which shot up seventy to eighty feet in the air, covering the Apaches in a tremendous brown cloud. One or two birds took the Walker method of planting the aircraft quickly into the dirt. These clouds would only climb to forty or fifty feet, and Tom could see through them to the aircraft. That was the technique they would use. It may be tougher on the airframe, but it was much safer on the pilots. They immediately shut down and did postflights.

As the area became quiet, Tom looked around. He climbed up on top of 220 and looked around. Absolutely nothing to see in any direction. The Fighting Sixth was the first asset in the corps to enter AA Gomez. They were eighteen Apaches, two Blackhawks, thirteen OH-58s, and the men that flew them. No ammo. No fuel except what was in the tanks. No support. Tom knew somebody had to be first. He just imagined it would be infantry or armor guys. He took another long look and saw his men gathering at the latrine. An uneasy feeling crept up inside him, and for the first time since Reforger '86, his stomach was churning. He looked down at his hands. They were trembling. It definitely wasn't DTs anymore.

CHAPTER 8

January 12, 1991
AA Gomez, Saudi Arabia

THE REST OF THE SQUADRON ARRIVED in Gomez by 1700. It took them less than twenty-four hours to get established. Lieutenant Colonel Hawk's priority was simple: get the unit flying. And that mission started almost immediately. The IPs, then the PICs, and then the remaining crew members would become "sand qualified" as soon as time permitted. Tom taught that strange considering they already flew into the area, but the guidance was for everyone to do a takeoff and landing in the sand.

Gomez was oriented to the north toward Iraq. The situation dictated that the squadron spread out as much as possible. In the environment they were in, it could have been miles. The overall shape could have been considered an oval with D Troop directly north, C Troop to the east, B Troop facing south, and A Troop oriented facing west. HHT was in the center, for it had all the classes of support, the chow tent, and the tactical operations center (TOC). From north to south, the AA stretched nearly a mile. From east to west, the assembly area was less than three quarters of a mile. A and C troops deliberately maintained close proximity to HHT to save time and resources. B and D troops were more independent, a reflection of their commander's attitude toward the squadron commander and his staff, the thought being, the further away my troop is, the less chance the commander will be in my AO.

In AA Gomez, Hawk went wherever he wanted and was equally abusive to all his subordinate commanders. The captains noticed Hawk had developed a much shorter temper these days. Chris Wise thought Hawk had a big wheel that the commander would spin first thing in the morning. Whichever commander's troop came up on top received the ass chewing for the day. Chris Wise also thought B Troop was on Hawk's wheel twice as often as his peers.

Tom Lawton and the Champions had been lucky early. First Sergeant Garcia had done a good job of keeping up with the sergeant major and anticipating what the colonel would look for. Top Garcia had the area squared away. The GP Mediums were both up, with camouflage in place. The two GP Small tents housed the leaders, Top and the platoon sergeants in one and Lawton and the lieutenants in the other. A smaller six-man tent was set up as the briefing tent or Troop TOC. The vehicles were always dispersed, and Garcia was great when it came to the crew chiefs. They were constantly on the aircraft or fixing up the area. He was good enough to recognize when they were tired or needed a break. To a man, they respected Roberto Garcia. Top knew Hawk's peeves were camouflage, trash, communications, and tardiness. Garcia ensured the radio, and eventually, the landline to the Squadron TOC were manned twenty-four hours a day. The troop members were never late or missing from meetings that were called spontaneously because of this effort by the first sergeant. The troops' minor success up to this time was due directly to the influence and dynamic leadership of First Sergeant Garcia.

This day would be spent flying the non-PIC crew members. All the PICs had been "signed off" as desert qualified on the previous day. Now the fun really began as the less-experienced aviators and front seaters got to try their hand at landing in the "dust bowl." Tom was anxious and was the first one off that morning. It was a beautiful day. The sun was coming up, and there wasn't a cloud in the sky. There was no wind to speak of, and the conditions were perfect for flying. Once he and Nichols were airborne, Tom didn't want to come down. He was in his element in the helicopter. Even though the view from two hundred feet was the same in every direction, just the fact that Tom was flying made him comfortable. As great as the view was at altitude flying in the front seat, landing was a different story.

When landing, the lack of visibility in the front seat was magnified. Upon decreasing speed, it was natural for the nose of the helicopter to come up. When this happened, the pilot night vision system on the nose of the aircraft took away even more visibility, making it extremely difficult to see the intended landing point.

As Tom came around for his first approach, he found himself tightening up on the controls. This only exacerbated his control problems. At sixty feet AGL, Tom saw the brown cloud forming. He continued to slow and felt the aircraft go through effective translational lift (ETL). The shudder of ETL was familiar to Tom, but he seemed to be staying in it way too long. He felt Nichols pull up on the collective as he arrested the descent. To his direct front, Tom couldn't see a thing. He quickly glanced out the side and could see the ground coming up much faster than normal. Nichols gave him assistance by continuing to let the aircraft drop. The natural tendency at the end of the maneuver would be to arrest the faster-than-normal descent. The seven-ton helicopter continued downward, and Nichols input a slightly noticeable forward cyclic to keep the bird moving forward. Tom was definitely uncomfortable by the input because he could no longer see a thing to his front. Tom got stiff in his seat as the big aircraft hit the ground hard. It wasn't hard enough to lock his shoulder harness, but it got his attention.

"I didn't like that one bit," said Tom.

"I know it feels uncomfortable, but you can't slow down, and you've got to plant it! If you let the aircraft waddle, you'll brown out more than what we just did and roll this baby over," explained the instructor pilot. "Then Walker will never let you have the controls."

Tom laughed and relaxed at the comment. "He rarely lets me have 'em anyway!"

"He will after I'm done with you. Let's go do it again," said the instructor pilot. "You have the controls. Remember, we want an altitude over airspeed takeoff. Let's get up about fifty feet before you nose it over."

The takeoff was much better than the landing. It was the same type of takeoff as a maximum-performance takeoff without the visibility. The next traffic pattern was much better. Tom was getting comfortable again. The second approach was all Lawton's. At ten feet, he glanced to his left and saw he had zeroed his forward airspeed, so he deliberately input forward cyclic. Almost too much, but Nichols caught the action and told him to perform a go-around. They continued with the traffic pattern, and Tom had some minor problems keeping his airspeed at eighty knots. Nichols kept Tom checking his horizon that seemed to help solve the constant changes in airspeed. With the forward airspeed corrected, Tom entered the approach and took it to the ground. The aircraft landed roughly, but with the rotor's right side up. "That's what we're looking for. What you just did. Now prove that wasn't a fluke. Let's do it one more time," said Nichols.

"Roger, one more time. A before takeoff check, please," said Tom.

The instructor pilot checked the instruments and looked around for more aircraft and had none in sight. "You're clear." The takeoff was virtually flawless. Tom took the liberty to extend the pattern and fly around some. He knew he'd be getting out soon, and he was enjoying his time in the air. It was the only place he could control the temperature of his environment. The third approach was much better. Although he knew he would never get used to the sight picture of the steep-angled approach and the abruptness of the landing, he knew that was the way to do it.

"Good job, sir. You're done," said Nichols.

Tom hesitated. He didn't want to get out. He looked in the mirror and met the instructor pilot's eyes.

"Come on, sir. I've got six other guys to do. If I let you fly much more, somebody else might miss his turn. Besides, the wear and tear on the aircraft needs to be kept to a minimum," said the instructor pilot.

Tom knew he was right. There'd be more time for this later. It just felt so good to fly again. The trip from Dammam didn't really count. Tom looked outside and saw Hart Osborn looking rather impatient. It was time to go. "If you can, let that new guy Harmon take about thirty minutes or so. Thanks." Tom disconnected his headset without waiting for a response.

Hart Osborn climbed in, and Tom went over and talked to Walker and Tucker. They talked about flying in the sand. As Tom was about to walk away, Walker asked him to walk with him, and the two turned away from the crowd that had gathered.

Walker started the conversation. "Sir, I . . . I'm not real sure how to start this off," said the big warrant.

Tom looked at him and could tell something was wrong. "What's up, John?"

The warrant looked around to see if anyone else was around. They continued walking toward Tom Lawton's tent. "I think I'm going through alcohol withdrawal," said John Walker.

Tom looked at the warrant and could tell he was serious. "How bad?" asked Tom.

"My hands were shakin' like leaves on a tree last night. I couldn't sleep worth a damn. And I admit I've got the urge for booze of any kind," said John. He added, "I ain't the only one either."

It was Tom's turn to look around this time. "You're right about that. Can you keep a secret?"

"Yes, sir," said Walker.

"I just got over the DTs myself. I had 'em pretty bad at Jubayl. I still have the urge for something to drink, but not nearly as bad as when we were in the port. I don't know about this stuff. I'm not a doctor. I think the only thing that can help is time," Tom said to the warrant. "Dr. Williams should be out here any day. When he comes, I can get you over to see him if you want?"

The warrant nodded. "I may want to do that, sir."

"Spread the word to the others. If you don't want to fly for a while, I'll understand. I'm feeling better after getting a pretty good night's sleep and flying this morning. It took my mind off . . . you know, wanting a drink. Not to mention, took me away from"—he waved his hand up in the air—"all this." He smiled at the warrant. "We'll start PT sessions soon, and that will help us sweat some of this out. How many others?"

"At least three," said Walker.

"You talk to 'em, John. I know where they're coming from. I'll do whatever I can to help. But we need to keep this to the doc or ourselves. He'd help us out if we need him." Tom thought about the alternative to the situation and added, "If we let this out, they'll ground every one of us." He didn't have to emphasize *us*.

"I know, sir. And I'm not using this as a cop-out." Walker slowed his walk. "I just felt that you should know because you'll be flying with me. If you don't want to, I'll understand."

"I told you before, I can't do this without you. We're in this together. All of us," said Tom.

"All right, sir. I'm sure we'll be better later on. It's just damn hard to concentrate right now. My control touch is shot to hell. Look." Walker held up his hands, and they were visibly shaking.

Tom held out his hands, and the trembling he had was gone. He was thankful the anxiety he experienced two days ago wasn't showing today. "They go away." He looked back and smiled. "Besides, your control touch will still be better than mine." They both laughed. "Go back to the fart sack and relax the best you can. Come see me tomorrow and I'll talk to Doc when he gets here."

The big warrant replied, "Roger, sir. Thanks. Thanks for understanding." He turned and headed for his tent.

January 14, 1991
AA Gomez, Saudi Arabia

THE DAYS STARTED TO BECOME ROUTINE again. They started at 0600 with a ritual known as stand to. The crew chiefs and pilots would get out of their bunks, go to the aircraft, and crank them up. Lieutenants Osborn and Timmons improved daily in their duties. Tom had complete confidence and trust in either lieutenant to handle any mission, big or small. Hart Osborn could probably command the troop if he were called on to do so. Walker and the other warrants that had been feeling "uneasy" were doing much better. They were not completely dried out but were functional. At this point, that was all Tom expected. Their status, if brought to Hawk's attention, would have had them grounded indefinitely.

As Tom walked back from his run-up of 220 with Walker, he couldn't help but notice his crew chief had flea collars on his boots. "Specialist Padillo, what is that crap you've got dangling around those Hush Puppy boots?"

"Those are flea collars, sir! We all got 'em on to keep the sand fleas from climbing up our legs," said the specialist.

Tom wasn't really pissed, merely confused. Tom said, "Look around you. You see any fleas?" Tom had read that the flea collars had a pesticide called Dursban in them. Troopers in other units were wearing them without authorization. Tom wasn't certain if the flea collars were a good idea. Between the flea collars and the DEET insect repellent, Tom was afraid the troops would get sick from the pesticides. "We've been here four days now, and I ain't seen bugs, critters, or varmints. Nor have I felt anything on my legs that indicates we need those things. Until somebody can show me a sand flea or a scorpion or a fuckin' rat, you guys keep that shit off your legs. Besides, those things are probably worse for you than a damn fleabite. Pass the word. Unless somebody is getting eaten up by bites, no more of those things." Tom shook his head and looked at Walker.

"Flea collars. They'll be callin' us the kennel over here. You ever heard of such a thing?"

Walker stopped and pulled up the pant leg of his flight suit. "Yeah, I have." He too had flea collars on his boots. Tom shook his head and kept walking.

Back at the tents, Tom walked in to the crew chiefs' GP Medium. He was nearly knocked over by the smell. It was a combination of sweat, funk, and bug spray. They were keeping the sides of the tent down to prevent the entry of unwanted insects. Tom understood their point but didn't understand how they could live with the smell. He called Garcia and brought him in. After Garcia stopped yelling about "fucking, bastard maggots," he listened to Tom long enough to get the message. They needed to get the place cleaned up and aired out and do laundry. The crew chiefs needed to knock off the DEET insect repellent and let the tents get air flowing through them. No one knew how long they would be there, and Tom felt that these conditions would only lead to sickness. Within thirty minutes, the task was accomplished, and the crew chiefs were doing laundry.

The warrants were slower to react, but two hours later, the unit was out of water. HMMWVs, or Hummers as the troopers called them, were sent to get water, and the word got out that the whole squadron was already running low. Tom sent Hal Timmons on a recon in an OH-58. Four hours later, he returned.

"No sweat on the water, sir." The lieutenant was positively beaming.

"What did you do?" asked Tom.

"I found a truck over by brigade headquarters. They didn't know where to go, so I . . . helped them get a recon of the AO!" said Hal.

Tom just looked at the lieutenant. "You gave a ride in your helicopter to some *water guy?*"

"Yes, sir," said the lieutenant. He added, "They didn't know where we were."

Tom thought about it. He thought about the ass chewin' he'd get from Hawk for this one. Then again, if Hawk knew, he would have gotten chewed by now. At least no one got hurt. Lawton thought he'd better keep a lid on this before it got out of hand. "I don't want you doing any more crap like that again, you understand?" Something on the lieutenant's face told Tom that he didn't understand.

Hal Timmons reached into his pocket. He pulled out ammunition. Timmons had .38 rounds, 9mm rounds, and 7.62 rounds. "Where the hell did you get that?" asked Tom.

"Some guys I gave a ride to," said the lieutenant, suppressing a smile.

Tom thought hard. If Hawk found out, they were screwed. Tom looked at Timmons and said, "You know what they say about the hard right versus the easy wrong?" The lieutenant nodded with a smile. "It would be too easy for us to sit on our asses and wait for the support to kick in, right?" Timmons was beaming. "Can you get more?" he asked.

"Yes, sir," answered the lieutenant while he tried to suppress a huge smile.

Tom did an about-face and walked away. If Hawk found out about this, Lawton would spend the rest of the war in Dammam. "All right, goddamn it! What are you waiting for! Go get as much as you can!"

"Roger that, sir!" The lieutenant saluted.

As he started to run away, Tom added, "And you better take O'Toole and Cross with you." Timmons laughed and saluted again. "And don't have an accident!" hollered Tom.

Thirty minutes later, a water truck pulled up and filled all the available water cans as well as the showers. Morale improved that evening when rounds were distributed. Everyone had their laundry done and had taken lukewarm showers. Timmons brought back enough ammo for everyone. They had enough to send some extra ammo cans to their sister troops on the perimeter.

Earlier in the day, a load of metal pallets arrived for the purpose of hard stands to park the helicopters on. The pallets were quickly laid out, and training to land on the pads immediately commenced. On his third approach, Chief Warrant Officer 4 Needles and one of the front seaters from A Troop got too slow. The rotor wash from the aircraft caught the metal and blew it straight up into the TADS. Lieutenant Colonel Hawk immediately ceased all flights to the hard stands until they were sandbagged on three sides. The results of this incident were one banged-up TADS bucket, one day spent filling sandbags by the entire squadron, and one very bruised ego for the squadron's senior instructor pilot. He handled the ribbing he took from the other pilots with calm understanding, knowing that it could have been them just as easily.

One thing good about the pallets was they soaked up heat all day long and put out a tremendous infrared signature at night. This was a definite plus. For that night, the night qualifications began.

To everyone's surprise, night flying was easier. Flying with the FLIR and using the picture it generated provided a better view so the pilots could see where they would land. Even without the metal pallets, the symbology generated in the Helmet Display Unit made for smoother approaches. Every pilot flew that night. The next day, they would start collective training.

0200, January 15, 1991
AA Gomez, Saudi Arabia

"SIR, THE AMMO'S HERE." IT WAS Specialist Cryder. He just woke Tom up.

Lawton had only gotten to sleep about an hour ago, but he knew what needed to be done. "All right. Thanks." He wiped his face. "Go to all the tents. I want you to get every swingin' guy out of the rack and let's get 'em loaded. Got that? Everybody. Even the scouts. Move."

The rumble of the HEMTT cargo truck could be heard coming. Tom quickly dressed and got outside. It was cold, and there was a steady drizzle of rain. Imagine that, thought Tom, rain smack-dab in the middle of a thousand square miles of desert.

Of course there were gripes and bitches. No one enjoyed getting woken up to go out in the rain. They were already out of the rack before the word came over the landline that the Hellfires and rockets would be loaded tonight. Fifty miles from the border, the Champions thought no way in hell Saddam was going to get to Gomez within the next five hours. He'd have to pass through the whole damn Fifth Corps. But an order was an order, and Tom wasn't going to fall on his sword over this one. He agreed with Hawk. Get them loaded at the earliest possible time.

The loading went slowly in the dark. The rain was no help. It made the missiles slippery and contributed to the length of time it took to load them. By five o'clock, they were done. Top had coffee ready for anyone that wanted it. Only a handful did. Sleep was the most precious thing at that point. It didn't matter that stand to was coming in an hour. A good CAV soldier in Indian country will take one hour of dry sleep in a heartbeat if he can get it. For the effort, Tom postponed the day flights until 1500. After stand to, he put everyone down again, and the Champions skipped the hot breakfast offered at the mess tent.

Tom briefed the first collective mission. He added a few twists to the routine. The scouts would go out fifteen minutes early and establish the perimeters off the BP. All crews would fly with armor plating commonly referred to as chicken vests. And talk on the radio was limited to only the Uniform frequency. The purpose was to get them in the mind-set to train the way they would fight. This was the first time many of them had worn the armored vest, and they needed to get used to it. The only reason Tom hated the vest was because it rode on his bladder. He had a notoriously small bladder, and with the vest on, he always had to pee.

They took the mission slow and easy. The results were positive as indicated by the after-action review. The consensus was they were ready to try it at night. Tom balked at first, not feeling they were ready. He looked at Nichols and Hart Osborn. They both nodded their approval.

"All right, we'll do it. But not tonight. I need to talk to the colonel about it." The crowd began to heckle Tom, so he got their attention. "Listen. Listen to me. He needs to know if we're going to try a troop mission. Take the next twenty-four hours for maintenance and we'll be ready for the night flight. Hal, get the water truck over here again tomorrow if you can and let's wash the aircraft. Lieutenant Osborn, you, Mr. Walker, Mr. Berstein, and Mr. Tucker get them ready to go. Mr. Harmon, I will talk to Lieutenant Colonel Hawk and see if I can borrow Chief Warrant Officer 4 Townsend, and we will do a six-ship night vision system mission. Get a good night's sleep and we'll see you all in the morning at stand to."

That night, after the command and staff meeting, Tom waited to talk to Lieutenant Colonel Hawk and Jerry Maurer about the flight.

"Sir, I'd like to fly a six-ship NVS mission tomorrow night. We think we're ready," explained Tom.

Captain Maurer couldn't believe it. "You guys are ready to fly collective night system already?"

"I swear we're ready, sir." Tom almost believed it himself. "I'll brief it down to the gnat's ass, sir. My guys think they can do it," said Tom.

Hawk wasn't so sure. Tom could see it in his eyes. He looked at the S3, who simply shrugged his shoulders and said, "Somebody's gotta go first!"

"All right. But brief me tomorrow afternoon on your plan," said the commanding officer.

Tom smiled. "Roger that, sir. Is 1400 good?"

"That's fine," said the commander. Tom started to leave, but Hawk called him back. Tom felt his stomach start to churn. "What's this I'm hearing about your guys giving rides to some of the support weenies?"

Tom started to think of some way to avoid the truth. But one look at Maurer told Tom that Hawk already knew. "Not really gave them rides, per se," Tom hedged. "We simply traded."

"You . . . traded?" asked the commander.

"Yes, sir. We . . ." Tom fainted a nervous cough. "We traded an area recon for certain classes of supply that we deemed necessary to support the mission." Tom added, "Sir." He could see the wheels turning in Hawk's mind.

Hawk looked at Maurer. "So that's where the ammunition came from?" The lieutenant colonel smiled. As quickly as it appeared, it just as abruptly faded. "You didn't give them rides in Apaches, did you?"

"Oh, no, sir! We can't afford the wear and tear on them for support weenies, sir!" said Tom.

The colonel nodded his understanding but then added, "You need to watch that shit! If something happens and one of those aircraft gets messed up, we'll all go to jail!"

Tom had one more thought but was almost afraid to ask it. He went for it anyway. "Sir, if I could find the guy with the grader, would it be all right if I . . . gave him a recon of the AO? He might be able to find us and get a berm dug around our perimeter."

Hawk smiled and nodded. "All right, Young Captain. But I want O'Toole to fly these guys. That way, if something does happen, you've got an instructor pilot at the controls."

Tom smiled back and said, "Roger, sir!" He started to leave when the Hawk stopped him again.

"One more thing. You've got five or six guys over there that think this is Club Med," said the colonel.

Tom was dumbfounded. "I don't understand, sir?"

"You got a bunch of warrant officers lyin' around, getting suntans, like they're at the beach or some shit. Get some discipline over there," said the commanding officer.

Tom was at a loss for words. Who the hell was doing that? The temperature barely got over seventy degrees. All he could muster was a meek "Yes, sir." He saluted and left.

Tom stormed across the assembly area and went straight into the warrant officer's tent. He wasn't sure what they were talking about when he walked in, but he was sure he didn't want to know.

Mr. Tucker was talking. "I'm serious, man. I heard that they put gerbils up their ass!" The tent erupted in laughter.

Tom was visibly pissed off, but the mood of his warrants took some steam off his anger.

"At ease!" hollered Mr. Weimer.

Tom did not say "Carry on" as was his usual custom. He slowly walked down the center of the tent. The pilots slowly but surely got to their feet and came to the position of attention. Tom started slowly, "I know I'm not the biggest prick in this man's army, and I know you guys aren't the biggest idiots. So why the *fuck* is anyone trying to get a suntan when it's not even that *goddamn sunny outside*? Can anyone explain that to me! Huh? What the fuck is goin' on in your heads? This is a goddamn attack aviation unit. You don't think people flyin' around here see what your doin'?" Tom got control of his emotions again. "I don't care who's doin' it. It just needs to stop. Any questions?"

No one said anything. Tom started to leave.

"We didn't know it was off-limits to suntan, sir," said Carl Tucker.

Tom stopped and looked at him. "Use your heads, fellas." Tom shook his head and continued walking. He knew he couldn't leave them when he was pissed off. They should have known better than to lie around getting suntans while everyone else in the AA was working. Hell, they should have known not to get seen. Tom was really mad at himself for not knowing what was going on in his own AO. He turned at the door and said, "I know how this lifestyle is probably gettin' on your nerves, but I'm livin' with Osborn and Timmons. So I'm sure you guys can keep your shit together!" That broke the tension. Tom shook his head and started out the door. "By the way, right before the squadron commander informed me in no uncertain terms that I've got a bunch of slackers, he approved our flight for tomorrow night. Get to sleep. You'll need it."

Just as he started to feel a little better, more bad news would come. He got into his tent, and Hart Osborn was there with Penny. "What's up?" asked Tom.

Hart Osborn took a deep breath and came clean. "Not much, sir."

"What?" Tom yelled. He knew exactly what Hart meant by the comment, but he was dying to hear the explanation. "What's the matter?"

"We've got four birds down, and two are down hard." Hart didn't want to be the bearer of bad news. But he had never had to fear being "the messenger" before. This time was different.

"Goddamn it!" snapped Tom. What else could go wrong? "I tell the pilots we're approved for tomorrow night's flight, and now you guys are telling me we don't have the aircraft to do the mission. That's just perfect, isn't it?" Tom threw his equipment on his cot. He tried to get control of himself, but he was tired, and he always got cranky when he didn't get enough sleep. Tom took a deep breath and rubbed his eyes. "All right. Let's hear it."

Hart could read his boss's mood and was very formal in his delivery of the bad news. "Sir, we've got one aircraft down for NVS problems. One has some of that rubber coming off one of the main rotor blades. 956 has a hydraulic caution light illuminating intermittently, and 439," Hart hesitated before saying, "has a cut on the right main tire that by the book is a red X."

Tom thought hard and looked at his lieutenant and shook his head. "What are you gonna do, Lieutenant?" Tom sat down on his cot and looked up at Hart Osborn.

Osborn was shocked by the question, and Tom could see that he expected to receive guidance. He'd never learn anything if he wasn't forced to think. "How do you want to fix these things?"

Tom could see the wheels turning in Osborn's mind. "Sir, I'll get with Mr. Walker and—"

Tom cut him off. "Mr. Walker needs his rest. He'll be test-flying all day tomorrow. The question was, what are *you* going to do?"

Hart Osborn was visibly flustered by the interrogation, especially in front of Sergeant First Class Pennington. He mustered up the fortitude to confront his boss. Hart said, "Whatever I do, I can do it without this crap," adding scornfully, "sir."

Tom had had enough. He got up off his cot and got in Osborn's face. "I'll tell you what you're gonna do. You're gonna lock it up right now!" Hart Osborn snapped to attention. He'd never seen Tom Lawton this upset before. "You're gonna tell me exactly what you're gonna do to fix the aircraft. We've got a mission scheduled that everybody and their brother told me they wanted to do tomorrow night. We have approval to do it. And now I've gotta go beg somebody else for an aircraft or only launch half the troop? I don't think so!" Tom let him think about it and backed off. Deep down he knew Osborn was doing his best. "So what's your plan?"

The lieutenant swallowed hard. "I need to let D Troop know about the hydraulics and the rubber coming off the blade."

Tom nodded. "Good. Is the tire flat?" Osborn looked toward Sergeant First Class Pennington for help. "I'm not asking him. I'm asking you. Is the tire flat?"

"I don't know, sir," said the lieutenant.

Tom Lawton backed up another step. "Thanks for being honest. Penny, is the tire flat?"

Sergeant First Class Pennington answered, "No, sir."

"But we're carrying that aircraft down?" said Tom to the sergeant. "That's pretty stupid. Unless that tire is seriously cut or ripped, why are we carrying it down? You know better than that, Penny. It'll be three months until we get a damn tire to replace the one that's on there."

"Roger, sir. I'll go look at it right now. If I can, I'll correct it with my pen," said the sergeant. Lawton knew that meant Penny would write "Status entered in error" in the logbook.

"As long as it's still safe. I'm sure if the tire is still okay, we can keep flying it. But let's get one on order tonight. I'll be more than happy to sign it off if the tire is okay. Thanks, Penny," said Tom, dismissing the platoon sergeant.

Penny looked at his platoon leader as if to say, "I let you down." He didn't have to say a word. Lieutenant Osborn hollered after him, "I'll be out in a minute, Sergeant." He turned his attention back to his boss, who had moved over to the cot again.

"We can troubleshoot the NVS tonight and try to locate the problem. Maybe one of the guys from D Troop is available," said Lieutenant Osborn.

"They're available unless one of the other troops get their services before we do," said Tom. He rubbed his head and realized he needed a shower.

"I'll get over there right now, sir," said the lieutenant, still at the position of attention.

"Relax, Hart." Tom looked up at the lieutenant. He came to the position of parade rest. "Look, I'm pissed about something else. Not our maintenance posture. We'll be fine by tomorrow afternoon. Getting back to the other subject, did you know we had guys sunning since we've been out here?"

Hart looked at his boss quizzically. "Sunning, sir? I had no idea."

Tom shook his head. "The Hawk jumped my shit about some of our guys catching rays. I went in and told them to knock that crap off. If you see them doin' stuff like that, make them stop, okay?"

"Roger, sir. Is that all, sir?" asked the lieutenant.

Lawton could tell Osborn still had his attitude. "No, that isn't all. I'm not pissed at you. I just . . . lost my temper about a couple of things going wrong at the same time." Tom got off his cot and walked over to Hart. "I'm sorry I snapped. I need to work on the mission for tomorrow night. I'd appreciate it if you could do what you could about troubleshooting the aircraft tonight. I don't like white light maintenance but understand the circumstances for tonight. Get what you can get done by 2200 and we'll do the actual fixin' tomorrow, okay?"

"Roger, sir," said the expressionless lieutenant.

Tom just shook his head. He'd pissed Hart off again and didn't have anything else to say to try and smooth the ruffled feathers. "I'll see you back here at 2200 then."

"Yes, sir." Hart Osborn saluted and walked out of the tent.

Tom slumped on the cot. He screwed that whole exchange up. Things were starting to get to him. He never used to get upset like that. He was tired, and he knew it. But he didn't have time to go to sleep. Slowly, he pulled open his maps and went to work. It would be another long night.

0615, January 15, 1991
AA Gomez, Saudi Arabia

FIRST SERGEANT GARCIA WAS DOING HIS morning task, burning the human excrement that had been deposited in the toilets during the last twenty-four-hour period. About a half gallon of diesel was poured into the metal drum which held the feces and paper. After it was lit, the first sergeant would spend the next hour stirring to ensure all the waste was burned. Of course he always had his coffee in hand.

Tom came out to join him in the task every other day or so. Shitty as the job was, he knew the first sergeant enjoyed being alone for this task. It gave him a chance to think and plan. Captain Lawton hoped it wasn't an intrusion whenever he stopped by to help Top "burn the shit." It gave the two leaders an opportunity to coordinate the day's actions.

After the day's tasks were discussed, of which maintenance was the priority, they would talk about the situation and try to predict what the unit or Saddam would do in the future. Top offered up some information Tom had not even considered.

"The sergeant major said they have some phones coming in. They should be ready today," said the first sergeant.

"Phones? Get out of here," said Tom.

"No, seriously. He said they'd be over by brigade headquarters. If we can find them, can we start sending guys over to use them?" asked Garcia.

Tom thought about the opportunity. He would love to get a call back to Germany and talk to Cindy. Take care of the troops first. "As long as all the work is caught up and a senior person goes along in charge. And one other thing. Make sure you brief them on weapons. Take the weapons and post a guard if you can't bring them into the phone area," said Tom.

"Roger, sir," said Top. Then the first sergeant changed the subject. "Well, today is the day."

Tom knew exactly what Top was talking about. January 15 was the date the UN Security Council had given Iraq to pull out of Kuwait. Every night, the troops would listen to the Armed Forces Network Radio (AFN) for updates of the situation. Tom proclaimed, "I don't think he's leaving."

"Well, I guess we're gonna have to kick those maggots out then!" said the defiant first sergeant.

Tom laughed. "I think we'll be ready if we're asked to go. I think we're gonna need about three more weeks until we're good enough."

"If the aircraft hold up too," said Garcia.

"Oh, they'll be just fine. We had them in pretty good shape before we got here. Every one of them still has a hundred hours left until phase. We'll probably need fifty hours remaining to phase inspections as a minimum before the fight. We can plan on slowing down operations in two weeks." Tom added, "It would be nice to do a live fire before the game kicks off too."

Top smiled. "You ever fired a Hellfire, sir?"

"No, I sure haven't. If everything goes the way it looks like it will, I'll have plenty of opportunity to shoot one. Hell, I might get to shoot a bunch!" Tom smiled. "Find out about the phones. If they're a go, start letting people go about 1400. I'm gonna check on maintenance and go over the mission for tonight one more time."

"Sir? You sure they're ready?" asked Top.

Tom smiled. "Ready? Of course not. But I'm not gonna let them know that!"

Osborn did his usual tremendous job at getting the aircraft ready for Walker to test-fly. D Troop was all over Champion aircraft as soon as the sun came up. The tire was bad, but not unflyable. Tom knew they were stretching the status with it, but it was better than letting it sit for who knows how long. The Hawk came and observed the mission briefing. He asked a couple of questions that Tom had not thought about. One was, were they going to go lights out? Tom thought about it, looked around the tent, and caught a couple of negative glances from his senior warrants. "Not on this first mission, sir. But next time we'll try it." Other corrections to the mission were rebriefed, and they were set. They were even going to use five of their own aircraft.

Everything went extremely well. They got off at exactly 2030 with all six aircraft. They hit all the ACPs on time and occupied the battle position the way it was drawn up on paper. The other Nightstalker aircraft were ordered to work to the west, and the Champions worked to the east. The aircraft separation plan that Maurer proposed worked. Lieutenant Colonel Hawk came over and observed the last thirty minutes of the mission and was pleased with the progress.

After the mission, the FARP was crazy. Aircraft were stacked up waiting to get fuel. Even with everyone flying, the refuelers managed to get all refueled within two hours. Tom made a mental note to bring it up at the next command and staff meeting. It was going to be difficult to turn the squadron around for a second rotation in the dark in less than three hours unless they practiced it a couple more times.

AAR comments from the Champions were surprisingly constructive. They were definitely getting their heads into the training. It was agreed that during the next mission, they would try blacked-out cockpits, then worry about external lights coming off next week. They just weren't proficient enough in the dark to be totally blacked out as an entire troop. Lawton could live with those kinds of assessments. Literally, live with it.

Sometime after midnight, the allies launched multiple air attacks against Iraq and Kuwait. Hussein had not left as the Security Council directed. Therefore, President Bush approved Operation Desert Storm.

January 18, 1991
AA Gomez, Saudi Arabia

THE UNIT WAS TAKING FULL ADVANTAGE of the phone system. As operations were becoming routine, daily trips were made to the phone site. The site was nothing more than four satellite dishes and two GP Medium tents full of phones. Within each tent were twenty poles that held four phones each. There was always a line going into the tents. There was always news to be shared and spread from back home, wherever that was. Many times, the calls back home were opportunities for families and friends to inform the soldiers of bad news, things that were going wrong, news reports, or how badly they were missed by their loved ones. Tom's first phone call was a bad one.

After a thirty-five-minute wait, he finally got to a phone. Three minutes later, he got through to Cindy in Germany. The connection was surprisingly good. "Hi, honey. How you doin'? It's me, Tom!"

"Oh my god! Tom, is that really you?" said Cindy.

It was so great to hear her voice. "Look, I can't talk real long. I hope everything there is going good," said Tom.

"I wish I could say it was. I just got back from the hospital in Nuremberg. Megan's got strep throat. The doctors here think that she might have to have her tonsils taken out," said Cindy.

Damn, thought Tom. "Have her tonsils out? Is she all right?"

"She's not too good right now. She hasn't been able to eat for two days. How are you guys? Lou has moved in with me, and she gets letters from Hart almost every day."

Everything she said from that point on was difficult for Tom to comprehend. His mind was on Megan. She must have been really sick to have the doctors say she needed her tonsils out. He snapped back to Cindy's voice. "You didn't get my letters?"

"No, I got one letter from you. I said Lou gets letters from Hart daily. He says you're driving him crazy!" said Cindy.

The rest of the conversation was more of the same. They only got to talk for another five minutes. Tom felt so bad for Megan, but there was nothing he could do in Saudi Arabia, except get home as soon as possible. The phone call made him homesick. It was great to hear Cindy's voice, but most of the news got him down. Megan's sick, write more, and they heard they would attack next week. He hadn't heard crap. Finally, he told her he had to get back, which was the truth. Tom mostly didn't want to hear any more. He wished he could be back in Germany with them. Tom told her he loved her, and Cindy said, "Don't worry about us. I love you too!" Tom waited for her to hang up. It was always hard to be the first one to hang up the phone.

That night, the squadron performed more individual training. All crews from all troops were flying as much as possible. They'd missed the day before because of more rain. Nichols was scheduled to get more time on Harmon, and every other crew was paired with their normal stick buddy.

About an hour and a half into their flight, Nichols was getting enough confidence in Harmon, the "Boy Warrant," to let him have the controls. After being cleared for takeoff, Harmon was executing a night vision system takeoff. The aircraft was just coming out of the cloud of dust and increasing speed to eighty knots when something got Nichols's attention. The instructor pilot just happened to glance out his right side in time to see a large black object headed straight for the crew compartment of the helicopter. He couldn't quite make out what it was, but he could tell it wasn't good.

"Break left! Break left! I have the controls!" screamed the instructor pilot.

Harmon had no clue what was happening. He released the controls and looked to his right. He nearly had a heart attack when he saw the two fuel blivets headed straight toward him. The aircraft was rolling hard to the left in an unusual attitude, and Tim Harmon braced himself for what was sure to be impact.

Nichols had the Apache rolled over in a ninety-degree bank while flying night system to avoid the sling load of a UH-60. He continued the hard roll and pulled all the collective he could without overtorqueing the aircraft. The blivets went right over the top of the aircraft. Instantly, the problem became altitude. Nichols spun his head to the left, which became down toward the sand. The position lights illuminated the ground enough for Nichols to see the dust rising from the rotor blades. The Blackhawk never even saw the Apache. The UH-60 flew on, unaware that the blivet they carried thirty feet below their belly had just missed another aircraft by two feet.

Nichols was shaken. In eighteen years of flying helicopters, he had never come that close to an accident. Tim Harmon was too new to flying to understand that he had nearly died. The young warrant officer did notify the chief warrant officer 4 that in no uncertain terms, he needed to get on the ground immediately in order to relieve himself. Nichols thought that sounded like a good idea.

Once on the ground, when the fear was gone, anger took over. Nichols stormed into Lawton's tent. The rage on his face was evident, and Nichols didn't need to yell to make his case known. He yelled anyway. "We damn near got killed by some fuckin' idiots that didn't even see us!"

The outburst had Tom's attention, and he tried his best to calm Mark Nichols down. "Easy, easy, Mark. Calm down and tell me what happened."

"I'll tell you what happened! Those fucking Blackhawk pilots have their heads so far up their asses, they can't see!" Nichols caught his breath and shook his head. Tom told him to take a seat on the cot, which was promptly refused. "They nearly hit us, sir! I mean, how hard is it to keep your head outside the cockpit and see what's goin' on?"

"Look, Mark, just calm down and talk to me. Tell me what happened. I can't help you if I don't know exactly what happened," said Tom. That appeared to sink in, and Mark Nichols started to explain the situation. He told Tom what had happened, how they had just missed the blivets, how the Blackhawk wasn't up on the common air traffic frequency the Apaches were using, and how they had nearly hit the ground during the unusual attitude recovery. Mark Nichols's hands were shaking as he spoke.

Tom said, "I'll go talk to Maurer, Mark. We can fix the commo problem. We can get the 60s to come up the common freq. I can't say if we can get their heads out of the cockpit long enough to see everybody else."

"We can deconflict the airspace then, sir. Those fuckers can do that shit somewhere else," said the instructor pilot.

Tom agreed. "That sounds like a good idea, Mark. I'll bring it up," said Tom, still trying to get the instructor to get control of his emotions.

"I didn't come to this hellhole to die in some stupid training flight. If I die, I want it to mean something," said Mark Nichols.

Tom was letting him vent, but that was enough. "Nobody is gonna die. Not in training and not in combat." Tom moved close to the instructor pilot to look him in the eye. "None of us came here to die." Tom let that sink in and then smiled. "I'm glad you're okay. I need to take what you've learned tonight and make sure other people learn it too. You understand? I'm not gonna let anybody die."

Something Tom said made sense to Mark Nichols. The event had scared him, but not enough for him to quit. "I know that, sir." He still wasn't completely cooled off. "It's just that those guys know better than to fly around like that."

"Just remember, Mark, it could have been an Apache that nearly ran into them," said Tom. "I'll talk to everybody at the next meeting. We can fix this. I'm just sorry you had the shit scared out of you for this problem to surface."

Mark nodded his understanding. Then he chuckled. "If you think I'm scared, you should see Harmon. He nearly shit his flight suit!"

Tom joined in the laugh then looked at the instructor pilot seriously. "You know," Tom hesitated to say it, but it needed to be said, "you two need to go back out and fly again as soon as possible."

Mark Nichols took a deep breath. "Yeah, I know it. But it ain't gonna be easy."

Tom smiled and slapped the instructor pilot on the back. "I know you're the best, Mark. And if you're ready to go up, Tim Harmon will go with you."

"Roger, sir," said the instructor pilot as he started out the door. "I'm still pissed off. But I don't want to hit anybody anymore."

"Get a good night's sleep, Mark," said Tom.

"Sir, thanks for listening," the instructor pilot said as he turned to leave.

"Good night, Mark," said Tom. Lawton got on his equipment and headed over to the Troop TOC. Specialist Padillo had duty and only caught Lawton's side of the conversation. Tom called on the landline to the Squadron TOC. "Is Captain Maurer there?" He apparently was asleep. "Go wake him up and tell him Captain Lawton is coming to talk to him. I'll be there in five minutes. Out." Tom just looked at Padillo and stormed out. The specialist had never seen his commander lose his temper before and didn't know what he was angry about. He just knew his captain was hot and headed to the TOC. He'd go tell the Top or Lieutenant Timmons after the commander left. They always appreciated knowing when the boss was upset. It was their job to find out why.

January 26, 1991
AA Gomez, Saudi Arabia

THE STATUS OF THE WAR WAS one of increasing escalation. Hussein had fired scuds into Israel, set some oil facilities ablaze, and sabotaged Kuwait's main supertanker-loading pier, the last event causing environmental chaos as millions of gallons of crude oil were dumped into the Gulf. Meanwhile, in the desert of Saudi Arabia, American and Coalition forces continued aggressive training while preparing for the war.

The squadron was beginning to train with the First Armored Division. Tom couldn't help but feel more comfortable with a division of tanks between the Fighting Sixth and the Iraqi Republican Guard forces. Tom was comfortable with little else that was going on.

He'd called Cindy two more times, and the phone calls just kept him uncomfortable with the way things were in Germany. She wanted to be friendly and positive, but it only made Tom homesick. His relationship with his troop seemed to be getting strained. As his nights became longer, his temper became shorter. There was the near midair which rippled not just through the troop but also through the squadron. A lot of grumbling went on about how the leadership was overcome by the events taking place. Of course, none of the rumors could be pinpointed to anyone in particular. Tom took each comment he heard to heart, feeling as if everything bad, he was responsible for it. Then the aircraft maintenance began to waiver. They were only able to keep three birds up for the last two days. All these negative things began to mount on Tom's strained shoulders. Tom was the type person that would dwell on the negatives and forget all the positives. If anything else were to happen badly, he thought he might lose it. Sometimes, if you start expecting bad things to happen, they will.

Because the Champions only had five Apache crews assigned to five of their Apaches, Hawk and Needles often used the sixth bird. Tom remembered offering to let the colonel fly his aircraft anytime, but he never wanted or expected to have him as his sixth crew.

Hawk and Needles were flying 956, observing an A Troop night system mission. They had been out for nearly an hour when they got a caution light illuminated for low oil pressure in the number 1 nose gearbox. This required the aircraft to be flown on one engine. Under the night system conditions, the instructor pilot chose to take it back to the D Troop area and perform a running landing. The word had come out on the landline, informing the camp that the squadron commander was about to do a roll on in the D Troop area, so everyone was out of the tents to watch. The aircraft touchdown would be visible for miles because of the dust, even in the darkness. Tom watched because he knew it was his bird. He grabbed a set of night-vision goggles and watched with baited breath.

The aircraft rolled onto the desert floor at forty miles an hour. Although a relatively smooth surface, rocks and dust flew everywhere. For nearly forty-five seconds, the aircraft rolled through the sandy desert, sending dust and dirt a hundred feet in the air for nearly a quarter mile. Tom sighed in relief as the aircraft came to a stop two hundred yards from the D Troop area. He was happy just to see it still upright. He had no idea what was about to happen.

"Sir, it's the TOC. The colonel wants to see you right now," said Specialist Cryder.

That was strange. It was nearly midnight. "Is it for all the commanders or just me?" asked Tom Lawton.

"I think it's just for you, sir," exclaimed the specialist.

"Roger, thank you. Tell them I'll be there in five mikes," said Tom. He had no idea what was going on, but something in his churning gut told him it wasn't good.

Cryder also could tell that something bad was going on. Top had told them that if something didn't seem right with the old man, get one of the lieutenants. As soon as the captain was out of sight, he went and got Lieutenant Timmons.

Tom entered the TOC out of breath. There, in a folding chair, was LTC Stanley Hawk. No one else was around. Tom hadn't had to deal with the Hawk when he was pissed off. But the look in the colonel's eye told him it was time.

"Sit down, Captain," said the commander icily.

The colonel said "Captain" as if it were a dirty word. Tom slowly walked to the front row of the briefing tent and took a seat.

"I don't know if you were trying to prove something to the old man or trying to kill me out of stupidity, but I'm holding you directly responsible for our maintenance problem tonight!" said the commander.

Tom was lost. He started to say, "What the hell are you talking about?" but something inside him told him to keep his mouth shut. Maybe it was just years of military service, but all Tom could muster was a meek "Yes, sir."

The colonel continued, "Upon postflight, we found the refill cap of the number 1 nose gearbox hanging off. All the oil came out of the gearbox, and we had to do a roll on to save your aircraft. What do you have to say to that?"

Tom couldn't think. What was there to say? The aircraft had probably been serviced, and the cap wasn't replaced properly. He did know that when his boss was like this, it was best to keep your mouth shut and hope for the best. His crew chiefs were responsible for the maintenance, and that meant him. He wasn't the kind of leader to point a finger at someone that was trying to do his best. Here goes nothing. "It's my fault, sir. My crew chiefs are my responsibility, and if they did the service, it's my fault."

That didn't satisfy the Hawk. He jumped out of the chair and yelled, "You're goddamn right it's your fault! What the hell kind of maintenance are you guys pulling!" The colonel continued the barrage, screaming, pointing his finger, and yelling as loud as he possibly could. After a minute, he regained his composure and took a deep breath. He walked around the tent slowly, not nearly as loud as before, yet the verbal assault continued.

Tom shut down his communication receivers. The colonel was in a transmit mode, and it was clear to Tom he did not want to receive any transmissions back. What was he supposed to do? Tom would throw in the required "Yes, sir" or "No, sir." But he wasn't really listening anymore. His stomach churned violently, and he could hardly understand what the colonel was saying. After ten minutes of venting, the Hawk finally sat down.

"This is what you're gonna do. You will proceed to the D Troop area. Find Captain Rooks and notify him that as of this moment, he is the owner of 956. You obviously can't maintain it. We'll see if he can do any better. You will also go to the S4 and get the paperwork drawn up to laterally transfer 956 to D Troop. Is that clear?" said the squadron commander.

Tom felt like throwing up. His boss had lost faith in his ability to perform his job. It didn't matter that he'd asked for more crew chiefs. It didn't matter that he'd asked for another crew member to fly with Harmon, and it didn't matter that a crew chief made a simple mistake. The only thing that mattered to Tom was that he felt incompetent. He again muttered, "Yes, sir."

Finally, the colonel said something about "relieving" Tom, but he didn't have time to train a new commander. But Tom didn't catch the threat because he was miles away. "That is all, Captain."

Tom Lawton stood up and saluted. The salute was returned with disgust and another sarcastic comment that Tom didn't hear. He did an about-face and headed out of the tent.

In a state of dazed confusion, Tom headed straight for D Troop. He couldn't clear his mind. All the things that were troubling him came together in the tent as Hawk ripped into him. Tom struggled to keep his composure. He wanted to hide, but the soldier that he was took over. He put all trouble and all pressure and pain he felt into a dark hole deep in his mind. Walking in a self-induced fog, Tom headed to Delta Troop.

Somehow, in the darkness, Lawton found Rooksy's tent; and to his surprise, the captain was still awake. "Sorry to bug you, Rooksy. The old man told me to come over here and let you know that 956 is yours. Effective tonight. I gotta get to the S4 and get the paperwork drawn up."

"What? What the fuck are you talkin' about? I can't take an aircraft. I don't have any crew chiefs for crewin' a bird, and I don't have the time to take care of it," said Captain Rooks.

"Look, I'm only tellin' you what he said," said Tom.

"Oh, for Christ's sake. He's just pissed about that nose gearbox cap. Give 'em a week and he'll forget all about it," quipped Rooksy. He grabbed Tom's shoulder and gave it a friendly shake. "Hey, man. This ain't nothing but fly crap in the pepper shaker, bro!"

"I hope so. He was mad as hell," said Tom, visibly shaken by the ass chewin'.

Rooks was an even keel kind of guy, and he gave Tom the best advice he'd had lately. "Fuck it."

"I don't think I can just say 'fuck it'!" said Tom.

"Yes, you can. Fuck this shit. Leave the helicopter here for a couple days. Let the boss get over this crap and drive on," said Rooksy.

"He said something about relieving *me*," said Tom.

"Now where the fuck is he going to get somebody stupid enough to take over your guys?" said Rooksy, smiling.

Tom thought about the comment. Maybe Rooksy was right. Tom just didn't feel like anything was right. He had to get out of there. "Thanks, Rooksy. I hope you're right." Tom started to leave and added, "You're a terrific friend. But I think I'm the one that's fucked." Tom turned and left the tent before Rooks could say another word.

Tom walked as fast as he could toward the C Troop area. Everything was coming down on him. The Iraqis hadn't even fired a bullet in anger yet, and he felt that he was screwing up. In the darkness, he came up to one of the Champion Apaches. It just happened to be 220. Somehow, he could read his name under the window on the cockpit. *Captain Tom Lawton-Champion 6.* He didn't feel like a Champion. And he didn't feel like being the Six right now either. And while he was on the subject, he didn't even feel like being in the army. He felt tired, confused, and pretty damn pissed off. What he felt like doing most was throwing up. He needed to get away. He needed to leave. Right then, right there.

Tom unzipped his flight suit. He began to hop on one foot as he untied his boots. He didn't realize he was talking and making sounds as he stripped. His anger began to grow, and soon it was rage. He threw his boots into the darkness. The flight suit came off and then the underwear.

"Sir, what the hell is he doing?" asked Specialist Cryder.

"I can't be real sure right now, Cryder," said Hal Timmons. Hal also had a pair of NVGs, and between the two soldiers, they thought they saw their commander taking off his clothes.

It was more than Tom could take. He took a couple of deep breaths and started walking in a small circle. The green army socks kept the small rocks from hurting his feet. But Tom's mind was so far away from Saudi Arabia that he didn't feel the pain his feet registered or the cold night air. His rage had taken away his rational thought. The hell with it. The hell with Hawk. And the hell with command. He was doing his best, and it obviously wasn't good enough. He needed to get out of there. He didn't know where he was going. He just knew he was leaving. Tom began to run.

"Where's he going, sir?" said Cryder. "He's headed outside the perimeter."

"I guess he needed to do some PT," said Timmons, trying to make light of the situation. "Call the OP and tell them to hold their fire if they see anything 'suspicious.' Don't tell them the nature of the wake-up call. You understand?"

"I know exactly what you mean, sir. But shouldn't we tell somebody?" asked Cryder. "Should we go get him? Is he gonna be all right?"

Hal ingested all the questions and came back, "No, we don't tell anyone. No, he'll come back after his run is over and . . ." The lieutenant pulled the NVGs away and looked at the trooper. "I hope so."

0213, January 27, 1991
Somewhere east of AA Gomez
Saudi Arabia

TOM LAWTON SLOWED DOWN. FOR SOME unknown reason, he felt better. It was as if God had sent him a personal message to "chill out." He began to walk. Tom Lawton was tingling all over. He had never felt more alive in his life than he did at that moment. Hell, he felt great. He put his hands in the air and started laughing out loud. He looked down at himself and realized the only thing he was wearing were the green socks on his feet, and he laughed even harder.

Then he looked to the stars and yelled as loud as he could, "I'm okay, Lord!" And it felt wonderful. He stopped and wiped his face. Tom could taste salt on his lips but couldn't tell exactly what it was. There was a combination of sweat and tears on his face. But he did know that it didn't matter. He was fine. He was alone and naked in the darkness, but it didn't matter. Tom Lawton looked up to the sky and looked down at himself one more time. It was as if the night sky had told him everything was okay. This is what he was, and he couldn't change it. He couldn't change the way he was because of the war or because of Hawk.

He thought for a moment that maybe this was God's answer to all his problems. Was this the Lord's way of answering Tom's mental anguish? It was unlike anything Tom had ever felt. All the pressure he was under was gone. He looked up into the night sky again. For the first time since he had been in Saudi, he really saw how magnificent it was. Tom had never looked at the desert sky like that before. The night was so peaceful and beautiful. Millions of stars were twinkling just for Tom. They covered him and protected him in his solitude. In their silence, he discovered the strength he needed to succeed.

It struck Tom that all those "problems" were really insignificant. Aircraft maintenance, training conflicts, equipment shortages, leadership questions, internal fears, and even Hawk's little tantrum were all no big deal. He only had one thing to do, and he was already doing it. Continue leading the Champions. That was it. Be the leader he was capable of being. Simply take care of the things he could and everything else would fall into place. The answer had always been there, but he was putting pressure on himself and creating problems that really weren't that big. He was the source of his own problems.

In the distance, he heard a helicopter. The sound of the blades and the cold night air immediately brought Tom back to reality. He laughed again and said to no one in the darkness, "Where the hell am I?" He took a deep breath and turned around 180 degrees. Luckily, the night sky provided him with enough starlight so he could make out his footprints in the desert sand.

Slowly at first, he started walking toward AA Gomez. What had just happened? Tom wasn't real sure. He only knew he felt better. Tom thought that it might have been some kind of religious experience. For that reason, Tom remembered his mother-in-law telling him that "God watches over all soldiers." Not being the most religious man in the world, Tom couldn't be sure. He looked to the heavens again and said out loud, "If that was you . . . thanks!" For the first time since they had arrived in the desert, his smile was genuine.

Tom hadn't done anything wrong. The fact was he was doing damn good. Tom thought about all the things that were troubling him, and none of them was that bad. Cindy was taking care of Megan, and they were both doing fine. The troopers in C Troop were doing the best they could. They busted their asses daily and never complained once. The maintenance would come around. It always did. So screw what Hawk thought. If he was gonna relieve Tom, that was his chance, and he didn't do it. Lawton started to jog, and the broad smile that had been missing for so long remained. He was looking for a job when he got this one. Nobody had died. And damn it, nobody was going to die. Not while Tom was still in command.

0245, January 27, 1991
AA Gomez, Saudi Arabia

FOR JUST AN INSTANT, TOM PICTURED the look on Cindy's face as she received notification that her husband had been shot by his own men. And even worse, he was . . . naked. He had to laugh.

He could see the OP in the darkness and avoided it. He split the difference between D Troop and C Troop and jumped over the berm. In the distance, he could make out 220, and he headed for it. Now if he could just find all his clothes, he thought he could put the whole night in the past and drive on.

As he got to the aircraft, a voice called out from above. "Hell of a night for PT, sir!" The voice belonged to Hal Timmons.

"Jesus, Hal! You scared the shit outta me!" said Tom.

The lieutenant was sitting up on the engine, cowling and snickering as his naked commander stood below him, shivering. "I took the liberty of gathering up your clothes. They're on the wing, sir," said the lieutenant. "I figured . . . man is he gonna be cold when he gets back!"

Tom started getting dressed. He could barely make out his clothes, and the cold night air was making him shiver. "What the heck are you doing awake?"

"Cryder told me about the call. I wondered if maybe . . . you needed to talk to someone. Remember, I owe you one," said Hal. "So do you wanna talk about it?"

Tom smiled at his lieutenant, who was showing how much he cared for his boss. "Yeah. Yeah, I do," said Tom.

"We heard about the nose gearbox cap. You can correct me if I'm wrong, sir. But isn't the pilot supposed to check that on preflight?" asked the lieutenant.

Tom thought about it and began to laugh. "Yes, he is," said Tom with a big smile.

"We just can't believe he chewed your ass for that!" said Hal.

"It was a good ass chewing. Before this, I always thought he chewed ass like Aunt Bee. You know, from Mayberry!" Then Tom went into a high-pitched squeal like Aunt Bee from *The Andy Griffith Show*. "Aanndddyyyy! Andy! Where's Opie, Andy?"

Both the pilots had a good laugh at Tom Lawton's impression of Aunt Bee. It was at exactly that point that Hal Timmons knew his commander was okay. In fact, he was better than he'd been in a long time. "You know somethin', sir, that's the first impression you've done since we got to the desert."

Tom thought about it, and Hal was right. "What do you mean impression? That's the Hawk callin' for his driver!" And the two had another good laugh. It felt good to laugh again. Tom knew what Hal meant though. "Hal, I'm okay. I was a bit overwhelmed for a while, but I'm better now. Thanks. Thanks very much for caring . . . about me."

"Shit, sir, we all do. If something happens to you, we'll get some pencil-pushin' geek in here who couldn't lead boy scouts to the brownie camp!" said Hal.

Tom smiled and put on his Kevlar. "Ah . . . Hal, who knows about my . . . little run?"

"Oh, nobody, sir. It's a big secret. You do know we have PT scheduled for tomorrow morning, right?" said Hal.

Tom remembered putting out the info that Hawk wanted the units to start doing PT every morning. "Yeah, I remember. 0700, right?"

"Yes, sir," said Hal. "How about Hart and I take the stand to tomorrow morning and you sleep in? I'll come and wake you up at 0645."

Tom liked the sound of that. "Okay, you got a deal. Wanna walk back to the tent with me, Lieutenant?"

"Roger that, sir," said the lieutenant.

Tom pointed up to the night sky. "Lieutenant, have you noticed the sky here? I mean, look at those stars!"

Hal Timmons looked up and then back at his boss. "Not really, sir." Then Hal stopped in place. "There seems to be a whole bunch more of them. And they look a lot brighter too."

Tom stopped and looked up at the night sky with his lieutenant. "I think of all the things are different for me now. The night sky will never be the same."

Hal looked at Lawton intently. "Maybe it's because there aren't any real man-made lights out here to interfere with the natural beauty."

Tom nodded in agreement and took one last look. "Come on. I better hit the rack, or I won't be good for anything tomorrow."

They walked back to the tent and talked about some of the things that had been troubling Tom. By the time they got to the tent, Tom was relaxed and ready for sleep. He hit the cot at three fifteen and was out by the time his head hit the pillow.

0645, January 27, 1991
AA Gomez, Saudi Arabia

"SIR, IT'S TIME FOR PT!" TOM could barely open his eyes, but he could tell by the voice it was Hal Timmons. When Tom finally located him, he could only see his head peeking through the front entrance to the tent.

"Roger. Thanks, Lieutenant. I'll be out in a minute," said Tom. He hurriedly dressed and stepped outside. Tom couldn't believe what he saw when he got outside. There, before him, were the Champions naked, all thirty troopers in formation, dress right dress, wearing nothing but sneakers and protective masks.

After he got his composure, Tom said flatly, "I guess I'm out of uniform! I'll be out in a minute!" The troop laughed and came to parade rest as Tom returned to his tent. He hurriedly stripped and returned.

With a broad smile, he took his place at the front of the formation and began the run. Someone behind started cadence, and the unit picked up the pace with vigor. Tom's route took them to the same place he'd been just hours before. He followed the tracks. Rather than risk a surprise attack and for safety's sake, he turned them around after ten minutes. It was too cold to be running without any clothing on.

Upon returning, Tom addressed the troops. "I don't know what to say," said Tom. They had obviously heard about last night's "exercise." "You guys can all stand at ease, and I mean at ease! I don't know what you heard from who or why, but . . . I appreciate the support." There were some "Hoaahhs" and some "Thank you, sirs." But Tom was unprepared for the sign of support he received from his men. "Well, I guess we better get showered up and dressed before someone complains that those guys in C Troop are sunbathing again! Heaven forbid I have to explain this if somebody gets sunburn from this! Dismissed!" Tom saluted and sought out his lieutenants. "Gentlemen, if you would join me in our AO, *bitte*!"

The three naked men entered the tent. Tom was smiling when he said, "I don't know whose idea this was, but if I go to jail, I'm taking both of you with me." Both lieutenants were trying to maintain the position of attention, but they could take no more. All three men burst out laughing.

"It was Hart's idea, sir!" said Hal.

"But you went along with it!" said Hart. "You and your CAV men doing CAV things crap!"

They started to get dressed, and the bonding experience was over. Tom got their attention with a fake cough. "I don't really know how to thank you guys. It's been a tough three weeks, and last night's little chat with Hawk was more than I needed. What you did . . . I mean, the support that this demonstrates . . ." Tom laughed again. "God, I hope I don't get fired now!"

"We talked about it, sir. You have the power of the rank, sir. That doesn't mean crap without respect. We all put our lives in your hands in the decisions you make," said Hal.

Hart Osborn added, "And we trust you with those decisions. We have faith in what you're doing and how you're doing it."

Tom Lawton wiped at his eyes and hoped the two lieutenants didn't see him. "I appreciate your faith, but I'm also aware I couldn't do this job without you two. Thank you, both, sincerely." Tom turned toward them and continued, "There's still much to do and little time. First, I will head over to the S4 tent and sign over 956 to Captain Rooks. Then, gentlemen, we will continue to focus on training this unit. Priorities remain maintenance on the 64s and NVG qualifications for the aerial observers. Hal, I want to be able to use our AOs at night so we can go with three aircraft instead of one."

"That's going to take a lot of time, sir," said Lieutenant Timmons.

"I know. You've got one week from tonight!" said the commander. "So get going!"

"Roger that, sir," said Hal. "And, sir, if I might add, damn good to have you back."

Hart added, "Yes, sir. But please do that Aunt Bee for me. I haven't seen that one, and Hal told me it was the best one you . . ."

"At ease, Lieutenant! No more impressions until you jerks get these guys ready to fight!" said Tom. "Now get outta here. I got work to do."

That night at the command and staff meeting, Tom nearly had a heart attack when Lieutenant Colonel Hawk made the statement, "We need to emphasize the proper uniform for PT." Tom thought the commander had found out about the morning's "nude follies." His fellow troop commanders all gave him a knowing glance and smirk but didn't say a word. Tom was relieved when the colonel followed up with, "Let's make sure everyone has their protective mask with them when they run!" Tom smiled with the knowledge that the Champions had gotten away with something. He was even happier when the subject was changed.

On the way out of the tent, Lieutenant Sheppard approached Tom. "Hey, sir, you got a minute?"

"Yeah, sure, Steve. What's up?" said Tom.

Steve Sheppard looked around as if he didn't want anyone to hear the conversation. "Sir, have your men been taking their PB tablets?" PB tablets, the technical name pyridostigmine bromide, were anti-nerve agent pills. Some soldiers had been taking the pills since their arrival in Saudi Arabia. They were given to the troops as preventative nerve agent tablets. PB tablets were to be taken on a monitored schedule with meals. That wasn't always the case. The supervision of the use of the tablets varied from unit to unit and ranged from strictly monitored to half hazard. These tablets were recommended for use as a preventative based on the potential that nerve agent would be used by the Iraqis. Up to this time, no unit in Saudi Arabia had ever reported the presence of nerve agents. If it had been reported, the whole shootin' match would have taken on a new perspective.

"In all honesty, Steve, I haven't been keeping track. I've been waiting for word of some kind to tell me when to use them. I thought nerve agents would have been used or the threat increased before I started making my troops take them. What's up?" asked Tom.

Steve took a deep breath and shook his head. "I can't say for sure, sir. Only I talked to a lot of people back at the port, up at brigade, and everywhere else I can, and it seems to me that the pills affect some people differently."

Tom wasn't sure what he meant, so he had to ask. "What do you mean 'differently'?" asked Tom.

"Some people get . . . physically ill when they take them. I mean nauseous, vomiting, disoriented, and diarrhea-type ill. It may not be a good idea for pilots to take this stuff if they have to fly. If people are getting sick, they shouldn't be in an aircraft, in the dark, flying anywhere near my tent . . . sir!" said the smiling lieutenant, only half jokingly.

Tom laughed and thought about the comment. The troop probably didn't need to have anyone, not just the pilots, take the stuff if it was making people sick. "I'll check, and if we're having any signs of sickness, I'll let you know. If they are causing problems, I think I'll turn off using those things. Thanks, Steve."

"Sir, this may only be a problem when individuals misuse or abuse the tablets. I don't know," said Steve.

"So I guess it comes down to only crappin' in your drawers a little from the pills now or crappin' uncontrollably when they drop chemicals on us with scuds, huh?" Tom laughed.

Schlep saw the humor and laughed at Tom's joke then added, "If they start throwing that shit around, sir, all the pills in the inventory won't help as much as your MOPP suit!"

Tom agreed wholeheartedly and came back with, "Hey, we're down to five minutes for everyone in the unit to be full up." The unit had been drilling once a day at putting on their protective gear. Sheppard was the guy responsible, and the training was paying off.

"Keep it up, sir. The only problem we're having now is the batteries for the M8 alarms are running low. They're becoming a very hot item across the theater. Seems like somebody is bogartin' them!" said the lieutenant. Tom had to think about what he said when Sheppard caught the blank look on the captain's face. "They're stashing them for themselves and not sharing, sir."

"Oh, I see." Tom smiled at the lieutenant and said, "If you run low, come see my first sergeant and he'll square you away, okay?"

The lieutenant merely smiled and shook his head. "Damn, sir!"

Tom walked back to the tent and thought about what Steve Sheppard had said. He hadn't taken any of the tablets yet. He was going to wait until he'd heard some unit had been hit with a chemical agent. What to tell his men was another thing.

When Tom got to his tent, Hart Osborn, Hal Timmons, and 1SG Bobby Garcia were there waiting on the results of the staff meeting. Tom quickly put out the information and then got down to business on the PB tablets. "Has anyone been taking these PB tablets regularly?" asked Tom.

Garcia was the first to respond. "Some of the guys have. I ain't takin' that shit unless you order me to!"

"Any effects, Top?" asked Tom.

Garcia nodded. "A couple of guys got sick to their stomachs and then got the shits."

"A couple of the pilots have had stomach problems and tightness in the chest after taking them," said Hal Timmons.

Tom got up and walked around the tent. "We haven't seen or heard anything to say the Iraqis have used chemicals to date." He continued to walk in a little circle as he thought. "We aren't at the front 'per se.' We've trained to react to an attack. And if this pill is giving people side effects, it makes sense that we shouldn't take them."

"Sir, we've been told to take them," said Hart.

"Well, *we* collectively have taken them and found them to cause problems more negative than positive. I don't think we should take them anymore. We're putting the crews at risk and therefore the mission. Put the word out to your platoons. If the time comes when we need to take them again, we'll go back to taking them. For what it's worth, I have not taken any and don't intend to."

"That's good enough for me!" said Hal. They all got up and saluted.

Hart Osborn couldn't resist one last jab. "So, sir, you want to go for a little run in the dark later or just sleep naked tonight?"

"Screw you, Lieutenant!"

0900, January 28, 1991
AA Gomez, Saudi Arabia

"GENTLEMEN! AND I USE THAT TERM lightly. I should call all you guys maggots!" yelled the first sergeant. He had all the enlisted soldiers in a formation. "I want each one of you to bend over and touch your toes." The soldiers all looked at the first sergeant quizzically. "Don't look at me like that, goddamn it! I told you to bend over." The soldiers did as they were told. "Now when I tell you to come up, I want everybody to say really loud . . . pop!"

The soldiers looked at one another and started to mumble and smile. The first sergeant said, "Ready . . . up!"

The soldiers came up slowly and with only mock enthusiasm yelled, "Pop!"

"No! No! No, goddamn it!" screamed the first sergeant. "When I tell you maggots to come up, you better say 'pop' loud enough so the Iraqi army fuckin' hears you! Now get on over!" The soldiers did as they were told, even though they were confused.

"All together, ready!" The first sergeant hesitated, then yelled, "Up!"

"Pop!" screamed the Champions as they came to attention.

"That's better, goddamn it!" said Top. "Now you know what that was? You maggots know what that was?" The soldiers all shook their heads negatively. "That's the sound of you guys pulling yer heads out yer asses!"

The soldiers didn't know whether to laugh or feel embarrassed. Top continued, "You might have heard the old man took a bad ass chewin' yesterday because somebody in this unit screwed up! But that ain't nothin' like the one I'm gonna give to the next guy who screws up like that again. You screw the pooch on aircraft maintenance again, and I'll have every one of you pulling yer heads out of yer asses in front of the mess tent at chow time! Get yer asses out on those aircraft and get them up by close of business or I'll rip yer lungs out!"

That day, Tom noticed the crew chiefs were busting their butts like crazy, trying to get all the aircraft ready for the night mission. Everything was FMC by 1500 that afternoon.

January 31, 1991
AA Gomez, Saudi Arabia

LIFE AT GOMEZ BECAME ROUTINE. STAND to, PT, shower, eat, maintain aircraft, eat, get mail, eat, go to the phones, fly, and try to sleep. Sometimes, the order would change, but at least it was consistent.

Nightly radio broadcast would keep everyone informed how the air force was doing. The S2 had briefed the unit on the total number of tanks and artillery pieces the Iraqis had, so a running total of the "kills" was recorded nightly. Bets were made on when the Allied forces would attack on the ground. Dates were marked on the TOC calendar. Still, no word came from higher on when the attack would start. Everyone could "feel" the time was near.

The soldiers did various things to occupy their time. On one such occasion, when Tom Lawton was on reverse cycle, he got up late and decided to take a shower. He walked quickly out to the shower stalls. No water was running, so he didn't think much about opening the door. To Tom's surprise, he found one of his soldiers masturbating. Tom was stunned and didn't know exactly what to say. At first, Tom thought he wasn't awake yet. Then somewhat irritated that the young man was "spankin' the monkey" in a common shower, Tom confronted him. "What the hell are you doin' in there?"

The soldier, obviously caught off guard and looking for some defense of his conduct, came up with the best one he could muster. "I'm just . . . relaxing, sir."

Tom responded, "I've heard it called a lot of things, but never 'relaxing.' You put that soldier to rest and get focused on what the hell you're supposed to be doin'. 'Relaxing' my ass! There's plenty of time for . . . 'relaxing' like that later." He wasn't really pissed at the young man. He'd heard it was a natural action. Not that Tom Lawton would know anything about such an activity.

The locals would often drive by the area in their Nissan pickup trucks, usually at Mach 1. They never stopped. They didn't have roads, and the troops often wondered how they knew where they were going. The berm was great for identifying Gomez to the local population. One day, O'Toole and Lawton took a scout aircraft south to see where the Nissans were headed. The nomads were aware the war was coming, and they had relocated south about fifty miles. The terrain actually changed there. The flat plain dropped off into a large valley or wadi. Families had relocated all their belongings into tents and established residence in this area. Small herds of goats and camels dotted the countryside. As Tom hung out the side of the aero scout, he noticed the younger children would wave. He also noticed the adults were less friendly. Some would wave, but they were obviously less than thrilled to have their lifestyle interrupted by the noisy helicopter. Lawton and O'Toole were careful to avoid the livestock, but that didn't seem to matter to the locals. Their seventeenth-century lifestyle was being interrupted by the twentieth century. And it was more an irritant than an inconvenience. These people were not the enemy. These people weren't spies and probably weren't providing information to the enemy north of the neutral zone. The villagers in Hafar Al-Batin were more likely to be spies. The men in the Fightin' Sixth never ventured into the village.

The warrants found various ways to spend their time too. Somehow, Joe Petty managed to catch a desert rat. The men played with the rat for hours. They tried to get it to eat and let it run through the tent and planned on keeping it. Tom wouldn't let them, fearing of lice or other diseases the rodent may be carrying.

That night, the men used a chemical marking stick to illuminate the rat's backside. The fluorescent glow could be seen for a quarter mile. They threw the rat outside, and it headed toward the D Troop area. They watched it for twenty minutes until it went out of sight. Ten minutes later, there was quite a stir in the D Troop area, lots of shouting and something that sounded like a round going off. Rooksy denied anyone in his troop had fired off a round, but it sure sounded like an M16. No one knows what happened to that poor rat, but the guards in D Troop were awake for the rest of the war.

The warrants also got a kick out of the tax break they were receiving. They named their tent "The Don't Have to Pay Taxes Tent." Scribbled underneath in small print was "More money for drinkin'!" The warrant officers of Charlie Troop maintained a sense of humor every day until the first contact.

One day, Tom found a piece of cardboard over his door that said Taxable Tent. The truth was that President Bush had activated a law that allowed officers to avoid federal income taxes on the first $500 of their income each month while in the theater. Enlisted men and, for some reason, warrant officers serving in the combat zone were allowed to avoid taxes on all income. Tom never chided the warrants. They, just like everybody in theater, deserved every penny they earned.

Mail call was always a great time. It had taken the mail system nearly three weeks to figure out exactly where in Saudi Arabia each unit was. By the third week of January, whenever mail came, it came by the ton. Letters, cards, and of course, packages. Big packages, small packages, solid packages, and crushed packages. Allen Berstein usually got five or six packages whenever the mail caught up. He would always share his goodies. Candy, gum, Cheetos, mouthwash, toothpaste, you name it and Berstein's family sent it. Records were set for eating pound bags of M&M's, only to be broken at the next mail call.

Of course the chocolate-covered liquors were big hits with the warrants. John Walker thought he could catch a buzz if he ate enough of the candies. All he got for his effort was a nauseous hurl and a path worn to the latrine for the next twenty-four hours. No buzz whatsoever.

The weather was strange. The men could tell a storm was coming for miles but couldn't tell whether it was rain or a "shamal." A shamal was a blinding sandstorm that was created by the seasonal winds on the Saudi peninsula. The thirty-to-forty-miles-an-hour winds could generate sand clouds over ten thousand feet high. A shamal may cover an area up to one hundred miles long and over fifty miles wide. Because of the altitude, daytime shamals could be seen for up to fifty miles, giving the unit plenty of time to react to the fierceness of the storms. The powdery residue kicked up by the winds played havoc with communications and entered every hole of the high-tech Apaches. After one of the storms, the crew chiefs would spend hours climbing in and out of the airframes, trying to remove as much of the sand as they could. Even after the aircraft were washed, sand could be found in any and all surface areas of the birds. Tom remembered having to go out and secure an aircraft during one particularly bad shamal. The optics of the Apache needed to be covered completely whenever the shamal came because the blowing sand acted like an abrasive on the lenses and mirrors. The orange outline of the sun could be seen through the blowing sand during the storms. The sand would blast at open skin or eyes, causing stinging sensations long after the storm was over.

When the rains came, they came in buckets. The amount wasn't so bad. It was the fact that there was nowhere for it to run off that was the problem. A rainstorm came the last week of January that created water fourteen inches deep in the tents. It took two days for the unit to physically dry out from the downpour. Tom remembered watching Hal Timmons sitting on his cot, pushing his wallet around like a toy boat. Eventually, the water would disappear nearly as fast as it came down.

February 3, 1991
AA Gomez, Saudi Arabia

THE SHAMALS WOULD GIVE SOME TYPE of warning, but the rains would come from nowhere. Tom and John Walker were flying a day training mission when they were caught in their first rainstorm in Saudi Arabia. John was the first to notice something was wrong. The aircraft had developed a small "shimmy." They decided to head back to the assembly area when they got a call from Champion 27. "Hey, sir. We got a loud popping sound goin' on. And it's not a compressor stall. It sounds like it's coming from the blades," said Ron Weimer.

"Roger, 27. This is Six. All Champions, we are to return to base ASAP. This weather might get worse, and I don't want anybody stuck out here," said Tom.

"Six, this is 25. I'm getting a small popping sound too. Do you want us to set it down?" asked Chief Warrant Officer 3 Dolce.

"Not unless you think it's unsafe. Let's get back and get them on the ground. Do not, I repeat, do not go to the FARP. Let's get home," ordered Tom.

Upon arriving, they discovered that each aircraft had various amount of the rubber stripping peeled off the main rotor blades. Tom's aircraft had one piece about four feet long hanging off the blade. After reporting it to D Troop, the decision came down to cut off the excess rather than try to repair the stripping. The removal of the rubber caused a minor out-of-balance shimmy, but it wasn't bad enough for the aircraft to need the rotor blades to be tracked. The discovery was just the tip of the iceberg. Each aircraft began to have the rubber stripping come off. If each blade were to be repaired or have the tape replaced, it would take a tremendous amount of man-hours and time, time the unit did not have.

February 13, 1991
AA Gomez, Saudi Arabia

COLONEL DENSON WAS BEST DESCRIBED AS cold and impersonal. However, the man did know how to fight. He wanted to make sure that everyone in the brigade had a chance to "ride the horse they were going to ride" into battle, with the guns ready. Denson wanted to run a live fire range, and every crew would get to fire a Hellfire missile. Throughout the brigade, maybe seven crews had ever fired a live Hellfire missile. They were reported to cost about $25,000 per missile, thus the limited number ever fired live.

The news flew through the camp, immediately starting rumors that two days later, the corps would roll north. The rumors were quickly squelched by a phone call back to Germany. The wives hotline hadn't heard anything about the war kicking off, so the rumors couldn't have been true.

During training, the unit was having problems getting the Hellfire missiles to acquire the laser spot. Sometimes, blowing sand prevented the missile from picking up the laser spot, therefore preventing a proper firing sequence. The instructor pilots discussed the matter and decided to try running fire. The other option was to fire from 150 to 200 feet above the ground, which no one found particularly appealing. To be stationary, two hundred feet AGL against an enemy with sophisticated air defense systems didn't seem like a realistic option. Guns and rockets were acceptable for stationary fire because they were considered "area fire" weapons. If crews could get a "solid box," they were cleared to fire from a hover.

Another option was discussed and later employed. To have a different aircraft, or perhaps a ground designator (GLID) from the CAV, lase the target for the firing aircraft. The OH-58D model scout helicopters within the brigade were used for this purpose. They were unarmed, except for two pilots with brass *cojones* and optics that could reveal the type of cigarette a man was smoking from two miles.

Hawk and Maurer decided to let each troop try to fire the missiles in whatever mode the crew preferred as long as it was known ahead of time, a record was kept for the results, and a comparison was made afterward to find out which method would be the most effective against the Iraqis.

A Troop was scheduled to fire first, and they chose to self-designate the target and use a stationary Apache as the designator. B Troop would fire second and chose to try running fire with one aircraft and to self-designate. The Champions would fire last. Tom wanted to use a 58 Delta as a designator for one running fire shot. Three crews would fire stationary hover fire, and two crews would fire using running fire at eighty feet, one with the 58D lasing and the other autonomously.

A makeshift range was made in the desert. Targets were established at various distances out to seven thousand meters. All crews were informed they would fire only Alpha-model Hellfire missiles. Some of the new C-model missiles were on the aircraft, but they were to be save for the two-way range. The C-model missiles had a lower trajectory and less of a smoke signature. A Troop fired from 1300 to 1330. They had some problems getting solid boxes until they got to 120 feet. That became an acceptable hover height for target engagement. The stationary designator aircraft was at two hundred feet and positioned laterally to the firing aircraft. The Assassins recorded four out of six hits, with the two long shots missing. Two aircraft had 30mm misfires, and one couldn't shoot rockets.

The Werewolves didn't have the same luck. They got on the range five minutes late at 1335. It took them ten minutes to get their first missile downrange, and it missed. Finally, they fired two missiles at the two-thousand-meter targets and got one hit. A subsequent target at four thousand meters was missed by ten feet. Their final crew was to fire a running-fire missile. For this maneuver, the crew would fly clockwise traffic patterns launching at fifty knots indicated airspeed and eighty feet AGL. On the first two traffic patterns, the crew couldn't get the box to go solid. On the third lap, with only eight hundred meters to the cease-fire line, the crew said they still couldn't get a solid box.

Someone from a Wolf aircraft made the mistake of saying, "Just shoot the damn thing!" The comment was understandable due to frustration while waiting to engage with rockets and guns. The problem was the comment was made on the Fox Mike command net. All hell broke loose.

"You will not just fire the damn thing. If you can't get your unit together, you will remove them from this range! Is that clear?" For an instant, no one knew who was talking. "Lieutenant Colonel Hawk, you and the B Troop commander will meet me at my location in thirty minutes. I will watch this next unit fire, and they better have their stuff together. Get these other guys off the range until they know what they're doing!" Tom nearly had a heart attack. It was Denson on the squadron FM.

Lawton knew everyone in C Troop was monitoring the squadron command push. The Champions knew better than to talk on the command frequency. They had heard every word. The aircraft were in a holding area on the ground five kilometers to the rear with one 58D-Condor 16 and two scouts to serve as range safeties on the flanks. Tom heard one of his guys say on the Troop Victor net go, "Yipe, yipe, yipe!" indicating they heard the ass chewin'. Then another added to no one in particular, "We better not fuck this up!" and Tom could only agree. He made a call. "All Champions, this is Champion Six on Uniform. It's showtime. I only have one word of advice. Don't hesitate! Treat it like it was the two-way range and get the shot off before one comes back at you. Don't let the observers make you nervous. Just do the job you're paid for and we'll do fine."

Then the call from Maurer came on the FM. "Champion element, this is Nighteagle Three. You are cleared to enter the range. Upon occupation, you are cleared hot for Hellfire engagements at all targets. Upon completion of Hellfire engagements, you are cleared to engage with area suppression weapons systems."

Tom acknowledged, "Bushmaster Three, this is Champion Six. Roger, expect occupation in three mikes, over."

Lieutenant Osborn and Mark Nichols led the troop onto the range and established the first firing point. Allen Berstein and Ron Weimer entered point 2. Tom and Walker took the third firing point, and Toretti and Tucker took the fourth point. Condor 16 occupied the point furthest to the east. Petty and Dolce waited one kilometer behind as briefed because they were to fire the running fire shot last.

Nichols came to a 120-foot stationary hover. Hart Osborn called, "Six, One-six is set, over." Hart Osborn picked his target and turned on the video recorder. An old car chassis at three thousand meters. Hart Osborn put his missile, rockets, and gun switches to the on position, moved the weapons activity select switch to Hellfire, prioritized which missile to fire, and positioned the crosshairs on the target. He lased the target and stored it in the fire-control computer. He quickly selected the Target-Nav index on the fire-control computer select wheel and verified the coordinates of the target. The symbology appeared in Mark Nichols's helmet display unit, informing the pilot which direction to turn to bring the aircraft into constraints. As Nichols brought the nose of the aircraft to the right ten degrees toward the target, Hart reached up and turned his master arm switch on and watched his symbology for cues and messages. The crew was on the target before Tom Lawton issued the order.

"One-six, this is Six. Target is one T-64, direction 185 degrees at three thousand meters, engage with Hellfire, over!" said Lawton.

"Roger. One T-64 at 185 degrees, three thousand meters," said Hart Osborn. "Target identified." Then Hart said on the intercom to Nichols, "I hope I hit this thing."

"You've got a solid box. Pull the trigger, Lieutenant!" said the instructor pilot.

Hart Osborn squeezed the laser and got correct range information. The box was solid, indicating the missile was receiving the laser energy. The lieutenant squeezed the trigger. There was a slight hesitation that surprised Hart Osborn. Then *whoosh!* The aircraft moved slightly around the roll axis as the ninety-nine-pound number 1 missile came off the pylon. The missile created smoke that temporarily obscured the front of the aircraft. The rotor wash cleared the smoke from the TADS line of sight, and Hart Osborn could see the target in his video display unit. He made sure the crosshairs were on the target and kept the laser trigger pulled as the missile climbed to its apex. Osborn continued to monitor the "time to go" message and held his finger firmly on the laser trigger.

"Steady, Lieutenant. Steady," encouraged Mark Nichols.

"I got it! I'm okay!" said the lieutenant testily.

Hart ensured that the crosshairs were on the target the entire last ten seconds. The missile impacted the chassis with a smaller-than-expected explosion. Hart came back one field of view to look for debris to come flying down and was disappointed. He turned off his recorder before he spoke to Nichols. "Did I hit it? It didn't even really explode!"

"Yeah, Lieutenant, that was a hit. There's nothing in that chassis to blow up. I know it looked pretty uneventful, but if that were a tank, you'd be getting secondary explosions right now. Nice shot," said the instructor pilot.

"Good job, One-six!" said Tom Lawton on Uniform. "I got that one on tape." Tom came on the intercom. "Our turn, John. Let's do it!" Tom called Champion 24 and asked for a spot. Allen Berstein was already searching the target area and found a target at three thousand meters. "Champion Two-four, this is Six. I have one missile, Charlie code." Charlie code was the identifier for Lawton's missile seeker.

"Roger, Six. Understand Charlie code. I have one T-64 at November-Kilo, five, four, four, one." Berstein paused and then added, "Nine, five, two, two. Altitude is two, five, five feet, over. Call when set."

Tom quickly wrote down the grid and verified what he heard. Then he put the grid and target altitude into the FCC. Quickly, he slaved the TADS to the grid. Bingo! There was another chassis. "Set. Call spot on, Two-four."

"Spot is on," said Berstein.

Tom turned on his laser spot tracker and verified that he was on the right target. "Roger, good spot." Walker got the aircraft in constraints, and Tom pulled the Hellfire trigger. "Shot, over!" Because Berstein was providing the laser spot, Tom merely recorded the engagement. With fifteen seconds left to impact, Tom said, "Spot on, over!"

Berstein acknowledged, "Spot is on!" Seconds later, another hit. "I've got one destroyed T-64 at previous grid, over."

"Outstanding, Two-four!" said Tom. "Your next engagement is one T-64 at four thousand meters, bearing 180 degrees. Fire when ready, over," ordered Tom.

Allen Berstein quickly prioritized his missiles and verified his laser was designating properly. He selected missiles and verified his recorder was on. His master arm was still on as he searched for his target. He kept reading the range, scanning the target area in narrow field of view to ensure he was looking at the correct distance. Target spotted, he lased and stored. Chief Warrant Officer 4 Weimer got him in constraints, and he was ready. He called Lawton, "Sir, I've got the target identified. Lasing with your code." Berstein paused and then added, "Set. Line me up, Ron." Weimer applied just enough left pedal to get the helicopter's nose directly on azimuth. Berstein squeezed his laser trigger and got a solid box. He pulled the weapon's trigger. Again, a slight pause for what seemed like an eternity. Then the missile came off the pylon. The smoke cleared, and Berstein locked on the target with the image auto tracker. He kept the laser energy applied to the target and watched as the timer counted down until impact. "Six, this is Two-four, target destroyed."

"Roger, Two-four. Nice shooting. Two-eight, this is Six," said Tom.

"Six, this is Two-eight, over," said Carl Tucker.

"Roger. Begin right closed traffic and contact, Condor One-six on Victor, over," ordered Lawton.

Tucker switched to Victor frequency and contacted the Condor 16 aircraft. Toretti began his racetrack pattern. They used a previously agreed upon laser code that the Delta would use to designate the target. The key to success would be the timing. Tom was hoping they could get it the first pass. But Tucker didn't get a solid box because they had never turned the master arm switch on, a mistake common during live gunnery, but one that could have been fatal in combat. They had to come around again. On the second pass, as soon as they turned inbound to the range, Toretti brought the aircraft up to 120 feet AGL and put it in a slow descent. He slowed to fifty knots. Tucker called he had a solid box with two hundred meters to the cease-fire line. With the aircraft down to forty feet AGL and the target obscured by the distance, Tucker pulled the trigger. Tucker said to Toretti, "Here goes nothin'!" The missile came off the rail, and Tucker called promptly, "Shot, over!" Toretti stayed with it to the cease-fire line. They turned all their switches off and called, "Switches cold!" to let everyone know they were not turning into the other aircraft with their weapons still ready to fire.

Condor One-six called, "Spot is on!" Tom Lawton had his recorder on and taped the hit in narrow field of view so Tucker and Toretti could review their "kill." "Good job, Two-eight. Champion 23, the range is yours. Execute one traffic pattern for safety purposes to familiarize yourself with the range. Good luck!" said Tom.

Joe Petty and Tom Dolce were ready to go. They had been observing from their position and were anxious to shoot. Because this was their second Hellfire, they were selected to try to fire the autonomous running-fire shot. Joe Petty needed to fire the missile early and then track it all the way to the target and still get cold switches before they turned at the cease-fire line. They chose to fly at ten knots above ETL. That way, they would avoid the shimmy of ETL, get a few more seconds traveling inbound, and still be in front of the blowing sand.

On the second pattern inbounds, Petty called, "Set!" The aircraft was coming in at about eighty feet so they could get eyes on the target.

Seconds later, the missile was coming off the rail. Tom could tell by the lack of signature it was a C-model missile. A thought went through his mind about the ass chewin' they would receive for wasting a Charlie on the range, but it went away quickly as he focused on the target that Petty was tracking. As long as it hits, all would be forgiven. Dolce continued on a slow descent and maintained the airspeed. The missile hit the target dead center and exploded with much more bang than the previous four. Petty called switches cold, and the aircraft turned outbound.

Tom was pleased. The unit fired five for five in the missile shots. Now came the guns and rockets. He called the troop on line and gave them direction to fire at will. It was as bad as he expected. Two guns didn't shoot, and one stopped firing after twenty rounds. The rockets all fired well, but not on target. Berstein and Tucker would have to spend the next two days bore sighting the rocket pods and getting the guns fixed. The unit went switches cold and left the range.

"That's a good job, Champion Six." It was Denson on the Command Fox. Tom looked at his watch. It was exactly 1430. "You've got your procedures down pretty good, but your aircraft need some work. Get to it. This is Six. Out!"

Tom said, "Roger." Not knowing if the Big Guy heard him or even cared. He thought he'd received a compliment for the performance of his men. Something that Denson rarely, if ever, did. Tom knew it was washed away by the performance of the aircraft. They would get that fixed soon enough. The weapons' problems weren't significant at that point. Getting it done before they hit the two-way range was the problem.

February 18, 1991
AA Gomez, Saudi Arabia

LIEUTENANT COLONEL HAWK HAD BEEN SOLEMN through most of the staff meeting, even when Chris Wise made cracks about the Super Bowl, knowing Hawk's team was the Buffalo Bills. The colonel seemed miles away. The game had become a big topic of discussion because the tape arrived the day prior and was being seen every three hours in the mess tent.

Tom Lawton watched the colonel intently. He wasn't himself. Stan Hawk was always confident. Always in control. This particular evening, he wasn't. The meeting concluded with the S3 telling everyone to start wearing laser glasses and their "chicken plates" whenever they do missions. The Champions had been in full battle posture for the last week.

After Jerry Maurer was done, he turned the meeting over to Bushmaster Six. The commander had some news to deliver, and it was apparent to Lawton that it was painful for him to deliver. Hawk started, "I have some news for you all. Two nights ago, the United States Army attack helicopters made their first night raids on Iraqi positions." The tent went wild. Everyone was excited at the news that some of their fellow aviators had kicked off on Saddam. The "It's about time" comment led directly to the next question that Hawk had anticipated. "Gentlemen, we are not in any increased posture." The comment deflated the atmosphere instantly. Tom looked at the colonel and could tell there was something else.

The commander cleared his throat, and the tent became silent. "On the opposite side of the spectrum, early yesterday morning, an Apache attack helicopter fired on . . . and inadvertently destroyed two American vehicles. Details are sketchy, to say the least. This is what I know. Two American soldiers died, and several others were injured. The unit was the First Infantry Division and one of the pilots was . . . the battalion commander." You could have heard a pin land in the sand. It was obvious that Hawk knew the other commander and had placed himself in the other man's boots. Hawk continued, "It was an evening mission, and there was a skirmish along the border. The Apache apparently became disoriented and fired upon what he thought was enemy tanks. They were friendlies." The colonel looked around the tent. "I have been informed that guidelines are being established which prohibit the commanding officers from engaging enemy forces." There was a low murmur in the tent.

Tom could tell the problem was twofold for his boss. First, a fellow commander and probable friend had been involved in a tragedy that Hawk alone could sympathize with. Secondly, because of the incident, Hawk would be unable to be forward, firing on the enemy as a leader should be.

After they were dismissed, it seemed that everyone had an opinion on the incident. When they got outside the tent, someone said, "How fucked up is that? Apaches shooting our own guys? That's messed up."

Tom couldn't tell who it was, but he was sympathetic to the commander's dilemma. "Look, we're not in any kind of position to know what happened. We can only accept the little information we know and try to make sure our guys understand it." For some reason, Tom added, "And that the same thing doesn't happen to us." The small crowd seemed to take the words to heart and soon went their separate ways.

Back at the C Troop area, Tom called all units into one tent and briefed them on what he knew. He concluded with comments directed at the pilots. "I honestly think that some problems like this can be prevented by concentrating on situational awareness. When you're monitoring the radio, plot what's happening on your maps. Events like this sometimes happen. We need to take the event, learn what we can from it, and try like hell to make sure it doesn't happen to us." Lawton asked for any questions.

A good one came from Allen Berstein. "Sir, do you think we can go out and record some friendlies in FLIR and then study the tape?"

Tom liked the suggestion. "That's a damn good idea, Mr. Berstein. Tonight, when returning from flying through the area, everyone try to get video pictures of hot M1s and M3s. We'll review them tomorrow. Also, we will go out in full blackout. No lights and bat wings extended in the front seats." He stood up and started out. "Let's stay focused on the mission. Gunnery was good, but we need to start thinking about shooting against the enemy."

Timmons asked the question everyone had on their minds. "When will that be, sir?"

Tom answered the best way he could, "Whenever it is, it won't be soon enough!" Tom smiled. "The sooner we kick their ass, the sooner Walker can get a beer and quit bitchin'."

"Hell, I'm ready to go tonight if I can get a beer, sir!" yelled the warrant from across the tent. Everyone laughed.

Tom thought about Walker's comment. He hadn't wanted or needed a beer in a long time. He found he could concentrate better in the cockpit. The urge was gone, and he didn't really miss it.

Tom had also noticed something else about himself. As the unit had gotten more confidence doing the routine tasks like communications, occupying battle positions, engaging targets, and other general pilot tasks, Tom felt he was getting more confidence. He definitely was more relaxed.

He looked down at his hands, and there was no sign of the previous uneasiness which he had experienced upon entering Gomez. Tom Lawton wasn't afraid anymore.

February 19, 1991
AA Gomez, Saudi Arabia

THE WORD CAME DOWN THAT THE unit was being assigned to the First Armored Division. It wasn't a real surprise, considering they were already colocated with the division in Gomez. The surprise came when they found out the unit would join the division in a "rehearsal." No one had ever heard of or seen a division-size rehearsal before, especially an armored division rehearsal. Hundreds of tanks, infantry fighting vehicles, and support vehicles moving through the desert, burning thousands of gallons of fuel every minute.

Tom took the news back to the Champions. As he got close to the area, he heard music. It wasn't a stereo, but a guitar. Listening closer, he heard two guitars. One voice he recognized as Hal Timmons. He went around the side of the tent that faced away from the center of the compound. To Tom's surprise, there was a handful of Champions sitting on stools and cots, singing and playing guitars. Hal was on one, and Joe Petty was on the other.

"Oh, hi, sir!" said Joe Petty. "Top found our guitars!"

"I see that, Mr. Petty!" acknowledged Tom.

"They finally found our Sea-Land vans in the Corps Support storage area. He found our stoves and some of the stuff we stashed for creature comforts and Lieutenant Timmons and my guitars!" said Mr. Petty.

"He got these for us because they were on top, sir!" said the lieutenant.

"How the hell you gonna haul these things through the desert, guys?" asked Tom. He really wanted to know.

"PFC McFarland said he would carry them for us in the scout Humvee," said Lieutenant Timmons.

Tom shook his head. "All right. But if anything of importance gets left behind"—Tom smiled—"it better be your shit, Lieutenant!" Tom looked at the two acoustic guitars and thought about the ramifications. Hell with the ramifications. The guitars were important to these troopers, so he decided to let the troopers have them. They had enough transportation with the three Humvees and the five-ton to get all their shit and more through the desert. Tom went to his tent, lay on his cot, and just listened to the music. The men were laughing and having fun. Tom Lawton drew in a deep breath and let it out slowly. It was the Champions that comforted him in the desert. For the first time in his military career, he was at peace.

That night at the 1800 meeting, Tom got some good news. Right before the meeting started, Hawk gave him back 956. The second bit of good news came in the form of another pilot. The new pilot was CW4 Lawrence Snyder. He was an Apache instructor pilot with tons of experience, including Huey Gunship in Vietnam. Tom Lawton had met him before and respected him immeasurably. Now Tim Harmon had a back seater to fly with and an aircraft to fly. As soon as he got the good news, the bad news came. Hawk and Needles would still be flying 956 when the unit went into combat.

After the personnel additions were announced, the main portion of the meeting started, and the atmosphere changed. The S2, Lieutenant O'Connor, gave the weather report and briefed the enemy situation in depth, including the latest battle damage assessment (BDA) provided from corps. That was the first clue that something was different. From then on, the meeting took a more serious air about it. When the S3 briefed, everyone found out why the tone had changed.

Captain Maurer briefed that the unit would be flying cover for the First Armored Division as the division did the rehearsal. The rehearsal was starting the next morning. A Troop had the first cover from six to eight, B Troop from eight to ten, and C Troop from ten to noon. The coordinates and frequencies were issued, and support was outlined. The division was to line up facing south. After the move south for fifteen miles, a wheeling-right ninety-degree turn would be made, and the division would roll on for another fifteen miles and hold at that position until the same maneuver was rehearsed the next day. The division would move with the cavalry squadron up front, serving as a covering force, followed by the maneuver brigades in sequence, First, Second, then the Third Brigade. The aviation brigade and the support trains, closely followed by the Division Support Command, would bring up the rear.

Lieutenant Colonel Hawk concluded the meeting by letting everyone know the obvious. After the rehearsal, it wouldn't be long until the ground war began. With the message the unit was one step closer to war, the troop commanders hastily broke up and headed to their respective areas.

Tom wasn't as excited as he thought he would be. In his mind, it was long past time to start. The unit had been told to slow down flying after gunnery to save wear and tear on the airframes and get maintenance to its peak. At that point, Tom knew the Champions were ready.

February 20, 1991
AA Gomez, Saudi Arabia

THE CHAMPIONS TOOK OFF AT 0955 and flew to the southeast. They met the Werewolves at the assigned location and took the battle handover without a hitch. The troop set up a wedge formation, with one scout on each flank and the third scout in trail. The unit flew racetrack patterns as it covered the division's move west. The division crossed the major north-south highway to King Khalid Military City (KKMC) and continued west. The division formation was, in a word, awesome.

Tom Lawton had never seen so much armor together at one time. There were hundreds and hundreds of vehicles stretching over five miles wide and five times as deep. The division cavalry and the three brigades stretched on for miles, with follow-on support units almost doubling the length. It took fifteen minutes to fly from the front to the end. The smoke and dust generated by the column were visible for miles. The division planners had the column split the difference between KKMC and Hafar Al-Batin, thereby preventing unwanted observers from either location an easy view of the movement. A second advantage to the rehearsal, the movement rehearsed was the same right-hand turn the division would use after crossing the border. The command and control procedures were the major pieces of the rehearsal that needed to be practiced. Communication was often garbled and confusing.

The AAR that night had two priorities. The first was to work the bugs out of the communications process. The second item that needed "tweaking" was refueling. The goal was to refuel on the move and be able to maintain pressure on the Iraqi Republican Guard forces.

February 20, 1991
AA Figaro, Saudi Arabia

THE NEW ASSEMBLY AREA WAS NAMED Figaro. The squadron picked up the same relative position in Figaro as they held in Gomez. The size was reduced almost in half, and the aircraft were parked outside the perimeter, facing outward. New infrared camouflage netting had been issued to suppress the heat signature the tents produced at night. Under the FLIR, the outline of the tents could barely be seen. The first night in Figaro, the support trains of the Fighting Sixth didn't arrive until 2200. So the troopers only set up the new camouflage and hoped the weather held. A fifteen-mile-per-hour wind blew throughout the night, but the forecasted rain never came.

Tom made sure the aircraft were tied down and put everyone down for the night before going to the TOC. The word was put out to sit tight for at least twenty-four hours, catch up on rest, and fix the aircraft. On the way back to his area, he checked on the guards at the OP. By the time Tom reached his cot, it was two o'clock. But he was restless and couldn't sleep.

Thirty minutes later, he got up to pee and realized he'd forgotten his bottle. He put on his boots and went outside to urinate. He was alone in the night, feeling the breeze. Being out in the darkness by himself, he remembered his "little run" back at Gomez.

Tom looked up at the stars and took in a deep breath. For some reason, Tom Lawton did something he hadn't done in years. He said a short prayer. "God, it's been a long time since I did this. I'm sorry it's been so long. I'm sorry I haven't gone to church either. I'm not going to make you any promises. Something I know I wouldn't keep, like . . . I'll go to church when I get back! I do have faith that you are watching over us." Tom paused and found it hard to come up with the right words. "Just give me the strength and wisdom I need to bring 'em all back. That's all

I need." He couldn't think of anything else to say. Tom added, "Amen," because as far as he knew, that was how prayers were supposed to end. He took one last look at the beautiful desert night and headed back to his cot. Unfortunately for Tom, thoughts of the approaching war kept coming into his mind. As hard as he tried to sleep, the prayer didn't help.

February 21, 1991
AA Figaro, Saudi Arabia

THE MEETING WAS MOVED UP TO 1300. It mostly covered supply and support information. After it was done, Tom quickly headed outside the TOC and saw an old stick buddy, CW3 Clayton Waters. He was one of the PICs in A Troop. Tom had flown with him for about six months before he'd settled into his limited flying position as the assistant S3.

"How the hell are ya, man?" said Tom. "It seems like years since I've seen you. What's up?"

"Howdy, sir! I guess you know more about what's up than I do." The warrant did his own impression from a Mel Brooks's film called *Blazing Saddles*. "Mongo just pawn in game of life!" said the warrant as he cocked his head to act like Alex Karras. Clay Waters had a tremendous sense of humor. At six foot three, his size intimidated many people. Tom had developed a special trust while flying with CW. He found the warrant easy to talk to and about the best night system pilot Tom had ever flown with. That's probably why CPT Phil Pearson, Assassin Six, chose CW to fly with. "How's it goin' with Champion Six?"

Tom smiled and said, "Same ol', same ol', man. We get the word when we get the word, ya know!"

CW nodded and said, "Yeah, don't we know it!" Then the warrant shocked Tom with an unexpected question. "So you still need a pilot down there in Charlie Troop, sir?"

Tom looked at his friend and said, "No, not really. Larry Snyder got sent down from corps, and I'm full up. Snyder and Harmon don't even have an aircraft to fly."

"I was just hoping I could come over to you," said the warrant.

"What's up? Captain Pearson's pretty damn good," said Tom. He could tell by the expression on the warrant's face that something was bothering him.

"We got a lot of problems over there," said the warrant.

"Lot of problems" could mean many things. "How bad is it?" asked Tom.

CW looked around to see if anyone else was listening as they talked. "There are some guys talkin' about fraggin' Pearson!"

Tom became pissed. "I don't know what that crap is all about! So he worked you guys hard, that's no reason for trash talk like that!"

"Yeah, I know it, sir. But some of the other guys are gettin' real tired of all the bullshit," said CW.

"And you don't think everybody else isn't tired of it too?" Tom scolded. "Look, you need to talk to whoever is blowin' smoke down there. This ain't Vietnam, and ain't nobody fraggin' nobody!" Tom looked at the warrant. "Do I need to tell Pearson or go to the CO?"

CW thought before he spoke. "I don't think it's serious yet. It's mostly a bunch of talk. It's enough to make it frustrating to be around. This whole thing is bad enough, but to have talk like that . . . it's just another distraction that we don't need."

"Do you want to tell me who the guys are?" asked Tom.

"No, sir," answered CW quickly. "Let me talk to them and tell them to put a lid on it."

"Otherwise, you owe it to Pearson to let him know what's goin' on. Hell, you fly with him! Suppose they try something around the aircraft and it's you and not him that gets hurt," said Tom.

That point got to CW. "I'll go talk to Captain Pearson, sir. I think it's mostly trash, but he does need to know."

Tom said, "He definitely needs to know, and you need to talk some sense into whoever is talking that crap." Tom continued, "We're all gonna get outta here in one piece. The warrant officers are the backbone of army aviation. The job can't be done unless you guys are a part of it." Tom let that sink in and saw it appealed to his friend's pride. "Besides, not much longer now."

"Okay, sir," answered the warrant.

"You get back to me tonight and let me know that everything is okay. Otherwise, I'll come over and talk to Pearson," said Tom. The warrant nodded his agreement, and Tom concluded, "You fly safe too! I'll talk to you tonight."

Tom saluted and then shook CW's hand. He turned to head back to the Champion area, shaking his head, when Nichols and Snyder came around the corner. He could tell by the expression on their faces that something else had hit the fan. Only this time, it was in C Troop.

"Sir, we need to talk," said Mark Nichols.

What now? thought Tom. "Can we walk while we talk? I'm ready to get back."

"Sure, sir!" said Nichols.

"What's up?" asked Tom.

"We might have a small problem," said Larry Snyder.

Tom shook his head. "A small problem, huh? What kind of small problem?"

Mark Nichols looked at Larry Snyder, and Larry said, "You go first. I just got here!"

"All right. Some of the guys have been talking—" said Mark Nichols.

Then Tom cut him off. "I've already heard enough about guys talking today. Get to the point."

"The point is, sir, some of the guys are whining about doing the cross-FLOT," said Mark Nichols.

The unit had five basic missions: the deliberate attack, the hasty attack, the movement to contact, the defense, and the cross-FLOT. A sixth mission was created since they had been in Saudi Arabia. It was called armed reconnaissance.

The cross-FLOT mission was an attack forward of the front line of friendly troops. It was designed to attack into the enemy's rear area and disrupt artillery, command and control elements, or rear echelon forces. Properly planned, the cross-FLOT could deal a lethal blow to the enemy and ultimately change the tide of a battle. If not properly planned, it could mean a lethal blow to the unit that crossed friendly lines and entered that enemy territory without proper support from artillery or preplanned coordination. Many things could go wrong, leaving the unit on its own deep-in-enemy terrain or without support when returning to friendly lines.

Tom knew exactly what Nichols meant. Someone had realized the Champions may be called on to do a cross-FLOT and they might get their asses handed to them. So many things needed to be coordinated: artillery, passage points in, passage points out, suppression of the enemy air defense, air force assets, jamming, synchronization at the engagement area, what weapons to use at what time, and the list could go on. Any mistake in one area could be critical to a crew or the unit that had gone deep. No one had told anyone in the unit to prepare for a cross-FLOT, so in Tom's eyes, there was no need to start pinging about something that may not even occur.

They arrived outside the pilot tent. "I don't care who it is. I want to talk to everyone," said Tom.

"I just thought it was something you needed to know before we kicked this thing off," said Mark Nichols.

"Get everybody out and find the lieutenants and bring them here too!" ordered Tom to Nichols. He then turned his attention to Larry Snyder. "Welcome to paradise!"

"Beats bein' up at corps, pullin' on my pud!" The warrant smiled.

Tom didn't want to ask the next question, but if anyone knew the answer, Larry did. "Did you have situations like this in Vietnam?"

Larry laughed "Sir, I take it by 'situations like this,' you mean guys that were afraid to go into enemy territory like these precious cross-FLOTs the brass would have us do? Sir, every day over there was in enemy territory. This can't compare. This whole war is different."

"Any words of wisdom then?" asked Tom, who was no longer smiling.

"I can't tell you what to do in this case, boss. I can only tell ya that I'll be with you whatever you decide. And if that means goin' into Indian country, I'm with ya!" explained the warrant.

That was all the explanation Tom needed. He had no idea what he was going to say until Larry had made that comment. All the pilots had assembled outside the warrant officer's tent. Tom had worked himself up into a tense mood, and it projected instantly to the assembled group. "I've been informed by some of your peers," said Tom, "that some of you might have . . . a problem doing the cross-FLOT mission." Some of the warrants looked harshly at Nichols. "In other words, a little bitchin' has been goin' on! I've never told you guys about the Four Riders of the Apocalypse. Bitchin' is just one of 'em. If whinin', moanin', and complainin' show up in the land of the Champions, we're all goin' to hell in a handbasket!" Tom let the comment sink in then got back to the point. "If you're going to have a problem with this mission, I need to know now."

John Walker spoke up. "I don't know what you were told," said the big warrant as he glared at Mark Nichols. "But you know we're gonna do whatever we're asked to do when we're asked to do it."

"That's not what you guys were saying in there before!" yelled Nichols. The comment led to anger and outburst from half of the crowd.

Tom quickly got control. "Listen! Listen to me!" The men grew quiet. "It doesn't matter what you feel right now. I need to know. If or when we are called on to do a cross-FLOT, are you gonna be counted on?" Tom meant it as a rhetorical question and didn't wait for an answer. "Because I've thought about it. The mission sucks! But if we're called on, we're gonna do it. And we're gonna pull it off. We can deal a blow to the Iraqis that they may never recover from. We could literally shorten the war." Tom looked at the faces. "I'm scared as hell of doin' this mission. But if called on . . . I'm gonna do it. I'm going to do it the best I can, and I'm going to make sure that each one of you comes back with me. Because my ass is coming back!" Tom looked for feedback, and he got it in the form of up and down nods and a couple of "Roger thats." He continued, "Look, fellas, we're CAV guys, and we're gonna do CAV shit! I'm not a politician, so I can't make speeches to fire you up or to try and inspire you to do something . . . beyond your ability. But this mission, if we have to do it, it's within our ability. We can do anything they ask us to do."

Tom looked around and was satisfied that the crisis had passed. To make sure or perhaps out of habit, he sought feedback from the crowd. He looked for someone to tell him, in his own words, what Tom had just said. Mr. Weimer would suffice. "Ron, can you try to put in your own words what I'm tryin' to say?"

CW4 Ron Weimer, a twenty-year veteran, scratched his chin and thought about the request. "Sounds like, quit yer bitchin', ya cowards!"

The group roared with laughter. Tom couldn't have said it any better. His three minutes of eloquent, heartfelt comments were completely washed away by the perfect one-liner that summed up his comments, feelings and thoughts all into one. "Nicely put, Ron!" Tom shook his head and finished up with, "I think we've said all we need to say on this subject. Dismissed!"

That wasn't exactly the term Tom wanted to use with his men, but it was appropriate. He remembered how he felt in Germany and when they first entered Gomez. Since the "little run," he hadn't felt nearly as anxious or felt the fear he used to feel. Lawton had become more confident, confident in himself, in his ability to lead, and in the abilities of his men. He could sympathize with the aviators that felt afraid. But as a leader, his position required him to mask any fear, great or small.

That night, Tom Lawton went over to A Troop to visit CW. The earlier problem they had discussed had vanished. CW said the pilots had gotten together and talked about their grievances with the troop commander. Two of the senior warrants and CW went to Pearson and told him the unit needed to talk with him.

"Pearson was pretty damn indignant at first," said CW.

"Oh, *indignant* you say. That's a pretty big word to tell me you pissed him off!" said Tom, smiling.

"Not really pissed off, sir. Pearson was just upset that there was so much pent-up frustration," said CW.

"So the meeting helped?" asked Tom Lawton.

"Helped a bunch, sir. We talked things out, and he came into the tent and talked with all the pilots. He talked to us like men, instead of robots." CW paused as if remembering the meeting and added, "It was good."

Tom then told CW about his little meeting with the Champion pilots and the comment that summed up his "eloquent" discussion. "Ron Weimer had the . . . audacity to say, 'Quit yer bitchin', you cowards!' I thought I was gonna shit!"

"Oh, *audacity*, eh! Sounds like a big word for *balls*!" Clay Waters laughed. Then he said, "I've got duty tonight, so I gotta get goin', sir. If I don't see you again, fly safe and we'll see ya on the high ground!"

"No sweat, CW. Keep outta trouble! I'll see ya soon," said Tom Lawton.

Before he left, Tom stopped by and talked to Pearson. He was happy about the afternoon's events. Phil was happy he had talked to his men and they had come to an understanding. Tom told him about the cross-FLOT anxieties of the Champions, and Phil said he could relate.

Tom didn't stay long. He wanted to get back and make sure the aircraft were all ready. The division had repositioned itself, so it wouldn't be long now. He might have time to get a quick letter written to Cindy and Megan. Tom had no idea how long it would be until he got another chance to write.

February 23, 1991
AA Figaro, Saudi Arabia

THE DAY WAS SPENT ACCOMPLISHING GENERAL housekeeping—taking care of the aircraft and the vehicles. Everyone expected the word to come down at any minute. While in Figaro, the men had the opportunity to feel the effects of the B-52 strikes. From thirty miles away, the ground shook, and the walls of the tents trembled. One particularly devastating drop produced vibrations in the tent for almost thirty seconds. This caused Carl Tucker to observe, "I'm damn glad I'm not on the receiving end of that!" It was later discovered that on the way out, the bombers dropped propaganda leaflets on the sight of the next day's intended drop area to increase the mental anxiety of the next day's targets.

The unit was issued special blue ropes with D rings to make "extraction harnesses." The rope was to be fashioned around the pilots waist to make a Swiss Seat, and the D ring could be used to fasten the harness onto the outside of any aircraft for extraction purposes. Tom had extreme difficulty getting his harness to fit comfortably and decided to simply carry it in the aircraft. Heaven help him if he had to use it.

The Champions spent the afternoon cleaning weapons, watching the jets meet the refuel tankers three miles overhead, and listening to Petty and Timmons strum tunes on the guitars. Tom found out that Petty used to play guitar in a rock band before he joined the army. When questioned about why he quit, Petty was indifferent.

"Sir, I mean we were on the verge of the big time. We'd cut a demo, and the money was right there. Two of the guys decided they wanted to play Christian rock music. That's just not me, sir. I didn't want to try to do it all over again, and the bills were coming due. So here I am," explained the warrant.

"Well, we're all damn glad that you decided to join us!" said Tom.

Specialist Cryder came up to the group slightly out of breath. "Sir, Top sent me over here to tell you there's a meeting in ten minutes and you and he need to go!"

"Got it, Cryder. Thank you. I'll meet Top at his tent in two mikes!" said Tom. "Hart, you have the controls. I'll be back as soon as I can, hopefully with some news."

Lieutenant Colonel Hawk started the meeting. "The Iraqis have been setting fire to oil wells all over Kuwait. Hussein has been given twenty-four hours to get out of Kuwait. Higher headquarters does not feel he will depart the AO, and they've had enough. The brigade has been ordered to provide one squadron to the armored cavalry regiment in the covering force, and the other stays with the division. Gentlemen, we will stay with the division." That bit of news allowed everyone to breathe a sigh of relief. The colonel made no secret that he wanted to do the covering force mission with the ACR. He accepted the assignment with the division reluctantly and said, "Our sister unit will move today to relocate with the Second ACR. Tomorrow morning, if the Iraqis have not pulled out of Kuwait, they will initiate contact against enemy forces at 0630. The ground war will begin." The tent erupted in "Hooaahhs" and "About time!" comments. Tom Lawton merely took in a deep breath, looked at Garcia, and exhaled audibly.

"It's time to do it, Top," said Tom without expression.

"About time we started kickin' off on that asshole, sir!" said Top to Tom.

The colonel got everyone quiet again and continued, "Tonight, we will execute an armed reconnaissance in sector for the division. We are to assess the enemy strength in sector. We will cross into Iraqi territory with one attack troop and move forward to PL Pear." The colonel pointed to the sector and the phase line on the map. The sector appeared to be about fifteen kilometers wide. PL Pear was thirty kilometers into the sector. Tom couldn't tell, but it sure looked like they would be going across the FLOT to him. "One troop will remain in a holding area five miles south of the border as reinforcements if needed." Everyone looked at each other to size up reactions at which troop would go. Hawk didn't hesitate. "Phil," he said as he looked at Pearson, "tonight, A Troop will conduct the reconnaissance by fire in sector to assess enemy resistance for the subsequent attack. Attempt to determine what enemy if any may hinder the breach operations that commence at 0630 tomorrow." Then Hawk looked at Tom. "C Troop will remain at Holding Area Cindy to provide reinforcements as necessary to A Troop."

Tom nodded at his commander and said, "Roger, sir. And the follow-on rotation for tomorrow?"

Hawk had obviously thought about that question and was prepared. "B Troop will be on hand from 0600 to 1400. A Troop, 1400 to 2200. And you're up 2200 to 0600. You have the night shift, Lawton."

Tom smiled and nodded his acceptance to his commander. He was glad to have the night cycle. The enemy air defense systems weren't as good at night. Better chance to get his men home in one piece. The advantage of the day mission would be better opportunity to clearly make out the targets and what type they were. At night, they just had to make sure the targets were enemy. Situational awareness was always the key to successful night operations. Tom would make sure the Champions had good SA.

Lieutenant Colonel Hawk concluded the meeting. "I need the commanders to stand by for final coordination. First Sergeants, please head back to your units with the details of this meeting and get the men ready. By this time tomorrow, we'll be at war, gentlemen!"

Tom remained at the TOC for an hour, finalizing the plans to support the armed recon and help Phil Pearson as needed. All the time his mind kept repeating, "We're really going to do this. This isn't training. This is for real now!" The excitement made it difficult to concentrate, but all the training helped to maintain an even keel. Because it was "real" now, surprisingly, things hadn't changed that much. The plans were the same, as if the mission had been for training in Germany. It was just a different terrain and the minor details that the opposing forces would shoot back real bullets.

Tom hurried back and found that Hart Osborn and Hal Timmons had already gotten the tent set up for the briefing. The map was in place, and the graphics were already posted. Lawton gave the briefing. It was short and to the point. The Champions were merely reinforcing A Troop and would follow on only if the Assassins got into trouble or found a very lucrative target. It took fifteen minutes, and there were only a couple of questions about radio frequencies. Tom apologized to Larry Snyder and Tim Harmon that he didn't have an aircraft for them and that the squadron commander would be flying with A Troop. The effects from the previous fratricide no longer applied. Hawk and Needles would use 956.

"Time on station for A Troop is 2200. We need to be in HA Cindy NLT 2000." Tom checked his watch and concluded the mission briefing with a time hack. "In ten seconds, it will be 1738." He paused then counted down, "Three, two, one . . . hack!" He looked around the briefing tent and concluded the meeting. "Just like we've been training to do, no speeches from me. I'll meet you guys on the radio at 1925." They knew what they had to do.

Tom got all his stuff loaded on 220 and helped Walker do the preflight. They decided not to go to chow. With a little bit of nerves and a sense of staying focused on the mission, Tom went to his tent for a few minutes but couldn't get comfortable. He even fixed his favorite MRE treat. Crackers, strawberries, sugar, and creamer when mixed together tasted surprisingly close to strawberry shortcake. It was the only way he felt he could reward himself for getting his unit ready. He'd done everything he needed to do personally. So he went to check on the pilots.

As he walked into the tent, the first thing that hit him was a stereo playing "In the Air Tonight" by Phil Collins. Top had obviously managed to bring back some other toys from the Sea-Land vans. He smiled and thought it quite appropriate for the situation.

"Sorry, sir. You want me to turn it down?" asked Allen Berstein.

Tom thought about it. "Naw." Then he walked over to Berstein's stereo. "As a matter of fact, would anybody get too upset if I cranked this puppy?" There was no objection. Tom cranked the stereo. Carl Tucker hooked up two small Bose speakers to Berstein's system, and they started the song again. The music could be heard all the way out to the aircraft where the crew chiefs were putting the final touches to the aircraft before launch.

Tom pulled up a seat on Walker's cot and made himself at home. The music was too loud for anyone to talk. The tent took on the atmosphere more like that of a professional basketball team's locker room than a tent in the middle of nowhere. Each pilot was doing little things that got him prepared to do his mission. Verifying coordinates, transferring the overlay to the map, and double-checking radio frequencies were all tasks, however mundane, required to guarantee success. Tom Lawton merely sat quietly, watching his men and listening to the music. This was where he wanted to be. This was where he needed to be.

Nineteen hundred came, and it was time to leave. In groups of twos, the pilots gathered their remaining equipment and headed out the door for their first combat mission. Walker and Lawton were the last to leave. Tom couldn't help but take one last look at the empty tent. It was too quiet now. An eerie kind of quiet. Tom turned hastily and headed out. He didn't look back. He quickly moved to catch up with Walker and get out to 220.

They mounted the aircraft and got the systems up. Tom glanced to the north at an ominous-looking sky. It looked like it would rain. They hadn't really discussed any weather-abort criteria because no one really expected weather to be a factor. This was the goddamned desert. There wasn't supposed to be any rain here.

Tom did one thing different than normal. Just before Specialist Crockett closed his canopy, he stuck out his hand to the crew chief. "I wanted to make sure you know how much I appreciate all the work you did to this bird to get her ready to fly!"

The crew chief took Tom's hand and beamed. "She'll take care of you, sir! And I know you'll take care of her!"

Tom smiled at the crew chief and said more confidently than he felt, "I will. We'll see you about midnight!" The canopy closed. And the Champions were off to war.

CHAPTER 9

THE CHAMPIONS TOUCHED DOWN AT EXACTLY 2000. Tom had every aircraft shut down to save gas. He went around to each crew to verify the aircraft maintenance was fine. Lieutenant Colonel Hawk passed the word that the division commander wanted to talk to every pilot involved in the operation at 2030. Tom passed the message, and the pilots all got together for the walk to the top of what was probably the only significant sand dune on the border of Iraq.

The dune was the only terrain feature for miles in any direction. They arrived ten minutes early. The commanding general was an impressive man, soft spoken and direct. His age was showing, but probably due to stress and a severe lack of sleep. In spite of his drained physical status, he was fired up and ready to scrap. Tom listened intently to every word the man said.

"This is the first time this division has been in combat since World War II. It was a proud unit then," said the general as he became choked up. "And I'm proud of you men now!" He continued to thank every pilot that would participate in the mission. As he came around to shake hands, Tom wanted to tell him that the Champions were only supporting the recon. But when the CG got to Tom, it didn't seem to matter. The fact that the commanding general of the division found it important enough to be there made it important to support the mission in whatever manner this man deemed necessary. He wanted his men to do "good things" on that first night of contact. And they all swore they would.

By 2100, the Assassins were at Readiness Condition 1 (REDCON 1), with blades turning and the weapons systems, navigation systems, and night vision systems at 100 percent. The Champions started at REDCON 3, which had them prepared to launch in thirty minutes. At 2130, they would accelerate their REDCON level to REDCON 2. All systems powered up without the rotor blades turning.

Tom used a PRC-77 portable radio to monitor the events rather than keep the aircraft running. When they moved up to REDCON 2, he would get in 220 and monitor the mission from the cockpit in case they had to pull pitch.

Prior to the start of the mission, the command radio frequency was constant chatter. There was confusion over whether or not the mission was approved and if they would launch or if they would be delayed. It was difficult to listen to because all the commanders from division to troop were talking constantly and stepping on each other. Tom tuned out most of the chatter and keyed on Bushmaster Six and Assassin Six. When they spoke, he concentrated on what they were doing and applied it to the map. With two minutes to go, the mission was finally approved.

The Assassins pulled pitch right on time. They immediately spread to a wedge formation with Pearson in the middle, flanked by two Apaches on each side. Lieutenant Colonel Hawk picked up a trail position five hundred meters behind and in the center of the formation. Tom watched the flight move out at fifty knots in a northeasterly direction. Something inside Tom wanted it to be the Champions heading that direction instead of the Assassins. But another part of him, the realist, was quite comfortable right where he was. He noticed the radios were quieter now. Pearson would have them talking secure on the Uniform radio. At this point, only Hawk and Pearson were talking on the Fox Mike command net. Tom took the radio with him to the top of the hill again to maintain line of sight between the aircraft and the portable radio. He watched impatiently as the aircraft moved out of sight. Their lights were off, and it was difficult to make them out in the darkness. Tom checked his watch nervously. Time to get to the aircraft. He quickly headed down the hill and jumped into the already-illuminated cockpit.

In the aircraft, the radios were nothing but noisy, confused chatter. The crews were constantly sending spot reports to Pearson, and he handled them cleanly. Tom took the reports and plotted the information on his own map. They had gone five miles to the north and were crossing into Iraq. All reports were negative. Only the berms and tank ditches were visible at that point. Ten minutes later, Tom could no longer hear any reports from the crews, only a few comments from the command and control Blackhawk circling near the border. The Blackhawk merely monitored the actions of the forward troop and served as a downed pilot pickup aircraft if needed.

The fact that Tom could no longer hear what was going on was driving him crazy. He started fidgeting in the cockpit. Walker could tell. "So, sir . . . did you hear the one about the guy and his parrot go into a bar? The bartender goes, 'Hey, you can't bring that shitbird in this bar.' And the parrot goes, 'I can't help it. He's my owner!'"

Tom smiled at the effort. "Is it that obvious?"

"There isn't a thing we can do unless that Blackhawk calls," said Walker.

Tom knew he was right. He exhaled loudly and put his hands on his knees. Then he noticed the raindrops appearing on the canopy overhead. "This is not good. Visibility is gonna go to shit."

"They gotta be to Pear by now, sir," said John Walker. "They'll be headed back soon."

Tom nodded in agreement and began to listen to the radios again. The raindrops got bigger and came down more frequently. Tom said to no one in particular, "This sucks!"

"Not like my first wife!" said the warrant from the backseat.

Tom had to laugh at that one. "We're moments away from goin' into combat, and you're thinking about that. Amazing!"

After what seemed like a week, a crackle came across the radio. They were coming back. A steady rain was coming down, and the wind was starting to pick up. Fifteen minutes later, they were overhead. Tom counted aircraft, more from habit than from fear that one had been lost. Five minutes after the Assassins were clear, the Champions departed. Not a moment too soon. The weather had gone to hell.

2245, February 23, 1991
Five miles north of AA Figaro
Saudi Arabia

"I CAN'T SEE SHIT, SIR!" SAID John Walker.

"All Champions, this is Six. Everybody, bring your position lights to full bright!" said Tom over UHF. Then he said to Walker on intercom in a voice much calmer than he felt, "I can only see black spots in the FLIR! I'm going outside!" The second statement let Walker know that his front seater was no longer watching the FLIR or on instruments. Lawton strained to see through the driving rain and darkness. He finally picked up the light of Nichol's right wing. Tom went back inside and slaved the TADS to the hot spot that should have been an Apache. "I'm inside!" It was nothing but a black blob on the screen. He quickly reversed polarities to white-hot. The picture became a large white blob. "Damn it, John! I can't see a thing either! Hold what you got!"

"All Champions, this is Six. I've got us about eight Ks north of the AA. I want nothing fancy when we get there. About three Ks out, slow to sixty and do a straight in. We'll refuel tomorrow morning. I repeat, do not attempt to go to the FARP!" ordered Tom. He shook his head. He'd flown in some nasty weather before, but never like that. It seemed like mud was hitting the TADS rather than rain. The rain would blow off the TADS due to forward airspeed, yet everything outside was the same temperature. This made the picture appear as one washed-out color. Occasionally, some blotches formed on the TADS, sticking to the screen out front. Whatever was hitting the TADS was thick and slow to come off. Tom remembered flying over the Tapline Road. It was the only linear hot spot for miles. They had dropped down to 150 feet because the only tower in the AO was on the north side of the Tapline Road, so they were clear of obstacles. The unit deliberately slowed to eighty knots and spread out to ten-rotor-disc separation to avoid any chance of a midair collision. All they could do now was wait until they were close to the assembly area. Looking at the ground for clues was not an option because there were no clues to be found.

Lawton called the TOC to say they were inbound with no intentions of going to the FARP. The call was rogered by someone in the TOC, but no one he recognized. He felt the need for some of Walker's humor, but none came.

Walker was up to his ass in alligators of his own trying to keep 220 right side up. The HARS had started acting up again, and the flashing velocity vector was making the usually flippant warrant extremely testy. "I can pick up Mark in the FLIR, but I can't make out the ground. If he buys it, we go in right behind him, sir!" said the pilot.

Out of instinct, Tom checked the altitude. One hundred forty feet and holding. The first thing he really remembered being taught in flight school was the fact that the air doesn't kill you. The impact with stationary objects on the ground is what kills you. Nothing in this desert was above forty feet high, so he felt as comfortable as he could, considering they were blind.

The Doppler finally indicated three kilometers out, and Petty called on the UHF. "Flight, this is lead. I've got three Ks out, and we're slowing to sixty knots." Joe Petty had dropped the "over" that normally accompanied radio traffic. Under the circumstances, Tom didn't have any heartburn with that. If and when they all got on the ground, he may or may not discuss the lack of military professionalism with the junior warrant. But at that particular moment, it didn't really matter. Getting wheels down was the only thing that mattered.

The radios buzzed acknowledgment to slow to sixty knots. Then there was only silence. Tom checked the altitude again, and they were down to one hundred feet. He quickly checked chalk two, and they were holding steady at the same altitude.

Two minutes later, an excited Joe Petty came over the radio. "I've got a vehicle straight ahead!" There was a pause. "I've got 'em! Flight, this is lead! We are on short final for a straight in to landing . . . headed . . . one-seven-five degrees. The vehicle is a Humvee with its lights on." There was a pause. "I've got the tents now. Lead will reposition to the east two hundred meters," said Joe Petty.

"Two will land to the right of lead, over!" said Hart Osborn.

"Chalk three is straight in!" called Walker.

"Four, roger! We will be right of three, over," called Weimer.

"This is trail. Roger," said Tucker.

Walker put the helicopter down with little finesse. "Nice one, Johnny!" Tom breathed a big sigh of relief and leaned back. He quickly looked to his right to see chalk four kick up dust and mud, indicating they too had landed safely. A few seconds later, he could make out their position lights. Thirty seconds after that, another cloud appeared as Toretti landed. Tom gave another audible exhale and a quick thank-you to God. The crew started there after landing shutdown procedures.

Out of the corner of his eye, Tom noticed the Humvee pulling up. He didn't think anything of it until the knock came on the canopy. He looked up to see a very excited and soaked Specialist David Horacio Crockett.

Tom opened the canopy and yelled over the still spinning blades, "Damn glad to see you! What's up?"

The crew chief stuck his head in the now-open cockpit and yelled, "Sir, you gotta come quick! A Troop balled one in!"

Tom was shocked, but the message sank in. On intercom, "John, you have the controls. I'm outta here for A Troop area. Have Osborn conduct the AAR! I'll be back as soon as I can." He looked in the mirror and got a thumbs-up from John Walker.

Tom quickly got his equipment and jumped out of the cockpit. "Sir, I got the Humvee to take you over there! Apparently, they rolled one over when they recovered from the mission. We don't have any details," said Crockett.

"Let's move!" said Tom.

By the time they got to the area, three vehicles had lights on what was obviously a crashed helicopter. The rain was still coming down in buckets. The image created by the lights was that of a beached whale with two huge harpoons sticking in the side, a sight more sickening than sad.

Confusion was all around the site. It seemed that people everywhere were hollering orders with no one in particular listening to anything being said. Flashlights waved beams of light in the rain without purpose or direction. Troopers were running in every direction. Tom quickly got out of the Humvee. "Crockett, I don't want you to stay around here. I'll just walk back when I'm done! Get with Walker and find out what got broken tonight. We need to be ready to go by dawn. Okay?"

"Roger, sir!" said the crew chief. Then he reached behind the seat and threw Tom a Gortex jacket. "I think you'll need this, sir!"

Tom absently looked up at the rain and back in the Humvee at the trooper. Somewhat sheepishly, he said, "Thanks, DC! I'll get it back to you. I promise!"

"No sweat, sir!" The crew chief saluted, and the vehicle disappeared into the darkness. Tom grabbed the closest person he could find. "Where's Captain Pearson?" "He's over there by the colonel!" said the shadow.

Tom jogged over to the front of one of the vehicles. Hawk, Maurer, Pearson, and Mike Leslie were all there. Tom didn't say anything. He just listened to the conversations to see what he could learn. After five minutes, he pulled Chief Warrant Officer 4 Leslie aside. "What gives, Mike?"

The warrant shook his head and said, "Apparently, they tried to come back to the same spot they left from. After they got down, they tried to reposition to this area. They became disoriented and rolled her over on her side."

Tom could sympathize with the pilots. "I know we had a damn shitty picture coming in here." Tom had to ask a question that he didn't want to. "Who was it?"

Leslie said, "Lyle and Klepowitz." He anticipated Tom's next question. "They both walked away from this mess!"

Tom smiled. "That's amazing in itself! There isn't much left." Then he saw Pearson walking with Kenny Lyle. He could tell by the hand movements that the chief warrant officer 4 was showing his commander what had happened to the aircraft. Behind them was CW2 Marty Klepowitz. Tom excused himself from Mike Leslie and went over to talk to the junior warrant.

"How ya doin', Wild Man?" asked Tom. Wild Man was a short and stocky guy with a gruff outlook on life. He got his name on the basketball court. He had a penchant for making sure that anyone that drove the lane would not make the layup. Often, he would follow up the obvious foul call by ranting and raving that he never touched the poor schmuck that lay on the floor.

In his ratchety voice, Klepowitz said, "Oh, just peachy keen, sir!" He smiled weakly and added, "I always wondered what fifteen million dollars' worth of crap looked like. And there it is!"

Tom looked at the wasted airframe and back at Wild Man. "At least you have your health!"

The shaken warrant laughed at the remark, then quickly soured. "Might as well have fuckin' bought it, sir!"

Tom shook off the notion that Klepowitz would rather be dead to the frustration and pain of the crash. "For what it's worth, I'm sorry this happened."

"Me too. I mean I'm glad to be standing here in one piece and alive," said the emotionally wounded warrant. "But I might as well have gotten hurt."

"How do you figure that?" asked Tom.

Klepowitz looked at the captain. "I'm done, sir! The war kicks off tomorrow, and I'm done. Ain't no way Lyle and I get another aircraft. I'll spend the rest of this war in a Humvee, settin' up tents and burnin' shit! But I won't get in another aircraft for a long, long time."

Tom considered the warrant's comment. He was absolutely correct. There weren't enough Apaches to go around the theater as it was. To lose one the night before was just bad luck. Tom knew the man was right about his fate, and a chill went done his back. It wasn't the rain, but the thought that it may have been one of his crews, or worse yet, it may have been him and John Walker.

"My old man always said, 'It's better to be lucky than good.' Now I know what he was talkin' about," said Klepowitz.

Tom agreed. "If there's anything we can do, just let me know, okay?" The drained young warrant tried to muster a smile. Tom was glad it was raining. That way, the tears that ran down Wild Man's cheeks could easily be mistaken for raindrops.

Tom went back over to the downed aircraft. For the most part, it was relatively intact. The avionics bays had not been compromised. An idea jumped to life in Tom's mind.

By the time he got back to the C Troop area, it was 0230. He quietly went into the warrant officer's tent. He somehow found Walker in the dark. "John? Hey, John?"

"Huh? Oh, what's the matter, sir?" said the sleepy warrant.

"Listen. Tomorrow morning, as soon as it's light enough, they're taking pictures of the wreck. I know we need a HARS, but is there anything else we could use?" asked Tom.

John Walker was still asleep, "Um . . . parts or boxes. Let me think." The warrant was on one elbow now and scratching his head. "Yeah! Yeah, there are a couple of things we could use!"

"All right! Tomorrow at six o'clock, I want you at the crash site. Take the parts we need to have and replace them with parts from the downed aircraft. They should have it upright by 0700. Got it?" said Tom.

"Yeah, yeah, I got it, sir!" said the sleepy warrant.

"I'll see ya in the morning. Good night!" said Tom.

Walker shook his head as if to clear cobwebs. "Just one thing, sir?"

"Yes, what is it?" asked Tom.

"There isn't any blood or guts on the aircraft, is there?" asked John Walker.

Oh shit! thought Tom. *They didn't know yet.* "It was Lyle and Klepowitz, and both walked away from it! The aircraft is a mess, but living space and forward avionics bays are still intact." Tom could see that answered the warrant's questions. "Go to bed."

John Walker just shook his head. "I'll say this for you, sir. You're focused!"

0630, February 24, 1991
AA Figaro, Saudi Arabia

THE DIVISION ENGINEERS BEGAN BREACHING THE berm precisely on schedule. Over one hundred lanes were created across the ten-mile front. The division moved forward with limited visibility conditions due to the sand and dust that was still blowing from the storm. The Second ACR was forward, and two heavy brigades were abreast in a wedge formation immediately behind the regiment. The terrain and weather conditions were the only things that slowed down the force. There was little to no resistance from the enemy.

Tom checked his watch. It was 0650 and time to go. The first sergeant came in the tent with coffee. "Morning, sir! Fine day for war, wouldn't you say?"

Tom still wasn't awake, and he despised it when the first sergeant was so jocular. "Just tell me when you need to have them down," said Tom. He knew that Top wanted the tents down so he could load them.

"Fifteen minutes, sir." Top smiled.

"Damn!" yelled Tom. "How about a bit more time to get my shit together!"

"Your lieutenants are already loaded, sir," said Garcia.

Tom rubbed his face and stuck out his hand for the coffee. "Weather?"

"Still shitty!" said the Top.

"Morale?" asked Lawton.

Top laughed. "Still shitty!"

Tom smiled. "That's what I like to hear. Consistency!"

Tom slugged down the coffee and gave a yell. He quickly shaved and dressed. He packed his equipment and carried it outside the tent. He had two separate piles. One was for the stuff he didn't need. The second pile included his protective gear, sleeping bag, a second flight suit, and a change of underwear. He didn't know when he'd see all his equipment again, and he planned on traveling as light as he could. He wasn't an infantry soldier, but some of the old war dogs from Vietnam had taught him how to pack light. He got everything he would need into his rucksack. Osborn and Timmons were outside and gave him morning status reports as they tore down the tent.

Hart Osborn said, "I don't know where he got them from, but Walker showed up with a HARS, an MRTU, and an FCC!"

Tom looked at his watch again. Ahead of schedule. "Good. He got them from 448. Lyle and Klepowitz rolled it last night. I had him go get some parts for our downed birds. After all, they won't be needing them. And yes, they are okay!"

Timmons laughed, and Osborn scratched his head. "Isn't it against every army regulation in the book to remove parts from a crash site until the investigation is completed?"

Tom didn't stop packing. He merely answered, "Yes."

"Oh! Okay, fine! It starts now. We just throw away the regs!" said the flustered lieutenant.

Tom stopped working and looked at him with a smile. "Yes!" The lieutenant shook his head and muttered something under his breath about going to jail. Timmons was nearly rolling on the ground in hysterics.

Tom went to the TOC for a situation update. Chris Wise was getting last-minute instructions. His departure time had been postponed to 0900. Hawk caught Tom's eye and yelled, "Lawton! Get over here! We got a problem!"

Oh crap! thought Tom. *He knows about the parts, and he's got a case of the ass.* "Corps won't let anyone sign for an Apache unless they're a troop commander. Because you're the last one up in the rotation, I need you to take one crew to the COSCOM site to pick up another Apache. You have to sign for it!" The colonel barked orders to one of the TOC commo specialist as Tom digested the order.

"You mean, you want me to go to COSCOM and sign for another Apache?" asked Tom, somewhat confused.

"Are you slow or something, Captain? 'Cause I know I didn't stutter!" said the commander.

"No, sir! I'll load up right away," Tom answered quickly then added, "The crew will be Snyder and Harmon, sir!" The colonel was busy with other business. "Is that it, sir?"

The commander was still distracted but answered, "Yeah, yeah, Tom, that'll be fine. After you sign for it, follow the division sector to the northeast until you find us. I'll have C Troop with me. Any questions?"

It was obvious Hawk didn't have time for questions, and Tom had a million. "No, sir!"

"Good. Get outta here. We'll see you in Iraq," said the colonel. Tom turned and started to leave when the colonel hollered at him, "Hey! You know it's no wonder those poor guys rolled that helicopter last night! They didn't have a single box in their FABs!" Tom stopped dead in his tracks. "You wouldn't know anything about that, would you, Captain?"

Tom turned and tried to read the commander's face. "I don't know anything about that, sir!"

"Is your shit all FMC this morning, Captain?" asked the commander.

"Yes, sir!" answered Tom honestly.

The colonel grunted and smiled. "Get the hell outta here, Lawton!"

Tom was upset that he was ordered to take a mission that he thought Pearson should have had to do. But it was an order, and he'd do it as quickly as he could. He got back in time to see the troop was completely loaded. Tom told Hart Osborn he was in charge and Snyder and Timmons would get a ride in an OH-58 to the COSCOM area where they would remain until the aircraft Tom signed for was ready. Hart was just as confused as Tom was but understood. Lawton gathered Walker, Snyder, Harmon, Timmons, and his observer, Sergeant Clark. They were off for fuel in fifteen minutes.

1335, February 24, 1991
VII Corps Support Command AA Jayhawk, Saudi Arabia

"HOW MUCH LONGER WE GOTTA STAY here, sir? This place gives me the creeps. Bunch of rear echelon mofos with too much goddamn time on their hands!" said John Walker. He was as impatient as Tom was. They had waited for two hours to see the senior warrant officer that was responsible for distributing all the Apache parts, components, and whatchamacallits in theater. It was time that could have been used flying north with the First Armored Division. Finally, two warrant officers came into the makeshift office.

"Either one of you Mr. Kratzenburger?" asked Tom.

"Yes, sir. That would be me," said the taller one.

"My name is Captain Lawton, and my commander told me to come here and sign for an Apache," explained Tom.

"Oh yeah! Can't believe you guys balled one up? You know we don't have any extra Apaches to give out as replacements to just anybody!" said the warrant.

Tom just looked at the man. He didn't want to get into a pissing contest with the corps maintenance officer. He knew he'd lose that fight in a heartbeat. And he really didn't feel like taking the time to explain to Katzenfarts that his piddly little replacement didn't mean shit to Tom and he wanted to be gone two hours ago. "Yeah, hard to believe, eh! How do I go about getting one of your floats? I know you have two. And my boss told me to sign for one. Can you help me out here? We're supposed to be in Iraq right now."

"Well, here's the problem, sir . . . ," said the warrant.

That was enough. "Look!" Tom started to move closer to the man but backed off. "I am not here to discuss . . . problems. I am here for solutions. If you can't help me solve the problem, please point me in the direction of someone that can."

"I can help you, sir! The aircraft you need isn't ready for combat yet. And it won't be for another two days," explained the warrant.

Tom paced. "I'll tell you what! Let me look at it. I've got a crew here. They can stay until the aircraft is ready. In fact, they'll help you in any way they can to get it up!"

The master warrant didn't like the plan one bit. But he was also to the point that anything he could do to get this peckerheaded captain out of his AO was fine with him. "All right, sir. Let's go see what we got!"

They went out behind the facility, and sure enough, there sat two Apaches. The entire collection of corps floats birds. They were beat to hell.

No armament systems, wing stores, or pylons, for that matter. They looked like they had been brought in on a lowboy trailer. Katzenfart got great joy from the expression on Tom's face. "There it is, sir. Which one do you want?"

Tom looked at Walker and then to Snyder. "You got ten minutes to give me a preference! Mr. Kratzenburger, if you get the paperwork started, I'll sign for it as is. Larry, you and Mr. Harmon stay with it until it's ready to fire. You know where to meet us!"

CW4 Larry Snyder shook his head and smiled. "North!"

"Roger that. John, I want to be outta here within the hour!" said Tom. That was a helluva a lot later than he wanted to be gone, but it would have to do.

1630, February 24, 1991
Phase Line Apple, Iraq

LAWTON AND WALKER PICKED UP LEAD, and Timmons, with his AO, Sergeant Clark, followed the Apache to a point on the Iraqi border. It was evident that hundreds of vehicles had gone through the berms. Tom looked down and gave thanks that they weren't down there trying to negotiate the terrain without an escort. The minefields were marked, and they did not appear to have caused the division the need to slow down one bit.

"Damn, sir. There are tracks for miles. I don't see anything on the horizon," said Walker.

Tom automatically checked the fuel gauge. Nothing to worry about there. Maurer had told him the order had been given that everyone would remain on the same frequency throughout the operation, so he wasn't worried about not being able to talk to anyone. What he found hard to believe was that he hadn't heard anything on any frequency yet. "One-six, this is Six. How about climbing to three hundred feet and let me know if you can talk to anybody?" Timmons rogered the call and began his climb. He stayed up for two minutes and got no one.

Every five miles or so, they would spot an occasional vehicle or two. Timmons would take a look to make sure the crew was okay. If they got a thumbs-up, they would continue to fly. He started marking the locations of broke vehicles on his map. The first thing Tom did was to verify the vehicle markings to ensure they were with the First Armored Division and not the Third.

Thirty minutes later, they finally came upon the support trains of the division. Fifteen minutes after that, they came to a welcome sight. An aviation FARP that was rapidly becoming crowded. Aircraft were flying in by the troop. Walker pulled into line at one of the points to wait his turn. Timmons did a quick recon, checking for markings on the other Apaches to identify any First of the Sixth aircraft.

"I got 'em, sir!" called the lieutenant. "They're over at the two o'clock position in a holding area. Looks like they're at REDCON 3, over."

Tom acknowledged and had Timmons get in line for fuel. He felt better knowing they had found the rest of the troop. Then he wondered what he'd missed. The thought that they had engaged anyone went through his mind, but Hawk said they had the night mission. He let the notion go. Little did he know of the events that had taken place.

1745, February 24, 1991
Holding Area Rattle, Iraq

LAWTON FOUND HAWK TWO KILOMETERS FROM the FARP. He was smiling broadly. He, Needles, Osborn, and the Champions had done a little "raid" into Indian country, and he had killed a T-62. The commander was the first to record a destroyed target. Tom agreed that's the way it should be. He was happy for his boss, but upset that he was sent on what he felt had been a bogus mission. Tom asked how the troop had performed, and Hawk was pleased. He said Osborn had killed a tank, but they hadn't seen much else. Many Iraqis wanted to surrender, but the troop had no means to take prisoners. Hawk relayed the information with coordinates to the CAV in hopes they could accept the prisoners. Tom was told to be prepared for the night mission. However, more nasty weather was rolling in that evening. Tom got the coordinates of the tentative assembly area for the night and was dismissed.

Lawton hurried over to the C Troop holding area. The pilots were all gathered around Osborn's aircraft and exchanging war stories from the first engagement. Hart Osborn's eyes were as wide as a kid at Christmas as he told the story of his first kill. Tom listened silently as Hart Osborn detailed the mission. Hawk had taken the Champions on a raid up to Al Busayyah. Tom wanted to be angry, but the reality of the situation set in. He was on another mission, shitty as it was, when the fight began. It dawned on him that he was happy that the troop had gotten "its feet wet" and even happier that they all came back.

Hawk termed the mission a raid, but it was essentially the new buzz mission, the armed reconnaissance. The fact that Al Busayyah was fifty miles into enemy territory was irrelevant. They moved forward seeking out targets, relaying information to the ground units moving behind, or destroying targets of opportunity. Years of planning, training, and coordinating cross-FLOT missions by the book were cast aside. When it came time to execute in combat, the playbook was thrown out the window. The play ended up being tighten down the chinstrap and run into the defense without blockers. Confidence is an immeasurable combat multiplier. Damn, he wished he had been there.

After another fine MRE supper, the troop cranked up and moved to the proposed site of the new assembly area. The weather was getting worse. The ceilings were coming down, and the winds were picking up. Needless to say, the entire unit had reservations about flying in nasty weather again. Even worse, in a combat environment.

1945, February 24, 1991
AA Stooge, Iraq

THE CHAMPIONS ONLY SPOTTED ASSEMBLY AREA Stooge because the ground element had already arrived and were setting up tents. This AA was different than the previous two. Because they were in close quarters, with division assets continuing to move around the area, all the living space was put close together on line in two rows with little space between tents. The vehicles were placed in rows surrounding the living area. Outside the vehicles were the aircraft facing outward as a safety precaution in case of an accidental discharge.

Tom met with the leaders and established the priorities. All maintenance and services on the aircraft were done, then the vehicles, followed by weapons.

They were to be ready to execute the division support mission at 2200. As Tom briefed, he got silence from his men because they were listening to the wind and the rain as it blew against the tent. He took Hart Osborn and said they would check what Hawk had heard. Heads shook when Lawton left, saying, "We still need to be prepared to go. Get some rest."

Tom and Hart stayed at the Squadron TOC, monitoring the radios with the operations personnel, assessing what was happening, plotting the spot reports, and trying to establish a picture of what was happening forward.

The division had stopped short of PL Colorado. They used the time to refuel and rearm any vehicles that needed munitions. Lead elements were approximately eighty-five kilometers from Al Busayyah. Reports from corps and division were monitored by the S2 in the TOC. They monitored a call that the Iraqi III corps commander had ordered his units in Kuwait to withdraw. By 2230, signs were showing that the Iraqi defense was crumbling. It had taken less than twenty-four hours for Hussein's army to crack.

If it was possible, the weather had gotten worse. Hawk called to brigade, and the decision was made to keep all aircraft down for the night. Tom looked at Hart and smiled. The fact that they had considered sending them out with such limited visibility shocked Tom. The accident just twenty-four hours prior probably aided the decision for the troop to sit tight for the night.

0030, February 25, 1991
AA Stooge, Iraq

TOM SENT OSBORN BACK A FEW minutes earlier to brief the unit and to get some sleep. They had only set up two GP Medium tents because they knew the living conditions were temporary. When he got back, only a handful of pilots were awake. Lawton told them everything he knew about current operations. Then he told them all to try to sleep. The unit had orders for stand to at 0500.

"So much for reverse cycle!" said Toretti.

"You might want to keep your camera ready for tomorrow. I think you might get some good photos in the next couple of days," said Tom. Toretti was the unit historian. Then he ordered everyone who was still awake to try and get some sleep.

Lawton stayed awake to update his personal map. He plotted the information he had written down on his kneeboard in the TOC. Tom heard the rain and wind howling outside. He finished off a bottle of water and nearly filled it up again with his own "nitrogenous waste." He had no idea where the latrines were and wasn't about to go look. By 0215, he lay down to try to sleep.

As he lay on the cot in his sleeping bag, his mind was racing a hundred miles an hour. Visions of the map and its graphics flashed through his mind as he tried to sleep. He checked his watch, sat up, and ate some crackers from an MRE. Tom pulled out his map and looked at it again. He couldn't sleep as he thought about the day's events. He wished he'd been with them on the first mission. At that point, it was too late to worry about the first fight and what he had missed. It was time for him to focus on what lay ahead. That just made his mind race even more. Tom said another prayer of thanks for the day's safe "activities" and felt better. Sometime around three thirty, he fell asleep in his flight suit on top of his bag. He had no way of knowing this would be his last opportunity to sleep on a cot for a long time.

0730, February 25, 1991
AA Stooge, Iraq

THE DIVISION CONTINUED THE ATTACK AT 0630. B Troop was mustered early to support the fight but still had marginal weather. All the ground assets were taken down and set to roll by 0800. They rolled forward as scheduled as the aircraft from A Troop and C Troop sat tight.

The weather didn't deter the ground forces. The division rolled forward, continuously lifting and shifting fires as units called back that another phase line had been crossed. The 1-1 CAV with the First Brigade right behind them was having tremendous success. By early afternoon, they had crossed the phase lines Colorado, Arizona, and Arkansas and were preparing to cross New Mexico. Tom monitored what he could hear, plotted the speed the division was moving at, and concluded they would be engaging Al Busayyah at any time.

Alpha Troop got notified to launch. Just as Tom suspected, the coordinates given to Phil Pearson were for Al Busayyah. The Champions were scheduled to attack next.

Early in the afternoon, the Assassins occupied battle positions in an area named Attack Position Python. Alpha Troop managed to get one thirty-minute attack on the Iraqi forces that had established a defensive position near Al Abash. When they were mission complete, Mother Nature had had enough. The fight belonged to the ground forces again. Heavy thunderstorms and shamal-type winds grounded most aviation assets. However, not every aircraft was grounded.

1600, February 25, 1991
Vicinity of Attack Position Python, Iraq

"I HAVE NO CLUE, SIR!" SAID Hart Osborn over the UHF. The troop was flying to the northeast in a raging forty-mile-per-hour sandstorm. Tom appreciated Hart's honesty, but that wasn't exactly what he wanted to hear.

"I'm showing us about two Ks from PL Cut and Shoot!" said Tom.

Petty came on the radio, "I'm on Cut and Shoot right now, sir!" Tom looked ahead. He had Osborn and Nichols in sight. The Apache was in a crab of about thirty degrees into the wind. He couldn't see Petty and Dolce in lead. The sand was too thick. For all Tom knew, Petty could have been two Ks in front of him. He quickly looked behind him and observed the two trail aircraft tight to him, also sporting a wicked crab into the wind. Tom Lawton had seen enough.

"Lead, this is Six. Put it down into the wind right where you are and let's sort this thing out!" ordered Tom. The unit would be safer on the ground. He checked his fuel again, and they had three-quarters of a tank. He called to Timmons, "One-six, climb up as safe as you can. Call the S3. Tell him we are down . . . vicinity of Phase Line Cut and Shoot. We're gonna ride the storm out!" Then on intercom, he ordered, "John, follow Mark and let's plant these things before somebody does something stupid."

The troop landed successfully and rallied at Lawton's helicopter. It was nearly chow time, but the wind was blowing sand so bad, only a couple of crew members even attempted to eat. Tom could see anxiety in the faces of his men. He'd had everyone bring their last-known grid coordinate and had the points plotted on his map. They had not received a global position system read out since they left the FARP early that morning. If they waited back at the last AA, they ran the risk of being too far behind the brigade to get a known location for the next FARP. Tom felt he had no choice but to move forward, but they had gone as far as they could. The weather had gotten so bad that they risked banging an aircraft if he continued. At least now they were down safe, saving gas and making an assessment of their situation, an assessment that took a peculiar turn.

Tom still had the majority of the pilots assembled at his aircraft when he heard the shouting start. "Look, I know where we are! I've been doing this long enough to know we are right . . . here!" It was Joe Petty, and he was apparently quite agitated that Mark Nichols had the audacity to question the location the junior warrant had indicated was the troop's present position.

"I'm not questioning where you think we are. I'm saying you're wrong!" said the instructor pilot.

"Well, fuck you, man!" The junior warrant threw his map on the ground and doubled up his fist. Hart Osborn sprang to his feet and stepped between the two men. "I'm tired of your shit, and I'm gonna kick your ass!" said Petty.

"Hey! Hey, you two, knock it off!" said Hart Osborn. Of course he couldn't stop it. Next thing Tom knew, the two were exchanging punches with the lieutenant smack-dab in the middle, trying his best to be a peacemaker.

Tom looked placidly at the event. Fatigue had overcome him, and his give-a-shit meter was pegged to full apathy. He turned to the rest of the assembled pilots who were growing anxious and said, "I've obviously lost control of those two." He looked at the combatants, and then toward the rest of his pilots, he said, "So do you guys think you could separate them before one of them gets hurt? We'd have a hell of a time trying to get another pilot to fly outta here!"

"You son of a bitch! Come on! You swing like a girl!" said the instructor pilot.

"Fuck you! I'll kick your little ass right here!" yelled Petty.

Tom lay back against the wing of 220 and took a pull on his water bottle. He was too tired to deal with the nonsense right then. O'Toole and Walker stepped in between the warriors and brought about a temporary peace.

Of course Nichols tried to get the last word in, and they went at it again. Tom let the dust settle. He walked over to the two warrants and said quietly, "Are you two through? If you are, why don't you both come over here, and we'll discuss what we're gonna do next!" Tom couldn't help but add, "When we get through with the war at hand, I will be the first one to enjoy watching you two beat the living shit out of each other. Until that time"—Tom pointed to the east—"the enemy is that way."

"He's so goddamn cocky and full of . . . ," said Mark Nichols.

Tom raised his hand, glared at the instructor pilot, and yelled, "It doesn't fucking matter at this moment, does it, Mark?" Tom got his composure back. His screaming wouldn't help matters one bit. "Come over here, both of you, and calm down!"

Tom took about three or four minutes to let the group calm down and get focused on their navigation problem. The points were all plotted on the map. Only one point was totally out of synch, so it was disregarded. Tom looked at the other four. There were no terrain features of any kind to use for reference, so he took the three points that were closest and used them to get an average starting point for their next takeoff. He told the three crews that if they were confident enough with their locations, they didn't need to change their points at all. The fact that they were less than five hundred meters apart made the arguments moot. If and when the weather cleared, they would be able to see for miles day or night. Tom told everyone they were going to sit tight until the weather broke, and then they would move forward and find the FARP.

After the plan was completely understood by everyone, Tom pulled the two combatants off to the side, and they talked. "I don't know how long this has been brewin', but it's over. You understand?" Tom looked at the two warriors with fire in his eyes that he never knew he had. "We don't have time for bullshit like this. If it continues, I won't bother to bring you up on charges." Tom knew what would hurt them more than Uniform Code of Military Justice actions. "I'll ground both your asses! You can tell your grandkids how you spent the war in a goddamn TOC, watching radios blare bullshit. You got me!" That seemed to hit home with the pilots. "I don't expect you to shake hands right now either. But if you do, that's good enough for me to know that it's over!" Seconds later, the two warrants grudgingly held out their hands and apologized to each other.

Then they apologized to Lawton, and he accepted. "I don't expect you to be friends, but we have a job to do. So let's do it, okay?" That was the end of the "brawl at Al Busayyah." Tom chalked it up to tension on their part and piss-poor leadership on his part. He expected the incident to get up the chain of command, but he decided he would never report it. Surprisingly, it was never mentioned again.

They sat in the aircraft waiting until the wind stopped. No matter how much they tried to plug all the holes, the sand found its way into the cockpits. Mother Nature placed a powdery film of dust on top of every flat surface in the airframe. Front seaters worked valiantly to try and keep the surfaces clean, to no avail. Ten minutes later, they were covered again. Eating and sleeping were impossible for the same reason. Tom tried to cover up his face and sleep in the cockpit, but the sand found its way into his mouth and up his nose.

Finally, at 1930, the wind stopped. The crews were quickly outside the aircraft doing preflights and getting ready to launch. They were off in five minutes.

2000, February 25, 1991
FARP Tango, Iraq

WITH ONLY MINOR DIFFICULTY, THE TROOP found the FARP. They immediately topped off their fuel tanks. Walker placed 220 with the left side low, and it made Tom uncomfortable. "What are you doing, John?" he asked.

"I'm putting the fuel opening higher to get as much gas in this puppy as she'll take. After today, I don't know when we'll see the next FARP, and I don't want be laughed at for running out of gas in combat," said the warrant.

Tom looked at the digital display when the refuelers finished. It read over 2,600 pounds. He'd hoped that all the fuel wouldn't damage the fuel cells or rupture any seals. It was a needless worry. The Apache had no problems, and the extra weight wasn't even noticed.

The Champions quickly repositioned and shut down five kilometers forward of the FARP. The squadron's ground forces were miles back. So the pilots made the best of their time by trying to sleep. They were scheduled to fly that night, and sleep was becoming a precious commodity.

Lawton, Osborn, and Timmons established a miniature TOC centered on 220's tail. Osborn pulled out a small American flag and posted it on top of the antennae on 220. It wasn't long before Maurer flew up in an OH-58 and briefed the plan for the evening. C Troop would have their first station time at 2200. One OH-58D was available and would meet them on command FM at that time. The mission was to move forward to the vicinity of Al Busayyah and suppress any enemy positions forward of the 1-1 CAV. Upon rearm and refuel operations, they were to be prepared to go out again. They asked, "How many times?" and "Who will relieve us?"

The S3 just nodded. "You have Alpha Troop coming out at midnight. After that, we'll see how it's going."

Tom rogered the mission, and they moved out to brief the crews. With the briefing completed, the news came on aircraft status. One HARS was acting funny, and Nichols's bird had the rockets stuck in the pods due to blowing sand. The sand had virtually cemented the rockets into the tubes. Tom made a mental note to ensure he covered his pods next time they had a shamal. Fortunately for 220, John Walker had laid his coat over the pod on the left side, and he had cleared the pod on the right side after refueling.

Again, they sat and monitored the fight on the portable FM. For some reason, John Walker asked Tom if he thought they were making a difference. Tom thought about the question and thought his pilot deserved a true answer. He looked at Hal and Hart as he spoke to the three men. "My dad always told me that there are two branches in the army. You got your infantry, and you got your infantry support. We are merely infantry support." Tom looked at the stars that started to peek through and continued, "It's like King of the Hill. Remember that game? If you don't have control, I mean feet on the ground on top of the hill, you don't win. Infantry guys put their feet on the hill. They don't come off the hill until they've won . . . or they've died. We owe our effort to every one of those guys to help them in any way we can to take the hill. In this case, the hill is Kuwait. This is the greatest collection of advanced weaponry that has ever been assembled, but without Joe Snuffy kickin' Akmed out of the damn dirt, we won't win. Getting back to your question. Yes, I'm positive we're making a difference. If nothing else, we can speed up the process for Snuffy to do his job!"

Walker grunted his disagreement. "Sir, you really believe that?"

Tom nodded. "Damn right, John. Without us, I think this war would take a lot longer."

Walker waved a hand, "I don't think it matters one bit, sir! All this technology! Crap! We don't need to be here. We should have just blown the livin' shit out of these terds with the air force and stayed home!"

"Can't do it! Got to have that king on the hill. And that king is the American infantryman. Not an Apache, not a bomb or a missile. GI Joe! And he needs every asset at his disposal to win. We are an asset that makes a difference," said Tom. He could tell his words fell on Walker's deaf ears, but it made sense to Tom. Timmons agreed, but Hart Osborn was skeptical. He obviously thought technology could win the war. Tom didn't want to discuss the philosophy anymore. It would be better discussed back in Germany when there was more time to go into depth. He turned his attention to the radio and began to mark spot reports on his map.

2200, February 25, 1991
AA Fargo, Iraq

THE CHAMPIONS LAUNCHED AT EXACTLY 2200. Osborn and Nichols stayed behind due to the fact their rockets were still locked into the pods from the sandstorm earlier in the day. Petty and Dolce were in lead. Berstein and Weimer were chalk two, then Lawton and Walker. Toretti and Tucker filled the trail position. Hawk had just landed and was not going out again until early morning. Maurer had the squadron fight from the right seat of an OH-58. He would go as long as he could go and told Tom to expect him off the net at 0300. The weather was still marginal, but the rain and wind had stopped. The clouds came and went, but they were high enough not to affect missile firing.

Immediately after launch, Maurer came up on the FM command net. "Champion Six, this is Bushmaster Three, over."

"Three, this is Champions Six, go!"

"Champion Six, this is Three. Wolf Six reports numerous stationary targets in the vicinity of, break." The S3 paused to check his map, then added, "PU065355." The Three let Tom write down the grid then continued, "Condor 16 will meet you on your Victor. The 1-1 CAV TOC is up on FM 35.65, over."

Tom quickly noted the information and called the Three. "Roger, understand Condor 16 on my Victor and CAV TOC on Three-Five-Six-Five, over!"

"Roger, Six. You have the battle!" said the Three.

Tom quickly plotted the coordinates of the engagement area and determined the position of the BP that B Troop had used. Tom decided to move three Ks south of the Wolf position and informed the Three and the CAV TOC. He made sure the CAV knew that the only aircraft in the vicinity were friendly and to keep their Air Defense Artillery weapons posture at RED. This meant the CAV air defenders should only fire with positive threat identification or if fired upon.

They approached the BP with caution, flying at eighty knots. Tom, who was using his night-vision goggles to see directly outside the canopy, could see the vehicles of the CAV as he flew over. He glanced underneath the aircraft to take a look at the view without goggles. It was pitch black. On the horizon, he could see an occasional flash from rounds impacting on the enemy positions. He quickly replaced the goggles and became comfortable again. Glances outside the cockpit revealed clouds to the south. They weren't low, but the bottoms of the clouds illuminated when the flashes from the CAV guns went off. Only Tom could see the reflections off the clouds and the bright white and green flashes in the goggles. The mixture of the weather and the flashing lights of cannons and artillery gave the battlefield a surreal quality. He had the feeling he was flying downhill. The illusion would come and go throughout the night. As they got closer to the enemy, Tom realized he enjoyed the beauty of the scene that he was witnessing, the flashes of color from the canons firing in the darkness, the light as it reflected off the clouds above. His visual senses worked overtime as the audio remained on hold. He could see the cannons fire but never heard them over the aircraft's rotor blades. In the distance, he could see the impacts and explosions of the rounds yet never hear any sound. This was twenty-first-century combat. This was why he'd trained for all these years. The fact that the enemy on the other end of these rounds was getting hammered started to sink in.

Condor 16 broke Tom's train of thought. "Champion Six, this is Condor One-six. I am set to the northern side of your BP. I have targets and can designate for you when set."

"Roger, One-six. You will be working with Champion Two-three. He will meet you on Victor after occupation. Can we get a sitrep, over?" said Tom.

"Roger, Six. The situation is negative enemy fire at this location. Targets are three to four Ks out, mostly soft-skinned vehicles and bunkers. The area appears to be a support area, over!" said Condor 16.

Tom thought it over. They were five kilometers from the BP. A glance out the window and he noticed no more friendly vehicles. Tom chuckled to himself and said to Walker, "Well, John, we are, for all practical purposes, cross-FLOT. And I feel like we're entering the range at Grafenwoehr, except for the churnin' fire in my gut."

"You just keep that feeling, sir. I was doin' just fine until you mentioned that!" said Walker.

"Except for the heartburn and the fact you couldn't get a tack up my ass right now, I'm fine!" said Tom. "Besides, those Delta Geeks are out here unarmed and unafraid."

"No shit. For the most part, they're unconscious too!" said Walker.

Tom laughed again and then realized it was time to get serious. He put the firestorm in his stomach away as best he could and got focused. "All Champions, this is Six. Two-three will fire one Hellfire designated by Condor One-six as a target marker. All targets will be south of that point. Use Hellfire to engage the first target in your sector thirty seconds after impact. All subsequent engagements will be at will. Use Hellfires only on hard targets. We don't know how long the support chain can keep us supplied, so try to make 'em all count! Any questions?" There were none. "Good. Call set. This is Six, out!"

The next calls Tom received were when the troop was set from north to south in the battle position.

"Champion Two-three, this is Condor One-six, over," said CW3 Clarence Dye.

"Condor One-six, this is Champion Two-three. Read you clear on Victor, over," said Petty. His thumb automatically turned on the video recorder as he told Lawton he was set in the BP.

After the initial contact, the crews abbreviated call signs. Dye said, "Two-three, remote mission, one missile, bunker, PU0638, 3643 . . . altitude, 0121, laser tracking line . . . 098 degrees, at my command, call when ready."

Petty wrote frantically. Dolce said, "Accept! Stand by!"

Petty quickly put the information into the fire-control computer, then called to Dye, "Ready."

"Fire, over!" Dye said.

"Shot, over." Joe Petty waited for ten seconds. Then nearly screaming at Condor 16, he said, "Lase now!"

"Roger, out!" said Dye calmly. CW2 Nelson Meyer lased the target. The Iraqis never heard Petty's Hellfire missile as it slammed into their bunker.

Tom heard the exchange on Victor and said to Walker, "Textbook exchange!"

Petty was observing and recording the target site as the impact occurred. The effects of the missile amazed him as it disintegrated the enemy position. "Whooaa! Fuckin' *A*, Condor! I think that's a kill!"

Tom glanced back to Walker. "So much for the textbook vocabulary exchange!"

"Nice spot, Condor! If you got another one, I'm ready!" said Petty. He was definitely into the flow of the mission.

Condor remained a bit more professional. "Roger, Two-three. Your BDA is one enemy bunker. By the secondary explosions, I would say the site was an ammunition point. Understand you need another spot on Alpha, stand by!"

Tom watched the bright explosions in the video display unit in awe. They continued exploding for ten seconds. He finally looked up, and from underneath his goggles, he saw a yellow speck on the horizon. The target was over two miles away. Tom looked back inside and got back on the VDU. He quickly found the remnants of the burning bunker as a huge white spot on his screen. He quickly scanned his sector. He moved south in the engagement area and picked the largest hot object he could find. The Iraqis were running around throughout the engagement area, not knowing exactly what had happened. Tom could tell by the movement of their heads that they had no clue what direction the shot had come from. He quickly checked the clock on the firewall. Five seconds.

"Fire!" yelled Tom. Simultaneously, the Champions fired one missile each. Thirty seconds later, three more enemy hot spots were in flames. Tom quickly scanned the target area again. The Iraqis were totally confused, but they did know one thing. They were getting out of the vehicles.

Tom switched from missiles to rockets. Walker had selected multipurpose submunitions. The rocket would fly to the target area and then release several small bomblets over a fifty-to-one-hundred meter area. Walker selected "fours" and lined the aircraft up on the target. Lawton picked what appeared to be a large truck. Walker got the range information, matched the target symbology, and fired. Out of the corner of his eye, Tom saw the flash as the rockets left the pod. The *whoosh* they created was a small distraction, but comforting to hear. The thought crossed Tom's mind, "'Tis better to give than receive!"

Seconds later, looking in the ORT, Tom could see the rockets open over the target and saw dozens of little hot spots land on the truck. Dozens of bomblets burst on the truck. Seconds later, another secondary explosion ripped the vehicle to pieces. "Damn!" said Tom to no one in particular. He quickly came outside of the cockpit to check on the other birds. They were all engaging the target area. He called on UHF, "Take your time and be selective. We're going to be here a while."

Twenty minutes later, Condor One-six had to leave the station for fuel. He notified Champion Six that he wouldn't be back and thanked Two-three for the missiles. The feelings of respect were mutual, and Two-three told Condor, "Anytime!" Then Petty went to work on the northern part of the engagement area with rockets.

Running out of hot spots, the Troop relocated two kilometers south and continued to engage targets there. They didn't achieve the same results they had during the first attack, but Tom still considered the follow-on engagement a success. No other targets had secondary explosions, and the enemy was definitely buttoned up. Fifteen minutes later, Tom received a Winchester call from 23, followed quickly by 28. With two crews down to only 30mm rounds, he called Maurer. The Three told him to break station and get to the FARP. Tom quickly looked at his fuel gauge and decided fuel was probably critical for the other aircraft. They departed ducks in a row and headed straight for refuel.

Miraculously, the FARP was set up exactly where the S3 said it would be. They were the only aircraft flying at the FARP. Alpha Troop was picking up the fight south of Tom's position. In the darkness, it took nearly forty minutes to refuel the four Apaches. As soon as they had fuel, they had to get missiles and rockets. The aircraft repositioned to the ammo site and shut down. The front seaters got out to assist in the loading effort. The back seaters ran the APU and watched over the loaders to prevent unsafe acts. The rearm point was not the place to do anything stupid. At one o'clock in the morning, this was a prime place for stupid things to happen.

By 0145, they were done rearming and moved to the holding area. Tom noticed the flashing velocity vector. "John, is the HARS screwing up again?"

"Yeah, it is. But I'm okay. I got it!" said the warrant.

Tom disagreed. To fly at night under the system with limited ground terrain for reference was tough enough, but with the system not working correctly was asking for trouble. "I know you can do this, but we don't know how long this fight's gonna last. After we land, get one of the scouts to get you to someone from maintenance and get another HARS."

Walker tried to protest, but Tom wanted to make sure 220 was ready to fight the next day. As they shut down, Osborn came over. "The Three's been trying to reach you. He says we need to go out again!"

"I was afraid you were gonna say that! Are you two ready now?" asked Tom.

"Roger, sir. We're up!" answered the lieutenant.

"Call the Three. Tell him I'm moving into 949. The HARS is tits up on this baby!" said Tom. "It'll take me fifteen minutes till I get there and get up, okay?"

Osborn nodded and hurried to crank up his bird. Tom got on the radio and called everyone to tell them the news. They had another station time in thirty minutes. Tom rubbed his eyes and looked at his watch. Nearly two o'clock. It felt like the night had been going on forever.

0235, February 26, 1991
Phase Line Texas, Iraq

THE CHAMPIONS WENT OUT FOR THEIR second mission of the night. The crews had changed somewhat. Lead remained Petty and Dolce, followed by Osborn and Nichols, then Weimer and Berstein. Tom switched into Tucker's front seat with Toretti and picked up the trail position. Physically, he was tired. He caught himself yawning a few minutes into the flight and shook his head to get awake. He also had Toretti turn down the heat in the cockpit. Tom wore an extra shirt as well as his jacket. He and Walker also flew with their jackets on under their flak vests. Toretti and Tucker flew in only flight suits with the vests and chicken plates. A minor difference, but Tom noticed it because of the sweat that was dripping into his eyes. He was pretty sure it was the cockpit heat and not his nerves. At the release point, he finally felt awake again.

The unit occupied a battle position that Alpha Troop had just come from. The 58 Deltas were done for the night, and the S3 said he was "going down" to get some sleep. There was nothing left to fire at in the position. After scanning the engagement area, they noticed no movement, only burning hulks of vehicles and bunkers.

Tom notified the 1-1 CAV TOC, whose sector they were in, that they were relocating three kilometers south and moving forward. The movement was deliberate and cautious. The four aircraft wheeled to the south at forty knots about fifty feet above the ground. Three Ks later, they wheeled left and came on line. Slowly, they moved forward.

Petty was the first to notice targets. "Six, this is Two-three. I've got targets direct front." The warrant quickly lased and stored two hot spots at four thousand meters.

Tom ordered the flight to halt. They climbed to 120 feet to observe the new area. Tom counted six hot spots, three of which appeared to be tanks facing south. Osborn's laser spot divided the engagement area up. Everything south of his mark belonged to Berstein and Lawton. Everything north belonged to Petty and Osborn. Tom turned on his video and moved his data entry keyboard select knob to record his present position. When the S2 reviewed the tape later, he would have a start point and know the orientation to the targets. He lased and stored the target farthest to the south in his first store position. Tom called the flight when he was set. "Champions, this is Six. First volley in thirty seconds at my mark. Ready, ready, mark!"

Tom watched his clock, and out of habit, he counted down, verifying the target in the VDU only once. Toretti already had 956 oriented on the target. Tom went back to the clock, counted down to himself, and yelled on Uniform, "Fire!"

Simultaneously, four Hellfire missiles left their rails, seeking their laser spots two miles away. Tom kept the laser on as he aligned the crosshairs on his tank. He couldn't make out the type, but with the gun tube headed south, he knew it was Iraqi. Seconds later, the screen on the VDU bleached completely white as the tank exploded in a ball of flame. Tom kept listening for the sound of the explosion from his tiny screen, but it never came. He scanned left and found another vehicle. It had wheels, so he selected rockets. Thirty seconds later, it too was in flames. Within ten minutes, all the vehicles in the entire engagement area were destroyed. Tom called to verify if anyone else saw movement, and there was none reported. He checked his watch, and it was 0353. Lawton contacted the CAV to let them know the coordinates of the last engagement, and they had definitely engaged tanks. They were Bingo for fuel, and two birds were Winchester for rockets.

They egressed the battle position as deliberately as they entered it. Tom received his battle damage assessment (BDA) and sent it to the CAV. The fact that they had engaged multiple tanks gave the CAV a heads-up of what to expect when they attacked in two hours.

Tom was on the verge of falling asleep when they started to pull into the FARP. It was a new experience for him. Tom had never come close to falling asleep in a helicopter before. The refuel went even slower this time. It probably took an extra thirty minutes because the fuel handlers were worn out. This was the third time Tom had refueled at this FARP. The FARP troopers had been rolling for God-only-knew-how-many hours before they got set up. In two hours, they would be on the move again. After hot gas, they went to the ammo point to get thirty-eight more rockets and four Hellfires.

It was still dark when they moved to the holding area. Tom called the TOC, which was nothing more than Lieutenant Shepperd and a junior NCO in a Humvee with a radio. He sent a sitrep and his BDA report and then said he would be down in ten minutes.

As the helicopter approached its intended landing point, Tom noticed too late that they were moving backward at about five knots. The helicopter hit harder than expected going backward. For some reason, Tom didn't get startled.

"Christ, sir! I'm sorry about that landing!" said Toretti.

Tom just chuckled. He looked in the mirror at the warrant. "If you think I could do any better right now, you're sadly mistaken. We're down on the ground safely. Another day, another thirty bucks and some change!" Tom realized he was too tired to give a damn about the style points for a pretty landing. The handicapped factor of six and a half hours night vision systems more than made up for the bounce.

"You'll have to excuse me for not hanging around for coffee, Mr. Toretti. I've got an appointment with my sleeping bag!" said Tom.

"I hear that, sir. Thanks. I enjoyed that," said the warrant with a big grin and tired eyes.

Tom walked back to 220 and thought about the comment. Toretti must be sick if he enjoys flying that much system time under those conditions. Tom began to think about sleep, and then he noticed the clouds above. He couldn't see stars in any direction. He got to the aircraft, quickly told Walker about the "festivities," and pulled out his bag. Tom popped open the engine cowling on number 1, spread out his bag, and took off his flight suit. Two minutes after he got into the bag, he felt the first drops of rain on his face. He tried to cover up, but to no avail. The drops became a steady rainfall, and minutes later, it started to get light. Thoroughly disgusted now, Tom climbed out of the bag and into the front seat again. He simply threw the bag over him and tried to sleep again. Unable to get comfortable, he gave up. He knew he was tired, but sleeping was not an option. He climbed out, put on his flight suit, and had coffee with Walker.

1000, February 26, 1991
Holding Area Charlotte, Iraq

THE FIRST ARMORED DIVISION HAD RUN up against the best the Iraqi army had, the elite Iraq Republican Guard. The tanks the Champions had engaged the previous night were elements of the

Madinah Division. What the division didn't know was that before the day was through, elements of the Madinah, the Tawakalna, and the Adnan divisions would all be in their sector. Refueling operations were completed early in the morning, and the division deployed with the First Brigade in the north, followed by the Second Brigade. A single, tank-heavy Third Brigade worked the southern sector on the boundary with the Third Armored Division.

The squadron was in support of both forward brigades, with Alpha Troop in the north and Bravo Troop to the south. C Troop was ordered to be ready for either sector at noon. Tom still had not slept but was aware of the orders and the fight. Timmons's scout had become the C Troop TOC and was parked in the center of HA Charlotte. Tom pulled out his last warm Pepsi. The only caffeine he would get after that would have to come from coffee, and Walker had plenty of that.

They hadn't seen any of the crew chiefs for what seemed like a week, and the Apaches were all past their normal ten-hour-service interval. Out of nowhere, two Humvees pulled up with water, MREs, engine oil, and other necessities to service the aircraft. The pilots nearly had a party. Tom had the aircraft checked out immediately. Up to that point, they had performed better than he'd expected. He wasn't sure how much longer the aircraft could go on without the much-needed attention. Crockett quickly checked both engines and gave Lawton a thumbs-up. He started cleaning the windows, which Tom hadn't noticed. They were streaked with brown water lines and spots that made it difficult to see.

"I don't know how to thank you two," said Tom to Crockett and Padillo.

Crockett knew. "Sir, when we get back to Germany, you can get me some of that Lichtenauer beer."

Tom laughed. "If that's all you want, you work too cheap!" Padillo was looking at Tom, and his smile faded. "What's the matter?" Padillo appeared to be stuck between wanting to say what he felt and wanting to change the subject. "Come on! What gives?"

"I don't know how to say this, sir, but you look like hell!" said the soldier honestly.

"I don't know how to tell you this, but I feel like hell too!" Tom laughed. "It's nothing that ten hours of uninterrupted sleep won't take care of. My butt hurts, my stomachs full of coffee and this Pepsi, and I haven't crapped for three days." They thought he was kidding. "I can hang until Saddam quits."

The specialist started rubbing his chin. "You need a mirror, sir?"

Tom rubbed his chin. Holy shit! He practically had a beard. Tom smiled at the man. "I guess my protective mask won't work worth a damn like this, huh?"

"No, sir! Top would give us hell if we had hair like that!" said Crockett.

Tom dug through his ruck for his shaving kit. "Again, it takes my crew chiefs to square me away. You guys are the best!" Tom started shaving.

Crockett watched his boss as he continued to wipe the windscreens on 220. "How's the fight goin', sir?"

Tom thought about the best way to answer. "We're kickin' their asses!" Then he added, knowing what the crew chief wanted to hear. "We might be able to slow down in three or four more days. At the speed we're moving, we'll be in Kuwait soon. The question is, are we gonna turn north? If so, we'll be ready. The aircraft and you guys are doin' great." Tom assessed his answer as honest and hoped it would be over in two more days. If he didn't get some kind of sleep soon, it would be over for him sooner than that.

The troop never had an opportunity to stay put for too long. The division moved too fast during the day. At noon, they were called out on a wild-goose chase to find six "reported" Iraqi tanks that were wreaking havoc in the division rear. Two hours later, with no fuel and no enemy tanks to be found, the Champions relocated to the new FARP, Sunoco.

Their timing was excellent. As soon as they finished, one attack troop entered the line for fuel, four Blackhawks and four scouts. No aircraft went to holding areas for fear of losing a space in line. When they repositioned to their new holding area, Cathy, brigade put out a call that the new FARP wouldn't be up for two hours. Within fifteen minutes, the lines at four of the points had six aircraft at each. Other brigade aircraft and some corps birds had gotten in line, and the FARP was a zoo.

Tom got word that his next "Be prepared" time was 1800, so he shut everyone down. With armored vehicles rolling and their proximity to the FARP, any form of sleep was out of the question. Tom, Hal

Timmons, and Hart Osborn decided to take a stroll over to look at the Iraqi prisoners of war.

The EPWs were placed in a makeshift holding area. A destroyed vehicle made one side, and strands of barbed wire enclosed an area about twenty meters by twenty meters. There were fifteen prisoners ranging in age from fifteen to sixty-five.

As they looked at the prisoners, one came up to them. "You have a cigarette?"

The threesome looked at each other, dumbfounded. Hal just happen to have a cigar, but no cigarette. "A cigar would be good," said the prisoner. Tom couldn't help but notice his English was great. It turned out that Khalil Al Hummadi was a student at Chico State University in California. He had come home to Iraq the previous summer and was immediately "drafted" for the invasion of Kuwait. He wasn't in one of the Republican Guard units. He was merely in a support unit for the Fifty-second Mechanized Infantry Division. He asked for water, and Tom gave him the rest of his bottle.

Khalil said he told the rest of his group not to worry and the Americans would come any day. That had been two months ago. The Iraqis were living on rice and beans for the last month. The officers had threatened to kill anyone in the group that had talked of surrender, but when the Americans came, "they ran like women." He wasn't sad, just hungry and ready to go home. "They took my undershirt. I used my . . . you call them Skivvies, to make a truce flag." Hal said that was a good idea and that if he had any clean Skivvies, he would have let Khalil have them. "Of course," Khalil said, "that would be fine, but no, thank you!" Hal figured it was a custom not to accept too much hospitality from an enemy that was kicking your ass. The truth was, Khalil thought Hal's underwear were as nasty as the man who offered them up.

Tom and his men thought it better not to ask too many questions of Khalil. They couldn't help him any more than they already had. Tom bid farewell and wished Khalil luck and safety. The three pilots agreed that if the shoe were on the other foot, they probably would not be treated as well by the Iraqis as they had treated Khalil.

2300, February 26, 1991
Holding Area Carlene, Iraq

THE TROOP HAD BEEN GIVEN ORDERS to attack into a new engagement area. The site was known as Objective Bonn. There was no doubt that this was the main battle area of Republican Guard forces. The Madinah and Tawakalna were pulling out of Kuwait in order to maintain as much of their force as possible. The shortest distance to Iraq brought the divisions right in front of the Seventh Corps.

The First Armored Division had moved to three brigades abreast in the attack. All three brigades had moved to Phase Line Libya. The division artillery was mercilessly pounding Iraqi forces in the northern part of the sector.

Alpha Troop was sent forward to provide eyes on spot reports for the DIVARTY commander and collect intelligence for the next morning's attack. C Troop drew the southern sector with the same mission. Tom was glad because he was becoming quite familiar with the night TOC personnel of the 1-1 CAV.

The ground fighting was more intense on this night. More tanks and artillery were exchanging fire. It was obvious that the enemy here was better prepared and would not capitulate as readily as the forces from the previous nights. The First Armored Division forces were more willing to "mix it up" too. The night's first mission was merely a reconnaissance forward three Ks of the CAV's observation posts. Headquarters was curious as to whether the enemy was preparing a counterattack. The troop established a picket line and observed actions to the south and in front of the CAV. There was no sign of any imminent attack, and after one hour, the troop was recalled.

0230, February 27, 1991
Battle Position Charlie 21, Iraq

SOMETHING SEEMED DIFFERENT WITH THE FOLLOW-ON mission. Tom couldn't put his finger on it. Nothing felt wrong, just different. There was more tension on the radios, and fatigue was showing on all the pilots, not just Tom. He chalked it up to the enemy's new resistance. They had been in the BP only five minutes when a frantic call came across the FM.

"We're taking fire! Taking fire!" It was the CAV TOC on command.

"Blackhorse TOC, Blackhorse TOC, this is Champion Six, over!" yelled Tom.

"Champion Six, this is the TOC. We are under heavy fire. I repeat! We are under fire. Origin . . . and type . . . unknown," said the voice at the TOC. He thought about Jed Stuart and hoped he was in a hole somewhere.

Tom notified the CAV they were moving forward. On line, the five Apaches moved forward to try to observe enemy fires that were causing the incoming on the CAV TOC. Osborn and Petty simultaneously noticed hot spots. Tom didn't try to set up anything fancy. "All Champions, this is Six. Fire at will!" Within seconds, Osborn and Petty had missiles in the air. It took Tucker longer to find targets. Allen Berstein said he had soft skins and fired three pairs of rockets. Tom lased the area and sent the grid back to the CAV in hopes they could redirect some artillery onto the area, countering the fires they were receiving. For five minutes, the Champions fired as fast as they could at every hot spot they saw. Tom still had five missiles left because he couldn't find anything left that appeared to be a "hard" target. They started to run low on rockets. Tom hesitated to move closer, knowing the CAV would fire at the grid he had sent at any time. They stayed two kilometers away from the area and slowed the rate of fire. Only two more missiles were fired, and there was no return of enemy fire.

The voice at the CAV TOC came on the FM command, "Champion Six, this Blackhorse TOC. Enemy fire has stopped. Our battery is prepared to fire. Can you observe?"

"Roger, TOC. That's affirmative!" answered Tom. Then he called the Champions to hold their fire so they could observe the artillery.

"Contact Redleg 25 on 32.55, over," said the voice. Tom switched to the new FM frequency and made initial contact.

"Champion Six, this Redleg 25, over," said 2LT Chad Barton.

"Redleg 25, this is Champion Six. Understand you are prepared to fire previous eight-digit grid. We are in position to observe, over," said Tom. "Call, shot!"

Seconds later, "Shot, over!" called the artilleryman.

"Shot, out!" said Tom.

"Splash, over!" said the lieutenant.

Tom looked to observe the target area and called, "Splash, out!" He found the round as it impacted. It needed to go deeper into enemy territory. "Redleg, this is Champion. Add three hundred, over!"

Surprisingly fast, Redleg had another round on the target area. It was right-on. "Redleg, this is Champion. Fire for effect, over!"

Within a minute, the engagement area erupted in multiple explosions. Tom turned the artillery control over to Hart Osborn and let him contact Redleg. The pit in his stomach that had been there previously was gone. The unit took turns calling for fire and mixing in occasional rocket shots on any suspicious targets that appeared man-made or showed signs of movement. With no rockets left and only thirty minutes of fuel remaining, they headed for the FARP. The CAV had received no more fire, and for the first time, Tom really felt like telling Walker this mission proved they had made a difference. But he was too tired. His butt, back, and mind ached. He tried to figure out how many hours he'd spent in the cockpit, but the math was too difficult. He was glad the Doppler told him how long it was to get to the FARP because he doubted he could figure it out.

1200, February 27, 1991
Holding Area Carlene, Iraq

THE DIVISION WAS HAVING TREMENDOUS SUCCESS against the withdrawing Iraqi Republican Guard units. The division had crossed three more phase lines and was on the edge of Objective Bonn. The only thing slowing the division down were the thousands of prisoners being collected. The ground brigades were engaging the Madinah Division in what was to be the largest fight of the war. T-72s, T-55s, armored personnel carriers, and SA-13s fought furiously as hundreds of vehicles attempted to get north of the American forces. The division commander called on every asset at his disposal to engage and destroy Iraqi forces along the entire division front. Fuel was becoming critical, and the goal was to put a final massive attack on the Republican Guards for the decisive blow.

One squadron had been sent deep on an armed reconnaissance. The goal was to find, fix, and destroy all vehicles attempting to get back to Iraq. The Fighting Sixth got the division support mission again. Hawk called on all three troops to move forward and engage with the forward brigades. His operation order called for a phased attack. A mass attack would have all three troops on line attacking at once. A continuous attack would place one troop attacking after another until the sequence completed the goal of the mission. A phased attack allowed for a mix. Either one troop forward first, followed by two troops or vice versa. Because B Troop was already on station, Hawk called for A Troop to deploy to the north at 1300 and C Troop in the southern sector by 1315. The S3 in an OH-58 was already out monitoring the fight. The squadron commander was in the only Blackhawk that was still operational.

Tom had finally gotten about three hours of uncomfortable sleep. But it was enough to get his batteries charged. He received the order and hurriedly copied new graphics. The fact that they had remained on the same frequencies for the last four days had helped shortened mission briefings and reduced the possibility for communications errors immeasurably. He hurried back to Timmons's scout for the briefing. To his surprise, Snyder and Harmon had arrived. The aircraft was loaded with sixteen Hellfires and no rockets, but it was with C Troop and not in the rear.

The crews had gotten just enough rest, preflighted the aircraft, and eaten. The scouts were very excited. For only the second time, they got to go forward with the Apaches. Tom split the Apaches into two teams of three Apaches each. The heavy Hellfire bird stayed with Osborn.

1315, February 27, 1991
Phase Line Monaco, Iraq

TOM COULD TELL THIS MISSION WAS going to be different. The radios were a nightmare. It seemed like the FM command had twenty people talking on it all at the same time. Trying to talk to the other troop commanders was impossible. Tom ended up switching to their UHF or VHF frequency to talk to them. They were late for pitch pull only because he couldn't talk to the S3. They pulled pitch and flew at 130 knots to the release point. Just as they slowed, Tom heard Maurer on the FM command. "You tell him to get those sons of bitches forward now!"

Walker was hot. "Who the hell does he think he is, fucking Patton?"

Tom just gave him a look to keep quiet. "Bushmaster Three, this is Champion Six. Somebody up here looking for sons of bitches? I guess we're not needed!"

There was a noticeable pause as Maurer, who realized he had broadcast the insult over the FM, tried to think of something cleaver to say to cover his error. After about five seconds, the flustered operations officer couldn't think of anything, so he decided to get down to business. "Where the hell are you, guys?"

"You've got us five hundred meters out your five o'clock." Tom wanted to add "shithead" but thought the comment might be unprofessional. As if calling one of your own units "sons of bitches" wasn't. They could discuss the proper use of radio terminology some other time, but right now, Tom needed to know where Maurer wanted him to go. Besides, it was probably just the heat of battle and the fog of war put together. After hearing the way the fight was going on the radios, Tom decided neither of those was it. Maurer needed steel on target about five mikes ago, and he wasn't getting it. The Champions were just what the Three needed.

"The Third Brigade is trying to finish off the Tawakalna elements in sector. Head south about three Ks and try to meet their Three up on 44.50. They keep saying they have tanks rolling north. You should have plenty of opportunity for engagements. There's weather coming in soon, so get your shots in and get out!" Maurer paused and then added, "Sorry about that call. Bushmaster Three, out!"

"No problem, Three. We don't sweat the petty stuff. We just pet the sweaty stuff!" Tom let him think about the remark, then added, "I might not be able to get through to you because these radios are nuts. I'll talk to you if I can, out!" He knew he wouldn't be able to get through after they moved. Call it a gut feeling, but he felt the Champions were on their own again.

The troop repositioned south, and Tom got the Brigade Three on the first try. He was up to his ass in gomers and didn't really want to deal with the Apaches. He basically said, find a spot and start shooting. There were targets enough for everybody. Tom rogered the transmission, and the

Champions moved forward. He had a scout on each flank and had the light team on the left in an echelon right and his team to the right in an echelon right. He was feeling cocky for the first time. The feeling would fade as quickly as it came.

The operations officer was right. The Tawakalna were saddled up and hauling ass for Baghdad. Every vehicle they had was loaded to the top with soldiers trying to get out. Osborn had the light team move right up and mingle with a tank platoon on line. Tom looked behind out the right rear and saw the Division Artillery's multiple launch rocket systems preparing to launch. Moments later, tank cannons were blasting, Hellfires were screaming, and MLRS rounds were fired like dragons screaming. Satan himself couldn't have matched the fires in hell to First Armored Division on this day.

For a few seconds, with the radios blaring the frantic and confused orders of desperate leaders, Tom just watched and listened. It was an amazing feat this so-called combined arms in action. The chaos generated by the unbridled carnage was hard to imagine. To actually witness the act left Tom momentarily in awe. On the other end of this barrage of unprecedented fires was an enemy that was getting pummeled in a scenario never before duplicated.

Walker interrupted Tom's reflection. "So? We gonna go kick some ass, or do you wanna pull out some wine and cheese?"

Tom just nodded and said, "Yeah, let's move over to the right!" He was still stunned by the events of his surroundings. He tried to get a call to Maurer and thought he heard him say he had to go refuel. He filed that in the "not important right now" file and picked up a firing position above two tanks. He surveyed downrange and saw at least five vehicles running north as fast as they could go. Mostly all the views of the enemy target areas Tom had seen so far were greenish-black tint on his tiny screen in the ORT. This scene was different. Every vehicle was within two kilometers, moving thirty miles an hour, and had Iraqi soldiers on top of it. Tom looked up from the VDU using his day TV image and could barely make out the tanks in the engagement area. He looked to the south and saw low, fog-like clouds from the developing precipitation moving at a pace nearly the same speed of the vehicles.

He went back inside and found a target. For just an instant, Tom hesitated to pull the trigger. He noticed the soldiers riding on top of the tanks, literally holding on for their dear life. He had an accurate range, and the tank was in the crosshairs. Then he remembered his own words. "Now is not the time to discover you can't pull the trigger." What if one of them had the opportunity to shoot down one of his crews? The momentary lapse of conscience subsided. He squeezed the trigger without further hesitation, staying on the target until it exploded into a huge fireball. The firing continued for another two minutes.

Then something caught his attention. Out of the corner of his eye, he saw a cloud of smoke and felt the aircraft shake.

"Holy shit!" yelled Walker. "We got incoming, and it's goddamn close!"

Tom was on the radios in a flash. "All Champions, this is Six! Back off! I say again, back off one klick!" He didn't need radio transmissions to acknowledge. He watched as the aircraft around him pivoted to the west and began to reposition. Tom looked to make sure everyone had the order. Only Osborn and Nichols were still lined up with the tanks. Tom called again, "Goddamn it, Two-six! Back off now!"

"You got the shot, take it!" said Mark Nichols.

"But the commander said to move back!" said the lieutenant.

"Look at that, Lieutenant! I see the tank in your screen, so are you gonna kill it or what?" said the instructor pilot.

Osborn got a good range to the target, pulled the weapons trigger, and kept the crosshairs on the T-72. Osborn could barely make it out as the smoke from the Hellfire obscured his intended target. He kept the spot on where he thought the tank should be. Soon enough, the smoke cleared, and the tank was in perfect position. Instantly, the vehicle erupted into flame. Hart Osborn said, "I got it! Now can we get the hell outta here?"

Tom watched helplessly as two more rounds impacted nearly on one of the tanks right beside Osborn and Nichols. Walker tried to say something, but Tom cut him off. "Wait one, John!" Lawton guessed it was Nichols keeping them in the firing position. Then on Victor, "Goddamn it, Mark! Get the hell outta there!"

Finally, the aircraft did a hard pedal turn and headed to the west. Nichols nosed it over, but not quite fast enough. The first round exploded right in front of the aircraft, and the second one just behind the tail boom.

"I can't see!" screamed Hart. As the aircraft cleared the smoke and dirt of the explosion, Nichols could see they were in a nose-down attitude. Just as Hart yelled to pull up, the engine-out audio started to sound out. Fragments from the incoming artillery rounds had ripped through the cowling covering the number 1 engine.

"We're all right! I got it!" yelled Mark Nichols.

The second round went off right where the aircraft had been. Fragments from that round hit the tail rotor and caused a vibration that was nearly uncontrollable.

"Tail rotor's hit, Lieutenant! I gotta put it down, or we're dead!" yelled the instructor pilot as he struggled to maintain control.

Hart Osborn was on the radio instantly. "We're goin' down!"

"Shit!" yelled Tom. Walker was way ahead of him and had turned 220 around to see the impact. Nichols had done a tremendous job getting the aircraft's nose up as the tail rotor started to come apart. The aircraft had just started to spin as it hit the ground. Somehow, it managed to go straight in as it impacted the desert. The last control movements somehow managed to keep the aircraft upright. Pieces of the tail rotor began to fly off uncontrollably as the aircraft began to self-destruct.

"Don't get out yet! Wait until the blades stop!" yelled Nichols.

Hart was shaken up from the impact but knew enough to acknowledge the instructor pilot.

"Lieutenant, I've got to zero the radios. Just get the hell away from the aircraft!" said Nichols. Osborn nodded and started unplugging his IHADSS helmet. He secured everything he could carry and his maps. As the blades finally came to a stop, Osborn jumped from the cockpit.

Nichols was already out of the cockpit and headed to the tail boom.

Tom's decision-making process was streamlined. Only one thing mattered, and that was his crew. "Light team, pick up an overwatch to the northeast! Heavy team, to the southwest! Don't let anything Iraqi come west until we've got Osborn and Nichols!" said Tom. Walker understood and didn't need to be told twice. He nosed 220 over and headed to the crash site. "Just get as close as you can to them! As soon as they're on, let's get outta here." Tom was back on the VHF. "Two-three, get the grid of the aircraft and send it to the Three ASAP! We're going to get the crew!"

Two more rounds of artillery impacted just one hundred meters from the downed aircraft. Walker brought 220 down to twenty feet off the ground. Fifty meters from the downed aircraft, he hit the left pedal hard and landed abruptly with the right side of the aircraft exposed to the waiting crew. Osborn and Nichols didn't need to be prompted. Nichols went around and climbed on the left side, and Osborn snapped the carabineer from his harness onto the right side. He got a thumbs-up from both sides. Within seconds, Walker was on the move again. Tom looked at the crew members, and they were holding on for all they were worth. Walker kept the speed down to sixty knots and about forty feet above the ground.

Petty came up on FM. "Six, this is Two-three! Do you want us to destroy the airframe, over?" It had been briefed to destroy any aircraft or vehicles that may be captured.

Tom thought about the request and the situation. The fog was rolling in heavy, and visibility was going to crap. The Third Brigade was not on the verge of losing the ground they occupied, so it seemed like an easy answer. "That's a negative! Do *not* destroy 444!"

"Champion Six, this is Champion Three-one!" It was CW4 Larry Snyder. "I contacted the Lizard Three, and he has the coordinates of triple four. He assured me they weren't going to lose this turf. As long as she doesn't take any more rounds, she should still be in one piece later!"

That was the best news Tom had heard lately. Nothing like having experienced professionals in your unit to keep you straight, thought the captain. "Thanks, Three-one!" Then he added to everyone on VHF, "We'll take them back to the Blackhawk and be back ASAP. Don't get any closer. Protect the flanks of the tanks and we'll be back in ten mikes! Six, out!"

They flew for three more minutes and finally got hold of the Blackhawk. Hawk and Maurer both received the news and were headed to the area. Walker set 220 down, and the two aviators climbed off. Tom motioned for Osborn to come up and talk to him.

The lieutenant climbed back up on the FAB, and Tom had the cockpit door open. Hart stuck out his hand for Tom. Tom smiled and took the hand firmly. "Are you okay?"

The lieutenant nodded, smiled, and mocked, wiping his brow. Then he yelled over the still-turning rotors of 220, "Thanks, sir!"

"Nice ride?" asked Tom, still smiling.

"Negative! I'd rather be inside!" yelled the lieutenant.

Tom grabbed at his sleeve and pulled him close. "I want you to get back up as soon as you feel you're ready! Okay!"

Osborn definitely understood the intent and nodded. Then he thought about what was just said to him and looked at his commander. *I have just been knocked to the ground by enemy artillery, and my boss wants me to get back up again? What is he, nuts?* Then the light came on.

Tom could see the expression in his face. What he just said had sunk in and was getting digested by the slightly rattled lieutenant. Then the face acknowledged agreement, and Tom knew that Hart understood.

"Roger, sir! I'll meet you at the FARP! Understand with Three-one?" asked Hart.

Tom just smiled, nodded, and saluted. Osborn returned the salute and jumped down.

"I didn't catch all of that, sir. But did you just tell that lieutenant that you wanted him to go out again?" asked John Walker as he lifted off.

"As soon as possible, John," said Tom. John was visibly confused. "He needs to get right back into the cockpit again or he'll be questioning himself for the rest of his life."

"Christ, sir! I bet Hawk won't let him do it!" said the warrant.

"Au contraire, mon ami!" said Tom with a weak French accent. "Hawk will be pissed at him if he doesn't ask to get back in the saddle. Mark my words. If the crew isn't hurt, he'll expect . . . no, he'll demand the crew fly again." Tom watched the warrant shake his head in disagreement.

Tom made sure that Nichols and Osborn were picked up by the Fighting Sixth Blackhawk and returned to the fight.

Lawton and Walker got back on station within fifteen minutes. Visibility had gotten worse. It was down to five hundred meters, and the helicopters continued to move north to try and take shots at the enemy. A Troop had already departed the northern sector for the FARP, and B Troop was ready. Tom noticed they were coming up against the Second

ACR's boundary and asked for permission to break station. Permission was immediately granted, and they returned to the FARP.

After refueling, Hawk met Tom and got a face-to-face debrief on the actions that caused 444 to get shot down. Hawk had already talked to Nichols and Osborn, and Tom's story verified the event. Now Hawk could explain to Denson exactly what happened.

Lawton looked for some sense of where the commander would go with the news that the Champions had lost an aircraft to enemy fire. As if Hawk had read his mind, the commander said, "I don't think Colonel Denson will have a problem with this. Especially since the crew is okay. I just want to make sure we have all the facts. You got too close." Then he added something that Tom needed to hear. "You did the right thing by getting them out that fast and not destroying the aircraft. Rooksy is looking at it."

Tom nodded and said, "Thanks for your support on this, sir."

"Oh! And one more thing. That lieutenant of yours wants to go up as soon as possible. You think he's all right?" asked the commander.

Tom smiled. "If he wants to get up, sir, I'll get him an aircraft for the next mission! And Nichols too, sir?" Tom added, "With your permission."

Hawk nodded. "As long as they're both healthy and can do the mission. Just put them with different crew members."

Tom could see the sense in that. "Roger, sir. Thank you!"

2200, February 27, 1991
Phase Line Monaco, Iraq

TOM HAD TO LOOK ON THE bright side. The Champions got to do one mission with six aircraft, and even though they got a bird shot down, both the crew members were just fine. He put Hart in the front seat of the heavy Hellfire bird with Snyder. Nichols jumped into Toretti's backseat. Harmon had a small disagreement with the new arrangement, but Toretti, who obviously was ready for a break, informed the young warrant he wasn't in a democracy.

The Champions drew one more mission: a screen along the forward boundary in the southern sector with an on station time of midnight. The division was prepping for the final assault to start the next morning, and the CG wanted to make sure he wasn't surprised by any Iraqi counterattack.

The weather refused to cooperate again. The FLIR managed to see through some of the thinner clouds, smoke, and fog. For the most part, visibility was less than one kilometer. Tom felt fortunate that the Champions had seen no enemy elements. At 0120, he called the S3 to tell him they were Bingo and reported the current situation and weather observations. He expected to be mission complete.

Maurer told him everyone else was down preparing for the major push the next morning. The Champions could go to REDCON 2 in the new holding area, but they couldn't shut down until 0500. Tom took a deep breath and told the Three they would monitor the FM command and maintain REDCON 2.

They headed to the holding area and found the scouts. Hal Timmons had the radio on. He monitored the call from the Three and was ready for Tom when they landed. The coffee was next to a small fire, and Timmons pulled out some M&M's for the group to munch on. The drizzle started about 0330, which merely added to the "joy" of the crowd. With the visibility still the same and the chances for launch becoming remote, Tom sent the crews to their cockpits. He would send runners if they were notified of another mission.

Hal didn't keep the fire going, lest some enemy troops that were bypassed get too froggy and take potshots at the pilots as they waited.

"They said the cease-fire is imminent, sir," said the lieutenant.

Tom looked at Hal and said, "About goddamn time, don't you think?"

Hal smiled. "Roger that, sir." Then Hal shined his red lens flashlight at his commander. "Jesus, sir! You look like hell!"

Tom just smiled and concurred, "Not you too!" He laughed and said, "I feel like hell."

"Why don't you come sit in the helicopter? This rain can't be helping you any," said Hal.

Tom declined the offer. "No way. My ass is killing me. If I don't get in the cockpit for a week, I'll be happy." Tom shook his head and looked at the lieutenant. "I think I've got hemis from hell. My stomach is on fire. I'm signed for a fourteen-million-dollar pile of junk"—Tom pointed into the night—"somewhere over that way. I haven't slept more than ten hours in five days, and I haven't had an ice-cold Pepsi in a month. Considering all that, I feel pretty damn good!"

Timmons chuckled and nodded at his boss. "I'm sorry about 444 getting hit."

Tom rubbed his head and felt how nasty his hair was and then rubbed his eyes to get the sleep out of them. He continued down to his chin to feel the growth of hair that he wasn't keeping on top of. He let out a deep sigh. "As long as Mark and Hart are okay, that's the only thing that matters." He looked up in the drizzle and wiped his face. "We got too damn close." Then he looked at Hal. "Too close."

Tom leaned back against the front of the scout and said, "If I could change one thing about the week, I'd have kept us back more in that BP. Maximum standoff range. I know better." He rubbed his nose. "But all the hindsight in the world can't change that." Tom's hands rubbed his eyes again, and he turned toward the front of the scout. Then he bent slowly at the waist. His head went down and started bouncing softly off the windscreen of the helicopter.

"Sir, we still have everybody. We did damn good. We kicked the shit outta one of the best armies in the world," said Hal, trying to cheer up his mentor.

Tom's head snapped up. "There you go again! I'm trying to be depressed, and you're cheering me up. Well, the hell with that, Lieutenant! Break out those M&M's and let's party. In another two hours, the division is gonna roll through what's left of the Republican Guard and run their asses all the way to Baghdad!" Tom clapped the lieutenant on the shoulder. "We did good!" Tom may have said it, but inside, he didn't feel like it.

0530, February 28, 1991
Phase Line Lime, Iraq

THE CHAMPIONS WERE TOLD TO GO REDCON 4 at 0500. Tom immediately headed to 220 to catch some sleep. He popped open the engine cowling that he was becoming so familiar with. As he stretched out, the rainwater kept hitting his face, but it didn't matter. He was out within a minute.

At 0530, the First Armored Division opened up with barrage of MLRS, 155mm, and eight-inch rounds that lasted until 0615. The big guns fired over a round per minute as they prepared the sector for the final onslaught. With the MLRS firing only one kilometer behind the area where the Champions were parked, the sounds of the firing were deafening. Tom Lawton remained motionless in his sleeping bag. For all intents and purposes, Tom was a casualty of fatigue.

At 0615, 2-1st CAV Apaches moved through the sector on an armed recon to destroy anything the artillery may have missed. There wasn't much left, only some soft-skinned targets that were immediately suppressed with 30mm. At 0700, the division's three brigades crossed Phase Line Italy on line and engaged the remnants of the Madinah Division. At 0800, the cease-fire went into effect.

Hart Osborn pulled out the small American flag he had carried with him and hung it from the top of his Apache. Then he quickly climbed down and got back into his sleeping bag. He joined the rest of the Champions as they lay in or around their aircraft trying to sleep as the division armor rumbled toward Kuwait.

CHAPTER 10

THE FIRST ARMORED DIVISION WAS RESPONSIBLE for destroying over 400 enemy tanks, 440 APCs, 100 artillery pieces, 1,200 trucks, and 110 air defense systems. There were over 2,200 enemy prisoners of war in the division sector with representation from the Madinah, Tawakalna, Adnan, and Hammurabi Republican Guard units. The division showed one M1A1 tank destroyed, two M3 Bradleys damaged, two AH-64s destroyed, and another five vehicles of various type damaged. Personnel losses included four deaths and fifty-two injuries.

The Fighting Sixth squadron's estimated battle damage assessment was 52 tanks, 103 APCs, 31 artillery pieces, and at least 200 trucks and bunkers. The videotapes needed to be reviewed to get a better assessment of the BDA, but for the most part, the contributions of the Apaches were considered significant. Of particular note was their ability to continue the attack at night when the division was reconstituting.

Tom Lawton finally was getting the rest he needed when Hal Timmons awakened him. "Sir, the crew chiefs are here, and you have a meeting at twelve. I thought you might want a little bit of time to get ready!"

Tom yawned and stretched from the inside of his sleeping bag and eventually came to life. "Thanks, Lieutenant." He checked his watch. "I never knew five hours of sleep could feel so good!" He looked around to see what was happening. Tanks and other vehicles from the division were rolling east at a steady twenty miles per hour. All the faces he saw were beaming, and *V* for victory fingers were being flashed. Tom would acknowledge the signs for victory with thumbs-up and waves to the various drivers.

Lawton quickly got into his ruck, got his shaving gear out, and removed the two-day growth. He found three MREs left and chose the ham slice rather than the chicken ala king or the omelet. He could eat the ham slice cold. He didn't want to take the time to try and make either of the other two meals edible. After personal hygiene, eating the MRE, and making sure the aircraft were getting their much-needed maintenance, Tom headed to the commander's vehicle for the meeting.

The first thing Hawk did was get everyone's head back into the war. He reminded everyone of the dangers that remained in the area and that they weren't even close to being done yet. The squadron was to occupy an abandoned airfield directly north of their current position. The problem was it would take two to three days to make sure it was clear of the enemy or mines. In the meantime, coordinates were passed out for assigned areas the five troops would occupy until they could relocate to the airfield. The priority was to get the squadron together again and prepare for the follow-on missions that were sure to come. Takeoff times were handed out and the new frequencies issued. With the information passed, Hawk congratulated everyone on a fine job. As the meeting broke up, Hawk caught Tom's eye and had him stand by.

"I just wanted to let you know that Colonel Denson is aware of the circumstances with 444's downing and he understands. He too agreed you did the right thing by getting the crew out. Rooks tells me he's got a lowboy coming to take her back to the rear, and that should be done in the next six hours."

Tom nodded and mustered a small smile. "Okay, sir. That's good news."

But the commander could tell the captain wasn't happy with the situation. "Look, Tom. There wasn't anything that you could have done. You had to get that close to see the targets. In combat, things get shot." He slapped Tom on the back. "The best thing is that all your people are all right. Get your head together because we still have a long way to go."

Tom accepted that. "Roger, sir. I'm okay." Tom smiled and saluted. Even though both of his chain of command had said they were "all right" with what happened, Tom still had a pit in his stomach every time he thought about the circumstances. He only felt better when he thought how much worse the situation could have been.

March 2, 1991
Assembly Area Conroe, Iraq

THE SQUADRON ASSUMED THE SAME POSITION they had when they were last together, but with more space between tents. News traveled slowly to the soldiers, and without a radio station to listen, rumors again swept through the assembly area. The cease-fire's broken. "We're goin' to Baghdad!" Republican Guard units had come together for a counterattack, and many other rumors were spoken but never panned out. But the worse rumors came from home.

The rumors from home were usually derived from a lack of communication between spouses by phone or mail. The major rumors included everyone's wife was running around on them and terrorist bombings were occurring all over Germany. Hawk finally called a formation and said that as soon as conditions permitted, soldiers would be allowed to make phone calls. He would check on the mail and personally get involved to make sure the unit's location was provided to the folks delivering the mail. That seemed to quell the rumor monsters temporarily. But they were never stopped.

The troop spent the days flying screen or recon missions throughout the sector. The one thing it allowed the pilots to see was the amount of damage the division had caused. Of particular note was a defensive line where the Iraqis had made a stand. They had established a standard two up and one back triangle formation. The defensive line stretched from north to south for nearly seven miles. Each vehicle, whether it was in a hull-down position or out in the open, was destroyed. The tanks usually had their turrets blown completely off.

Lawton was flying with Toretti, who was getting pictures to use in the unit historical files. The troop would shoot two rolls per day. One afternoon, they came upon a dead Iraqi soldier. The man had somehow survived the attack that had destroyed his vehicle, and he had attempted to get away. The tracks in the sand came from the tank about nine hundred meters away. It was at this spot the soldier had lain down and died. The sight of the dead man stirred emotions inside Tom that he hadn't had before. It was the epitome of the enemy's struggle. Stationary equipment, in a defensive posture, that couldn't survive the onslaught of the Allied forces that his country was facing. When his vehicle was destroyed, he only wanted to get away. Lawton asked Toretti not to take any more pictures of the dead soldier. They headed back to the assembly area, satisfied that nothing was left of the "infamous" Republican Guard in the sector. The vision of the dead man was forever etched in Tom's mind.

The next issue to cause a stir was war booty. Throughout the division area, empty bunkers from Iraqi support units and various headquarters elements were now available for US troops to enter and search. Various items of Iraqi equipment such as NBC equipment, Russian radios, AK-47s, pistols, license plates, and helmets were showing up in the assembly area. Anything the enemy had was beginning to show up in American soldiers' hands. The possibility that the bunkers may be booby-trapped rarely crossed the troopers' minds as they went in search of war treasures. The Champions, being typical soldiers, were not exempt from attempting the searches.

One afternoon, Tom just happened to be looking for some of the pilots when he was informed by one of the crew chiefs that four of them had taken a Humvee and gone in search of bunkers. Tom immediately went from zero to pissed off until he realized he was simply worried about his men. Naturally, the crew chief knew the location of the bunker area and could take Tom directly to the site.

Upon arriving, Tom couldn't help but notice at least a half dozen other vehicles were around the same area, doing the same thing. He pulled up behind the Humvee with the C-5, 1-6 CAV bumper marking. John Walker was emerging from the bunker with a big smile and two armloads of Iraqi equipment. As soon as the warrant saw his commander, his smile faded. Right behind him were Petty, Berstein, and Tucker.

"What the hell do you guys think you're doing?" yelled Tom.

Petty was the first to answer. "We were just getting some of this stuff, sir." The warrant held out the AK-47 he had and an Iraqi helmet as if showing his boss the items would help him calm down. He continued, "Look, sir. There's a bunch of other people doing it too!"

Tom started to feel like a parent. The saying "If everyone jumped off a bridge, would you do it too?" came to mind. But he was too pissed. "That doesn't make it right! I don't give a damn what other people are doing!"

Tom collected himself. "I only care what you guys are doing. I want you to get your stuff and get the hell out of here. You got two minutes to get this vehicle rolling back to the AA." Tom looked at the faces and made sure they understood his intent. Slowly, the warrants turned and did as they were ordered.

As angry as he was, curiosity still got the best of Tom. He walked down toward the bunker and looked inside. Whoever had been there left in a hurry. There was a plate of rice and half-cooked chicken still out on the table. There were crates of equipment inside that had not been opened. The desire to see the contents pressed Tom, but after just chewing out his pilots, he knew better than to enter the bunker.

Walker said, "Sir, those crates have markings that say they came through Jordan. I thought they were on our side in this one?"

Tom just looked at the warrant and walked back to his Humvee. "None of that shit matters now, John. The only thing that matters is you guys staying healthy. Get your shit and get back to the assembly area." There was a slight hesitation. Tom yelled, "Let's go!"

The warrants could tell by Lawton's tone that he was as serious as he had ever been. They made sure they had all their equipment and loaded into the vehicle. The Humvee cranked, and they were headed out of the area as three other vehicles entered.

That night in his tent, Tom was writing a letter to Cindy when Joe Petty came to the door. "Sir, can I see you for a minute?"

Tom was in much better spirits now and said, "Sure, come on in! What's up?"

The warrant was struggling to find the words. "About this afternoon, sir, I understand what you mean." Tom knew what was on his mind, and his smile faded. "I, I'm sorry we went over there. It was a stupid thing to do, and I wanted to apologize."

Tom got off his cot and went over to his rucksack for some M&M's. The candy had become an addiction. He couldn't chew ass on one of his subordinates when they knew they were wrong. As a sort of peace offering, Tom broke out the candy and offered it to the warrant. "Sit down, Joe." Tom took a deep breath and started, "We just made it through a week of pretty intense combat, flying in the dark, bad weather, enemy shooting at us. Hell, for all we know, our own guys were shooting at us." Tom paused to let the comment sink in and said, "And now you . . . gentlemen . . . want to go and risk your lives in those bunkers. For what?" Then Lawton hit Joe with a low blow as he pointed to the letter he was writing on his cot. "I'm not gonna write your wife a letter and tell her that you died because you were stupid."

Joe looked up and met his commander's eyes. "I never thought about anything like that. We were just . . ."

"It doesn't matter what you were doing. I just don't want you doing it anymore," Tom said. "You pass the word that the ol' man was pissed, and I better not find anybody else doing that crap." Tom took some more candy and continued, "My only goal is to get everyone back. To think that we made it through the war with everyone, only to chance losing a life or limb on a . . . goddamn scavenger hunt really pissed me off. There's no need for it." Tom caught himself before he got too angry again.

Then for some reason, Tom found he couldn't stop his mouth from asking the question, "So what kind of stuff did you get?"

Petty laughed and told his boss about the shirt and radio he got. Walker got a radio and an NBC mask. He also said the crew chiefs had crates of bayonets. Tom could only shake his head in disbelief. He quickly reminded Joe not to tell anyone he asked what they got but to pass the word to stop going through the bunkers. Petty promised he would and left.

Tom shook his head in amazement. He was serious about not wanting anyone hurt doing something stupid. But he became a bit upset at himself for his attack of human nature. Who cares what they got? As long as nobody got hurt. Then he couldn't help but think, *I wonder how many bayonets they got?*

Hawk was aware of all the booty being confiscated by the squadron troopers and quickly put the word out to cease the practice. The corps headquarters put out a policy that no war contraband could be kept. An amnesty box was established, and soon items formerly belonging to the Iraqi army began to show up in the box. Eventually, the policy was established that having an Iraqi weapon of any kind was punishable by an Article 15 or a court-martial depending on the circumstances. When they discovered that the unit had over five hundred brand-new bayonets still wrapped up and covered in Cosmoline, Hawk got permission for every soldier to get one. Some soldiers tried to stretch this exception and were eventually caught.

The best way to prevent the bunker searches from occurring was to get the troopers away from the environment. The unit couldn't move to the abandoned airfield soon enough. All the commanders in the squadron welcomed the news. However, the issue of collecting war trophies was a struggle for weeks. Units were witnessing morale drops across the theater because the situation was handled differently in each unit. Each commander seemed to handle the situation differently until higher headquarters got around to issuing guidance that restricted the collection of all items to only those with historical significance. Even then, the commander's intent was usually stretched to support troop morale.

March 3, 1991
Juylil Air Base, Iraq

THE TROOP FINALLY GOT ORDERS TO move to and occupy the Juylil Air Base in southeastern Iraq. They flew over remnants of Iraq's army and followed power lines north to the Baghdad highway. At the release point, they made a southern turn and entered what was left of the air base. A quick flyover provided the helicopter pilots a chance to see the destruction the US Air Force had inflicted upon the Iraqi war machine. All the perimeter buildings were destroyed, and the runway was cratered in three spots.

The CAV was set in positions north of the base. A small POW compound had been constructed just off the road leading into the base at the north entrance, and it appeared to have about three hundred prisoners. There was an armored brigade on either side of the base, which gave the aviators the "warm and fuzzy" feeling they needed considering they were only a couple hundred miles from Baghdad.

The Champions occupied an area to the northwest of the airfield. The aircraft were parked on the tarmac, which made takeoffs and landings much less challenging than taking off from the sand. Numerous areas around the base had been lined off with white engineer tape, marking suspected minefields.

On the first couple of days, the troop adjusted to its new surroundings, conducted physical training, and watched the engineers fix the runways. They soon found another pastime, watching camels walk through the minefields. They would watch in amazement as camel herds and the Bedouins that herded them walked through the marked-off areas without a scratch. Attempts to communicate with the herders proved fruitless. Either they didn't understand or didn't care. They continued to walk the herds through the restricted areas. To them, life went on as it had for decades.

After three days, the engineers had the runways fixed. Within hours, C-130s were landing night and day, with visitors and VIPs getting their first views of the defeated country. Colonel Denson could be seen either welcoming or sending off the many VIPs out on the tarmac. Pictures were taken, and stories were exchanged by warriors and REMFs as well, some just tall tales and others total bullshit.

While at the base, the troop had a standard security and screening mission. The sector ranged from the Basra highway north to the Euphrates River and west to the Talil Air Base.

March 4, 1991
Juylil Air Base, Iraq

SOMETIMES NO FLY AREAS WERE DESIGNATED and published, specifically for the helicopters. Warnings were issued not to overfly a facility named Khamisiyah. The facility was apparently a weapon storage area for the Iraqis, and the US Army engineers were scheduled to blow the area up in the afternoon. Tom made it a point to stay well west of the sites when there was announced demolition occurring. From the air, the dust cloud created by the explosion was visible for miles. Lawton insisted that no one left the compound to get an up-close view of the destruction.

When they weren't flying, Tom, Hart, and Hal had the distinguished task of writing awards for the troopers. Brigade wanted to get started on the awards process, and within days, paperwork was generated to provide the troops with the recognition they deserved for their superhuman effort. Without computers, the awards needed to be handwritten and virtually took forever. The fact that they didn't have anything else to do with their time made the initial effort seem rewarding. Before they left Juylil, the fifth and sixth rewrites of the awards had been submitted and, as a matter of routine, "kicked back" by the brigade adjutant for lack of "viability."

The whole awards fiasco became another point of contention and quickly created an "us versus them" scenario. The Vietnam-era pilots had established standards that were much different than the ones established for the Gulf War. Eventually, guidance came from higher that outlined how, who, and what awards would be given. After the twelfth rewrite, the Champions finally started to get approval for Air Medals and even some with the "V" device for valor. Bronze Stars were submitted for a majority of soldiers in leadership positions and eventually approved. The whole process would take months and left many soldiers confused and bitter.

For Tom's part, he could only compare the awards process that occurred to what he remembered from his father's return from Vietnam. A veteran of over three hundred combat hours in Vietnam, Tom's father received a Bronze Star with a "V" and numerous Air Medals. The fact that he had an opportunity to receive one Air Medal seemed to be all the honor he needed, lest the awards seem not up to the standard established by previous recipients. Tom was honored for the awards he was nominated for but always kept the perspective that previous veterans had toiled for months to get the same recognition. One week of hell in the desert didn't quite equate to 365 days of hell in the jungles of Vietnam. This was the only war in town, and someone else would eventually set the standards. Attempts were made to recognize the troopers that had performed in an outstanding manner, and that was all that mattered.

After three weeks, the unit received notice they had to relocate all Allied forces out of Iraq and into Kuwait. And when it finally came down, they had twenty-four hours to move out.

March 20, 1991
Juylil Air Base, Iraq

THE VEHICLES WERE LINED UP ON the runway and prepared for an early-morning departure. The plan changed only in the order of departure. The normal procedure of A Troop departing first was altered as C Troop was first to depart. Tom was thankful for the opportunity to lead the relocation mission, but he had forgotten the risks that came with being first.

The FARP rolled early to establish a refuel point halfway between the air base and Kuwait. The plan called for it to be set up when C Troop entered the area. Thirty minutes later, the second troop would come in, followed by the trail element. As fate would have it, the FARP was late getting set up, which proved to be unfortunate.

As the Champions entered the FARP, the area was still being surveyed for safety. Lawton and Walker had just entered their refuel point when they noticed a fuel handler running like a bat outta hell across the area. Walker said, "Something doesn't look right, sir? There's a problem out there!" He planted the Apache hard into the desert. Tom immediately agreed when he noticed no fuel handler come up to the cockpit. Tom quickly unhooked his helmet and got out of the aircraft. He couldn't see anything definite and merely sensed something was wrong. He made a motion with his hand under his neck to let Walker know he wanted him to shut down.

Then he saw what had happened. Lawton quickly jumped on the FAB and told Walker, "Relay to all Apaches to stay clear of the FARP, then call that Blackhawk in! We got a man down!"

Tom jumped down and ran over to the sight of the fallen trooper. Three other soldiers were there. The NCOIC had stepped on or kicked a cluster bomb. This sent alarms and panic through all the soldiers in the FARP. They had been in such a hurry that they had not properly cleared the area or searched the location for mines or bomblets. A cluster bomb didn't care if you were Iraqi or American. There were thousands of them scattered throughout the desert. The FARP just happened to position itself on a site that had previously been struck by the US Air Force.

SFC Leroy Childs's boot had been ripped open by the force of the blast. Blood, bone, and skin were sticking out of an opening that had once housed the sergeant's toes. The crimson trail that was left behind the sergeant indicated he had dragged himself about ten feet before collapsing. Childs was screaming and hollering for a medic. Two other fuel handlers were trying to treat the NCO who was close to shock. The medic that traveled with the FARP arrived with his first-aid bag and quickly took care of the wound. He applied pressure and elevated Childs's leg. Tom grabbed the next two soldiers and had them do what should have been done in the first place. They quickly checked the surrounding area and made a landing area for the Blackhawk to land. The ten troopers from the FARP got on line and quickly walked the area. Looking for anything that resembled a bomb or unexploded ordinance, the men marked the suspected areas with tent pegs and eventually white engineer tape. Too many bomblets were discovered in the area, and Tom called Hawk to get the FARP moved.

The one great advantage to an aviation unit is mobility. As soon as the aircraft arrived, Childs was on the Hawk and headed to the Division MASH. If they were in any type of unit other than aviation, Childs may have lost his leg or his life.

They had to move the FARP three clicks to the south to get clear of the bomblets. It delayed the FARP process two hours longer than planned, but it was finally safe for aircraft to enter.

When they entered the assembly area in Kuwait, the vehicles had already been dismounted, and the tents were going up. The unit had not gotten the word on Childs, so no mine sweep had been accomplished. As soon as the aircraft landed, the word was passed about Childs and the cluster bomb. It seemed a little late, but the troopers got on line and walked through the entire compound searching for any suspected explosives. Luckily, none were found.

March 21, 1991
Assembly Area Dodge, Kuwait

DODGE WAS SET UP MUCH LIKE the last two compounds during the war. All the tents were in the middle with a lot more space between them than the previous sites. The aircraft surrounded the area and faced outward. There was one significant difference: the center of the compound was marked by a new addition. The flight surgeon had "acquired" a Bedouin tent.

The doc's tent was a square blue-and-white-striped canvas tent about ten feet high, with a flag at the top. CPT James K. Hubert, the flight surgeon, shared the space with CW4 Mike Leslie, the squadron safety officer. The tent soon became the focal point for meetings, health concerns, general lounging, and of course, bullshit sessions. It wasn't hard to locate the Fighting Sixth with the huge blue and white circus tent in the middle of the assembly area.

Tom was quite glad to have the flight surgeon catch up with the unit. There were a couple of things he needed a professional's opinion on. Late in the evening, he went to the "Big Top" for some counseling. He had finally gotten caught up on the rest he had needed, but there was one ailment that had not improved.

Tom knocked on the door to the tent. "Who the hell are ya, and what the hell do you want?" came the cry from inside. It was Leslie. For a moment, Tom thought the surgeon wasn't in.

"Don't pay any attention to him. Get the hell in here whoever you are," said Doc.

"Hi, Doc," said Tom tentatively. "I . . . I just wanted to check out your new digs. Just as nice as everybody told me!"

"You want something to drink?" asked Hubert. From the layout inside the Big Top, Tom expected a Martini, but Doc only offered a Pepsi. "What brings you to our den of inequity?" asked the flight surgeon.

Tom took the Pepsi and said, "I don't know. I . . . I just thought I'd see how the surgeon was living. That's all!"

Leslie looked at Hubert. "I don't think that's it, Doc! He looks like he's sick or somethin'!" chided the warrant. "Get one of them big-ass needles out and show it to him. If he ain't sick, that needle will get him that way!" He laughed.

Tom didn't see the humor. "All right! All right already." Tom rubbed his chin and started to speak. "I . . . I think I've got . . . hemorrhoids! There! Ya happy?" Both Doc Hubert and Mike Leslie roared with laughter. Tom added with a disgusted voice, "I don't see anything funny." Tom just looked at the two men laughing like hyenas. "Hell with it! I'll leave!" Tom turned and started to leave.

"No, no, don't go. Christ, we thought it was somethin' serious like . . . ," said Doc as he thought, "like . . . the clap or somethin'!" The hyenas began to laugh again.

Tom didn't appreciate the humor at his expense. "Look, can you take a look, or should I just come back later?"

Hubert finally turned into the professional that he was. "Naw. Take down the flight suit and lay across this table." Tom did as he was told. "Don't be shy! Pull down them drawers and let me take a look!" Tom breathed in heavily and did as he was told. The doctor and his "assistant" began to examine . . . the situation.

"I don't mind you lookin', Doc, but does Leslie have to examine me too?" asked Tom.

The doc just grunted. "He ain't gonna get too close, trust me on that!" The doctor examined the area. Tom's uncomfortable feeling turned into pain.

"Damn!" said Mike Leslie. "That's a good one! You could win a prize if we were having a contest!"

"That's just great. Somethin' I can tell my grandkids!" Tom began talking like an old man. "Back in the big one, WW Gulf, I won a medal . . . for havin' the biggest hemorrhoid in the damn desert!" Doc and Leslie chuckled at the routine but continued to examine the problem.

"Looks like the work of the ether bunny!" said Leslie. Tom was confused.

Doc Hubert played along with the warrant. "It's possible." Doc looked at Tom. "Are you a sound sleeper?" Tom shook his head. "Are you . . . comfortable . . . with your tent mates?" Leslie snickered, and the joking continued.

Tom asked, "What the hell are you guys talkin' about?"

Doc looked at Leslie and nodded. "The ether bunny, huh? You think this could be a case?" Slowly, the men turned and examined Tom's ailing rectum once more.

Tom couldn't take it. He started to get up. Then the two practicing proctologists laughed out loud and told Tom to relax. Tom lay down again as Doc told Tom a tale.

"Apparently, back in the rear," started the doctor.

He was interrupted by the still-laughing warrant. "No pun intended!"

The doctor elbowed the warrant and continued, "A medic was taking liberties with some patients."

Tom asked, "What type of . . . liberties?" He had to ask, but based on his prone position, he knew what the liberties were.

"He was using ether to knock out patients after they were asleep and then . . . having his way with them!" said Leslie.

"Get the hell outta here, Doc!" said Tom in disbelief.

"I'm serious. The patients were waking up with . . . discomfort in their anal area," said the doctor.

Leslie added, "They were coming in for sore feet and leavin' with a sore ass!"

Tom said over his shoulder, "I can assure you, there hasn't been any visit by the fucking ether bunny in my . . . rear area." The two men chuckled at Tom's explanation.

"I can only tell ya what we heard," said the surgeon.

"You might wanna keep that one to yourself, Doc!" said Tom.

After what seemed like an hour, the doc finished up. "Well, I don't think we need to cut that puppy." Tom audibly exhaled. He'd heard the horror stories from some of the senior pilots. "Here are some suppositories and some cream. You need to keep it clean. Try not to do anything too strenuous and lay down whenever you can." Tom nodded.

"So you were expecting me to have something . . . worse?" asked Tom.

The doc laughed again. "You'd be surprised. I didn't think it would be possible for soldiers to get sexually transmitted diseases out here, but there getting them. Fungus, growths, skin diseases. Most of it from not bathing enough. They don't like to take showers."

"Next time you get in your troop's tent, take a good whiff. It'll stink like Doc's socks! Here, smell this!" said the warrant as he held up a sock which was shaped like a foot was still in it.

Tom smiled and said, "I'll take your word for it." Tom finished dressing and started out the door of the Big Top. "I'd kind of like to keep this . . . you know . . . private!"

"Oh, you can trust us." The surgeon nodded.

Then Leslie added, "We're professionals!"

Tom just looked at the two men and knew it would be all over camp. The question was, how long would it take before the Champions found out?

One of the best aspects of the modern weapons is their ability to record events on video. The Apache had the ability to record about thirty minutes of every flight, and during that time, it recorded everything good as well as bad. Everything the machine recorded from pictures to the locations and directions, to the target array and of course the dialogue was on record.

During the downtime in Dodge, the troops reviewed all the tapes from the battles. Tom found it a painstaking task, but necessary. He reviewed most of the tapes with his crews. He found it disturbing to watch the Osborn and Nichols film after he had ordered them to back up. Mark Nichols managed to pull the tape before he jumped onto 220. On the tape, Osborn kept the crosshairs on the tank even though the fog obscured it. The fact that Nichols told the lieutenant to take the shot and disregard his commander's comment did not go unnoticed by Tom. Specifically put, "Fuck him, Lieutenant." In the crowded tent, he let it go. The other warrants gave the crew a hard time and made catcalls, but it unsettled Tom that the crew failed to move when ordered, and the way Nichols put it, stung. Nichols could only cast his eyes down when Tom looked at him. The facts couldn't be changed, and nothing more needed to be said.

Tom watched nearly every tape, especially the night engagements. He would check the grids of the BPs and the direction and distance to the targets against his maps. He didn't know it at the time, but it would help him and the Champions in a way he never imagined.

March 24, 1991
Squadron TOC, AA Dodge, Kuwait

ASSEMBLY AREA DODGE WAS ESTABLISHED JUST inside the Kuwaiti border of the Wadi Al-Batin. The Wadi was the only terrain feature for miles. On the map, it appeared to be some major terrain feature, perhaps equal to a small canyon. In reality, it averaged a couple hundred meters wide and maybe fifty feet deep at the deepest point where the Kuwait border met Saudi Arabia, not nearly as impressive as it appeared on the map.

The Wadi is where the unit deployed to when it left Iraq. The area would become "home," if only for a short time. The shorter, the better.

Tom was in his tent, lying on his stomach, recovering from his malady when Garcia came in the tent. "Hawk wants to see you ASAP." Tom didn't have to ask. Garcia said, "He didn't say what it was about. But you know it ain't good, sir!"

"Captain Lawton, this is MAJ Reuben Morales and CPT Jesse Winston. They're from Seventh Corps, and they're doing an investigation," said Lieutenant Colonel Hawk. Tom shook hands with the two men. He noticed that neither man wore wings on their "chocolate chip" uniforms. The major was infantry, and the captain wore the insignia of the armor branch. The colonel continued, "They want to ask you a few questions. Gentlemen, he's all yours." Then Hawk left the tent. Tom sat down and tried to look relaxed. But he knew if they were from corps, they were there for a purpose, and it wasn't anything good.

Major Morales started, "First of all, let me say, nobody is accusing you of anything." Tom quickly closed his mouth before it opened any further. The word *accusing* hung in the air like a noose. "Were you conducting night operations on the twenty-seventh?"

Tom had a chance to review the operations of the week thoroughly by then, and he knew the exact time the men were questioning. "Yes, sir," he answered flatly.

"Did you fire Hellfire missiles during those operations?" asked Morales.

"Yes, sir," said Tom.

"Are you positive of the targets you engaged? We're they . . . enemy targets?" asked the investigator.

Tom hesitated. Then with just a bit of attitude, he answered, "Yes, sir."

"Look, Captain Lawton, you're not making this any easier," said the major. "We're just trying to get to the bottom of a friendly fire incident, and we think you can help."

"Friendly fire," said Tom with a chuckle. "Friendly fire isn't really . . . friendly, is it?"

The major saw no humor and became tired of the captain's highly visible attitude. "Four M1A1s were hit," said the major when Tom interrupted.

"Hit or killed?" asked Tom flatly.

The major looked at Captain Winston as if allowing the captain to speak. Captain Winston said, "They were hit, and there were some casualties."

Tom nodded and said confidently, "Then it wasn't us."

Not the answer the major wanted to hear. "How can you be so sure, Lawton?"

Tom wondered how long it would be until the guy lost his temper. He'd found the button to get the major spun up. He leaned back in his chair. "If we hit them with Hellfire missiles, they'd be dead."

It was obvious that the comment didn't satisfy the two men. "We need proof if you have it," said Winston.

"I guess you think because Apaches had one-night fire fratricide that we're responsible for all of them, is that it?" said Tom, showing his displeasure at the tone of Winston's comment. He got up out of the chair. "Well, it wasn't us! I'm sure of it."

"At ease, Captain!" said Major Morales. Tom stood down and took his seat again. "Your commander said you might have some tapes we could review of the time period in question?"

Tom shook his head and looked down at his feet. "I guess you need someone to go with you to interpret them too? Has Lieutenant Colonel Hawk approved this?"

"He will, Captain Lawton. And we don't need you to review the tapes. We have Apache standards personnel available to review all the tapes. We just need you to get them for us," said Morales.

Tom knew they were right, but he didn't want to make it too easy for them, considering they appeared to be trying to burn him or one of his pilots for the fratricide. "I've got to get with the S2. He has the tapes now. It'll take me about ten minutes. I believe we have eight or ten tapes from that night. So if you'll excuse me, I can't say it's been a pleasure, sir."

Morales put his hand out to stop Tom. "I say again, Captain, we're not trying to put the blame for this incident on anyone. We're just trying to find the truth."

Tom looked the major in the eye. "The truth is on the tapes." Tom continued walking. "You won't find what you're looking for on them." Then he turned and added, "Sir."

Two days later, the tapes came back without Morales or Winston. The tapes had not provided the answers the two men wanted. There was no apology for the implied accusation, but Tom knew better than to expect one.

March 25, 1991
AA Dodge, Kuwait

THERE WERE OTHER THINGS FOR THE unit to see when they reviewed the tapes: violence, destruction, and death. There was plenty of that to go around. Among the tapes reviewed, the troopers in Charlie First of the Sixth got to witness the perfect engagement.

B Troop just happened to have the mission to overwatch the Basra highway the day the Iraqis decided to test the resolve of the American forces. Orders were not to let them leave with any equipment. Orders were orders, and CAV soldiers did as they were ordered to do.

The Champions saw the tape of CW3 Andy Holton and CW3 Terry LaTear. LaTear was in the front seat. LaTear was an old Cobra guy through and through. He had been a gun IP for three years before his transition to Apaches. To say he knew what he was doing was an understatement.

When the first Iraqi vehicle made a threatening move, an American ground vehicle blew it to bits. LaTear's targets were center mass of the column. As the gunner, he talked Holton through his whole procedure. Slowly, meticulously, and without malice, they destroyed eight Iraqi vehicles in less than five minutes. Each missile hit the target at center mass. By the third destroyed vehicle, the Iraqis figured out the best position to be was anywhere but a tank. If it was armor, it was going to die, and they knew it. The Iraqi troops jumped from the tanks like they were already on fire. LaTear was so calm and so good at what he was doing that he became a legend in the attack community. He merely shrugged off the label as "doing my job," but it was so much more than that.

On the videotape, LaTear demonstrated the unique ability to visualize the entire engagement in his mind. He remained focused on each missile engagement and was not distracted by the destruction around his targets. He never hesitated. Perhaps the most important aspect of the engagement was that he had no pity. Terry LaTear had become the techno-warrior the army wanted the twenty-first-century soldier to be: skilled, technically proficient, tactically superior, intelligent, and extremely deadly. It was a perfect and lethal combination.

The technology had created that lethality. However, the technology could only be controlled by the men that were pulling the trigger. Human error, usually a split-second loss of concentration or just dumb luck, prevented the technology from achieving even higher rates of destruction. Tom got to hear firsthand another cause for error, the same thing he had been struck by on his daylight engagement—having a conscience.

Lawton was alone in his tent that night, writing a letter to his father, when Carl Tucker came by. Tom could see he was troubled. After getting Mr. Tucker a seat, the warrant finally came out with what was on his mind.

"Uh, sir, you got to watch a lot of the tapes, right?" said Tucker. Tom nodded. "I've been watching a couple of mine the last two days, and there are things that have been bothering me."

Tom thought he knew where Tucker was headed but let him go there at his own pace. "I've seen close to a hundred of them now. They're starting to get boring," said Tom, not really meaning it, thinking that might be the best thing to say to the man sitting across him.

The warrant exhaled loudly. "There's this one where I'm lasing the target area, and it's night. I think it was the third or fourth mission, I don't remember. And there's a guy, kind of lost, not knowing what's going on. As I'm getting my range, I see this guy out in the open. He could tell we were out there. I could tell he was looking to see if he could find us." Tucker demonstrated what he had seen. Carl Tucker faced Tom. The warrant sniffed at his nose, and his eyes watered over. "I didn't see any gun, but I shot at him anyway." Tucker wiped at his eyes. "I fired rockets downrange right after that, and . . . after they hit, I was glad I didn't see him anymore."

Tom got off the cot and handed Tucker a fresh bottle of water. "You know, Carl, I've seen dozens of engagements like that. I saw one where two guys are running like scalded dogs trying to get somewhere. Hell, anywhere but where they were, they didn't get there. The 30mm just walked up on them, and when the smoke cleared, they weren't there anymore. You can hear the gun shooting and what the pilots are saying. These are two guys with kids. You can't hear the other end, but you can see what's happening. What you see doesn't match what is happening." Tom searched for the proper words. "I can understand it." He looked at Tucker. "Yet I'm not sure anybody else could." The warrant nodded in agreement.

"But as long as we don't get to likin' it"—Tom got Tucker's eyes up to his own—"we can live with our actions."

Tom let the comment sink in. "I can only say that those guys are combatants in a combat zone, and they made a choice sometime before they died to be where they were." The warrant nodded his agreement. "If one of those bastards gets in a hole and comes out shooting fifteen minutes later when we're closer and kills one of us . . . you know we'd feel a lot worse." Lawton wanted to change the tone of the conversation, so he hit Tucker's water bottle with his own. "Here's to the enemy. They died fighting for their country." He didn't intend it to be a coldhearted salute, merely an acknowledgment of the respect for soldiers that had fought for their country. In another time and place, it may have been them.

Tucker accepted the toast, but Tom could see he didn't feel much better. "Carl." The warrant looked up again. "We don't have to like doin' this. No army manual says you have to enjoy killing. God help us if we ever get that way. I want to make sure you know that you're not the only one who feels like that." Tom started to tell Tucker about his own hesitation but thought better of it. "If you want to go talk to Doc or the chaplain, I understand." The warrant got up and started to smile again.

"No, that's okay, sir." He shook his head as he started to leave. "I just needed to tell someone . . . what was goin' on inside my head."

"If you need to talk any more, my door, or should I say, my tent is always open," said Tom. He shook Tucker's hand, and the warrant was gone. Tom thought about Tucker's remorse for a while. He understood what Tucker was going through. He'd heard many comments in the TOC watching the tapes. "Would you take . . . such and such shot?" or "I would have never pulled the trigger on that shot!" But when it got right down to the rubber meeting the road, no one knows what they would have done unless they were in that particular situation. To Tom, keeping his men safe justified what he'd done, but he took solace in the fact that he didn't enjoy it.

Tom lay down on his pillow and was ready to try and sleep, but something was in his pillowcase. He reached inside and found a box of Preparation H. He should have known Leslie couldn't keep a secret. Lawton laughed out loud. The reality of his pain and the planted medication took Tom away from the discussion with Tucker. At least, temporarily.

March 26, 1991
AA Dodge, Kuwait

FOR THE THIRD DAY IN A week, they were confined to their tents. The oil well fires were being put out, but other problems still existed. At one time, over five hundred fires blazed across Kuwait and Iraq, creating an environmental disaster that took months to extinguish and years to recover from.

When the winds came from the east, oil droplets that were not burned would climb up into the sky. They would move with the winds until nature decided to let them fall. Billions of these tiny oil droplets fell throughout the area west of the fires. When the winds came from the east, the Fighting Sixth was confined to their tents. When nature called and one-stepped outside, the thick, nasty scent of oil would be drawn into the soldiers' lungs. The bitter, grotesque black liquid could be tasted. And as the troopers walked around their tents, the droplets could be seen on top of the tents.

At night, the Champions could see ten or twelve oil fires burning in the distance. When they climbed up on top of an Apache, they could see over thirty fires burning in the distance.

March 27, 1991
AA Dodge, Kuwait

THE PHONES HAD BEEN TURNED ON again, so numerous trips were made to the corps phone center. Humvees were loaded to the brim with troopers on their way to and from the site. A sign-out point was established in the logistics tent, but it wasn't always enforced. Decentralized command and control was creeping into the area, and the soldiers were taking full advantage of it.

HHT had sent a truckload of soldiers to the phones. Ten soldiers departed with ten M16s. Ten soldiers returned with only nine M16s. The soldiers covered the fact the weapon was missing and quickly returned to the phone center to try and recover it if that was in fact where the weapon was lost. Two hours later, they returned without the weapon. What was waiting was one pissed-off SGM Bartholomew W. Love. The soldiers had no choice but to come clean and say the weapon was lost between Dodge and the phone center. Three vehicles were dispatched to trace the route the soldiers took. A complete search of the assembly area turned up nothing.

Then the thought that maybe another soldier had stolen the weapon came to somebody's mind. Within minutes, the entire squadron was on line to have each weapon checked by serial number and matched with its proper owner. After no match was produced, the unit was put on line and did a walk-through of the entire assembly area once again.

The unit ended up spending two days searching for an M16 that was never found. Hawk reported the incident to higher headquarters. The response back down the chain was Article 15s for the soldier and his first-line supervisor. On the positive side, the unit didn't lose another weapon.

Lawton spent the early part of the evening by himself. He was upset about having to put his troops under the microscope for the missing weapon. Tom was sitting on top of 220, watching the fires from the oil wells. He heard music coming from the warrant officer's tent. It was Joe Petty doing a pretty good lick on the guitar. The song was "Life by the Drop" by Stevie Ray Vaughan. It was a big O'Club song with the CAV troopers of the 1-6th. On any given night in the club, you were guaranteed to hear the song played no less than five times. Petty played it damn well.

Tom started to think about his phone call earlier in the day. He'd gotten through to Cindy, and they were fine. She sounded great. The big rumors floating around Katterheim were the unit was headed to Saudi Arabia any day and that terrorists were planting bombs in all the casernes. Both of those were nothing new. It was just comforting that there weren't any new rumors flying around.

The next rumor that did get Tom's attention was the fact that since Cindy and Lou were living together, they were lesbians. Tom laughed at the thought. He told Cindy he was glad that "somebody was getting something." At this point, sex had been so far from his mind that he'd forgotten all about it. Tom told Cindy about some of the happenings in camp, and she was happy that everyone was doing well. She told him that Hart Osborn was sending a lot of letters, making Tom's writing prowess feel meager. She also said that Hart was always "bitchin'" about Tom's leadership style. Tom laughed off the comment. He suspected Hart had a problem with Tom's style but didn't expect him to write his wife about it. That was all they had time for, so they said good-bye, and Tom promised to call and write soon.

Then his thoughts went back to sex. The girls said they were partying and having fun on the weekends now that Cindy was working. He hadn't missed the booze at all. But thoughts of sex started his mind going places it hadn't been in a while. He suddenly realized he was becoming excited and repositioned his legs as he sat. Tom always figured that the rumor about saltpeter in the MREs was a lie. Now he had evidence. He seemed to be functioning normally. He thought about finding someplace to go do some "relaxin'," but a noise behind him quickly changed his plans.

Lawton didn't notice the two men coming up behind him, and he couldn't quite make out the voices. He did notice the guitars had stopped. That explained why one of the voices turned out to be Joe Petty. The other was Carl Tucker.

"Hey, sir. I hope we're not disturbing you," said Tucker.

Tom quickly dismissed the thoughts that he had previously entertained and said, "I wasn't really doing anything." Though it was dark, Tom could make out the pilots and climbed down off 220 to the wing and took a seat. "What's on your minds?"

Tucker started first. "I told Joe what we talked about. And today, we had an experience that we felt we should talk to you about." He nodded to Joe to go ahead.

Joe Petty looked uncomfortable. Even in the dark, Tom could see the tension in his face. Mr. Petty started slowly. "Sir, this afternoon, when we were searching for the lost weapon, Mr. Tucker and I went outside the compound." Tom frowned at the thought but remained quiet as Mr. Petty continued. "There's a group of ruins over that way"—he pointed northeast—"that we went to look at and see if maybe somebody went there or took the weapon there. Hell, I don't know for sure, but we ended up that way!" Tom laughed at the comment, trying to help Mr. Petty relax.

"As we came up on the ruins, there was a bunch of loud barking and growling and loud squealing from a donkey. The dogs didn't sound like normal dogs. More like a pack of wolves!" Tom remembered flying over a couple packs of dogs in Iraq. The dogs' lives had been altered by the war, and they were starving to death. He had wondered if they had turned into flesh eaters. Petty continued, "We came around the corner, and there were about a dozen of them little bastards attacking a donkey." Tom was surprised but not stunned by the news. It merely proved his suspicions that the mutts had become flesh eaters. The next question he asked himself was, would they eat humans? "Sir, you wouldn't believe it unless you saw it yourself. I mean these little bastards, no more than this tall"—he held his hand up to his knee—"were growlin' and nippin' at this poor donkey."

The warrant looked at Tucker for support. Tucker picked up the story. "The donkey must have stepped on a mine or a cluster bomb because the left rear quarter of this guy was gone."

"I mean to tell ya, sir, not a thing left!" said Petty. "And this whole pack of mutts was bitin' at its other leg, tryin' to bring it down."

"The donkey couldn't defend itself," added Tucker as if justifying the future of the tale.

"We tried to scare the dogs away, and the little bastards wouldn't have any of that," said Petty. "They started to growl at us and come toward us."

"I started to get a little nervous at this point," said Tucker.

Petty continued, "I pulled my 9mm and shot at them until they left."

"We tried using rocks! But only the gun seemed to work," added Tucker.

Tom wasn't surprised. "It sounds like you were justified in using the pistol, Joe! If it was for defensive purposes, nobody will question it."

"I was hoping you would say that, but that's not what I'm worried about. The next part is what I wanted to talk to you about. After the dogs finally ran off, the donkey was in bad shape, still alive, but mangled." Petty was hesitant to add, "I didn't know what else to do."

"I couldn't do it, sir! No way!" said Tucker.

"Couldn't do what?" asked Tom.

After a short hesitation, "I shot the donkey," said Petty.

"Damn straight, sir. He put that pistol up to that critter's head and put him out of his misery!" said Tucker. "I couldn't do it!"

"You shot the thing?" asked Tom.

"Yes, sir," said Petty. "I knew it wasn't gonna live. No vet or doctor on the planet could fix it up." Tom shook his head. "It just . . . just looked at me." Tom could tell Petty was hurt emotionally by the incident. "It didn't have a chance, sir!"

Tom didn't know what to say. He could blow it off and laugh about it, but this was more than morbid humor. He could chastise the warrants for not being the steely eyed killers of crippled animals that they should be, or he could take a middle-of-the-road approach. The middle of the road seemed appropriate.

"I think you did the right thing, Joe. If you left it alone, the dogs would just come back again and finish him off. I don't think the mongrels really care if dinner is dead or not at this point!" said Tom. "I'm hoping that you buried it!"

"We covered it with some of the stuff from the ruins, sir. I don't think the dogs can get to it." Tucker looked to Petty for agreement.

"No way, sir. We packed a bunch of crap on top of it," said Joe Petty. Then he reflected, "I just don't understand how I can pull the trigger on . . . men and blow them away without a second thought and have . . . difficulty dealing with this?"

Tom chuckled at the comment. "I think it's called a conscience." Tom thought about his own moment of waiting that fraction of a second before pulling the trigger. "If it makes you feel any better, I think it's good that you had the courage to pull the trigger in this situation. And yes, it was the right thing to do. You probably should have shot some of those little dogs too!"

The warrants laughed and agreed with the suggestion. Then Tom asked, "You don't think you'd have a problem pulling the trigger at the enemy again, do you?"

The warrants looked at each other and said together, "No, sir!"

Petty added, "It's easier, you know, emotionally to shoot an enemy target than to shoot a stupid animal that's inches in front of you!"

Tom had to agree with that. Because the stupid animal doesn't know any better. The enemy had a choice. "Well, unless you have any more to talk about, I was wondering if you knew 'Desert Skies' by the Marshall Tucker Band? I heard you playin', and I was just wonderin' what your repertoire consisted of?" asked Tom.

"Heck yeah, sir! Being from Tennessee, I have to know Marshall Tucker and the Charlie Daniels Band too!" said Petty with a big grin.

"What's say we put this donkey thing to rest and go listen to some tunes?" said Tom.

"All right, sir. Thanks for listening," said Petty. They walked back toward the tent, and about a minute later, Petty had another question. "So, sir, you need any more of that Preparation H?"

Tom couldn't help but laugh. "Yeah, I do. To shove up your ass, Petty!"

"Why me, sir? I didn't know anything about your problem! It was Carl who told me to ask you," said the warrant. Only three years in aviation and he was already polished at the art of the three standard replies: lie, deny, and make counteraccusations.

They went back to the tent, and Petty got out his guitar again. Hal Timmons stopped by and accompanied him. Then the crew chiefs that were done reviewing their forms came over. McFarland brought his drumsticks, somebody pulled out a harmonica, and the Champions had a mini jam session outside the "nontaxable" tent.

Tom couldn't remember all the words to "Desert Skies," but he did remember the last part. And it was good to hear half the troop join in:

> *So won't you bury me, with my chaps on,*
> *And my six gun strapped to my side,*
> *So I can watch the moon hidin' in the desert sky!*
> *Hidin' in the desert sky!*

They stayed up until about twelve that night, singing songs and telling stories. Tom had a voice that only a mother could love, so he mostly listened and laughed. The bonding was good for relieving the strain and pressure of the situation. Some commanders felt that distracting a warrior from his focus would cause that warrior to perform poorly in a war environment. Tom felt if the warriors could live together and become a unit they would fight for, then they would go into hell for each other. Different philosophies for different commanders. Tom's philosophy had proved successful so far. He let the men sing.

March 28, 1991
AA Dodge, Kuwait

THE CHAMPIONS FINALLY RECEIVED WORD THAT they would depart for Saudi in two days. They had one more day to overfly the battlefield areas. Toretti had his camera and got great pictures of all the crews overflying the carnage that was once the Iraqi Republican Guard. The destruction that remained nearly a month later was unbelievable. Hulls of vehicles littered Iraq and Kuwait for hundreds of square miles. Depleted uranium rounds destroyed many of the vehicles. Mixed with other battlefield debris, pollutants, and toxins, it couldn't have been a safe environment. Lawton was glad they would soon be gone. There was too much potential for bad things to happen.

Tom wondered what happened to the bodies. He thought about the dogs that Petty had shot at. He wondered if he could ever look at dogs the same. The war had taken the animals over the edge. They had become insane from hunger. Where were they getting their food? Tom shuddered at the thought of the dogs eating dead bodies. He was glad they didn't fly over any more of the dog packs after Petty's incident. Lawton thought the pilots might be tempted to kill them.

The flight finished uneventfully, and a troop formation was held. Many pictures were taken of the crews and troopers in various poses. Victors over an invading enemy horde. Champions one and all.

Tom was never one for speeches, but he took exception this time. He put everyone at ease and had them gather around 220.

"First of all, I want to thank each and every one of you for your effort and your support. The mission could not have been accomplished without the tremendous energy and professionalism you all selflessly demonstrated." Tom paused and looked at Garcia. "Not many of us were involved in Vietnam, but for those who were, this is probably a special feeling for them. The United States Army is where it belongs. On top. Recognized as the finest army in the world." Tom let the applause go for a few seconds.

"Right now, it may not seem like much. I don't think we can understand the magnitude of what we accomplished, and believe me, it took everyone here working together to accomplish it. This tremendous victory may be seen as a defining moment in history, a moment that we can be proud of and tell our grandkids about." Tom began to think he was sounding corny, but to him, it made sense. He could see on the faces of some of the soldiers that it made sense to them too. "In ten or twenty years, I hope every one of us can look back at this victory with the same sense of satisfaction and appreciation we feel right now because we did good!" There was more cheering. "I'm serious, gentlemen! We did damn good. Never forget that!" Then something in the back of his mind told Tom to add a reminder. "Just remember . . . we ain't on the plane yet!"

Garcia waited until some of the troops got through shaking Lawton's hand. "Sir, I thought you didn't make speeches?"

Tom looked at the ground and didn't realize he was mumbling, "I just said what I felt, Top." He rubbed his eyes and looked at the burly Hispanic man. "I couldn't have done this without you, Top. Thanks."

"Bullshit, sir! I think you guys could do this without me!" Then Garcia, the veteran of two tours in Vietnam, said, "Next time, you're gonna have to!" Both men laughed. "Come on, sir. Let me buy you a Pepsi!"

March 30, 1991
AA Dodge, Kuwait

HAPPINESS IS SEEING A PLACE YOU detest in your rearview mirror. There was a collective sigh of relief when the last aircraft from C Troop pulled pitch from AA Dodge. With the ground vehicles all gone and the other troops' earlier departure, C Troop was the last one out. Only one Blackhawk with support personnel was still there to ensure complete withdrawal of all Fighting Sixth forces.

The unit did a quick overflight of the area and headed southwest down the Wadi Al-Batin for Saudi Arabia. The radios were quiet, and a sense of relief was all one could feel. Saudi Arabia was one step closer to home.

CHAPTER 11

March 31, 1991
The Wadi Al-Batin, Kuwait

THE CHAMPIONS FOLLOWED THE WADI AL-BATIN southwest. It was an easy flight to navigate because it was the only terrain feature to follow for miles. They overflew dozens of blown-up and destroyed vehicles. Every guard post was damaged or destroyed. It would take years to rebuild Kuwait.

Tom wasn't sure if the men were simply happy to get out of Kuwait or happy that they were one step closer to Germany. The unit still carried a tremendous feeling that comes from being a victor in war. Their performance had peaked at the perfect time. The Champions became the professionals they had always wanted to be. The confidence that they had the ability to destroy their enemy with impunity was a bad thing. Perhaps the best thing that happened was 444 getting shot down that fourth day of combat. It gave the men, especially Tom, a taste of reality that they desperately needed. Tom wondered if the reputation the US Army had achieved would carry through to the next major conflict. Just as all wars are different, Tom knew the army would have to change if it was to do as well when the next conflict came.

The flight entered Saudi Arabia. It was obvious they had crossed the border because the damage ceased. They crossed the Tapline Road for the last time as they headed south to King Khalid Military City. The area provided to American forces was set up northwest of KKMC, a community of tents broken down into boroughs, and each borough represented a unit. The aviation brigade would share the compound with the Third and First Armored Divisions. The aircraft had metal sheeting to park on in a separate area designed to hold aviation units. It was miles to any kind of support area, and it took approval from a senior commander,

O-6 or higher, for troops to visit any facilities in the area of KKMC. After landing, Tom got out, took a look around, and was immediately reminded of "Andersonville." KKMC would never be quite as bad as Andersonville was, but it was damn close.

April 1, 1991
KKMC, Saudi Arabia

IN THE MILITARY, NOT ONLY IS the first day of the month payday, it's also the day when promotions and awards are given. It just so happened that 1LT Hartley Osborn had been given "the special trust and confidence" of the president of the United States of America deemed necessary to get promoted to captain. Lieutenant Colonel Hawk had a ceremony, and most of the officers found time to attend. "Captain" Hart Osborn was properly humbled and honored for the promotion, and to Tom's amazement, Hart thanked Lawton for everything "Tom" had done. "Like showing me what it's like to fly 'outside' an Apache!" Hart couldn't help but emphasize calling Lawton Tom. He called him Tom about five times, validating to himself and the gathered crowd that he was a peer. And now he and Tom were equals. Everyone congratulated the newest captain in the United States Army. Tom merely smiled and shook hands with his "peer," knowing their relationship would never be the same.

Tom Lawton had been identified as having accumulated enough hours to become a senior aviator. Lieutenant Colonel Hawk seemed too eager to pin the senior aviator "blood wings" on Tom. But Tom had always been a team player, and getting blood wings was one of the things an aviator would do to be on the team. It wasn't as bad as Tom knew it could have been. Hawk merely pounded Tom's wings once into his chest, just enough so the wings stuck there. Tom could hear Mike Leslie yelling for Doc Hubert, "You better get in here, and I think he's gonna pass out!" Tom didn't pass out, but he was glad the event was done. Tom didn't bother to pull the wings out. He was proud to be wearing them. He'd flown under a lot of shitty circumstances with little fanfare to achieve the goal. He happily shook hands but kept other hands at a distance, lest they think they deserved an opportunity to unseat the wings from his chest.

When Doc Hubert came by, Tom asked him quietly, "You got anything for this? It's gonna hurt like hell later!"

"The only thing that can make that feel better is in Germany! And you'd need about six of 'em before it would stop hurting!" The doc laughed. "In all seriousness, I got something to take care it. Plus we need to wash it out. How's the other area?"

"Oh! That's as good as new!" Tom lied about his hemorrhoids. They were better, but the flight down had "aggravated" the situation. Tom promised he would come by and have his chest cleaned.

Tom thought about Doc's other solution. It seemed like years since he'd wanted a beer. Now it didn't seem to matter. Booze was a nonfactor. They hadn't had alcohol for over three months, and they were all doing fine. Walker had lost about twenty pounds and was looking downright svelte. He wondered how long he could go without beer. It would be challenging when they got back to Germany, but he vowed right then that he would try as long as he was in command. He'd proven to himself that he could lead without "the crutch." How long could he keep it up?

April 2, 1991
KKMC, Saudi Arabia

ONE OF THE BEST WAYS TO pass the time away in the desert was at the "barber shop." WO1 Harmon brought his barber kit with him from Germany. It didn't take a cosmetology degree to cut hair the Desert Storm way. Hell, put the clippers on high and roll along the hair until it all came off. What Lawton found comical was watching Harmon work. So intent on perfection, he would sheer off everything, then walk around behind his work with comb and scissors like a real barber. The first minute actually got rid of all the hair, and the next ten was spent bullshittin' about the weather, politics, Iraq, or gerbils. No topic was off-limits, and everything was open for discussion. By the time they got to KKMC, Harmon was getting pretty damn good at cutting hair. Harmon could give a haircut and still leave something on top that resembled hair. The fact that having a shaved crop was better hygienically speaking than longer hair was irrelevant.

Tom went in for his weekly haircut and fell waist deep in a conversation on the future of the army. O'Toole was on his proverbial soapbox. "I'll tell ya what they need to do! They need about 250,000 stark raving lunatics! Keep 'em pent up . . . away from normal people, pay 'em $50,000 a year, and turn 'em loose on any enemy that thinks they got the balls to fuck with us!" O'Toole was met with a chorus of "Shut the hell up!"

"I'm serious! Get rid of all the extraneous bull the army has. Hell, make it two hundred thousand soldiers, pay 'em what they're worth, and kick all us old farts out!" said the warrant. At that point in time, drawing the army down from nearly one million men to two hundred thousand seemed ludicrous, but O'Toole did have a point. The folks that remained in the army would be able to get paid what they deserved. Less people would spend time away from their families. Temporary duty here, there, and everywhere all at a moment's notice and for God only knew how long would be limited.

The drawdown would be driven by politicians trying to save money, but at what price in the long run? Could a price be put on field time training at NTC or Hohenfels? The pressure of an "up or out" climate or the thought of being held accountable for having one soldier fail to perform even the most menial task at any level would cost leaders their career. Whatever the price was, it was a helluva lot more than Tom would get paid.

"Sir, O'Toole's so full of crap, Tim can't cut his hair 'cause he keeps getting shit in the scissors!" said Walker. The tent broke up laughing at the slight.

"What do you think is gonna happen to the army after this, sir?" asked Tim Harmon, still cutting the air around Ron Weimer's head.

Tom had to think about his answer. Because of the delay, it seemed every head in the tent was on him. "I hate to say it, but Mr. O'Toole has a valid point."

"See! See! Screw you, guys!" yelled O'Toole as the tent broke out in mock chaos.

"Wait! Wait! Let me finish!" said Tom as he let the tent get quiet again. "Historically speaking, the US Army always has . . . what's the term . . . *downsized* after a major conflict. There isn't a doubt in my military mind that we'll downsize again. Some of that is because the technology is so much better now. The army doesn't need as many people. Secondly, it costs a hell of a lot of money to keep an army this big." Tom listened to the grumbles and continued. I think the army leadership has learned that to go down too much too fast is bad for the country, and they won't let it happen like it has in the past. But you have to admit it, fellas, the technology is good enough to put a bunch of us on the streets."

"So you're saying we fought so good that we worked ourselves out of a twenty-year retirement?" asked Carl Tucker.

Tom shook off the question. "I can't say that for a fact, Mr. Tucker, but I will say some other military jobs are obsolete." Tom could see the wheels turning in the pilots' minds. "Here's an example, JAAT." For years, the focus of close air support was the joint air attack team, a lethal combination of air force assets, usually A-10s, army artillery, and attack helicopters. "Now correct me if I'm wrong, but I didn't see a need for a flying bathtub with a cannon strapped to it loitering around for fifteen minutes, making me pull off a shot I could take so he can fly in for two minutes and shoot two tanks and leave." Tom got concurrence from around the tent. "In the future, that damn Longbow Apache will shoot fire and forget rounds picked out by ground designators that digitally transmit the target coordinates to our fire-control computer. The platform may be ten Ks away from the target area, firing radar-guided missiles. There won't be a need for the air force in the close fight. In return, they probably won't send us in the deep fight, but we all speak army, so we should be doing the close fight on nearly every mission."

"So you got rid of A-10s, sir! What about the army?" asked Reimer.

"Light fighters with computers, that's the way were headed. Techno-warriors souped up by superconducting chips and laser-guided munitions," Tom said before he meant to. "Sounds like science fiction, but it's a lot closer than you may think." That quieted the tent. "You may be right, Mr. Tucker, about working ourselves out of a job! I think we can only afford the army to cut down to five hundred thousand." Everyone in the tent thought that was a feasible number. "I could just as easily see a cut down to somewhere between Mr. O'Toole's guess and mine."

"I still think that's too much. We always need infantry to occupy the terrain we fight for," said Ron Weimer. Chief warrant officer 4s don't stay around that long because they're dumb. "Somebody, a lot of somebodies, has got to do the tough jobs. An army of four hundred thousand isn't enough. No way."

"There are people who believe that the weapons can do more than the men," said Tom flatly, more or less opening up the floor for a new topic. The room was silent. "Soldiers are only respected when they are needed. Weapons are respected all the time."

Weimer said, "Sir, you're talking about Armed Forces Day, static displays, and all the dog and pony shows we do, right? The people see the weapons and learn some of the capabilities. They probably get 'warm and fuzzy' by all the gee-whiz gadgets but don't respect us for all the sacrifices we make."

"That's the way I see it. Granted not all Americans, but a lot. There's an old saying that I don't remember word for word, but it goes something like, 'In times of trouble or of war, God and soldiers we adore!'" said Tom. "I guess you could add, 'In times of pacifism and of peace, at arm's length, the soldiers keep!'" The tent filled with understanding, yet nervous chuckles. "Another analogy is that the military is like a mean dog. Kept on a leash in the backyard because he's ugly and deadly, but when there's trouble in the front yard, the dog is brought out front to solve the problem."

"I think they brought every ugly dog in the pen out for this fight!" said Carl Tucker.

"Well, all I'm saying is there ain't gonna be as many doggies the next time there's trouble in the front yard!" said O'Toole. He was met with a chorus of "Shut up."

Tom laughed as the group waved off the comment. Walker looked at Lawton and said, "Don't mind him, sir! He's got PISS!"

Tom nearly blew the Pepsi he was drinking out his nose. "What?"

"He's got the PISS, sir!" repeated Walker.

"What's that?" asked Tom, not sure that he wanted to know.

"He's got post-Iraqi stress syndrome!" said the warrant. The comment created a chant of "PISS! PISS! PISS!" from all the attendees.

"That's right, sir! I'm sufferin' from too much stress. By the way, did you sign my retirement paperwork yet?" asked O'Toole. Tom just shook his head negatively and started to drink his Pepsi.

Then Walker changed the subject. "So you guys know how to tell which gerbils been tubin'?" The tent erupted in laughter again.

Tom stood up. "On that note, gentlemen, and you too, Mr. Walker, I shall take my leave. I will come back at a later time for my haircut." Tom headed out the tent. Walker called the tent to attention as his commander departed.

Tom said, "Carry on, you knuckleheads!"

As he got outside, he heard Walker say in a loud voice, "Now we know how to get the commissioned guys out of the barber shop."

Tom wanted to stay and enjoy some more of the camaraderie, but duty called. It was about time for the evening meeting.

That evening, about 2200, Tom, Hart, and Hal were just about in the rack when a loud bang that sounded like a bomb rang out from the warrant's tent. The three officers scrambled to get dressed and rush over to see what had happened. Fearing the worse, they entered the tent panting and carrying the first-aid kit.

At the far end of the tent, a half-dozen warrant officers in various stages of dress were laughing hysterically. It took Tom a minute to digest what was going on. As he walked to the far end of the tent, he could see Tim Harmon and Carl Tucker covered with some kind of red liquid. Lawton quickened his pace to the scene unfolding before him. "What the hell happened? Are you guys all right?" he asked to no one in particular.

The laughter continued, with fingers being pointed to the stove. From behind him, Mark Nichols spoke. "It's okay, sir. Dooberhead left some beans on the stove." Then Nichols started to chuckle. "The can started making noises and . . ." Then Nichols cracked up.

"The fuckin' can exploded, sir!" Berstein laughed.

"As soon as I touched it to take it off, boom!" said Harmon. "Sorry to get you excited, sir!" Tom looked around the tent and saw beans and sauce everywhere. Harmon and Tucker were covered. Carl Tucker didn't see too much humor in the incident. After Tom was sure everyone was okay, he found it kind of funny too.

He shook his head. "Your beans, Mr. Harmon?"

"Yes, sir!" said the warrant sheepishly.

"Your mess! Get it cleaned up ASAP," said Tom. He turned and saw Timmons covering his mouth to hold in the laugh. Hart Osborn was glaring at the junior warrant. "Come on, gentlemen, let's get some sleep."

April 4, 1991
KKMC, Saudi Arabia

THE DAY HAD STARTED OFF NORMAL enough. About 1300, O'Toole started throwing up and having diarrhea. By 1500, O'Toole was having dry heaves, and Nichols was throwing up. Three hours later, O'Toole was hooked to an IV, Nichols had dry heaves, and Weimer was throwing up. Whatever the "bug" was, it worked like clockwork and was moving right down the line in the warrant officer's tent. By 2000, half the tent had it, and Hubert had a quarantine sign hanging over the Nontaxable sign.

Tom stopped by to visit but didn't stay too long. Timmons and Osborn were told to stay out. Whatever the virus was, it had somehow made the jump to the enlisted tent the next day, and it made the rounds through their area. Ten minutes later, Tom went back to his tent depressed that his troop was basically "down" due to some kind of bug that had hit the whole troop.

"Man, this sucks!" said Tom to his two friends.

"They still blowin' chunks, sir?" asked Hal Timmons. The colorful CAV terminology was more than Tom needed, but he understood what Hal meant.

"It's like a damn hospital ward over there. Half the tent is on IVs, and the other half is bedridden. Same, same with the troopers. The only person that didn't get it was Toretti, and he's on the very end of the appointment schedule." Toretti's bunk was the last one next to the door.

"Maybe the virus petered out?" said Osborn.

"Yeah, that's possible," said Tom. They had heard about bugs like this from other units. "I guess we've just been lucky so far."

"Sir, I'm gonna go check on my guys," said Timmons. "But only for a second. I don't want any of whatever it is."

"See ya in a few," said Tom. The tent was quiet for a minute. Tom had an eerie feeling that something was up with Hart but had no idea what it was.

They had a run-in back in Dodge. Osborn had asked Staff Sergeant Ramirez to do something, and Osborn intended for it to be done right then. Ramirez, overtasked with requests from Top Garcia, Lawton, and for some unknown reason, the sergeant major, basically blew off the lieutenant. Osborn got hot and wanted to give him an Article 15. Six months ago, Osborn had written Ramirez up for a recommendation as Aviation NCO of the year in EUSAEUR. Tom took the middle ground, trying to support both the lieutenant and the NCO.

Lawton called Ramirez into the tent for the Article 15. Tom read it. Ramirez pleaded his case and admitted he was wrong and that it wouldn't happen again. Tom found him guilty but gave Staff Sergeant Ramirez a suspended sentence. Lawton said he understood the situation but needed to support the lieutenant. Ramirez understood what Tom's situation was, appreciated the leniency, and promised not to screw up again.

Needless to say, Hart Osborn was upset about the decision. He felt Tom had failed to support him. They had a small argument about it in Dodge, and Tom wondered if that was still bothering Hart.

Before he could ask, Hart Osborn broke the silence. From out of the blue, Hart said, "I've asked the colonel for the S4 job." Tom was stunned. Tom knew that Larry Krause was headed back to Germany to be with his wife for her delivery, but he didn't think it would be so soon. "He said it was mine as soon as you can let me go."

Tom was hot. "Is this about the Ramirez thing? Is that was this is about?"

"That has nothing to do with this!" said Captain Osborn.

Tom was beside himself. "I'm surprised you bothered to tell me! Were you gonna move out in the middle of the night or what?"

To his credit, Hart Osborn remained calm. "That's what I was waiting to tell you. I didn't want to bring it up with Hal here."

"I don't suppose Hawk provided you the name of your replacement, did he?" asked Tom sarcastically.

"No, Tom, he didn't," said Hart.

Tom decided to let it out. "Damn it! Why didn't you tell me?"

Hart Osborn didn't waiver. "Because you wouldn't let me leave." Tom thought about the comment. He had to admit Hart was right. "Tom, it's got nothing to do with Ramirez. It's got nothing to do with differences between you and I. It has to do with me wanting to move on." Tom had calmed down and was listening now. Osborn continued, "This is a promotion for me! I want you to be happy for me. The colonel thinks I can do a good job." Hart started to pack.

"I'm just upset at the way it's happening," said Tom.

"I've learned so much from you. But I've been a platoon leader for too long. It's time for me to move," said Hart.

Tom thought about his forty months as a platoon leader. He loved every day of it. Tom had to admit the last couple of months he was ready to go. Hart had been a platoon leader for nearly thirty months, which was a long time. Tom still felt that Hart should have told him earlier. "I just wish I would have seen it coming."

"Tom, there was nothing you could do. I just asked today. And I know you. You're not gonna keep me here, especially when it sinks in that this is a good thing for me," said Hart.

Tom had to admit Hart was right. Perhaps it was Tom's own selfishness that wanted to keep Hart in the troop. It would mean more work for Tom, and he would lose that special camaraderie a commander develops with a platoon leader. More than that, he'd be losing someone that he felt he had mentored and developed into an outstanding officer. "You don't have to leave tonight. I can help you move. You can even leave your shit here!" Tom said.

Hart thought about the offer and declined. "I need to move over to the S4 area and get into the operations over there. If I'm gonna do it, I need to do it all the way."

Tom nodded his agreement and chuckled. "If it was me, I'd do the same thing." He went over to help Hart get his bags together. "You know, I've never had a primary staff job. I have no idea what an S4 really does."

Hart smiled and said, "You and me both!"

"I will tell you this. Anything that I or the Champions can do for you, all you need to do is ask," said Tom. "I owe you that much."

"No problem, Tom. I know that," said Hart.

Tom realized he was getting too sentimental for his own comfort. "Just one other thing, we can't do a proper farewell because I didn't get you an award. Since you are the head 'loggy toad' in the squadron"—Tom bent over and picked something off the ground—"you can have my socks!"

Osborn laughed and put his hands up. "No, thanks! I've had all of your socks that I can stand!"

Tom threw them back on the ground. "Hart," he got Osborn's attention, "in all honesty, you were ready to command an attack troop before we got down here. I've got nothing but respect for you and the effort you gave the troop." Tom held out his hand. "Thanks."

Osborn looked at the hand and grabbed it slowly. "You taught me more in the last six months than I learned in my first two years as a platoon leader, and I thank you for that." Then he added as he let go, "You have an unorthodox way of working, but you are people oriented, and that's what makes you the leader that you are. I'll try to keep a piece of that unique quality with me when I get command."

Tom said, "And when you get it, you kick it in the ass!"

Hart grabbed his bags and said good-bye. He was out the door before Tom could stop him. He looked around the empty tent. God, he wished he were back in Germany. He wished he had Cindy's arms to crawl into. He did the next best thing. He got out some paper and wrote her another letter. That was as close as he could get.

0215, April 7, 1991
KKMC, Saudi Arabia

THE MOVEMENT OF THE TENT AWAKENED Tom. Without prompting, Hal Timmons popped out of his bag too. The wind was howling, and the sides of the tent were beginning to flap violently. Outside, Tom heard a steady roar. The noise was unlike anything he'd ever heard before. It didn't have the volume of a train, but it came from everywhere. The north side of the tent began to blow horizontally. Tom and Hal got out of their bags and jumped on the flapping tent in a fruitless attempt to keep it from flapping more violently. For a full minute, the tent flapped violently as the relentless wind howled its anger. For an instant, Tom wanted to get his Kevlar and get it on his head. The thought of a tent pole flying through the side of the canvas side of the tent went through his mind, but he knew that if he let go, the tent was gone, maybe Hal with it. The two men lay there holding on to the tent as if it were a life raft, trying to yell above the wind's roar, neither knowing what the other wanted to do.

Slowly, the wind subsided. It slowed to about fifty knots and, within two minutes, down to ten miles per hour. Hal found a light and turned it on inside the tent. Tom looked through the dust in search of some clothes to wear. His equipment was scattered everywhere, and he couldn't find his flight suit. Then it hit him. If the tent looked like this, what about the aircraft? What about his men? He grabbed his sweat clothes and sneakers and hurried outside.

Garcia was already outside with a flashlight. "What the hell was that?" asked Tom.

"I'd have to say that was the mother of all shamals, sir!" said the first sergeant. "Nobody is hurt, but we got shit scattered for ten fucking miles!"

Tom observed Top's flashlight as it moved about the wreckage. Half a dozen tents, big ones, were down. People were milling around, dazed by the severity of the intense storm. "As long as none of our people got hurt, Top. I'm gonna run out to the flight line and see if we got hit there too!"

Tom picked up a jog as he headed to the aircraft parking area. Flashlights were shining like spotlights in every direction. The first aircraft he came to was a Blackhawk rolled over on its side. His first impulse was to check to see if anyone was inside. Then he saw the ropes dangling off the main rotor blades. It had been moored, but no mooring could have withstood this wind. Rooksy came up behind him. "Goddamn it! That's my Hawk!" Tom wanted to stay and comfort his friend, but his mind raced to his own Apaches. He moved on without a word.

Tom headed down the row behind the Blackhawk. With all the lights shining, he could make out the airframes. The Apaches were all still upright, but the rotor blades had been snapped like toothpicks. He could make out the symbols on the engines' cowlings and saw they were Alpha Troop aircraft.

Tom slowed his pace as he came to the C Troop area. His aircraft were all on the north side of the row, unscratched. To the south were the B Troop aircraft with main rotors pointing in every direction like huge praying mantises with their limbs broken and pointing to the heavens, tie-down ropes dangling in the ten-knot wind.

Lawton checked every one of his aircraft, and the Champions had somehow escaped without damage. The wind had taken away some of the covers, but nothing that couldn't be replaced. Tom headed back and found Chris Wise. He had a flashlight and was assessing the damage.

"I hope it's not as bad as it looks, Chris," said Tom.

Wise shook his head. "Mostly the blades. I think we're better off than that Blackhawk." Wise's light showed the main rotor blades of his aircraft snapped one-third of the way down the blade and pointing upward at an awkward angle. Chris was taking the event the only way he could. "Damn good thing this happened after we got out of Iraq, or we'd be hurtin' right now!" Tom smiled and nodded.

When he got back to the Blackhawk, Lieutenant Colonel Hawk, Rooksy, and the sergeant major were all there. There wasn't much more that could be done in the darkness, so the plan was to reassess the situation first thing in the morning and start getting as many birds up as possible. The UH-60 had received the most damage, and the rest of the squadron got off with only blade damage. Rooks couldn't help but bring up the fact that this was the third major windstorm on the third different continent that the unit had suffered through. They were going through the unit training plan at Fort Hood, Texas, when the Mother's Day Massacre windstorm of '89 occurred. Then in spring of '90, they were hit by a freak windstorm outside of Hohenfels. Now a freak shamal in Saudi Arabia. Rooks said, "If we go to Africa or South America next year, I'm asking for a transfer!"

Tom's perspective was different. It was damn good it had not happened two months ago. Mother Nature had done more damage to them in five minutes than Saddam had been able to do in months.

In the morning light, the majority of the damage remained broken rotor blades and blown-off covers. Tie-downs were broken or snapped, and the scouts had weathervaned or slid into the direction of the wind but weren't really damaged. The fact that not one person in the squadron was injured was a miracle considering they were in tents. One of the division CAV units had a couple of injuries from flying debris. All in all, it could have been a major disaster. It would only take parts and time to get everything fixed. The unit wouldn't be able to get into the port for another week.

April 11, 1991
KKMC, Saudi Arabia

THE OFFICIAL END TO THE PERSIAN Gulf War was announced. At KKMC, the unit began to receive broadcasts on armed forces radio. Lawton was reaching into his kit bag when he heard the news. A sharp pain, like a tack, hit him on the back of the hand. He didn't know what had happened, so Tom began to look in his kit bag for a piece of metal or something that may have caused the sharp pain. He picked the bag up and saw nothing inside. He turned it upside down and jumped back quickly when something fell out.

Tom nearly reached for his pistol when he saw the scorpion. It was at least four inches long and pitch black. He quickly slammed a boot on it, crushing the monstrous insect before it could run off to hide. He moved his foot and looked at the pile of goop he had made on his wooden flooring, then looked at his hand. There was a big red welt forming on his left hand in the soft tissue between his thumb and index finger. He rubbed it and could feel the tingling start. The sting began to swell immediately.

Lawton started to panic, thinking that he may die from a stupid scorpion bite. Tom quickly got on his equipment and headed for Garcia's tent. Suppose he fell over right there dead, no one would know. He grabbed his shaving kit and quickly dumped all the contents on his cot. He carefully scooped up the scorpion remains, lest a resurrection were to occur. He placed the goop that was once the scorpion, placed it into his shaving kit, and quickly sought out his first sergeant's guidance.

Top was understanding and told Tom the chances were good he wouldn't die. But the captain needed to get to an aid station and get treatment. Top Garcia got Crockett and a Humvee to take Lawton to the station. By the time they got there, Tom's left arm was tingling, and his hand felt like it was asleep. A mild case of nausea was starting, but for the most part, he was okay.

Thinking abstract thoughts of a humiliating death, he decided if he were to die from a "goddamn bug bite," he was gonna "goddamn die with his men!" The doctor tried to assure him he probably wouldn't die, but they didn't know for sure and wanted him close should something happen.

Tom nodded politely at the thought of something happening, grabbed his gear, and told the captain he would get back if it got worse.

Tom got back in the Humvee, his left arm dangling, his hand swollen, and trying to keep from puking. He told Crockett to get him to the shopette. The specialist got his commander Tylenol, Pepsis, and a huge bag of M&M's.

"If it were any other war, it would be beer, whiskey, and cigarettes, but this is the only thing we can get," he told Crockett. "If I'm gonna go out from a bug bite, I'm going out doin' stuff that will make me smile."

Crockett started the Humvee, and they headed back to the AA. "If I had any beer, sir, you know I'd let you have it!" The crew chief smiled.

"Thanks, but I'll be just fine. Goddamn doctors! They don't know shit!" Tom was agitated, but not nearly as pissed as he was letting on.

"If you die, sir, can I have your watch?" asked Crockett with a broad smile.

Tom burst out laughing. "You'd probably take it before you called the medic, wouldn't you?"

"Not me, sir!" The specialist smiled. "Not as far as you'd know!"

Tom popped his first Pepsi and took four Tylenols. "Don't you tell anybody I'm self-medicating or they'll ground me. Then you'd get some other jerk to come be your commander. He'd probably put you up for an Article 15 for that nasty breath you got!" The crew chief laughed. "You go ahead and laugh! Let's go back to the shopette. I'll get you a damn toothbrush and some of that gel crap to scrape those teeth!" Now Tom was laughing too. "Here I am sufferin' and you want my watch! Damn!"

The pain was subsiding by the time they got back to the tent. Tom put out his hand to Crockett and told him thanks for the support "or lack thereof!" He gave the man a Pepsi and headed to his tent. He made sure Hawk was aware that he'd been bitten and told the commander that as far as anyone knew, the scorpion sting wasn't fatal and there was nothing to do but wait. Tom got out his paper and tried to write, but his hand was numb. After five minutes, he threw the pad across the tent and started eating the candy.

Hal Timmons had gone to the port. Hart Osborn was the S4. He was alone in his tent, suffering from a stupid bug bite in the middle of a desert surrounded by fifty thousand GIs that wanted his watch. He had to laugh about the situation . . . or he'd go over the edge. Just like the other fifty thousand GIs, Tom was ready to be home.

April 15, 1991
KKMC, Saudi Arabia

LAWTON RECOVERED FULLY FROM THE WOUND. Two days later, his hand was still numb and tingled, but the nausea had stopped. In the meantime, there was some good news. The squadron was notified that SSG Hector Ramirez was named the EUSAEUR Aviation NCO of the Year. Tom was happy that Ramirez had won the award and noticed that CPT Hart Osborn was one of the first guys to shake his hand. Ramirez knew that it was Osborn that had written up the recommendation and subsequently turned in the award. It was one of the few bright spots during the stay at KKMC.

There was one other. The enlisted soldiers and warrants from all five troops were busting their tails trying to get the aircraft ready after the windstorm. Tom had heard music being played in the evenings by Petty, Timmons, and a couple of other people he didn't recognize. Petty approached him with the fact that members from the Third Armored Division Band had been bunking about two hundred yards away and wanted to put on a little "jam session." The band members would be leaving in two days. Tom saw no harm in it and said, "No problem. Not too loud, not too big, and do it after work so that anybody that wants to listen doesn't get reamed by their commander!" Petty agreed and put together a small performance.

There was an open space next to the aircraft parking area. Top gave Petty the five-ton truck and a Humvee to use as a makeshift stage. Ramirez worked some magic and got power to the whole area. Five soldiers from the Third Armored Division Band joined in playing bass and electric guitar and three soldiers on horns. McFarland borrowed drums from the band, and Timmons played some rhythm guitar. Petty played lead and sang most of the songs.

The session started off small with the Champions and some D Troop mechanics listening as the guys play. Petty played some early Beatles, mostly acoustic stuff, and then Hal Timmons sang a Jimmy Buffet song. Soon there were a hundred soldiers watching.

Petty started to get into it. He got on the electric guitar, and the place started rocking. They did a couple of Georgia Satellite numbers and followed that up with a Buddy Holly tune. Then Petty embarrassed Tom and dedicated "Desert Skies" to his boss. Tom went up onto the makeshift stage and took a bow.

Tom didn't stay. He merely thanked everyone for his or her support and added, "Hope y'all enjoy the show!" Tom gave Petty one of those "Don't do that again!" looks and quickly got down.

Joe Petty picked up where Lawton left off. "I just want to say thanks to the guys that crewed the birds and the refuelers. Y'all didn't get to pull the trigger, but we could never do our job if you didn't do yours. On behalf of all the pilots in the squadron, thanks a bunch!" Petty stepped back and got a tremendous ovation. He introduced the members of the band and continued, "We've been workin' on the next two songs for a couple of hours, so don't get upset with us if we don't do it right. You guys know C Troop of the Fighting Sixth is called the Champions. But at this particular moment in time, each and every one of us is a champion!" Petty stood back to enjoy the applause. He was a natural. Tom felt deep down Petty had chosen the wrong profession. "When I get to the chorus of the second song, I'm sure you all know it. Please feel free to sing along. Let's wake up Saudi Arabia!" More hoots and hollers.

Joe Petty stepped away from the microphone, coughed a small throat-clearing burst, and then slowly moved forward. He sang from the heart, a song that every soldier recognized. McFarland started a heavy backbeat. The song was "We Will Rock You" by Queen. The troops, up to three hundred of them, went nuts. Petty sounded off like he was at a tryout to replace Freddie Mercury.

> *Buddy you're a boy make a big noise*
> *Playin' in the street gonna be a big man someday*
> *You got mud on your face, you big disgrace*
> *Kickin' your ass all over the place . . .*

The troops roared their approval and instantly picked up the beat. When it came to the lead guitar solo, Joe Petty was a little rusty, but it didn't matter.

He had the crowd ten thousand miles away, rocking at their favorite stadium. And for just a few minutes, they weren't in Saudi Arabia anymore.

When he finished, the crowd cheered their approval. But they knew enough about the music to stop as if choreographed and let Petty start "We Are the Champions." And for every word of the chorus, three hundred voices joined in. Louder and louder it grew. By the end, another hundred had come from their tents and joined in. The music stopped, and Petty just turned the microphone on the soldiers. The troops sang the chorus all the way through, swaying to and fro, surprisingly enough, in time. Tom remembered being impressed, thinking they were only in time because they were all sober. They cranked up the chorus one final time with music, Joe Petty ripping the guitar for all it was worth.

When it was done, all the members of the "session" received a thunderous applause. Petty finished up with, "You guys get home safe, and we'll see ya in Deutschland!" The crowd begged for more. To his credit, Petty said they didn't know any more tunes and the Arabs would probably call the military police if they kept it up. The troops finally realized the good time had come to an end and began to slowly leave.

For an hour, the escape from reality took the troopers away. It was as if all the carnage created over a month ago was years behind them. It was a great chance to get morale up, and everyone warmly received the effort. It wasn't until months later that Lawton found out that even the chain of command enjoyed it.

April 19, 1991
KKMC, Saudi Arabia

THE ORDERS FINALLY CAME DOWN TO move the squadron to the port of Dammam for redeployment. Since the storm had done so much damage to the blades, it took an extra week to get new blades to the assembly area and on the aircraft and all the birds test-flown. They had just finished the last test flight when the word reached Hawk that the squadron needed to be ready to move. A controlled form of excitement came over the area as the unit packed up. They realized they would soon be out of the desert and one step closer to home.

CHAPTER 12

April 20, 1991
Khobar Towers, Dhahran, Saudi Arabia

THE SQUADRON PARKED THE AIRCRAFT AT an airfield about thirty minutes away from their assigned quarters at Khobar Towers. The towers were eight-story high-rise apartment buildings in an area of the city just off the Persian Gulf. The towers' complex was a group of about twenty buildings all built exactly the same. Inside, they had elevators that naturally took forever to get to any floor. The apartments had many rooms with carpeting, but no furniture to speak of. Each troop brought their own cot and personal equipment with them and staked out their own little corner of paradise into whatever space they could salvage. Weapons were brought upstairs, and each man was responsible for the care of his own "Betty." After two days, when a routine was established, Hawk decided weapons could be collected and a guard placed on them, rather than risk another fiasco like they experienced in Dodge.

The view from the top of the towers was beautiful. Visibility was always perfect. You could spend hours sitting up on the roof, watching the ships move up and down the gulf, empty when coming in and full to the brim with oil when they departed. Hundreds of ships in the course of a week. Lawton had heard that oil had hit forty dollars a barrel. Tom Lawton wondered how many spies of industry or various foreign governments perched on rooftops such as this to count, verify, catalog, and classify the ships that moved through this strategic area. Then he wondered how much money all that oil equated to. He was sure that somewhere, someone would pay an awful lot of money for information like that. He didn't dwell on the thoughts, because in the grand scheme of his world, he didn't really give a damn. If it were another time and another place, more money could be made if the towers were a four-star hotel. Tom could be observing the scenery from a lounge chair, with loud music playing and a beverage of his choice. But not here and not now. The CAV was still running through his blood.

In his world, he had one more major step to accomplish, and that was getting everyone home. As close as he was to fulfilling that mission, he wasn't comfortable enough to think he was out of the woods yet.

To the north of the complex was a square. In this area, capitalism reigned supreme. Of course the Army and Air Force Exchange Service (AAFES) was there in force, offering all the necessities that soldiers desired, except "girlie magazines" and alcohol. Wolf Burger stands and specialist shops selling locally made products, art, and of course gold were centrally located in that area.

The gold stands were making a killing off the soldiers. Some soldiers knew absolutely nothing about the art of bartering. Of course the Arabs were good at it, and like all salesmen, they could spot a sucker a mile away. The Champions weren't the first unit to come through, but the vendors could tell who the new soldiers were. The gold was sold by the gram. It made no difference what type, design, or beauty of any piece of jewelry. It only mattered how much it weighed.

On the first day at Khobar, soldiers thought they were getting a good deal for twenty-one or even twenty dollars a gram. The first troops to purchase were excited and overjoyed with their purchases. So were the vendors. At the Khobar market, the lowest prices found, usually by soldiers in units just about to ship out, who learned the "art of the deal" and the best place to buy, was fifteen dollars a gram. Some soldiers spent thousands and thousands of dollars on gold.

That evening, Tom had an informal briefing to his troopers about the scams, the vendors, and the happenings in the mall area. He didn't put them on restriction, figuring that if you tell a soldier not to do something, he will try to do it. Rather than order them not to, he tried to appeal to their wallets and their common sense. Most had a couple thousand dollars saved up, and they would have more than enough chance to spend it in Germany. That seemed to keep the buying sprees in check, at least for a little while.

April 23, 1991
Dammam, Saudi Arabia

LAWTON GOT WORD THAT ANY SOLDIER that was of the Jewish faith would be afforded the opportunity to join other soldiers of the faith on a cruise in the gulf. Tom told the first sergeant and Hal Timmons to find any Jewish soldiers in the troop and see if they wished to attend.

The word quickly spread, and Allen Berstein was the only troop in C Troop that met the requirement. He was approved to go and wasted no time packing his gear. He felt he could trust Cross and Tucker to watch over his stuff and swore that he would come back as soon as possible. The other warrants laughed at the thought of coming back to Khobar Towers for any reason.

"You're outta your mind, man! I wouldn't come back here until it was time to go," said Tucker.

"And don't even think of us. We'll be here. Toiling in the hot sun. Getting your aircraft ready to redeploy," said Wes Cross with all the sarcasm he could muster.

Berstein would have none of it. "I'll be back, and if there is anything I can get for you guys, I will. Trust me."

Walker hollered from across the room, "Don't listen to that shit! He's headed to the 'Jew boat,' and he wants you to trust him! Let me watch your shit! At least I could get somethin' from the mall for your rucksack."

Berstein became a bit nervous at the thought but didn't need to worry. The feeling that anyone had an opportunity to get out of the towers for anything other than washing aircraft appealed to all the troops. He headed outside for his ride and got nothing but handshakes out the door.

"Don't go meetin' any Jewish princess on the Jewish love boat, or we'll sell your shit!" yelled Walker as Berstein loaded his vehicle.

"I doubt I'll even meet a woman on the boat, so cut me some slack, okay?" pleaded the warrant. But with a last parting shot, he said, "If I do, I'll try to poke some fun at her for you guys!" He just made it into the truck before Walker's empty Pepsi can hit the window.

LTC Stan Hawk got all the commanders together and offered to take them to dinner. It was an offer none of the men refused. Two nights prior,

Denson had taken his staff and the squadron commanders "out on the town" as his way of thanks. Now it was Hawk's turn to offer a thank-you dinner to his men.

The evening started out with a ride in one of the Nissan Pathfinders the Japanese had provided to the "war effort." Dammam was a huge city that could have easily passed for any major city in Europe. And if more trash was lying around and the water was to the west, it could have passed for some cities in Southern California. The setting was not quite the same because California cities would have beautiful women everywhere. There were *no* women there.

They parked in an area equivalent to any parking area in America, an area about three hundred yards by five hundred yards. The difference between American parking lots and this particular Saudi parking lot was quickly explained. This lot was turned into the "judgment area" on the weekend. On Saturdays, when punishment was handed out, this particular parking lot was the main square where the Saudis conducted beheadings. It didn't feel any different until Tom found that out. After Hawk told the men what the lot was on Saturdays, it took on an eerie quality. The captains couldn't help but look at the ground and try to find blood trails. Apparently, the blood was sprayed away with water, and the entire lot was cleaned up immediately after the event.

They walked across the street into the business area. The area was a mall-type square with various shops throughout. There were two major differences between the downtown area and the mall at Khobar Towers. The downtown area had produce for sale. Strange-looking fruits and vegetables with sweet, pleasant smells were available everywhere. Tom had no idea the country had any type of produce, much less in volume and quite a variety. After nearly four months of nothing but desert, it was hard to imagine the country had any produce at all.

The second difference was the prices. There were about eight or nine gold shops in this area. The vendors weren't nearly as hardworking as the vendors at Khobar. They were patient and enjoyed the bartering, but not that much. They didn't want to play the game. They knew where their profit margin was and didn't go below it. The captains did a quick recon and headed onto dinner.

The Arabian Cafe had all the atmosphere of a European restaurant specializing in seafood, but there was a less-cordial atmosphere. Plush carpeting, a giant fish tank, dimly lit, and plenty of English-speaking people. There were only a handful of women in the room of forty people. All the people wore suits or dressed up for the evening, except the soldiers. They stood out in their "chocolate chip" BDUs. They were never approached by any other guests nor attempted to converse with others in the crowd.

Seafood was the favorite choice among the soldiers. Tom Lawton had prawn and lamb with rice. Everyone else chose shellfish or the fish special for the evening, a type of grouper in a traditional sauce. The drinks were limited to water, soda, and tea. Taking the boss's lead, no one even tried to order wine, and beer was out of the question.

After dinner, talk turned to business, the victory in the desert, the future of the captains, and of course the future of the army. Hawk was in his element. He was happy that all his troops were there and had performed superbly in combat. It was his first opportunity to say thank you for the job well done. Hawk proposed a toast. "Gentlemen, I want to thank each of you for your effort and the effort of your troopers. A toast to the men and women of the Fighting Sixth."

All the captains raised there glasses and said, "To the Fighting Sixth!"

"Colonel Denson also sends his thanks to you all. He's happy with the job you did and told me to let you know you all have tremendous careers in army aviation because of your outstanding leadership during the war," said Hawk. Tom didn't know how to take the comment. He would leave Saudi Arabia with one less aircraft than he came. Granted the airframe was recovered, but he would probably never see it again. He knew Denson, and he knew his memory for negative things like "a damaged aircraft" because you got too close to the enemy. Tom put the notion out of his mind and tried to enjoy the evening.

"Tom, I want to thank you for letting Hart Osborn move to the S4 job. He's doing a lot of great work there," said Hawk.

"He deserved it, sir. He did an outstanding job at the platoon leader position for so long that once he made captain, I couldn't justify keeping him," said Tom.

Hawk nodded his agreement and changed the subject. "I guess my award for the commander with the best performance for the week would be . . ." Hawk made a mock drumroll. The captains all smiled and looked at one another. "Captain Promotable Darren Rooks." The small group was pleasantly surprised by Hawk's selection and gave a sincere clap. "Our operational readiness rate for the week of conflict was 92 percent FMC. We fired over 150 Hellfires, a ton of rockets, and over four thousand rounds of 30mm, with only a handful of gun malfunctions. A damn good rate and an obvious indication of the hard work our maintenance people did. Thanks, Darren. It wasn't really a tough choice with stats like that. But if we were in Germany, I'd buy all you guys a beer." The colonel got a bit choked up. "Words can't express the . . . feeling of loyalty and honor I feel. I will hold my head high and personally thank each one of you for a job well done."

Everyone was humbled by the colonel's emotional talk. It was Chris Wise that broke the humility of the moment by changing the subject. "So what do we do for an encore, sir?"

Everyone chuckled. "You drive on like the outstanding soldiers that you are! You take the lessons learned from this one, and you prep for the next one. It's that easy." Tom agreed wholeheartedly with the comment. It sounded a helluva a lot easier than it was.

Rooksy got a chance to say thanks as usual. Rooks thought about his troops and their well-being. "I appreciate the recognition, sir. But in all honesty, it's the troops that did it all. I think that if any of them were here, they'd want to know the answer to that same question. They all keep stirring up the notion that there's gonna be a drawdown of the army after this and that a whole bunch of troops are going to be asked to leave. You heard anything about that, sir?"

"I haven't heard anything about a drawdown, per se. But historically speaking, after a major conflict like this war, the United States Army cuts down its personnel numbers. I can't imagine that we would cut down too much, especially in the aviation community, because of our flexibility, mobility, and the punch that we can pack. I can see some forces being . . . thinned out," Hawk said. Then he added as if an afterthought, "I don't think we did so well that we worked our way out of employment." He smiled, believing what he said.

The whole war was so unrealistic until the damage and the bodies were seen in the daylight after it was done. Weeks and weeks of pounding from the air. A mass of Allied Troops unlike anything since the Second World

War. A terrain perfectly suited for the use of modern weapons systems and the platforms the United States had been developing for a decade. Hawk spoke about getting ready for the next one. There was no doubt in anyone's mind at the table that the next war would be more difficult than this one had been. The thought of preparing for it so soon hit home with Lawton. War would always be a never-ending struggle, a constant circle of events. Peace, crisis, war, crisis, peace and the process would start all over again. It all seemed so futile. Tom cleared the thought. This was something no "warmongering CAV trooper" should be thinking. But he was.

After dinner, they had about an hour to wander around downtown and see the shopping areas again. As they walked, Chris Wise asked Tom, "You really believe what the Hawk said?"

"Which part?" asked Tom, not knowing where Chris was headed with the question.

"The part about no downsizing in aviation. That and the fact that we're all okay!" said Chris Wise.

"I'm pretty sure all the captains in command are okay. You gotta admit, years from now, when they look at our OERs and read our records, troop commander during Desert Storm will be a great bullet. That's why all the guys from the states flew into Iraq when we were there. That's why people all tried like hell to get these commands that we have." Tom looked at Chris and smiled broadly. "I think we're just fine. Some other poor schmucks that had recruiting, reserve duty, or ROTC, any of the three *R*s, will be gettin' their résumés together, but not us!"

Chris Wise smiled and almost believed what his friend had said. Yes, the chain of command was right. They'd take care of their guys.

Soon they were back in the shopping area in the main part of town. Many soldiers were out now including enlisted personnel, with patches indicating their units on their sleeves. The patches covered most of the divisions as well as the corps elements still in country. Hundreds of troops, but none from the aviation brigade, except the small group of commanders.

Phil Pearson found Chris and Tom window-shopping. "I found it, fellas! The place to shop for jewelry! Come on!" Wise and Lawton looked at each other and shrugged. They followed their excited friend to a shop about fifty yards down sidewalk.

"Thirteen bucks a gram! Thirteen!" said Phil with a huge grin.

"I'm there!" yelled Chris Wise.

Tom just smiled and followed the two men in. They browsed for about five minutes. Then they couldn't take it anymore. Each man got a sales representative and began the process. Fifteen minutes later, they were outside.

Phil Pearson had purchased two necklaces and two bracelets. Tom purchased one large necklace, one thin eighteen-inch necklace, and three bracelets. Chris Wise went completely nuts. He bought five necklaces, five bracelets, three rings, and one ugly pendent. Then he charged the whole purchase to his Master Card as if he were at Walmart. The volume purchase did have its advantage. The vendor only charged him twelve dollars a gram. Tom wondered what Cindy would do if a $3,000 charge from Akmed's Jewelry Shop in beautiful downtown Dammam just happened to pop up on the bills. Tom wasn't too sure, but he knew that he'd need a flak vest to face her.

The giggling commanders joined the rest of the group and quickly got into the squadron commander's Toyota, as if they had just robbed the merchant's store. They were all sufficiently dumbfounded when Rooksy notified them he'd gotten almost the same purchase as Wise but only paid ten dollars a gram.

The thought that some of the soldiers back at Khobar had paid twice as much left a bad taste in Lawton's mouth, but there wasn't much he could do. Downtown remained off-limits to the cavalry soldiers, and he doubted he could get back downtown to make more purchases. The fact that he'd made some good purchases for Cindy, Megan, and his mom would not be advertised, but he knew he would tell his soldiers to barter more before buying at the towers' square.

April 24, 1991
Khobar Towers, Saudi Arabia

IT DIDN'T TAKE LONG FOR THE soldiers to get a line on the phones. Every chance they got when they weren't preparing the aircraft for redeployment, the troopers spent in the mall area or on the phones.

For all the long-distance calls, there was a price to pay. A price that none of the troopers would ever imagine.

After the usual fifteen-minute wait, the soldiers entered the phone area to grab one of the open phones that was hung on a pole that had four phones attached to it. When the soldiers were connected with the AT&T operator, they would give the operator their phone-card number. It didn't take long for some genius soldier to figure out how to screw his buddy.

The bastards would wait at one of the poles and pretend to be talking. They would listen for the other soldiers to give their AT&T phone-card number, write it down, and use it later to run up enormous charges. When their troopers got home to their loved ones, they would also come home to enormous phone bills. Needless to say, it put many strains on married couples and damaged dozens of credit ratings. The army's Criminal Investigation Division eventually caught the guilty parties.

Of course when the phone calls got through and someone with bad intentions didn't overhear the calling-card numbers, the information from the home front would contain bad news.

On this day, Tom got through to Cindy, and they talked about what was going on at both ends of the call. Cindy said that things were relatively okay, but the rumors of adultery still ran rampant. She'd said that she and Lou had remained faithful, and Tom had no doubts about that. And even if she hadn't been faithful, he was happy that she'd said she had remained true. But other spouses were falling by the wayside. She wouldn't name anyone in particular, and Tom refused to speculate. Tom didn't want to know the names or get any information on the situation as it was presented. Even if the rumors involved his own troops, he knew they would be home soon enough.

Cindy told Tom about one wife that had gone so far as to videotape herself having sex and mailed the tape to her husband in the desert, stopping long enough in the middle of the act to tell her husband she'd had enough and wanted a divorce. The thought of that happening to one of his troopers made Tom go pale. "She'd had enough! What about the guy?" Cindy didn't know how it turned out, but any way couldn't have been good. The talk changed to getting home soon, but the thoughts remained about the rumors of adultery. The story of the video spread throughout the Khobar Towers. It was dismissed as bullshit by everyone but was viable enough to create doubt in every married trooper.

From that point on, videotapes affected everyone differently, especially the tapes received from loved ones back home. It caused everyone to want to review their tape alone first before sharing it with other soldiers.

Tom concluded by asking Cindy when she'd heard they would be home. "The latest word is early May! And don't you worry because we'll be here," said Cindy.

"I know you will, babe. Whenever it is, it can't be soon enough. I love you!" said Tom. He waited for her to say it back and, as usual, found it hard to hang up after she said it. God, how he missed her.

April 28, 1991
Khobar Towers, Saudi Arabia

THE ROUTINE WAS NOW FIRMLY ESTABLISHED. Get up, eat, get on the bus, and go to the airfield and wash aircraft. All day wash aircraft. The Environmental Protection Agency or the European equivalent wanted to ensure that no foreign matter of any kind was brought into the continent from any source. The fact that the rotor blades had stirred up dirt, sand, and microscopic grit that could have carried material that endangered the continent was lost on the troops. They only knew that they were washing the hell out of the aircraft and they never passed the inspection standards set by the overseeing bodies. They handled the inspections like they handled most everything, initially with disgust, followed by acceptance, then by the determined spirit to make it better than it was before. The fact that it took nearly eight hours of washing per airframe to even get close to meeting the standard gave the troops a target to set records.

Crew chiefs climbed on, around, and into the airframes to remove every speck of dirt and dust collected in five months of flying under the worst conditions imaginable. Everyone from privates to the squadron commander pitched in. After five days of relentless washing, the last aircraft was finished. Only the flight from the airfield to the port remained.

The trail party under Rooksy's control was responsible for port ops. Only twelve people would remain in Saudi Arabia to ensure the port operations were successful. After that last flight, it was only a matter of time until they headed for Germany.

That evening, the "wash patrol" happened to get back just as Allen Berstein got off the truck that had brought him from the "love boat." He had a huge smile on his face and was obviously darker than he'd been when he left. He caught hell from the rest of the troop.

"What the hell is this?" yelled Walker. Berstein just smiled.

"Was there a George Hamilton look-alike contest on that boat or what?" asked Cross.

"No, not really. But we did have a lot of time to . . . hang out!" Berstein laughed.

"Hang out my ass! Did you get laid?" asked Walker. Berstein just smiled. "You son of a bitch! You got laid, didn't you?"

Berstein's huge smile spoke more than any words he could have said. The group of pilots and crew chiefs faked attacking the poor warrant. But he was still smiling like he'd won the lottery.

Walker continued as he held Berstein in a headlock. "She was fat, wasn't she? Even if she wasn't, you better say she was fat, or I'll rip your head off!" Berstein was laughing too hard to speak. To his credit, he never admitted whether he had sex or not. It didn't even matter. Just the thought that someone had sex while they were there brightened the spirits of every trooper. Morale was at a new high.

May 4, 1991
Khobar Towers, Saudi Arabia

THE ORDERS FINALLY CAME THROUGH. THE Fighting Sixth was next on the list of units to depart Saudi Arabia. It seemed to take forever. Ron Weimer described it best. "If I had terminal cancer, I'd want to spend it in Saudi Arabia because it takes forever for anything to happen."

There was a controlled form of excitement over every soldier in the squadron. The chatter was quicker and faster paced. Every person that got on the buses seemed to take one last look at Khobar Towers and then break into a huge grin. It would be a place that no one would miss.

The buses rolled to the same airport in Riyadh that they had arrived at. Four busloads of deliriously joyful CAV troopers with one thought in mind: getting back to Germany. They off-loaded the buses and filed into the waiting area. The waiting area was a Quonset hut with some wooden chairs. They didn't name it the waiting area for nothing. They went through two manifest calls, and customs checked everyone's bags for foreign objects and weapons. After this time consuming ordeal, they waited some more. Dogs were brought in to smell the bags for drugs or other contraband.

After two hours of waiting inside, the soldiers finally got the opportunity to go outside. The cigarette smokers were in heaven again as they got to take their last couple of smokes before they got on the plane.

Suddenly, there was a big commotion at the next hut over. Two Humvees of military police showed up and went inside the building. Ten minutes later, they came out with two soldiers in handcuffs, followed by a small group of officers. One of the military police was carrying two AK-47s and a bag full of something else, probably pistols. The group in trail was the platoon leader, the company commander, and a battalion commander.

Hal Timmons tapped on Lawton's shoulder. "I'm glad you talked me outta taking those parts from that AK-47. I think they might have found them, and I'd be like those guys," he said as he pointed to the group getting into the Humvees. Hal had taken apart one of the AK-47s he'd found in Iraq and gotten the firing mechanism out that made the weapon fire on automatic. The FBI and ATF didn't particularly care for the AR-15s sold in America that became modified to fire on automatic.

"I guess somebody didn't get the word!" said First Sergeant Garcia. "So far, we're clear." The Top smiled. "Sir, I was talking to one of those guys inside. He told me last week they found a female soldier with a bag full of money." Tom raised his eyebrows and looked at Garcia for more details. Top looked around as if he didn't want anyone to hear. "He said she had over $10,000 in her duffel bag!"

"What the hell was she doing with that kind of money?" asked Tom, whose curiosity had the better of him.

Again, Garcia looked around. "Apparently, she'd been . . ." Top made a gesture with his hands and hips that was vaguely familiar to Tom, but it'd been a long time.

"No shit!" said Tom.

"She musta been 'loving' her way through the forces!" said the Top.

Tom smiled at Garcia. "I guess Berstein wasn't the only one that had sex in theater."

Garcia laughed. He looked around again. "Look on the bright side, sir. At least it wasn't a guy they caught with the money!"

Tom shook his head. "I hadn't thought of that particular twist, but now that you mention it, I'm glad it wasn't any of our people," said Tom.

Top covered his mouth to keep from laughing. "I don't think we got any fags, sir!"

"I don't mean with the sex-for-sale garbage. But any of those other things, like weapons or war trophies," said Tom. He knew the army's policy on homosexuals and how much it was frowned upon. He snickered at what Top had said. For all Tom knew, he could have served with any number of homosexuals and never known. Sex was the last thing on his mind during "hell week." "I'm sure some of our guys tried something stupid, but I can hope they didn't, right?"

"Yes, sir. If they did, they'll get caught too," said Garcia. Tom nodded. That was the fact, probably because they would run their mouth to the wrong person. Garcia put out his cigarette. "Hey, sir, we got movement inside." Just then, a bunch of "Hooaahhs" came from inside the building. "I think we might be gettin' on that big bird home!"

"After you, First Sergeant!" Tom smiled as he let the Top head inside.

"I hope I get a fucking window this time! I'll be damned if I'm flyin' all the way to fuckin' Germany and I don't get to see some goddamn water!" said Garcia.

Tom laughed. "I'll trade if we have to. Just get on the damn plane!"

May 4, 1991
Riyadh Air Force Base, Saudi Arabia

THE 747 TOOK ABOUT THIRTY MINUTES to load. Then the fourth as well as the fifth flight manifest check took another thirty minutes because the numbers didn't come out the same. The crowd was annoyed at the delay and was becoming restless.

As if on cue, Walker got the group going. "Hey, you think you could break out them beers?" he shouted to the stewardess.

She must have had many crowds like this before. She merely smiled at the large man and said, "I'm sorry, sir. There will be no alcohol served on this flight." To which the crowd booed. The flight attendant, having done this route before, knew what the troops wanted to hear. "But I heard the welcome home parties in Germany are worth the wait!"

The group surrounding Walker cheered at the response. Walker, obviously feeling the effects of female-induced testosterone surge, came back with, "Would you care to join us?"

To which the professional, seasoned, and still-smiling stewardess responded, "I'm sorry, sir, but I have to wash my dog when we get back!" The guys broke out in laughter as Walker sat speechless in his seat. The stewardess smiled, turned, and walked away. Not one to quit, Walker hollered after her, "Can I help?" The men laughed again.

After an hour in the seats, the vibrations trembled through the aircraft as the engines of the huge jet came to life. Anxious troopers strained to look outside. Excitement filled their voices as they detected movement. The stewardess finally got on the intercom and gave the standard overwater safety brief. As the plane taxied to take off, a calm anticipation overcame the passengers.

"Ladies and gentlemen, this is Captain Steve Harland. Riyadh Tower has cleared us for departure. Please fasten your seat belts. Our next stop, Nuremberg, Germany!" The passengers roared their approval.

Five seconds later, the huge jet was at full throttle, lumbering down the runway. At maximum gross weight, the aircraft needed every foot of the runway to get off the ground. Immediately after the wheels broke the surface, the aircraft erupted with hoots and hollers as soldiers of all ranks, races, and religions cheered their approval.

Somewhere in the back, Mike Leslie could be heard over the crowd as he yelled, "*Adios*, motherfuckers! We're goin' home!"

As he heard the wheels groan to signal they were stowed in the belly, Tom let out a big sigh of relief. Garcia was next to him in the window seat with a huge grin on his face. Tom leaned over and got one last look at Saudi Arabia. That was the best view he had seen in a long time. The flight plan took them across thousands of square miles of desert, a desert that had changed each man and woman on the plane forever. Nothing really noticeable on the outside, but inside, in their souls, it had touched them all mentally, physically, and psychologically. For better or worse, they would never be the same.

CHAPTER 13

May 5, 1991
Nuremberg, Germany

FOR THE FIRST TIME SINCE HE could remember, Tom Lawton had been sleeping soundly. The yells of joy woke him from a sound sleep. The 747 touched down once then bounced and landed again. The rough landing didn't mean a thing. They were home, and they knew it. The whole plane erupted in shouts of elation. The captain came on the intercom, "Ladies and gentlemen, welcome to Germany!" More shouts of happiness and high fives all around.

The aircraft taxied to parking, and the doors opened to a beautiful seventy-degree afternoon in Southern Germany. The soldiers quickly departed the plane, got their gear, and jumped on waiting buses. Thirty minutes later, they were at Katterheim.

1530, May 5, 1991
Hangar 3010, Katterheim, Germany

THERE WERE BANNERS WELCOMING THE BUSES, and the parking lot was crowded with hundreds of friends and family members. Tom immediately spotted Cindy, and she looked beautiful. Due to his sense of responsibility, he waited until all his soldiers were off the bus. Out of habit, he checked the seats. When he got to the top of the steps before leaving the bus, he took a deep breath and wiped away a tear that had formed in his eye. He was really home.

Cindy had tears streaming down her face as she ran to greet Tom. He grabbed her and held hugged her as tight as he could. Tom could no longer hold back the tears that were building up in his eyes. He whispered into her ear, "God, I missed you, honey!"

"I missed you too, Tom. I missed you so very much," she said, unable to look into his eyes. Tom kissed her cheek. "It's just . . . so great to hold you again."

Tom didn't say anything for a few seconds. He just held her tightly and let her skin touch his. He breathed in her fragrance and let the fresh, clean smell of his beautiful wife enter his nose. He put his face in her hair. Eventually moving to her face, their foreheads touched, and he looked into her eyes and smiled. "Damn good to see you! What the hell is your name again?" She laughed. Then it dawned on him. Something, rather someone, was missing.

Cindy caught the expression on Tom's face. She looked over her shoulder. There, watching her mommy with an elevated view from Lou's arms, was Megan. "She may be a little tentative at first, Tom. Just go slow with her for a while."

It took Tom a second to digest what she said. When it hit him, Tom was shocked. Why wouldn't his own daughter recognize him? He walked over to Megan. Lou let her down slowly. Tom could see Megan was struggling to remember. Cindy watched from behind, giving Megan a chance to warm to the "stranger." The little girl was hesitant as the "strange" man came close. Tom stopped and bent down. For just an instant, the fear that Megan may not recognize him swept over Tom. Struggling to keep his composure, he bent down and looked into the eyes that were perfect reflections of his own. He didn't know where he got the strength, but a smile came to his face, and he said, "Hey, baby, how you doin'?"

A beaming smile appeared in the little girl's eyes before it swept over her face. "Doddy!" And she jumped into his arms. Tom couldn't help it. The tears came out, and it felt damn good. Megan knew it was her father. She didn't know where he'd been or what he'd done. None of the past mattered at that moment. The only thing in the world that mattered was they were together again.

Tom quickly wiped his eyes, lest someone see this "techno-warrior" with his heart hanging out. There should be none of that in "this man's army." The hell with that, thought Tom. He reached back for Cindy, and she was there, right where she needed to be.

They stayed together hugging, the threesome holding each other for a few minutes without any words being said, as if they were the only people on earth. Tom gathered himself and looked up. There was Lou crying her eyes out. Tom stuck out an arm and waved her over. Lou Ann slowly walked over and joined the crowd. Tom pulled her into the group and said softly, "Hart did good! He'll be home real soon." Then Tom gave her a soft head-butt, pulled her close into the tightly gathered cluster, and said, "I figure since you two are rumored to be so close, we might as well really give the Caserne something to talk about!" The three adults laughed.

Megan just grabbed Tom's face and looked into to his wet blue eyes. She kept saying, "Doddy home now!"

Tom would nod in agreement. "That's right, baby, Doddy home now!"

Then Cindy pulled away a bit, as if she realized they weren't the only people alive. "I bet you want a beer! We got tons of beer for you guys. Do you want a beer?"

Tom looked at her smiling face and looked around, noticing that the crowd had suddenly become more jocular. "I don't think so, honey." Then he added, "Not until I leave command. I survived without it. I just want to find out for myself how long can I go without it." He looked at her and smiled. "I'll drink again sometime, just . . . when I'm ready."

Cindy was stunned. "No beer!" After she realized that he wasn't kidding, Cindy smiled and gave him another big hug.

"I'm going to start running again too!" Tom smiled, believing it as soon as he said it.

Cindy looked up at him again, and with tears in her eyes, she said, "Oh, Tom, you are back." Tom waited for her to add, "And better than ever," but was glad she didn't.

Tom put a finger under her chin and said, "As soon as we can, let's get outta here." He didn't have to add why. Cindy knew. He'd just come from five months in a war in a foreign land with little or no privacy. Months of turmoil and strain he'd never experienced before. She knew he had wanted to talk to her about hundreds of things, but they never had time. She knew that his mind wasn't on anything except the peace and quiet that their home had to offer. Cindy guessed he wasn't interested in sex either, not just yet. She would take care of that when the time was right.

For his part, Tom wanted nothing more than to sit in a tub or take a hot shower for as long as he could. There were a thousand things he wanted to do. Tom's list was long and had no real priorities. Only one for the moment—he needed to get away.

The squadron didn't have aircraft, and they all had plenty of time off coming. Hawk gave the squadron four days off. Of course it was the troopers that got four. The leaders needed to be back after three days. That was okay because there was another four-day pass coming, followed by a much-deserved leave. Hawk was observant enough to notice that everyone wanted to be gone. They stayed around for forty-five minutes, and then he dismissed them, drawing a thunderous applause from the gathered spouses and friends.

2130, May 5, 1991
Lawton quarters, Katterheim Caserne

TOM HAD JUST FINISHED READING MEGAN a story and put her to bed. Cindy was at the doorway watching him tuck her in. Tom kissed Megan on the cheek and came to the doorway with a big smile on his face.

"I missed that," he said. Then he grabbed Cindy's hand and headed down the hallway. Tom was as happy as he had been in a long time. The couple lay on the bed and just held each other. Tom didn't want to talk about Iraq, but the conversation ended up there. He didn't feel like anything he did needed to be brought up with Cindy. They did talk about some of the fun things, like the antics of the warrants, shopping for gold, how well the helicopters did, and of course the outstanding performance of all the troopers.

Tom made a conscious effort not to bring up any events during the five days of the war or any topics involving injuries or death. He wasn't ready to talk about it, and Cindy didn't want to hear about it. The time to share the dark side of war would come much later. There was too much positive information to talk about.

Cindy smiled at the stories and shared some of the "hot gossip" that was taking place at the caserne. They talked for about two hours until there was mutual silence. Tom looked over at his wife and smiled. She returned the smile and asked, "What?"

Tom tried a Clark Gable impression. "You know, it's been a long time since I've let a woman . . . take me. But in your case, I'm willing to make an exception!"

Cindy smiled and laughed at the attempt, and then she slowly reached up and kissed him. "If you're gonna let me take you, I think I can handle the challenge!"

Tom quickly took off his clothes and jumped under the covers. He pulled the covers up to his eyes and said, "Be gentle with me!" and he batted his eyes.

Cindy laughed and got off the bed. She turned away from him and looked over her shoulder. Slowly, she began to take off her clothes. Tom didn't realize that he was slowly lowering the covers from his face. When she was done, she slid into bed next to him.

"You know I'm . . . way out of practice!" said Tom with a broad smile.

Cindy kissed him and climbed on top. "I guess you need to keep practicing until you get it right."

And practice they did, over and over . . . until Tom got it right. Then they did it again to make sure it wasn't a fluke.

1500, May 14, 1991
Jordan Gymnasium, Katterheim
Caserne, Germany

LIEUTENANT COLONEL HAWK CALLED EACH TROOP into the gym for an hour to give out the awards. Charlie Troop received the exact same awards as the other line troops. For the most part, the awards were presented in groups by the type of award being given. They all received service awards for Desert Storm and Desert Shield. All the aviators received Air Medals, and ten received valorous awards. Tom Lawton and five other Champions received Bronze Stars.

Tom felt tremendously honored to have received the medals. He remembered when his father returned from Vietnam. The local paper came to the Lawton house and made a big deal about his father's Bronze Star and ten Air Medals. Tom could visualize the whole scene as if it were being repeated twenty-five years later.

There was talk of a Distinguished Flying Cross for Tom and John Walker. Tom talked with Hawk and explained that he didn't want one. The event the crew was to be recognized for was the recovery of the downed crew. In Tom's opinion, since the aircraft had been shot from the sky because he didn't get them further from the enemy artillery, he was glad he wasn't getting relieved of his command. To receive an award seemed too ironic for Tom to accept any form of recognition. Anyone else would have gotten Nichols and Osborn out, and if Tom had used better judgment and been a few seconds quicker, they may not have gotten hit. Hawk disagreed, but Tom finally won out, probably because Denson got involved and put out the facts about DFCs in Vietnam. Whatever the cause was, it was all right with Tom. He didn't want an award that he didn't feel he deserved. The fact that his father had been through a hell of a lot tougher scrapes during 365 days in Vietnam weighed heavily in Tom's mind. The Bronze Star was a beautiful award, but deep down, Tom knew he was just doing his job.

After the ceremony, Hawk addressed the gathered crowd and offered thanks for the outstanding effort. He also thanked the families that "kept the home fires burning." After the ceremony, he called Tom and Hal Timmons over to see him. "I have a replacement for Hart Osborn." Tom was shocked. "You both know LT Scott Gallagher." Tom nodded. Gallagher was a good officer that had received the ultimate "shit sandwich." While in the desert, he was notified he had been passed over for captain. To his credit, Scott Gallagher sucked it up. In true CAV warrior spirit, he drove on as if he'd never heard the news and actually performed quite well according to his troop commander. "Lieutenant Gallagher will report to you on Monday."

"Roger, sir! Great!" said Tom.

"I didn't think there would be a problem with you. I'm guessing he'll put in his paperwork to get out. The problem is we will get a new list soon and he might get picked based on his performance in the desert." Tom and Hal nodded in concurrence. "One other thing. Colonel Denson has been picked out to be the First Armored Division chief of staff." Tom wasn't surprised, but Timmons was confused. "He did a good enough job to be recognized for his efforts and will be changing on the third of June." Hawk looked at Lawton. "Denson wants to say thanks to all the troop commanders in particular for the great things you guys did."

"He can thank me with a one block on my OER, sir!" joked Tom.

Hawk smiled right back. "I think we can all expect that, Tom!" The colonel started to walk away. "What that means is we can expect to be practicing change-of-command ceremonies for the next two weeks!" Lawton and Timmons just laughed at the suggestion.

Tom thought of something else. "Sir, who's the new Six?"

Hawk said, "Some guy named Oscar Guyton. He's coming out of the Pentagon."

Tom looked at Timmons and shook his head. Timmons looked at his boss and said, "I don't know him either, sir. But I'll bet you my CAV coin that because this guy is coming out of the Pentagon this quick, he's gonna be fired up to make changes. He's gonna want to whip us into shape!" Then he laughed out loud. "I bet he can't lead flies to shit!"

"Let's give the guy a chance. He can't be that bad," said Tom.

Unfortunately, he had no idea how bad it would get.

June 3, 1991
Katterheim, Germany

TIMMONS WAS EXACTLY RIGHT. GUYTON WAS a horse of a different color, somewhere between turquoise and pink. He definitely wasn't army green. Immediately after the change of command, he called all the commanders down to troop level into a closed-door meeting. Not one word was mentioned about the past. It was all "we will do" and "in the future." He spent thirty minutes talking about how he wanted things done. Guyton reiterated more than once that if the troop commanders didn't want to do things his way, other "jobs of less significance" could be found. The threats were repeated, yet he never once mentioned training, flying, or taking care of subordinates. Tom shuddered at the thought of having to get into combat with this boss.

Denson was a great leader because he let the troop commanders do their job. He never went down to the troop commander's level unless he absolutely felt it was necessary. Tom knew that was one of the reasons the brigade had succeeded in the war. Denson didn't get into the nuts and bolts of the troop units. He provided a big picture for guidance, gave orders, and demanded they be followed. If it wasn't, you could expect to be fired.

Guyton was into the weeds. Everybody's weeds. He quoted the maintenance readiness stats of some of the units that had already been flying, readiness rates which only created the appearance he was trying to impress the assembled group with his meticulous memory. To top it off, the squadron didn't even have the aircraft back, and Guyton was giving Hawk crap about his personnel being on leave.

Guyton also mentioned the hot thing in the Pentagon was a plan to downsize the army. The paperwork would be out soon, and anyone that didn't want to keep up with the standards Guyton would set could expect to "receive a personalized copy" of the process for separation.

Without knowing it, Tom Lawton may have subconsciously decided his future at that meeting. Maybe it was just fate. Hal Timmons's comments about trusting "higher" never seemed more truthful. Tom shook the negative vibes from his mind and vowed to support this new boss just as he expected the new boss would support him. But the nauseating feeling in his stomach refused to go away. He had no choice. This was the guy he had to follow.

June 9, 1991
Katterheim, Germany

THE TROOP LANDED AT 1715 WITH all the aircraft except one. Of all the bad things that could happen, the fact that an Apache showed up in Amsterdam with an AK-47 inside its belly was beyond belief. To have it be a Champion bird just added to the problem.

Lawton got his first office call with COL Oscar Guyton that evening. Tom and the Hawk sat outside the man's office until 1945. Hawk had to go in first and spent fifteen minutes behind closed doors.

Finally, Tom was called in. He didn't have to report, but Guyton in no way, shape, or form made him feel at ease. Lawton longed to have Darth Vader looking at him across the desk. But Vader was gone. It was "Guymeister Six." That was the new name the warrants had tagged the stoic, Ichabod-Crane-looking clone with. Guyton gave the appearance of a vulture as he peered over his bifocals with eyes that had little life.

"Captain Lawton," said the colonel. Tom shuddered. He knew he was in deep shit because the Guymeister knew his name. "I read the report, and I'm not very pleased with the news."

"I know what you mean, sir. I'm not real happy about it myself," said Tom, trying to smile and ease the tension.

Guyton would have no levity. "I also know about you're record in the desert and the aircraft you lost due to recklessness." Guyton pulled off his bifocals and continued, "I don't know what kind of outfit you run, Captain, but nonsense of this nature will not be tolerated." The colonel stood up and walked to the front of his desk. "I hold the commanders at troop level responsible for the actions of their troop. It appears that one of your troops violated a general officer's direct orders about returning war trophies from the Persian Gulf Theater. What do you have to say to that?"

Tom looked at Hawk. He was in hull defilade. The term was used by tankers to indicate a defensive position that affords little opportunity to get hit. Hawk was hull down all the way to his high and tight. "I think it was someone else, sir."

"What makes you think that, Captain?" sneered the colonel. "It's your aircraft, and I think one of those wiseass warrant officers of yours tried to sneak this weapon in country."

Tom looked into the Guymeister's eyes and smiled. "I think your wrong, sir." Tom wondered where Guyton came up with "wiseass warrants."

Guyton got off the desk and walked behind Lawton. Tom remained facing forward. "You have more faith in your men than I do. Your troop lacks discipline." He came around to the front and moved directly in front of Tom. "This is what you will do, Captain. You will conduct a commander's inquiry about the incident. You will report back to me in twenty-four hours with whatever information you have. Then we'll decide what we'll do about this. Do you understand my guidance, Captain Lawton?"

"Yes, sir," said Tom.

The colonel made a weak attempt to smile and said, "We'll get to the bottom of this soon enough."

Tom looked at the colonel and came to attention. "If that's all, sir, I'd like to start my inquiry, and I'll report back here tomorrow evening."

"Oh, that you will, Captain. I want you back here at 1700," hissed the commander. "Dismissed."

Tom saluted and walked out with Hawk. When they were outside, he said to Hawk, "Goddamn, sir, I thought for a minute that I put that fuckin' gun in there!"

"Tom, I tried to explain it could have been anyone. He wasn't very willing to listen," said Hawk.

"Shit, sir. Where they found the AK-47, it would take two or three people four or five hours to get the 30mm off, stick that gun up there, and replace it again. Any maintenance guys, civilians, or my crew chiefs could have done it. This is screwed up, sir," said Tom.

"I understand. Just ask around and find out what you can," said Lieutenant Colonel Hawk.

Tom just shrugged. He wasn't so sure he'd find out anything.

June 10, 1991
Brigade commander's office,
Katterheim Caserne, Germany

TOM COULDN'T HELP BUT NOTICE THE two military police investigators in Guyton's office. He knew right then it didn't matter what he had found. The colonel had already decided to call in outside investigators to solve the problem. Tom reported to the commander and outlined what he'd found out.

"Sir, I've interviewed the crew chiefs, my pilots, and the crew for 956, along with various maintenance personnel. I don't have any definitive answer to who put the weapon in the belly of the aircraft. When we left it in Saudi Arabia, it was clean and had passed inspection," said Tom. "I want to add that I understand it is my responsibility, and if anyone should get punished for this, I guess it should start with me, sir."

"Oh, that's so noble of you, Captain Lawton. But it's not you I'm looking for," said the colonel. Lawton kept waiting to hear the word *yet*, but it never came. "I didn't think you'd have much luck, so I called in these investigators from Würzburg. They have the responsibility to find the culprit or culprits of this crime. You will assist them in any manner they need."

"Roger, sir," Tom said. He shook hands and offered, "Anything I can do to help, gentlemen."

"That's all for now, gentlemen. Lieutenant Colonel Hawk, please stay," said Guyton. Tom started to salute, but the colonel was already back to his desk. He shook his head and headed out the door with the two investigators in tow. He briefed them on everything he knew and gave them the names of crews, maintenance personnel, and anyone else the investigators thought they needed.

Tom felt he was doing as much as he could. He maintained the belief that none of his troopers was responsible for the incident. The military police appreciated the help and vowed to try and turn something up but reminded the captain that the chance of catching whoever did this were remote. Lawton merely responded, "Did you tell that to my boss?" He could tell by the look on their faces, they hadn't had the chance to say anything to the Guymeister.

This was just the beginning of run-ins between Guyton and commanders across the caserne. If it wasn't Hawk's squadron, it was the sister unit. And if it wasn't the lieutenant colonels, it was the captains that were subject to the micromanagement style of the new brigade commander. When that style failed, he turned to a different method of management. The technique of "leadership by intimidation" became commonplace, and no leader was exempt from Guyton's wrath. Lawton's initial experience was the tip of the iceberg.

June 19, 1991
Katterheim, Germany

THE INCIDENT INVOLVING THE AK-47 QUICKLY went to the back burner when the unit began flying again. Since they had left Germany, new "no fly" areas had come up around the region. The unit had not had a lot of flying time before they were ordered to start performing troop-level missions.

The Champions were on their first flight as a troop since the desert. Weimer and Berstein were in lead, followed by Lawton and Walker, Nichols and Gallagher, and Toretti and Harmon in trail. They received clearance for takeoff, and everything seemed fine. Weimer called for takeoff, and the four ships departed straight out from the runway on a 270 heading in a staggered right formation.

At three hundred feet above the ground, Weimer banked to the right to bring the flight to the north. Unfortunately, this was the spot to turn for the old traffic pattern. The town of Fleigerstein had a new no-fly area that was implemented while the unit was in Saudi Arabia. Out of habit, Weimer had turned before the town rather than extend his pattern for five more kilometers. As soon as he turned, Tom knew they were in trouble. There was only time for him to utter, "Oh, shit!" on the intercom.

Because of the formation they were in, with Walker flying tight off Weimer right wing, they had no choice but to turn to the right with lead. The flight had no option but to turn with the Weimer.

Tom looked in the mirror at Walker and simply said, "The question is not whether we are fucked, but how bad?" Tom didn't have to wait long to find out. Ten minutes later, a call came over the FM radio ordering the flight to return to base immediately. When they finished refueling, Tom had Walker taxi to parking as quickly as possible. Hawk was already there. They were to report to Guyton's office immediately.

"Is this going to be some kind of habit, Captain Lawton?" said Colonel Guyton.

Tom naturally had a smart-aleck response to the colonel's jab, but under the circumstances, he decided keeping his mouth shut might just keep his job. "No, sir."

"You know our kind German hosts have those no-fly areas posted for reasons. Not for some high-strung, out-of-control captain and his troop of undisciplined pilots to disregard recklessly," said the colonel.

"I understand, sir," said Tom.

The Guymeister asked for an explanation. Tom tried his best to explain the actions of his troop and how he had a chief warrant officer 4 in lead to avoid just that kind of problem. It was an accident, and he swore it would never happen again.

"I think you should probably lead your unit rather than fly in the middle of the formation. And this chief warrant officer 4, doesn't he read the NOTAMs that are posted to explain the changes in our flight training area?" asked the colonel in a condescending tone.

Tom had had enough. "Sir, in the past, we've found that it's easier to command and control the troop from the middle. And Mr. Weimer's record is spotless. He is one of the best pilots in the brigade!"

That didn't sit well with the Guymeister. "Command is not supposed to be *easy*, Captain. And Mr. Weimer is no longer 'one of the best' now, is he?" Tom looked at the Hawk, who might as well not even be there. He looked back to Guyton. "Mr. Weimer is grounded until he passes a check ride. You, Young Captain, probably need to relook your policy of commanding from within the flight. Apparently, it doesn't work with your management style."

Tom wanted to tell the colonel that he wasn't a "manager." Managers work at fast-food places. He wanted to say he was a "leader" and a damn good one. But when the reality of the situation hit Tom, he knew better than to say a word. He smiled and replied, "Roger, sir. We'll take a look at that," knowing he had no intention whatsoever of changing a technique that proved to be successful.

"You're dismissed, Captain Lawton. Lieutenant Colonel Hawk, would you join me for another minute," directed the commander.

Tom saluted and left. When he was outside, he stopped by the adjutant's office, shaking his head and trying to smile. Tom noticed the female major wasn't smiling, and there were two other people sitting in her office with clouds hanging over them.

Major Stevenson caught Tom's attention and stepped outside the office with Tom in tow. Tom was very familiar with Major Stevenson. She had helped him get the awards through in the desert. He found her to be extremely competent and objective. On this particular day, she looked fried. Tom said, "Ma'am, I know we have to stop meeting like this. But if I come up here for much more of this, I might as well get a part-time job in the Three shop!"

Emily Stevenson found no humor in Tom's comments. "You aren't the only one, Captain Lawton. Believe me. For the last week, it's been nothing but negative actions. I've been in here from 0600 to 2100, and he's always here. He never smiles. It's difficult to make the transition from Denson's style to Colonel Guyton's."

"Ma'am, you need to stop makin' derogatory remarks like that and get back into the gym like you used to," said Tom, still holding his smile.

"If I had the time, I would," she said and then changed the subject. "How'd it go in there?"

"Grounded Weimer," Tom said flatly. "Basically, he told me to look at making some changes, changes I am . . . reluctant to make."

"He's all for changes," said Major Stevenson. She looked around the hallway. "We're in the process of making major swaps, from troop to troop, at all levels of personnel."

Tom understood what she was saying. It also explained her long hours. "How many per unit? A line unit?"

"You can plan on 60 to 70 percent," she said.

Tom was stunned. "Shit! We just figured out what we were doing with the people we have. Now they're gonna change everybody?"

"It's the best thing for your unit in a long run," Major Stevenson explained. "You all came over from Fort Hood together, so your DEROS date is the same. We take out half the unit so not all of it leaves at once. Doesn't that make sense?"

She had a point, and Tom knew it. To break up the Champions seemed to defeat the purpose of getting a unit collectively trained. They had just come from combat and were the best they would ever be. Now they were going to be split up. Tom didn't see this one coming, and it hurt. For the army, it was the best thing to do. Tom could accept that and was thankful to Major Stevenson for the heads-up.

Emily Stevenson looked down the hallway again and saw no one around. "I also have some information on two new drawdown programs if you're interested?"

Tom looked at her and smiled. "Drawdown? You mean get out?" Tom laughed and said, "I love this shit! I don't think I'm ready to leave yet, but I'll keep it in mind."

"If you show up here too many more times, Captain Lawton, it won't be an option," she said honestly.

Tom's smile faded. "I don't plan on being back here. Not under circumstances like this."

"You think these guys planned on being here now?" She pointed inside her office. "Think about what I said. There are options. If I didn't have fourteen years in, I'd be looking at them real hard."

Just then, Lieutenant Colonel Hawk came out of the colonel's office. Behind him, Tom heard the Guymeister holler, "Major Stevenson, send in Captain Pinkham!"

"I gotta go. Hope to see you again under better circumstances!" said Major Stevenson.

Tom waited for Hawk. "Sorry, sir. I guess I can't seem to stop stepping on my crank!"

They walked out the front door. Hawk said, "You don't need to worry about this stuff. Tom, you keep driving on, doing what you do best." Then the colonel pulled out a cigarette and lit it.

Tom looked at his boss. Hawk's eyes were very far away. Hawk didn't even smoke in the desert. "Sir, you need to put those things away."

Hawk chuckled and put his arm around Tom. "Did you really quit drinkin'?"

"I wouldn't really say I quit, sir," said Tom. "I'd just say I'm taking a sabbatical for a while."

"Well, I won't give you shit about booze if you don't give me shit about cigarettes!" said Hawk. Then he squeezed the back of Tom's neck playfully. "And quit fuckin' up, you bonehead!"

Tom laughed and walked with his boss. He felt a little better about Hawk than he did last February. They had become closer since they fought together, but Tom would never be too close to this boss. After he was ripped for the loose nose gearbox cap, Tom was emotionally scarred. It took a near nervous breakdown, running through the desert naked, a "message from God," and a week of war before Tom could even talk to Hawk. But since they were visiting the Guymeister on a regular basis, Lawton felt they were getting closer.

"By the way, be prepared to conduct a personnel swap with the 229th," said Hawk. "I know what you're thinking, and this swap has nothing to do with Weimer and the latest adventures of C Troop."

"We're going to swap personnel to prevent wholesale departures of personnel at the fifteen—to eighteen-month mark, right?" said Tom confidently.

"Pretty smart, wiseass!" The Hawk laughed.

Tom had to ask. "Have they already been determined? Or do we low-life troop commanders get a say as to who we want to keep?"

Hawk looked at Lawton without stopping and said, "There's nothing you can do about this. The names will come out next week, and the swap will be made the following Monday."

Tom Lawton nodded his approval. "Good thing I don't get paid for the decisions I make at my level. I'd be broke!"

Hawk missed the joke. The colonel took a large puff on his cigarette. Lawton wondered how much say the Hawk had in the swap, and from his reaction, Tom guessed it wasn't much.

July 4, 1991
Stewart Jones Park
Katterheim Caserne, Germany

TOM TOOK THE FOURTH OF JULY as an occasion to get to know the new people and their families. The Champions had a farewell party the previous Friday, and it turned into a drunken festival of true CAV proportions. Tom and Cindy left early, and he had somehow managed to stay sober. The toughest part was saying good-bye to Walker, Berstein, Toretti, Tucker, Cross, and Weimer. Larry Snyder came down from corps, and the warrants had a great reunion. They talked about the CHEMRAT and the exploding beans and dozens of other events that Tom knew nothing about, nor did he care to. When Walker brought up "gerbil talk" in his loud booming voice, Tom knew it was time for the Lawtons to leave.

In exchange for the wild, rowdy, single crowd that Tom had originally commanded, he received four young chief warrant officer 2s, complete with families. The rowdy CAV guys were gone, and Tom now commanded a troop of fathers with kids the same age as Megan or younger. He couldn't help but feel Guyton had directed that these young pilots be put into Tom's troop. If he was such a "bad manager," why did he get all this inexperience? Lawton smiled to himself. Tom knew he was good enough to make them a unit, and one day, they'd be just as good as his first set of Champions.

Lawton was impressed with three of the newbies right away, CW2 Richard Burslie, Matt Mahar, and Paul Heinz. They fit in quickly, and Burslie was a PIC. Tom shifted Petty to the backseat, and Mahar became his front seater. Heinz flew with Dolce, and they struggled to get along.

The new scout pilot came from the division CAV unit down the road, and Jed Stuart had already told Tom about his newbie. A Cobra pilot by nature, CW2 Riley Rossovich was like a lost puppy. He felt totally alienated by all the techno-warriors that flew the Apache. The rest of the troop could smell his anxiety. He immediately became estranged from the rest of the unit, and Tom vowed to fix it.

"Mr. Rossovich! Got a minute?" called Tom across the pavilion. Riley Rossovich came over and brought his twenty-year-old spouse with him. Tom introduced Cindy, and they all shook hands. Cindy took the cue from Tom and asked Mary Ann Rossovich to go for a little walk.

"I understand you're Cobra rated. Is that true?" asked Tom.

"Yes, sir, and I miss them. Don't get me wrong, the scout is fine, not I like the thought of being able to shoot back!" said the twenty-three-year-old.

Tom laughed. "Don't we all!" Tom got up and asked Riley to come for a little walk. They talked awhile, and then Tom got down to the point. He explained the feelings the other warrants had and what was going on. "Do you want to fly the Apache?"

Rossovich was direct. "I don't know if I'm smart enough, sir." Tom laughed out loud. "I'm serious, sir. I only got a high-school education from Podunk Alabama!"

"Just answer the damn question, Mr. Rossovich!" said Tom, still smiling.

Riley thought about it and said, "Yes, sir. I surely do!"

They talked some more, and Tom told the warrant to get his paperwork together to get the transition. It wasn't Riley's decision to make if he was or wasn't smart enough for Apaches. Someone else would tell him if he was "unable to perform to standard." Until he tried, he would never know. "Besides, you might surprise yourself!" said Tom. The warrant agreed and vowed he would try to get the transition. From that point on, Riley Rossovich was a different pilot. He felt like an equal, and his adjustment to the new unit became easier. The fact that Tom had Joe Petty to talk to and use his warrant officer "influence" on the other pilots helped.

The next week, things were considerably better. The atmosphere around the hangar began to get comfortable again. As fate would dictate, that comfort would again be interrupted by turmoil.

July 14, 1991
Hohenfels, Germany

THE CHAMPIONS HAD BEEN GIVEN A mission to support the Hohenfels training area as an OPFOR aviation unit. To accomplish the mission, Tom sent Lieutenant Gallagher, Chief Warrant Officer 4 Nichols, Chief Warrant Officer 3 Dolce, and Warrant Officer 1 Harmon. What started off as a routine, run-of-the-mill training exercise quickly turned into an event of monumental proportions that would send ripples throughout the training community in EUSAEUR.

As the OPFOR, the pilots were unaware that they were "in the box." The "in the box" status indicated the aviators were actually participants in the training, subject to all the rules and regulations the commander at Hohenfels had in place. One of the rules was no participants involved in training were allowed to drink alcohol.

After the first day's training, the four men headed to the local pizza parlor on the caserne. They should have known something was wrong when they sat down with their beer and the rest of the soldiers left the eatery. They had just started their meals, and Nichols and Harmon had opened their second bottle of German beer when the doors came open.

Eight military policemen came in the parlor from the front door and four more from the back. The senior military police approached the four men and asked them, "Are you gentlemen here for training?"

Lieutenant Gallagher, the senior aviator, the person responsible for the conduct of the men, answered, "Sure enough, Sergeant. We're the OPFOR pilots. Is there a problem?"

The sergeant, who took his job a bit more seriously than the aviators were taking theirs, said, "Sir, I'm afraid I have to inform you that you are in violation of the CG's memorandum on the consumption of alcoholic beverages during training. I'm going to have to ask you all to come with me. We need to go down to the military police station and conduct breathalyzer tests. Please come with me, gentlemen."

To their credit, the men left without a scene. Nichols tried his best to explain to the sergeants that they weren't "officially" in the box. Gallagher was trying to keep the situation from escalating, to no avail.

The results of the breathalyzer showed all three men had consumed alcohol. Tim Harmon, with a face that could barely pass for eighteen and a mere 140 pounds soaking wet, blew a .08 on the breathalyzer. After only one and a half of the locally brewed German beers, the junior warrant was "impaired." The news hit Katterheim by 2100.

2230, July 14, 1991
Katterheim, Germany

TOM COULDN'T HELP BUT NOTICE MAJ Emily Stevenson was still at work. She didn't say a word as Tom and Lieutenant Colonel Hawk entered her office and sat in the two chairs. From inside the brigade commander's office bellowed the voice of the Guymeister, "Get the hell in here!" The first thing Tom noticed that was different was that Guyton had cursed. On every other occasion, Guyton had remained professional. He'd gotten some heat over this incident. And when the flames are turned up at higher levels, it's generally the people below that get torched.

Guyton ordered Tom to report. Tom did as he was told and stood at the position of attention. Guyton was in fine form. As soon as he started, Tom had visions of Hawk ripping him in the tent in Saudi Arabia. Lawton remained expressionless as the commander circled him and offered rhetorical questions and solutions to a problem that didn't exist five hours ago. Guyton alluded to Tom's lack of control, personnel that were "incompetent," and "piss-poor command presence" that have caused all of "his problems."

For twenty minutes, the colonel railed. Tom could see out of the corner of his eyes, even Hawk had tuned out. Finally, Tom got the chance to rebut his commander's allegations. Lawton agreed his men were wrong, and he agreed he did not brief them on the consumption of alcohol. "Therefore, sir, I'm the one responsible for their actions. Any punishment you deem necessary, I should be the one to receive it."

Guyton yelled, "You bet your ass you'll receive it!" Then the colonel regained what little composure he could. "I don't know what I'll do just yet. It may be time for you to find a new line of work, Captain Lawton."

For the first time, Tom looked directly into the commander's eyes. "Sir, I think you're blowing this thing out of proportion."

"Goddamn it, Lawton! If the commanding general of all the training in Europe calls me, telling me there are aviators from my brigade getting drunk at one of his training installations, I'd say it's already out of proportion!" said Guyton with rage. "And at face value, you are bringing negative attention to brigade. And I won't tolerate it!"

Tom tried one last time to soothe the beast. "Sir, you could have stuck up for them and said they weren't clear on their status in the box."

"Oh, that would be special! Tell the CG my people don't know the rules!" hissed Guyton. Then the light came on. The whole thing was about Guyton and how the incident appeared to higher headquarters. "I'm not going to defend the fact that your troops were intoxicated," continued the colonel. "But anything I can do to diffuse this situation, I'll do." Guyton went over to his desk and got on the phone. Lawton looked at Hawk, who just shook his head.

The colonel made a call and explained to someone on the other end that "his personnel" were unclear of their position during the training and the policy letter didn't identify the opposition force training personnel as being part of the training team. Guyton rogered a couple of times and hung up the line.

Guyton cleared his throat and said, "There will be a new policy letter from EUSAEUR stating that all personnel, no matter what the purpose is, will refrain from alcohol use at either Grafenwoehr or Hohenfels. For now, the matter can be handled at my level." Guyton got up and walked around his desk again. He looked at Hawk and then at Tom. "I'm tempted to give you a letter of reprimand for your failure to adequately brief your personnel. But for right now, consider tonight's . . . counsel sufficient punishment, Captain Lawton."

Tom didn't fully realize that he was being let off the hook. "Roger, sir. I still will accept any punishment you have and ask that my soldiers be given another chance."

Guyton walked over, got in front of Lawton's face, and hissed, "The next time I see you or any of your so-called soldiers in my office, you can expect to be relieved for cause. Do you understand me clearly, Captain?"

Tom looked right back at the commander and said, "Clearly, sir!" He saluted and left. Lieutenant Colonel Hawk had to stay behind to catch his own form of hell, as was the custom he had come to know since Colonel Guyton arrived.

As soon as he closed the door, Major Stevenson was there with some papers in her hands. "You might want to read these when you get a chance. People are lining up around here to take the opportunity. You need to take a look at them."

Tom read the subject. The paperwork was titled Voluntary Separation Incentive. Lawton looked at the major. This time, he didn't say anything negative about getting out of the army. Tom nodded and said, "I'll let you know, ma'am." He started to leave and then turned and said, "He told me next time would be the last."

Stevenson had worked for Guyton long enough to know the colonel was serious. "He means it, Captain Lawton. Don't mess up again."

Tom nodded and tried to smile. But it wouldn't appear. Tom shook his head and walked out. He looked at the papers Stevenson had handed him and started laughing to himself. Tom was happy because he was still in control of the situation. He didn't have the urge to strip and run naked through the caserne. His mind took him back to that night in the desert. When that night ended, he was so at peace with everything. Lawton knew there was nothing Guyton could do to him that would make him feel as bad as he had felt emotionally that night. Tom smelled the fresh night air of the German countryside. Cindy was home, waiting to hear the results of his ass chewin', and it was time to get there and tell her the results.

Tom looked at the papers in his hands one more time. All these meetings in Guyton's office seemed to be circumstantial to Tom. They could be explained to a reasonable commander. Lawton felt that even Denson would have supported him. Lawton began to think about what Stevenson said. She'd been around Guyton more than anyone. Emily Stevenson didn't feel Guyton was reasonable. Tom was torn between the thought that he was still a good commander and the fact that his new senior rater thought he was a piss-poor manager. Tom knew he wasn't a manager. He was a leader, sure of his men and sure of himself. Not so sure of his relationship with Guyton.

The hell with it, thought Tom. He was damn good at his job, and he knew it. He cranked up the car and headed home, vowing not to change one bit. When he arrived at his quarters, he went straight to the garbage can and threw the papers Stevenson gave him in the trash.

0930, July 28, 1991
Katterheim, Germany

FOR TWO WEEKS, THINGS WENT ALONG fine. Tom began to think he could survive his command, even with Guyton breathing down his back. He was feeling almost comfortable when something happened to take that feeling away.

Hart Osborn had called from the S4 shop and said he had some pictures he wanted to show Tom. It was a relatively slow day, with mostly maintenance going on, so Tom decided to go take a look.

He went to Hart's office, but no one was around. Lawton looked around and didn't see any pictures but figured he'd wait around a few minutes for Hart to return. Soon enough, Hart Osborn showed up. "Hey, Tom, how's it going?" He went behind his desk and started going through his inbox. It became apparent. He couldn't find what he was looking for. "You don't have the pictures, do you?"

Tom looked at Hart with a confused expression. "No, Hart, I haven't seen any pictures."

"I had them right here on the top of my inbox," said Hart Osborn.

Tom became nervous. "They're gone?" he asked.

Hart checked all his drawers and said, "They can't be. They were just here ten minutes ago."

"How many pictures, Hart? What were they of?" asked Tom.

"They were pictures of the Halloween party last year," said Hart, almost unconcerned.

Tom turned white. "Were there any pictures of me in costume?"

Hart smiled. "Damn straight there were! We got three pictures of you in all your glory dressed up as a sweet transvestite!"

"Oh shit!" Tom began to go through Hart's drawers. He started to look everywhere in the office. "You don't understand, Hart. If those pictures are seen by . . . some other people who don't understand the situation . . ." He didn't have to finish.

Tom saw the light come on in Hart's face as it became red. "Oh man! I'm sorry, Tom. I'm really sorry."

"Look, we gotta find those pictures. We need to find them real quick. If somebody else finds them, there's gonna be a whole lot of questions. Questions that some people won't give a damn how I answer," explained Tom.

"I'm sure they're around here somewhere. Just give me some time and I'll find them," said Osborn.

Tom didn't have a choice. They had already looked everywhere in the office, but the pictures were nowhere to be found. Hart asked Tom to give him one day to find the pictures. Reluctantly, Tom agreed. He had no choice. But a voice inside his head told him the pictures would find Tom. It was only a matter of time.

1015, July 28, 1991
Brigade headquarters
Katterheim Caserne, Germany

"SIR, I WAS WONDERING IF YOU had a minute?" asked the captain as he stuck his head in the door.

Guyton looked up from his desk. With a disgusted look, he answered, "If you have something with regard to the matter we discussed last week, I suppose I can make time for you, Captain."

"I think I have something you might find . . . useful, sir!"

1615, August 3, 1991
Katterheim Caserne, Germany

TOM LAWTON STARTED TO THINK EVERYTHING was going to be all right. Hart Osborn had not found the pictures, so perhaps they had disappeared altogether. That's when the call from Hawk came that told him they needed to report to Guyton's office at 1700 hours sharp.

When Tom hung up the phone, he had a sick sensation in his stomach. Hawk had no idea what the two men needed to be in the commander's office for. Tom was quite sure why they were going there.

1700, August 3, 1991
Brigade commander's office
Katterheim Caserne, Germany

GUYTON CALLED FOR THE TWO MEN to enter and made Tom report to him. Guyton was sitting behind his desk with his glasses on. For the first time since Tom had known him, Guyton had the semblance of a smile on his face. Tom concluded it was a rather morbid sight.

Tom reported, and Guyton surprised him again. "Why don't we have a seat, gentlemen?" The colonel moved from behind the desk and took a seat in one of the four chairs available in the office. Lawton and Hawk took seats, but they were by no means "at ease."

"Captain Lawton, it has recently come to my attention that you were quite a partier," said the colonel. "Yes, quite a partier." The colonel had a sickening smile on his face as he reached into his pocket. Tom's heart dropped when he saw pictures in Guyton's hands. Guyton threw about half a dozen on the coffee table. Lawton didn't have to ask what they were. Hawk, confused throughout the whole melodramatic episode, bent over to look at the pictures on the table. Guyton kept two pictures in his hands as he stared at Tom with a sadistic smile.

"If you like those, Stan, I'm sure you'll love these!" said Guyton. Tom remained silent. "I'm trying to figure out if you've got . . . a psychological disorder of some kind or if you're just an alcoholic."

Tom looked at Hawk. The squadron commander had a strange look on his face that quickly changed to one of confusion. Tom said weakly, "It's a Halloween party, sir. None of my soldiers were there." As soon as he heard himself speak, he knew he was on the defensive. He knew his explanation could never justify the behavior in the eyes of his superiors. He could have been at Mardi Gras in the French Quarter of New Orleans, and Guyton would not have understood.

"This is supposed to be some kind of costume or something?" asked Hawk.

Tom nodded without his customary smile. "Yes, sir."

Then Guyton chimed in, "And we have these. Apparently, doing shots of some kind. Habits that can be associated with an alcohol problem." Tom was tempted to say he'd been sober since December, but he was beginning to see the way this hand was going to be played. "So what is it, Captain? Are you some kind of alcoholic or just a pervert?"

Tom felt the words cut like razor into his heart. Was this how it was going to end? He answered meekly, "I'm neither, sir. Those were taken at a Halloween party." Tom swallowed hard and tried to change the subject. "How did you get them, sir?"

"My source is irrelevant, Captain Lawton. What is relevant"—Guyton leaned forward and hissed—"is the fact . . . that I've got you by the balls."

Tom's mind raced at a million miles an hour. Where was Guyton going with this? What did he want? He knew the colonel was enjoying the hell out of watching Tom squirm.

For a split second, Tom wondered what exactly it was that was keeping him composed. Guyton was positively beaming at his little discovery. How could Tom not break down in a total loss of composure? It was being in command. He was still the commander of the Champions. He was instantly taken back to the desert. He remembered the peace he had found the night he ran naked into the darkness. Try as he could, he couldn't hold on to that image. That peace and clarity.

Everything he had worked for was being pulled away from him. It started the first time he'd been in Guyton's office. This wasn't command anymore. This was no longer service to the country. This was a personal mission by Guyton to get rid of the people he didn't want in "his army." To get rid of Tom Lawton. If being in "his army" meant being subject to scrutiny every single time you did something, it wasn't worth it. He remembered the vows he made before going to the desert. First, Guyton had forgotten his roots and no longer worked "for" soldiers. Secondly, by the time Guyton was through with Tom, his men would probably lose confidence in his ability to lead as well.

Lawton ran a quick decision matrix in his mind. He added up all the positives about being a commander, all the great things about the army, all the things that were so clear in Iraq.

Then he started adding up the negatives, things that had started eating at him the last two months. He thought about Cindy and Megan. He remembered when he was told that he wouldn't succeed much higher in the army because Cindy was a working wife. Visions of Major Stevenson and the paperwork flashed in his mind. He thought about the other captains sitting outside Guyton's office, waiting to be relieved. There really wasn't much of a decision to make. The cards were dealt, and it was time to fold.

Tom came out of the position of attention he had been sitting in. The only thing he could shoot for was leaving with dignity. He was still too much a soldier to show disrespect, lest he would get other charges added with Lieutenant Colonel Hawk as a witness. Hawk wasn't a part of this, and Tom knew it. He looked straight at Guyton and crossed his legs. "What do you want, sir?"

The colonel was taken by the frankness that Tom spoke with. He sat back and rubbed his chin. "You know I could charge you with conduct unbecoming an officer. I could probably get you sent somewhere to . . . dry out. But that may be too embarrassing for the command. I could give you a letter of reprimand, but that doesn't do me justice." Tom thought about each alternative and quickly considered how to address each one when the colonel let something slip. "I don't need to have a big, messy situation like this." A spark went off in Tom's mind. Suddenly, Guyton came clean. "I want you out of my brigade! That's all I want, Captain Lawton. I want you gone. You've never done anything good for me, so I'll give you the opportunity to choose."

"I'm listening, sir," said Tom as emotionless as he could be.

"You can either transfer somewhere else in the corps, or I'll seek as many charges as I can on the information I have. These pictures and . . . the less-than-stellar performance you've had since you came from the desert," hissed the Guymeister.

Tom ran the choices through his mind. To take the transfer meant the end of his career on Guyton's terms. Guyton would let him go and no doubt throw in a bad OER for good measure. That didn't matter because the new commander would call Guyton in a heartbeat to get the "real poop" on why this captain was made available for transfer. Why would a captain leave command after just over a year, unless he had problems? That option sucked.

As for charges against Tom, what did he have? All the events that brought Tom into Guyton's office had extenuating circumstances. If he did have a psychological disorder, the colonel would need more evidence than some photographs that mysteriously showed up in his possession. And if he went with the story that Tom was an alcoholic, he had dozens of witnesses that would say Tom hadn't had a drink since he left for the Gulf. He had an idea, but he needed time.

"Sir, those don't sound like very good choices. Are they the only options you're gonna give me?" asked Tom.

"You're lucky if I allow you to transfer, Lawton. Your options are limited, Captain," said Guyton with a sad attempt at a smile.

Tom said, "I could use the night to think about it, sir."

"I suppose I can wait until tomorrow, Captain Lawton," said the colonel. "Just let me know at 0900 how soon your office will be empty, okay?"

Tom slapped his knee, acting as if he were happy. He wasn't, but there was no need to let Guyton know that he had gotten under his skin. "Roger that, sir!" He got up quickly and was obviously in a hurry to leave. He looked at the photos on the table and hesitated for a second.

"These will be in good hands, Captain Lawton. You can trust me on that." Guyton smiled.

Tom smiled right back. "Oh, I'm sure I can, sir." He got his hat and left.

Outside, he quickly went to the hallway. He was too pissed off to understand that he had just had his military career taken away from him. For an instant, something inside made Tom want to go back in and tell Guyton that he was wrong and that it was all a mistake. Tom would work harder and do whatever he had to to keep his command. But reality took over.

Lawton's command was over. That was a fact. He probably had no future left in the army. But the colonel had said something in the office that stuck in Tom's mind. A seed had been planted that was starting to grow. He headed toward Stevenson's office. He didn't know if he could pull it off, but if things worked out the way he wanted, there would be nothing to pull off.

Tom knocked on the brigade adjutant's door. Major Stevenson was still in. "Excuse me, ma'am."

"Well, do you still have a job?" asked Major Stevenson.

Tom thought about how to respond. "No, ma'am. I guess I don't!"

Stevenson looked up from her desk and smiled at the captain. "I'm sorry, Captain Lawton."

"Hell, ma'am, there wasn't anything you could have done to prevent this thing from going down," Tom said as he moved to the chair beside her desk. "I could use your help with some paperwork now though."

"Sure, anything I can do," she said.

"I could use another copy of that VSI or SSB paperwork if you have any?" asked Tom.

"I just happen to have about twenty copies," said the major. She reached for a copy on top of a pile on the corner of her desk.

Tom took the paperwork and asked, "I could also use a couple of addresses if you have the time to help me look them up?"

The major looked at Lawton without hiding her confusion. "Addresses, huh?"

Tom was already scratching the names of the addresses he wanted. "If you don't know where they are, I'd appreciate it if you could tell me where I could find them."

Stevenson saw what Tom was writing and began to smile. "I think I might know where some of these are."

Tom smiled back. "Thanks for your help, ma'am." For just an instant, Tom wanted to ask her if she knew how Guyton had gotten the pictures, but she probably didn't know about them. Otherwise, Tom was sure he would have gotten some kind of comment.

Lawton got the addresses and thanked Major Stevenson for her help. He gathered his things and left before Hawk came out of the office. He didn't want to see Lieutenant Colonel Hawk, lest he get more questions that he didn't want to answer. It was out of Hawk's hands as well. Colonel Guyton and no one else was playing the game.

1930, August 3, 1991
Katterheim, Germany

AS SOON AS TOM WALKED IN the door, he headed for the refrigerator. Cindy wiped her hands and watched her husband without expression. He pulled out one of the two beers that were left in the fridge. He popped the top and took a long pull on the cold brew.

Cindy was shocked and asked, "Did we have a bad day, dear?"

Tom sat in the chair next to the table and looked at Cindy. "If I were to leave the army, would it . . . bother you, honey?"

A huge smile came over Cindy's face. She dropped the towel and ran over to Tom. She threw her arms around him and gave him a big kiss. "Oh, Tommy, it wouldn't bother me one bit!"

Tom smiled and gave her another little kiss. "You know, we would become civilians. The only civilian I know is my mom!"

"Well, Tom, seeing that you come home and drop that kind of bombshell on me, I guess I can return the favor." Cindy smiled.

Tom went to the fridge to get the other beer and offered it to Cindy. "Sure, hon. I'm ready for anything. You want this other beer?"

"Um, no, I won't be drinking for a while," said Cindy with a smile.

"Excuse me?" said Tom.

Cindy walked over to him and gave him another kiss. "I'm pregnant."

Tom's mouth popped open. "You're what? When did . . . ? How are we gonna afford . . . ?"

She put her hand over his mouth. "It's gonna be okay!"

"I guess I have a designated driver again!" Tom laughed.

Cindy smacked him playfully on the arm. "You better enjoy it now, because after this one, you're gettin' snipped!"

Tom gave her a big hug and looked at her seriously. "You know this one will be born a civilian!"

"Enough with the 'civilian' stuff. I think we can survive," said Cindy.

Tom lost his smile and looked at her. "Yeah, I think we'll survive. But there's something I have to do first, honey." He told Cindy about the pictures and that Guyton had them. Tom told her about the meeting in the colonel's office, and then he told her what he was going to do. Cindy's response was exactly what Tom expected. She supported Tom's plan wholeheartedly. By her nature, she was a fighter. In this case, she wanted to take it a step further and try to burn Guyton. Tom stopped that notion because there was no way they could turn the tables on him. If

Tom's plan worked, it would be enough just to get out of the army without ending up in Leavenworth.

Tom quickly ate supper and began typing. He had the paperwork from Major Stevenson to fill out and some letters to address. All the while, Tom wondered if the plan would work. Tom took a break and stepped out onto the back porch. He looked up at the night sky. There were too many lights around the housing area to really see the stars. Lawton just wanted to see them, hoping against all odds they would give him an answer. There were some clouds and a couple of jets flying toward Nuremberg, but no solution to his problem. That night, the sky didn't provide an answer for Tom's "situation." The sky wasn't the same as it had been in the desert. It would never be like that again.

Tom went back inside and began to type. His only wish was to salvage his reputation. He wanted to walk away from the army that he loved and still keep his dignity. The more he typed, the more he convinced himself that his little plan might actually work. By midnight, he knew he had nothing to lose. One way or the other, Tom Lawton's career was over.

0900, August 4, 1991
Brigade commander's office,
Katterheim Caserne, Germany

GUYTON STILL HAD THE SADISTIC-LOOKING SMILE on his face. He was so giddy, he failed to notice all the paperwork in Tom's hands. Hawk was there but stayed in the background, choosing only to be a distant participant. He also had a smile on his face, but only because he had done his part for Tom. There was nothing else Hawk could have done anyway. Guyton was pulling the strings, or so he thought.

"Well, Captain Lawton, when are you . . . moving out of your office? Do we need to get started on an OER?" The colonel beamed.

"Sir, the change of command date is August 31, and you don't need to start an OER," said Tom flatly. Then he put a group of papers on the colonel's desk. "All you need to do is sign this paperwork."

The colonel looked confused and asked, "What paperwork? What do you mean change of command?"

"Sir, those are the papers I filled out last night requesting the voluntary separation incentive. As you can probably see, Lieutenant Colonel Hawk has already signed his portion," said Tom.

"What the hell is this, Stan?" barked the colonel at Hawk.

"Hear him out, sir. I think you'll find his offer . . . reasonable," said Hawk.

"Like hell I will!" yelled the commander. He turned to Lawton. "You are a sorry excuse for an officer!" Guyton tried to gain composure but failed. "What the fuck do you mean offer?"

"I mean, sir, a deal. Between you and me," said Tom.

The colonel sat down again and hissed at Hawk. "I'll deal with you later, Colonel. There will be no deals, Captain. I have your worthless ass, and you know it."

Tom pulled a dozen envelopes out of his pocket and held them up. "I don't think so, sir." Tom threw the envelopes on the desk one at a time, just quick enough so the colonel could read the addresses.

"What the hell is this?" asked Guyton.

"Oh, just a little story, sir, about a decorated Gulf War veteran. Seems there's a colonel that has it out for his ass. Seems that the colonel had planned to reassign a group of troop commanders for the purpose of . . . who really knows what?" said Tom, trying to act tougher than he really was.

"That isn't true! There is no plan! That's all horseshit, and you know it!" yelled the colonel.

"The *Washington Post* and the *New York Times* don't care if it's true. It makes a good story," said Tom. Tom pointed to the letters. "I hope I have the right addresses on those congressmen too. Besides, the crap you have on me is horseshit too. But nobody cares about a captain. A colonel that's abusing his power is another story. Just the congressional investigation alone will keep you from being a general. As if you deserve to be one."

"You little son of a bitch," gasped the colonel. Then his mind started to work. "But I'll get you an OER, and you're finished in the military."

"I don't think I'll be taking that OER, sir. Eighty-nine days. It gives you time to put in whoever you want in command, do a proper inventory, and make sure the whole deal doesn't seem . . . out of the ordinary," said Tom. "I don't want an OER, and I don't want to stay in anymore. You get what you want, and I get what I want." Then he added, "Sir."

"You piece of shit," said Guyton.

Tom reached over and grabbed the letters. "Maybe I am a piece of shit, sir. But what I am right now is due to what I've been taught." Tom stared at the colonel and added flatly, "And how to be a piece of shit is the only lesson you've taught me." He turned and started to leave. "It's a better way out for both of us if you just sign those papers." There was no response, only seething indignation. "I guess we go down together. But I'm not going without a fight." Tom looked at Hawk and turned to leave. "I'm sorry, sir. I appreciate your sticking by me through all this, and I wish you all the best. Thank you." Tom was just about to open the door when Guyton stopped him.

In a quiet voice, Guyton said, "All right."

Tom turned around and saw the colonel signing the separation papers. Tom walked back over and took them. "By the way, sir, you will be invited to the change of command." Tom smiled. Then he added, "If I could make a recommendation, sir. CPT Hart Osborn would make a tremendous troop commander." Tom couldn't help but push the envelope a little.

"Just get the hell out of my office. I'll put whomever I want in command and not you or anyone else will decide who that will be. You're both dismissed," said the colonel.

"You can keep the pictures, sir. They don't matter anymore," Tom hollered over his shoulder.

As they headed out the door, Tom turned to Hawk and said, "I'm sorry I got you into this, sir." He quickly dropped the papers in Major Stevenson's box and gave her a thumbs-up. She smiled and was quickly back to the business on her desk.

"Tom, you were a damn good commander in the desert. If I can get you out of here with your ass in tact, I feel I owe you that much." He smiled.

Tom handed Hawk the envelopes. Hawk felt one and stopped. He looked at Lawton. "You need these?"

Tom grabbed them and ripped one open. He held up one of the letters so Hawk could see it. The piece of paper was blank. "I couldn't write anything down last night, sir. As much as I wanted to bring it all up, I didn't want to put anyone through this crap. What good would it have done?"

Hawk laughed. "Remind me not to play poker with you!"

Tom stuck his hand out. "I want to say thanks again for supporting me, sir." The colonel shook his hand and patted him on the back as he walked away.

Tom was almost outside the building when a voice from his past came up. It was Charlie Sweat. "Hey, Tom! How's it goin'?"

"Oh, about as well as it could be!" lied Tom.

"You just came from the colonel's office?" asked Sweat.

"Yes," said Tom, starting to get nervous by Sweat's peppiness. How did he know about Tom being in the colonel's office?

"What happened?" asked Sweat.

"I'm going to leave command, Charlie," said Tom.

Sweat looked stunned. "Because of the pictures?"

How the hell did he know about the pictures? Then the picture started to come clear. The pieces fell into place. Hart's desk. Sweat had taken the pictures from Hart Osborn's desk and brought them to Guyton.

"You know about the pictures, Charlie?" asked Tom.

"Um, yeah, sure. It's all over brigade," said Sweat.

"How'd it . . . get all over brigade? You didn't manage to bring the pictures up here for the colonel to see, did you?" accused Tom. He took a step closer to Sweat.

Sweat may not have been a team player, but he wasn't a liar. "I didn't think he'd do anything with them!"

Tom grabbed Sweat by the collar. "You didn't think he'd do anything with them?" Tom shook his head and pushed Sweat backward. "You thought maybe the colonel needed to know what kind of officers he had in his command, didn't you? You . . ." Tom couldn't finish what he wanted to say. He stepped back and patted down the collar that he had previously held so tightly in his hands. "You didn't really think you'd get the command back, did you, Charlie?"

Sweat pushed Tom's hand away. "He's the brigade commander. He's got the right to know what's going on in his own command."

Tom laughed. "And as long as he's got a prick like you to keep him squared away, he'll know everything, won't he? His command's gonna be a tight group, won't it? You selfish fuck!"

Sweat's true emotions came through. "We don't need people like you in the army. And we sure as hell don't need you in command!" said Charlie Sweat. "I heard about you in Desert. I heard how you lost it, running naked through the fucking desert! Another week of combat and they'd have put you in a funny farm, Lawton!"

Tom started to draw back and punch him. But he could see himself getting court-martialed. He could see that pompous fuck Guyton smiling like some kind of omnipotent being over his glasses while Tom got sent to Mannheim. Lawton did the only thing he could. He laughed in Sweat's face. "As whacked as I was," Tom said, "I was still ten times the commander you ever were." He turned and walked away.

He needed to tell the squadron S1 that his paperwork was in. On the way to the adjutant's office, he saw Hart Osborn.

Hart called him into the supply office. "I think I know what happened to the pictures!" said Osborn. "I think Sweat came by right before you did. He was in the office about five minutes before you got there."

Tom put his hand on Hart's shoulder and said, "I know."

Hart was confused. "You already know?"

Tom explained everything to his friend. He finished by saying, "I turned in my paperwork to get out. Guyton signed it, and I'll be gone in . . . twenty-seven days."

"Oh man. I'm sorry, Tom. I'm so damn sorry," said Hart as he shook his head.

"Look, it doesn't matter. I've already talked it over with Cindy. She's a go at the civilian station. By the way, I'm going to be a dad again," said Tom with a big smile.

"Congratulations." Hart smiled.

Tom sighed. "The army is gonna change, Hart. It's probably already started. There's gonna be a need for a smaller, more technical force, and I don't think I fit that bill. I've always been people oriented and thought the army was that way. It's already changing from taking care of people to taking care of business." Then he chuckled. "As long as it's always there to take care of the country, I guess it doesn't matter who's in it or how big it is."

Hart agreed and then looked at Tom. "You know I had some problems with the way you led the troop in the desert. But you were damn good at it."

Tom looked at Hart and stuck out a hand. "I think every person that ever commanded would like to know what his troops thought about him while he was their commander. Even if I wasn't, it's damn nice of you to say that, Hart." In his best Spanish accent, he said, *"Muchas gracias. Adios, amigo!"*

Tom headed down the hall and told the S1 his paperwork to separate was approved. He then informed Major Maurer that the C Troop change of command was set for August 31. He headed out to the flight line and told Garcia. Lawton asked Garcia not to tell anyone until he knew who the new guy would be.

Then he went out and flew with the Champions. It was a simple day multiship mission that Gallagher was in charge of. He couldn't help but critique the lieutenant on his selection of battle positions and brought up the map to show an alternate position that might have been better.

This was what he would miss the most. After the AAR, he went home to be with Cindy and Megan. He needed to get used to his new lifestyle.

CHAPTER 14

August 28, 1991
Hangar 3010, Katterheim Caserne

"I'M GLAD IT DIDN'T TAKE US too long to do the change of command inventory. I guess it helps that I still have all the stuff I'm signed for." Tom smiled. CPT Sammy Thompson smiled back at Tom. Tom couldn't help but think that his peer was . . . damn good looking. He quickly dismissed the thought and got back to business.

Thompson reminded Tom of the Apache still at the repair facility "Except for AH-64, one each, serial number 444!" Thompson had a good sense of humor and was pretty tough-minded, qualities she would need to be successful as the first female attack helicopter troop commander. Sammy was an ROTC-commissioned officer from Embry-Riddle Aeronautical University, a university with a world-renowned aviation program. She was a licensed fixed-wing pilot with over 2,500 hours. She was jump qualified and air assault qualified and could cuss like a pirate. Tom thought she'd make one hell of a good Champion.

Tom said, "Don't worry about 444. They keep promising me, 'You'll get it next week.'" They laughed together at the thought. "Is there anything else I can help you with?"

"Sure, Tom. Do you have any advice . . . you know, that will help me . . . if the shit hits the fan?" she said.

Tom could tell she was serious, so he tried to lighten up the mood. "You mean all the other stuff I've been teaching you isn't worth something?"

"Yes, it is. But I want to know stuff that will keep me, or rather us, stay alive in a combat situation," said Sammy.

Tom thought about it. He should have known he wouldn't get off easy. "All right." He noticed Sammy pulled out a pad and got ready to write. It always impressed Tom when a junior officer got prepared to take notes from a mentor. He tried to make sure the lesson was worth it.

Tom started, "It comes down to the basics. I'm talking not just the be, know, and do stuff. Even more basic than that: shoot, move, and communicate. The key for you as the commander is in priorities. As the trainer, you should make sure your unit is trained to execute missions in the following order. Be able to shoot straight, put steel on target, and get first-round kills. Next, they must be able to move in all environments, especially night and under limited visibility. And finally, they must be able to communicate. Not just to you, but for you, in case you are disabled, off the net, or on vacation." Tom smiled to let Captain Thompson digest the information.

He continued, "Now the key for you to succeed is a little different priority. Communicate, move, then shoot." He watched her puzzled expression. "There's no way you can possibly train to handle the radios the way they are in combat. They're nuts. I mean crazy." He smiled and saw her finish writing. "Four or five conversations can be going at once. You need to be able to digest and transmit the information you get to whoever needs it at the appropriate time, either up or down the chain of command. That's the toughest part of the fight.

"By the nature of aviation, you will be able to move wherever and whenever you need to. After you get there, you must be able to shoot, and that also means first round on target just like your troops. The items are the same. It's just a different priority for the commander," said Tom. Then he looked at Sammy to nail the point home one more time. "You've got to be able to communicate, because if you can't, you're not commanding. Makes sense?"

Captain Thompson finished writing, looked up, and smiled. "Makes a lot of sense. Now what about peacetime operations?" she asked.

Tom looked at her and hesitated just a little before continuing, "Okay, peacetime. You aren't George Patton," he said flatly.

Sammy Thompson frowned. "What's that supposed to mean?"

"Hey, relax!" said Tom. "Nobody else is either. My point is, only a very few special people are, and notice I didn't say men!" Tom smiled. She was relaxed again. "Not many people are that kind of warrior. The rest of us need help. It takes courage to ask for help, especially when the going gets rough. You could ask for help from higher," Tom said, but the comment from Hal Timmons jumped into his head: never trust higher.

Tom quickly put the thought away. Tom decided that it wasn't the time and she wasn't the person to discuss this sensitive issue with. He provided her with another option. "You might get help from your peers." Tom had visions of Charlie Sweat's smug, holier-than-thou face the last time he saw him. Then he gave her the best option. "Or you can ask for help from the people that will always help you, the soldiers that work for you."

Captain Thompson nodded approvingly at the suggestion. "I can believe that one."

"They will always help you if they can," said Tom. "You take care of them, and they will take care of you. From the first days of soldiering, troops will always take care of their leaders. As long as there's faith and trust that the leaders will take care of them, soldiers will take care of their leaders."

"I guess you know I'll do my best to take care of the Champions," said Captain Thompson.

"I don't have any doubt about that, Sammy," said Tom.

There was something else troubling her, and Tom could see it. "More questions?"

"Yeah, just one. What about Guyton?" she asked.

For an instant, Tom thought about telling her the truth, but he didn't want to go into the whole story. It was too personal, and there were enough rumors running through the caserne already. There were rumors about why Lawton was leaving and that Colonel Guyton wanted him relieved. Of course, questions about Tom's sexual preference were being raised and that the Lawton marriage was a cover-up. Other claims were made that Tom and Cindy were really bisexual and that Guyton was doing him a favor by letting him out quietly. Tom wondered how long it had taken Charlie Sweat to think of that one.

The truth wouldn't work here. Tom did what came naturally. He laughed. "Sorry, Captain Thompson, some of this crap, you're gonna have to find out for yourself!" But Tom didn't want to leave it like that, so he thought of something that Steele had told him. "A few years ago, the Marine Corps had a commandant named P. X. Kelly. He said something profound that I didn't really understand until a couple of years ago. I don't remember the quote exactly, but it essentially says, 'Expect every rank you make to be your last and make your decisions accordingly.' What it means to me is, as a captain, a troop commander, I make decisions based on what's best for my troopers, not higher level. Not decisions I make just to get promoted. Make captain-level decisions and you can't go wrong. Some people try to make decisions they can't make or shouldn't make. If your decisions are right, you'll get promoted. If you can't make the right decisions as a commander at this level, you probably don't deserve to lead troops at a higher level."

After a few seconds, she accepted the answer. She stuck out her hand. "Thank you for everything. I won't make you any promises, but I swear, I'll take care of them."

Tom nodded as he pulled his hand away. "You do that, and they'll keep you from having to get too close to Guyton."

"I guess your new guys couldn't take care of you," she said. "I mean with Guyton!"

Tom looked at her for the first time with the hardness that had come from his experience as a commander. "It wasn't the troops that let me down. They would never do that." Tom looked away, not wanting to explain. "Let's just say, for the sake of simplicity, it was me." He wanted to clarify all the misconceptions she probably had, but he knew it didn't matter. People would think whatever they wanted, and it didn't matter to Tom. The fact was, he was leaving command and Sammy Thompson was taking his place, handpicked by Colonel Guyton. She would do fine. Tom thought that Guyton probably already had her OER written. He decided it was time to leave. "Best of luck, Sammy," he said. He turned and walked out of his office for the last time.

August 30, 1991
Katterheim housing,
Germany

TOM AND CINDY WERE LYING IN the bed. Tom put the letter he was reading down. The return address was from Texas. The letter made him smile, but his attention returned to his wife. He started rubbing her belly, and she was lying back, as usual enjoying it. She asked, "You're not really gonna miss this, are you? The army?"

Tom looked up at his wife. "I'm going to miss some of it," he replied.

Cindy looked confused. "The loss of personal freedom. The rumors. The phone calls at all hours. Getting your butt chewed for things you have no control over. Responsible for everything and everybody. Peers that aren't friends and friends that aren't peers," said Cindy.

"That last one is an anomaly. Friends are always friends. Some peers are merely acquaintances!" He chuckled. "I'll miss the friends. The action." Tom pondered and added one more, "I'll miss serving my country." Tom glanced at the large picture hanging on the wall. Toretti took it in the desert. It was all the Champions when they were in AA Gomez. Unknowing, fearful, yet confident. Their broad smiles covering the nervousness that churned inside. Men with hope. Men with a destiny to fulfill. He snapped back to reality. Tom looked back to Cindy. "You don't have to go tomorrow if you don't want to."

"Oh, I'm gonna be there all right. We're going to see this thing through to the end. And I'm with you all the way," said Cindy.

"I know you are, honey," said Tom. "And just in case you didn't know it, I love you for it." Tom gave her a kiss, rolled over, and turned off his light. Cindy couldn't sleep, so she grabbed a book and started reading. It only took Tom about five minutes to fall sound asleep. Cindy noticed he was smiling while he slept. Tom hadn't done that for years.

0730, August 31, 1991
Hangar 3010, Katterheim Caserne, Germany

TOM LAWTON GOT INTO 220 FOR the last time. Mark Nichols was in the backseat. They went out for one last flight, just so Tom could say good-bye to the aircraft that had performed so well for him in Iraq. They went south, well away from the caserne, over Ansbach and Gunzenhausen Lake. The beautiful German countryside basked in the glow of the sunny August day.

Nichols gave Tom the controls, and he put her through the paces. For some unknown reason, on this day, Tom felt he had "it." During the hard banks and steep turns, Tom couldn't help but notice he had the aircraft in trim, as if it were a part of him. Tom did a high "G" maneuver, and Mark

Nichols gave him a thumbs-up. "A 2.4, sir. You gotta do the negative." They had just pulled two and a half "Gs" in a helicopter, and now Nichols was encouraging Tom to do a negative "G" maneuver.

Tom hated it because it made his stomach flip and everything in the cockpit would fly around. Plus, the movement of the collective was abnormal. He always thought that you needed to let the power out, but at the top of the maneuver, he had to force himself to keep the collective still. It was his last flight, so he entered the maneuver at 140 knots and nosed the aircraft up. At eighty knots, he came over the top and nosed it over. Everything in the cockpit flew up in the air, and Tom's stomach joined it all. The aircraft headed back to earth as God intended, and gravity returned to normal.

"Nice one, sir!" Nichols chuckled. The instructor pilot did the maneuver on a daily basis and was used to it.

Tom wasn't used to it and knew it was time to head back. He straightened out the mess in the cockpit and looked it over like it was his bedroom in his parents' house the last time he left it. He wanted to remember it that way. The fun was over, and the finality of everything was setting in. Tom was quiet for the rest of the flight.

They landed at 0915. Tom reluctantly climbed out. Lawton had actually had "it," that special feeling of being one with the aircraft for just a short period of time. If it was to be his last flight, it was a great one. It was such a shame to get that feeling and have to leave it behind. Tom rubbed his hand along the side of the aircraft. He looked around to ensure he had the privacy of the moment. Quietly, so no one would hear, Tom said, "Good-bye, old friend." He turned and headed to the hangar. He didn't look back.

Tom Lawton went to his old office and quickly changed into his Battle Dress Uniform. His boots were spit shined. His hair was cut to his customary high and tight. He checked his mustache to see that it met the standard set by the Department of the Army. A knock came on the door. It was Roberto Garcia. "Come on in, Top."

"Sir, the men are set downstairs. I know you said you wanted a couple of minutes to talk to them," said Garcia.

Tom put his Kevlar on his head and quickly checked the mirror to make sure it looked straight. "Thanks, Top. Could you make sure . . . I'm not too messed up."

Garcia checked over his boss and made a slight adjustment on the Kevlar. Tom smiled at the assistance. Garcia stepped back. "Looking good, sir." Lawton started to turn, and Garcia made a little cough. "I . . . I just wanted to say," started the first sergeant, "I don't know what the hell happened or why. I think you were one of the best captains I've ever worked with." Garcia laughed. "I've worked with thousands of 'em too!"

Tom stuck out his hand and said, "Roberto, I've only worked with a couple hundred first sergeants, and I can honestly tell you, you are the best." Tom shook Garcia's hand firmly. "The army used to be focused on threat analysis. Today, it's more focused on urinalysis." Both men chuckled. Tom swallowed hard, looked at his first sergeant's eyes, and said, "We had a tremendous run, and more of that can be attributed to your leadership than mine. For that, I am truly thankful." Tom dropped the handshake, looked at the NCO with tears in his eyes, and gave Roberto Garcia a hug.

Lawton pulled away and took a deep breath and rubbed his right eye. "Enough of this sentimental crap. I need to get my game face on." Tom's familiar smile appeared. He turned and walked out of the Champion Six office, Sammy Thompson's office, for the last time. Roberto Garcia turned out the light and locked the door.

The Champions were in formation when Lawton and Garcia showed up. Timmons called the troop to attention. Tom quickly gave them at ease. "Damn! Look at you guys! All dressed up. Must have some place to go!" The troops all laughed.

"Not as far as you have to go, sir!" said Padillo from his position as the guidon bearer. "We heard you was goin' to Texas. That true, sir?"

"That's true. We got a little place in East Texas," said Tom loud enough so everyone could hear. He turned to address the crowd. "Yesterday, I got a letter of acceptance to an attack helicopter battalion in Texas." Tom let the information sink in. "I just wanted you all to know, I don't plan to get totally out of the business." Tom heard the "Roger thats" and "Good deal" cries from the troops. "I'll probably check into a teaching job and coach a little hoop on the side. So if any of you need to look me up, I intend to be around."

Tom walked a little closer to the assembled mass. "I do expect one thing from you guys." The troop grew quiet. "I expect you to treat your new commander with respect and honesty." He looked at the faces and knew he didn't have to say any more. "Except for my family, you know you guys mean more to me than anything in the world. You always did." Tom sniffed a little and moved anxiously in front of the group. "I'm leaving because it is the best thing for me, not because of anything that anyone here did or didn't do." Tom stepped back. "You were 'Champions' in the past, and Captain Thompson has assured me you will remain 'Champions' in the future." The troops understood that meant she intended to keep the name. There was a big "Hooaah!"

"I'm leavin' real quick after this, but I wanted to take the time to tell each and every one of you that I appreciated the effort you gave," said Tom. Then he went through the ranks and shook hands with each man and gave words of encouragement and thanks.

When he got to Joe Petty, his hand was trembling, so he looked at the most experienced member of his troop in the eye and said, "I expect more outta you than anybody else. When it happens again, I expect you to be a leader."

Joe nodded. "Sir, I put my packet together for Officer Candidate School. I'm hoping to be a lieutenant within the next year."

Tom's smile reappeared. "Outstanding! I wish you the best of luck." Tom grabbed the warrant and gave him a hug. "Damn it, Joe. You'll be great!"

"Thanks, sir. I hope so," said Joe Petty. They looked at each other and knew there was nothing more to say. "Best of luck to you, sir."

Tom continued through the rest of the troop. Much too soon, it was time for the change of command to start. Garcia came and got Tom and brought the formation to attention. Tom Lawton took one last look at his Champions and then headed to his position in the ceremony.

Before Tom could get in position, COL Pete Denson intercepted him. They were well away from anyone else. Tom stopped and looked at the man, not knowing what to expect.

Denson cleared his throat and looked at his feet. "You should have come to me, Lawton. I could have helped you out of this mess you were in." Tom could tell Pete Denson had received his information on Tom's "mess" from Guyton. "There must have been another way to work this out."

Tom shook his head. "Only if you were in command, sir, would I even bother to stick around." His familiar smile appeared, relieving the colonel of some unnecessary tension. Tom was actually comfortable with his old boss.

Denson fumbled to find words and then said, "What the hell happened here? I've only been gone for a couple of months and the whole brigade seems completely different."

Tom thought it was time to lay a bit of enlightenment on his former commander. "Sir, it's not just the brigade. It's the army." He could see by the confused expression that Denson didn't understand. Tom shook his head again. "It's like this."

Tom looked over at the assembled crowd and decided he had some time. He inhaled deeply and said, "In your war, your girlfriend was back in the States praying for you to come back after 365 days alive and healthy. In this war, girlfriends were in the tent next door, praying the condom worked last night." The colonel started to get a little angry, but Tom continued, "When you were a captain, you could get drunk, and your buddies would get you home and take care of you. Now if you get drunk anytime at all, somebody wants to put you in rehab or ruin your career." The colonel's mouth closed, and his eyes narrowed. Tom wasn't done. "And one more thing, sir. Thirty years ago in the army, a commander would put his butt on the line to protect his people." Tom nodded toward Guyton and said, "Now a commander will put his people on the line to protect his butt." Denson glanced at Guyton then back to Tom. The colonel's anger faded. The captain wasn't trying to whine or blame someone else for his situation. He was being honest with a superior officer that needed to hear the truth, and Pete Denson respected that. "You didn't lead like that. I know you probably haven't heard any of the stuff that's goin' on around here." Tom smiled at Denson and added, "But at least you treated everybody the same. Like crap!"

"That wasn't without purpose, Lawton. It seems to have worked pretty good last spring, right?" Denson managed a little smile as his mind went back to Iraq.

"You got it, sir! Every one of us knew where we stood with you. It isn't like that anymore," said Tom.

It was as if the smoke had cleared the battlefield for Pete Denson. "Well, I'm sorry your career is over. I still think if you'd have come to me earlier, I could have prevented this," said the colonel.

"Sir, the best thing you can do is to take a look around here and prevent anybody else from getting," Tom hesitated before saying, "in the same situation as me."

Colonel Denson nodded and smiled. "I think I'll do that. You know you did damn good down there in Iraq with that bunch of outlaws you had." The colonel smiled and extended his hand to Tom. Lawton looked at the outstretched hand and took it. "You let me know if there's anything I can do for you on the outside, okay, Tom?"

Tom saluted crisply and said, "Thank you, sir!" He turned and headed to his assigned position. Then it hit him. The old warrior called him Tom. Denson actually knew his name. It was too bad that Denson hadn't let Lawton know before then how good a commander he thought the captain was. It may not have changed a thing, but Tom Lawton was the type subordinate that worked better with a pat on the back rather than a kick in the ass.

1000, August 31, 1991
Hangar 3010
Katterheim Caserne, Germany

THE CEREMONY GOT UNDER WAY. LAWTON stood tall in his place as he waited to give his comments. He couldn't help but notice the Apaches in the background. The joy of his last flight was still fresh in his mind. Slowly, visions of good times, as well as bad, flashed through Tom's memory. The negative events of the last three months tried to push all the good times away, but Tom shook them off. He tried to stay focused and found it difficult. Finally, it was Tom Lawton's turn to say farewell.

Tom stepped to the podium and closed the book that was lying there. He had no need for a written speech. Tom knew what he wanted to say. Tom stood tall and forced the customary smile to appear on his face.

Tom looked to his right and began, "Colonel and Mrs. Denson, Colonel and Mrs. Guyton, and friends of the Champions, I'd like to thank all of you for coming. This ceremony typifies the ever-changing United States Army. Through all the changes that will take place, I am positive they will be what's best for the country."

Lawton's glance came straightforward. With no one in particular in mind, Tom let the bitterness he felt appear. "As we become a more technology-dependent and modern force, the leaders of tomorrow will be faced with the choice of the people versus the advancing technology. Though the choice will be difficult, I can only hope the choice will be what's best for the soldiers. Their initiative, dedication, and spirit are what make our army great. Without those assets, we will never attain the heights we are capable of. The people are what make us work." He wanted to say more but decided he'd better not. He could feel Guyton piercing him with his eyes. Screw him, thought Tom. Guyton should be the one speaking out for the soldiers, not some captain that was, for all intents and purposes, spent.

Lawton changed the subject without a glance at his tormentor. "My heartfelt thanks and my respect go out to CPT Sammy Thompson as she takes command of C Troop, First of the Sixth Cavalry." Tom looked back to the assembled troop. "To the Champions, I wish you all only the best. It's easy for any commander to stand before his unit and say they were the best. I don't have to prove that to anyone here, because I know in my heart, we were." Tom nodded to Garcia at the front of the formation. "I challenge you to maintain the standard we have established, not just for Captain Thompson, but for future Champions of all ranks. It was each and every one of you that made my time in command a joy." Tom became a little choked up. "It's always been about the troops. That's the way it should be."

Tom coughed his throat clear. "There's one more person I must mention. I couldn't have gotten through my time in command without Cindy's love and loyalty." He looked over at Cindy and said, "Thank you for everything, honey." He felt tears welling in his eyes as he looked at Cindy, who was wiping away her own tears. Tom had to lighten the mood. In three hours, they would be flying to Frankfurt. "I want the window on the plane." Most people in the crowd knew a plane ride was waiting for the Lawtons, and they chuckled at Tom's stab at humor.

Tom was silent for a moment as the crowd grew quiet. He regained his composure and addressed the troop again. Tom could sense it was time for him to go. "Fellas, back in March, people were fond of saying we went to Iraq, we won a war, and we got the T-shirt to prove it. Well, I'm here to tell you, we did a lot more than get the damn T-shirt! I want you to promise me that you'll never forget what we did and how good we were!" There were about a dozen "Hoooaahs" from the Champions and in the crowd to Tom's right. "History will look back on what we did and acknowledge that at that time, the United States Army was the best military in history. There may never be another more complete victory in war than what we achieved. We were Champions." He got nods and agreement from many people in the audience. "We were all Champions."

Emotions swirled inside him as the end of his command arrived. Dozens of visions flashed through his mind. Hart Osborn, Hal Timmons, Joe Petty, Top Garcia, and all the people, sights, and sounds of the last year. It all seemed like a dream. As much as he didn't want the dream to end, it was time to wake up.

Tom Lawton struggled to come to the position of attention and felt a single tear trickle down his cheek. He quickly reached up and wiped it away. Tom swore he wouldn't do that. People might think less of him if he was seen crying.

Then it hit him. The hell with what people thought. The only thing that mattered was he could look at himself in the mirror. His eyes swept over the Champions. All the soldiers he had commanded had gone to war and come home alive and in one piece. Cindy and Megan were there and could be proud of his accomplishments, and he was leaving the army on his own terms. After all was said and done, Tom was proud of the service he had done for his country. At that moment, he realized how proud he was of himself. Tom was on top of the world for the first time in his life. He was filled with confidence and strength that he never knew he had.

Yet deep inside, he knew the feeling wouldn't last. It was time to leave. Tom went out as only a soldier could. The familiar smile appeared on his face, and he snapped to attention. He swiftly drew up his hand to salute his men for the final time. Another teardrop slipped down his cheek, but this time, he did nothing to stop it. In the strongest voice he could muster, Tom Lawton yelled, "I WILL ALWAYS BE A CHAMPION!"